Author Biography

Margaret Henderson Smith, a psychology graduate, taught in a priority area primary school before establishing her own Private Pre-school and Care & Service Agency.

Now retired she lives with her husband in Wirral where they enjoy walking and sailing.

Whilst teaching, her love of writing prompted her to set up and edit a school magazine which was judged the winner in a regional competition organized by the local press. A Question of Answers is her first novel.

With love and thanks to
John
Jane & Richard
Gail & John
Elizabeth & Derek

for their interest, support and encouragement

and
In memory of Pepper

Edited by Jane A.Williams

A Question of Answers

Margaret Henderson Smith

Published 2008 by arima publishing

www.arimapublishing.com

ISBN 978 1 84549 328 8

Printed and bound in the United Kingdom

Typeset in Garamond 11/14

Swirl is an imprint of arima publishing.

arima publishing
ASK House, Northgate Avenue
Bury St Edmunds, Suffolk IP32 6BB
t: (+44) 01284 700321

www.arimapublishing.com

Chapter 1

Harriet ripped the lottery ticket into a pile of pink dust. 'Sod you!' She ground her elbow into the mound and looked down just in time to see the confused look on the cat's face as it hurtled towards the door shedding its paper trail like a jet's engine.

'And you can sod off too!' she shrieked. 'Cats! Just like men! Bloody purrrfect!'

Now Harriet wasn't given to swearing unless extremely provoked. Well, yes, it was common parlance at work, in the staff room of course. Most of the time she pretended not to hear it, unless deliberately provoked by Mr. Sanderson who couldn't resist the toss of blonde hair as her lowered lashes swept every last expletive to the ground.

'What's so special about New Year's Eve anyway?' she rattled to herself. 'What's so different about that?' She glowered at the phone secured to the wall like some grey plastic idol, some silent, uncooperative arbiter of her fate. Then it rang! For a brief moment Harriet froze in disbelief, her elbow still planted in the table she swung round overcome by an uncontrollable compulsion to answer it just as the cat came shooting back. Then like some deflated exhibitionist on the nursery slope she sprawled across the floor turning it into a meowing rug before heaving herself up to the threat of the final ring. 'New Year, New Bloody Kitchen. Sod off!' she shouted.

The doorbell rang and in a hasty attempt to recover her equilibrium she smoothed her ruffled hair, pulled her jumper down and cleared the guilt from her throat as she turned the latch. It was Mark back earlier than she'd expected.

'That was quick,' she said accusingly. 'I thought you were shifting all the boats this morning.'

'Only Greg and Pete turned up,' mumbled Mark. 'Greg looked as grey as that,' he said, pointing to the phone.

Harriet's heart leapt. She didn't want it to ring now!

'And Pete couldn't remember why he'd come in the first place!'

'Had a better time than us then Grey Greg and Prostrate Pete?' Harriet snapped. 'Well you were the one that backed off Harriet, don't blame me!'

Of course Harriet had backed off. She hated New Year's Eve at the sailing club. She was still nursing the cringe wounds from last year's shells shot from the mouths of the wealthy, the competent, the competitive and the downright snooty.

'Your boat still looks bloody new Harriet, not managed another launch yet? Still drying out Harriet?' Harriet couldn't stand Tarquin Bridgewater.

Of course they hadn't managed another launch. Harriet had avoided it like the plague since Mark pushed off in too much of a damned hurry and Harriet to the jeers of the whole club had landed in the drink!

Not that there had been much time for sailing last year. The girls had finally left home and Harriet and Mark overcome with TV inspired enthusiasm, intent on capturing the rising market decided to revamp the whole house. This would enable them to downsize whilst making a phenomenally large profit. The board still sits like a flag in rigor mortis, as dead as their hopes.

Posh cousin Clarissa also announced her marriage last year. Harriet got roped in for making the bridesmaids' dresses. She'd have felt a little less put-on if she'd been doing them for *her* girls, but no, the endless miles of machine stitching was all for the benefit of two rather large girls, so plummy they could only be photographed with a wide-angle lens and so fussy Harriet was almost tempted to offer them matching mouth zips! Anyway, weddings were a moot point with Harriet.

Then there was school. Harriet was having the utmost difficulty keeping up with all the requirements. Her day's work really began at 4.00 pm, with the back seat of her car loaded to the hilt it felt like the challenge of Everest most nights. 'More time now both girls have gone,' she used to think, but really it didn't make much difference. She felt as though she was drowning in a sea of kids and admin and the boat of enthusiasm had finally succumbed to the ocean of despair. Apart from Mr. Sanderson of course. He frequently threw a lifeline. Little did he know how often he saved her from drowning in that dark, deep water. She knew he liked her, at least she thought she knew he liked her. Why would he survey the whole room and rest his eyes just a little longer on her. Oh yes, with mathematical precision Harriet knew just how much more of his attention span was hers!

'Any sign of Bob and Tricia down there?' Harriet enquired cautiously.

'Who?' shouted Mark, pulling at the front door. 'What happened to Pepper? She looks like an old pan scrub! Where did all these bits come from Harriet?'

'Bob and Tricia, I asked if you'd seen them!'

Harriet was hoping he hadn't. She didn't like Tricia very much. She'd seen her thirsting for attention. Laughing just a little bit longer at Mark's quips than anyone else. Sending his ego off the planet with her inappropriate gushing at his sailing skills. Pity she hadn't been the recipient of the ice-cold plunge! Harriet allowed herself to muse at the thought of her running mascara creating a massive delta through those rouge brushed cheeks. Then she began to feel uncomfortable at her amusement and suppressed the carefully cultivated thought into the 'only fiction' mind file. 'Mustn't make this into a big thing,' she said to herself.

'Didn't Tricia say she was collecting the kids from her mum's while Bob nurses his hangover?' queried Mark. 'Anyway, I thought you were going to see yours this morning. Been any phone calls?'

Harriet stopped in her tracks. Had he come back early expecting her to be out so he could talk to Tricia on the phone? Harriet went sick. Her stomach was trying to cling on to the inside of her knees but the fluctuating wobble hurtled it to the floor and she clenched her arm round her waist for fear of Mark seeing the gap!

Then as if its limelight had been usurped the phone suddenly shrilled.

Solidified, Harriet and Mark flicked a reciprocal glance, then both taking off at the same split second terrified the cat who misjudged it, shot across their path and sent them both flying! Harriet and Mark fought their way up from the now neurotic heap of fur.

'This thing needs hoovering,' said Mark, lightly. The cat almost sneered and then shot through the cat flap.

'Happy New Year!' they chimed simultaneously. 'Though it's not exactly the best start,' bemoaned Harriet. In spite of that they both agreed to try to make it a good one.

Chapter 2

'Good, but only as good as Mark wants it to be,' thought Harriet as she emptied the pedal bin, shaking the last pink shreds of hope for the week down before she tied off the bin-liner. 'And bloody boring.' She shocked herself again at such obvious signs of limited vocabulary. She never used to be like this. In years gone by Harriet was almost emotionally fulfilled and certainly well occupied with her babies. She enjoyed nurturing the girls to maturity and dreaded the day the house silenced of their laughter, their chattering, their squabbles. Rachael and Clare were both independent now, fortunate enough to be embarking on promising careers and each had an eligible young man in tow. Harriet and Mark were jolly pleased with all of those things, if only they'd opted to live a little nearer. They were both in Surrey, too far for Harriet. After all, they were still Harriet's babies, Mark's daughters, but Harriet's babies.

'Back to work tomorrow,' said Mark as he squeezed past Harriet and the pedal bin. 'It's alright for you, you've got another week off. Teachers, they don't know they're born!'

But Harriet well and truly knew she was born. She'd barely started her first year at university when she'd become pregnant with Rachael.

'Well I hope he's going to marry you, especially as he's now ruined any prospects you might have had of a career,' her mother had said. 'You'll be back home then, until that good-for-nothing finishes his training and gets a job.' Harriet had no choice. Fortunately Mark was in his final year. She knew those months were difficult for her mother, especially when the baby arrived. She hadn't moved with the times. It was as well Mark had been able to get work as soon as he'd graduated. They'd not been in 4 The Willows long before she was pregnant again.

'You could have gone far Harriet, if he hadn't ruined your career. No chance now,' she would say. But Harriet proved her wrong. She'd managed to get herself into training college once the children had started school. She'd got her teaching qualification but didn't do much with it until the girls were older. After undergoing various attempts at refresher courses she finally arrived at Stetmead Street Primary, an inner city school whose families suffered much deprivation.

'If you can teach here Miss Glover, you can teach anywhere!' said Mr. Sanderson on her first morning. Harriet wasn't so sure. She'd watched the determination on the prematurely lined faces of mothers herding their tiny offspring through the rusting but elegant arched gates. They stood like a monument to equality, spiking the cold blue sky with aspiration whilst trawling the lifting tarmac with derision.

'You're new 'ere, arn you Miss? My Mum says you'll need a rocket up your arse to teach us lot!'

Harriet wasn't new any more, but she was still filled with that same nervous apprehension on entering those gates. She didn't want to be reminded of the brevity of the Christmas holiday.

Mark, on the other hand was very laid back about his work. He was in research. Something to do with global warming. Harriet still wasn't quite sure what he did exactly then neither did Mark! At least he wasn't telling *her.* They seemed to meander their way through the day, the week, the year without undue pressure. It was just a bind having to turn up at all! The pay cheques, though not brilliant, knew their way to the joint account, unlike Harriet's. Each one the culmination of another month of struggle and according to Harriet, each one going to be the very last. If it wasn't for Mr. Sanderson she would have gone long since.

Harriet could never quite understand how this gorgeous six-foot blonde had extracted from the higher socio-economic strata to become a primary school headteacher. Of course he'd already done the leafy suburban bit with great success, but to hunger for the challenge of an inner city school was beyond Harriet. She was there for the money, basically. Joris Sanderson, Harriet considered, was selfless. He was one of those rare species of male that actually actioned his words. He was, at least in this small microcosm of society, going to make a difference. His belief in equality and social justice for all was the light that guided his whole being. And, of course, according to Harriet, that's why he wasn't married! She likened it to the priesthood. He was living a life totally dedicated to fulfilling those most honourable values, without encumbrance. Needless to say, she hadn't quite got her head round such a good-looking guy being so distractingly available. Yes, that's why Harriet was still there! As well as needing the money, of course, Harriet was determined to help him in every conceivable way. She was always first to volunteer for the extra-curricular activities as long as Mr. Sanderson was going to be around. It had even been known for Harriet to offer a hand during the school holidays, unknown to Mark, of course. 'That's jolly sporting of you Harriet! I'll give you a call as soon as I know what's what!' Closed classroom doors, echoing corridors, the odd mop head and bucket to avoid. No distractions, just the sweetness of the vacuum, like virgin snow, waiting for his footsteps. Harriet was *desperate* for the phone to ring.

In theory, Harriet was available too. Harriet and Mark had met in 'supplies', section G – L, on her first day at university. Harriet was short of a spare light bulb.

'And you're Harriet, who?' mumbled the janitor.

'Oh, Glover,' she smiled, 'South Block 2.'

Her right heel lifted and having fulfilled its obligation to allow Harriet to stretch forward returned to position with haste, jabbing the unfortunate chap behind who, in his haste to rescue his foot, sent Harriet flying. 'Jerk,' Harriet bristled to herself, 'why couldn't he keep his big feet to himself?'

An embarrassed Mark helped her to her feet.

'I'm quite alright, thank you,' Harriet said rather coldly yet amidst the flood of irritation she couldn't help liking his smile.

'Look,' he beamed, 'really sorry! Let me buy you a drink, I'd feel heaps better!'

'C'm'n. I haven't got all day. What is it you want?'

'Bog rolls,' beamed Mark.

'Name and Block?'

'Mark Glover, Block…'

Harriet couldn't believe her ears! 'But then there were a lot of students and it wasn't such an unusual name.'

Harriet had always been apprehensive about leaving home and going to university. Both her elder brothers had sported 2:1 degrees and Harriet, for the sake of family honour, had felt obliged to follow them. James and Paul were both married now. James had submitted to plummy Geraldine, who'd managed to produce the vilest of offspring, Clarissa. They lived on the edge of expensive suburbia. Theirs was the beauty of green pastures and rolling hills, with all the conveniences of life just a stone's throw away. Paul, on the other hand had settled for a rather timid girl, Susan. 'But obviously not so timid in bed,' Harriet used to think. She knew she was just a little bit jealous of Susan. With four children and only Paul's salary theirs was the overstretched semi. 'Quite ordinary, really,' Harriet frequently mused. She felt Paul hadn't quite aspired to their parents' ambitions. Harriet certainly hadn't!

'I think Susan might be expecting again,' her mother had recently whispered in shocked bursts down the phone.

'Again?' questioned Harriet, battling with envious disbelief.

'Well she is married, Harriet,' retorted her mother in an instant side-swipe. 'Why don't you call in tomorrow morning and tell me what you think. I'm sure I'm right! And by the way Happy New Year to you all!' A reprieved Harriet placed the receiver only to struggle with a surge of conflicting emotion.

'Well, it's not for the want of trying, Mummy!' Harriet caught in the mental fury of indignation silently argued with everyone and anyone who could have had any bearing on her present existence. Of course Harriet had wanted to marry Mark, but he turned out to be the biggest commitophobe on the planet. There was absolutely no reason for it. His parents were happily married. His brother Sean managed to seal it in church even. Harriet can remember it so vividly. Angela, like a beautiful wave, sweeping down the aisle in a sea of white. That was the day, really the one and only day in all those years that Mark just vaguely hinted Harriet's turn would come. Harriet was still waiting, but she wasn't sure why. She'd long since tired of Mark's insistence that there was no point.

'We're a pair of Glovers already,' Mark would say. 'Can't change that!'

She knew he hated ceremony, change, being cornered. But Mark was the guy that all the girls liked and Harriet, being Harriet, wasn't going to lose him; not to any one of them. 'Even if it meant, well, even if it meant….' Harriet thought about the light bulb.

'If I hadn't needed a bloody spare,' Harriet hated the dark, 'I probably wouldn't have even met him. If he hadn't shoved his clodhopping big feet under mine I'd have just gone.' She rose to the final straw. 'If the spare bulb hadn't been bloody broken because of his bloody big feet we might not have spent the night together in bloody bed!' Harriet felt her language was well justified. 'Anyway,' she thought, 'why should I want to marry him any more?' She felt he'd long since extinguished the spark from their relationship. Not 'Glovers' just Gloves now. Boring old gloves! Yet, despite her 'old glove' analogy, Harriet wasn't about to let go of Mark. 'Huh, Tricia Harrington, she can go and fish somewhere else, too. Can't think what Bob ever saw in her!'

Chapter 3

With no call all week from Mr. Sanderson, Harriet could only assume that he'd not been able to find the time for school work over the holiday, although she was quite sure he wanted to get the Parents Association on to its new footing as soon as they went back. There was still a lot to do and Harriet had offered to help with all the letters that needed to go out. She puzzled over it as she drove to school.

Harriet wound her way round the grey tables and chairs bracing herself for the swing of the classroom door. 'Ugh! First day back. I really don't want to be here,' she thought. Just missing Harriet, the door swung open creating a vehement rush of cold air.

'What's this all about then? What a damned cheek `e's got! Who does `e think`e is? Jumped up stick of git!'

The words were shot simultaneously with the paper straight into Harriet's face. She peered between an army of cheap jewelled hands, chipped coloured nails and dangling, grubby sleeves, to see a forest of A4 paper waggling menacingly, each one spearheading anger into the bristling air.

'Does `e think we don` know `ow to bring up our own fuckin` kids, or what? Parenting classes, `e could do with `avin` a few `imself, might show `im `ow to do it!' Harriet went pink as the instantaneous roar of laughter filled the corridor.

'She could probably do with a few lessons an` all!'

'What, with `im!' came a shriek from the back.

Harriet was mortified. In two seconds they had gone, marching their way to the Head's office leaving in their wake a trail of undignified fury.

'Sara Atkins,'

'Yes Miss,'

'Danny Bustard,'

'Miss,'

'Sabaru Camaboolla,' began Harriet.

'She's not `ere Miss.'

'Oh yes she is Kevin, I saw her go into the toilet with a banana, Miss. It was my banana. She pinched it,' came a determined little voice.

The children's laughter filled the room and Harriet struggled to gain control but her mind was elsewhere, desperately trying to sink the pain of missed opportunity.

'Who did help him, then?' She frantically scratched around for an explanation as the day ticked by. She hadn't seen him all day, she hadn't heard what had happened to the angry parents either. She opened her car door, hurled the books in to the back and started the engine. Her mind was still wrestling with it, tossing it back and forth when to her horror she saw the two huge white trunk-like arms of the lollipop lady coming towards her. She hoisted her pole at the windscreen, wobbling the big round end at Harriet, blocking her vision. Harriet stopped abruptly and opened the window, to be met with a red, round, angry face pushing into hers.

'Just look where you're going!' it shrieked. 'Nearly `ad me then you did.'

Harriet apologised profusely and drove off choking the tears away. She stopped at the lights, automatically glanced at the familiar looking 'For Sale' board pressed against the empty showroom window just on the corner and decided Bryce Rae Roberts weren't capable of selling anything! As the lights changed to green she suddenly remembered the phone call on New Year's day. A sense of warm rapid relief surged through her. 'Of course, while Mark and I were flattening the cat in a scramble to answer it, it rang off.' She knew that was him trying to get hold of her. 'Mr. Sanderson never tries twice!' She drove home, wondering why it hadn't occurred to her before.

Much cheered and armed with mountains of work, Harriet opened the front door to the phone ringing. 'It's him,' she thought. 'He hasn't had a chance all day. He's going to explain!' But it had slipped Harriet's mind that Mr. Sanderson hardly ever explained anything, unless pressed to do so. She hurled her bag, coat and books at the stairs and grabbed the phone in eager anticipation, hardly aware of the sliding heap behind her.

'Harriet,' bounced her mother. 'I thought you were calling in on New Year's day. I even phoned to see where you were!'

Heart sink. Harriet deflated like a pricked balloon. This hadn't been Harriet's day. She turned to face the misery of the avalanche she'd just created when the phone rang again. She couldn't believe her ears!

'Yessssss!' she hissed. 'That's him!'

'`arriet, is Mark in yet?'

'No, he bloody isn't,' snapped Harriet. Then she rapidly recoiled. 'Sorry Tricia, it's been a bad day. First day back and all that.'

'That's OK `arriet, it's just that Mark offered to lend his winch to Bob and I'm phoning to see when it would be convenient to collect it.'

'He'll be home in about an hour.' Harriet was trying to control her trembling voice. 'I'll get him to give you a ring.'

'Thanks, `arriet, see you!' Harriet was seething. She couldn't decide what was worse, being ignored by Mr. Sanderson or now having final proof of Mark's infidelity!

The doorbell rang. It usually did between 4.00 and 6.00 p.m. This was the optimum time for flogging double-glazing, a block paved drive, or new guttering. Harriet was incensed. She floundered over the mountain of books, topped by her bag and coat. She pushed forward the letter-flap, saw a hand clutching a clipboard and screeched 'Sod off!' Immediately the bell rang again. 'I'll give it him!' She grabbed the handle, swung the door back sharply, opening it as wide as she could.

'Oh, hello Mr. Sanderson, er, I didn't expect…'

'To see me, Miss Glover?' He took over her surprise. His expression was as stern as she'd ever seen it. 'Can I come in?'

'Er,' Harriet was tongue-tied. Her brain could not produce an instantaneous excuse for the heap on the floor. 'Err, do mind that lot, I er…'

Harriet's mind was swimming. 'I've just told him to sod off! Sod off, as in sod off!' The thought swirled around her head. He'd never called on her before. Wow, had she dreamed of such a day. So many scenarios! Harriet's brain couched in its rose pink face felt as though it was on elastic strings. She desperately tried to concentrate. 'What had he come for?'

He picked his way through the heap on the floor, stepping very gingerly over the strap on Harriet's handbag and finally sank into the sofa. He began leafing through the sheets on his clipboard. 'Harriet, it didn't go down too well, did it?'

Harriet felt another blank coming on. She wasn't sure what he was referring to.

'I was attacked this morning, Harriet, by a mob of outraged parents! Do you know anything about it Harriet? That Bustard boy's in your class isn't he?'

'Er yes,' replied Harriet clutching on to the straightforward question, 'Daniel, yes he is.'

'His mother, Mrs. Bastard er Bustard, Harriet, is she a bit of a ring-leader?'

Harriet studied the carpet intently.

'Need to win her round. We're not letting go of this one, Harriet. Catch her in the morning will you before assembly and tell her I want a word. Find a few stars for the lad and make him milk monitor, or something. That woman told me to "button it" Harriet. Would you believe it! Not nearly as bad as you telling me to sod off though!' He shot a broad grin at Harriet as he raised himself to his full height.

'See you in the morning, Harriet. I'll let myself out.'

Harriet watched him pat their boat as he made his way to the gate. Then, over the hedge she just saw him nodding to someone as he got into his car.

'Who was that?' thought Harriet still dazed by the whole experience. Then she saw Tricia's bleached blonde head of hair bobbing up the driveway. Harriet rushed out to greet her on the path, as that's where she intended her to stay. No way was she going to invite Tricia Harrington in, especially not with Mark due home.

'Wow, `arriet, who was that gorgeous hunk?! He's just smiled at me. Where have you been hiding `im, then? Promise I won't tell Mark. Not this time, anyway!' she added.

Harriet wasn't of a mind to tell Tricia Harrington who he was. She decided a mantle of mystery was just the thing to keep her guessing. Anyway, Harriet was furious that she'd almost succeeded in stealing those final precious moments from her. How could she be the last one he smiled at? She decided not to tell Mark either, for the moment. This she would keep to herself. It was not for sharing. Tricia left the question in the air as Mark drove in.

'Any chance of the winch for Bob?' she shrilled, not giving Mark a chance to get out of the car. It wasn't nice but Harriet was rather pleased Tricia was making such a pain of herself. Mark definitely wouldn't like it.

'In the garage Tricia, we'll get it now,' he said, and off they went with Harriet left standing there.

'Isn't he wonderful, `arriet? He wouldn't let me `elp him carry it.' She turned to Mark. 'Ooh we owe you one for this Mark. Drinks on us!'

Harriet looked confused.

'Burns' night `arriet. I `ope you `aven't forgotten! Kilts only Mark on Saturday night and don't forget we're open to guests. I've ordered tons of those haggises. I've told everyone to ask around. Mine's a mini-kilt,' she shouted. 'Of course I'll be wearing my knickers, though. *You* needn't bother Mark!'

'Bloody cheek!' Harriet quietly fumed. 'And her in a mini kilt! Not with those peg legs,' thought Harriet as she heard Mark slamming Tricia's car boot. 'Too thin by far.'

Harriet's rage suddenly evaporated in the realisation that Tricia had swiftly moved her thoughts away from Mr. Sanderson. She wondered just how much haggis Tricia had ordered. She decided Tricia had probably over-egged it to compensate for last year's fiasco when the Club cook, desperately short, was obliged to cut the small black balls into quarters to meet the demand. He'd had to flatten it on to each plate to encourage a meeting with the mashed potatoes and everyone received a huge dollop of turnip to compensate. As Refreshments Liaison Officer it was obvious to Harriet that Tricia wasn't going to be caught out again. She wasn't quite ready to vacate her post. She felt it gave her some standing at the Club and Harriet knew the position was up for re-election at the forthcoming A.G.M. Tricia couldn't afford another crisis. Harriet really didn't wish to bail her out. She certainly wasn't going to go guest gathering. She wasn't going to provide her with even more flirting opportunities. She considered that Bob was a perfectly good husband. At least he married her, but Harriet couldn't for the life of her think why. Anyway Harriet really wasn't in the mood for the Burns' night bash. She wanted a quiet weekend just to analyse a little more the meaning of Mr. Sanderson's unforgettable smile.

Chapter 4

The necessity for milk monitors had long since passed, but the next day Harriet announced to all the class and Danny that she would like him to be the register monitor.

'I done wonnu Miss,' he bawled and he shot into the playhouse refusing to come out. 'That's a good start,' muttered Harriet, still distracted by the thoughts of Mrs. Bustard and Mr. Sanderson thrashing it out in the office. Harriet marched to the playhouse and stretched over the precariously secured corner. As she leaned on the offending strip of wood designed to anchor both sides together, it shot into the air winging towards Danny who was crouched under the window on the other side. Danny did a quick dodge only to be attacked again by Harriet hurtling towards him like a demented surfer to the sound of the whole house clattering on the floor! The classroom door swung open.

'Do you make a habit of building floor traps for people, Miss Glover?' The class silenced as Mr. Sanderson lifted the house panels to safety.

'Out you come, er…?'

'Daniel,' said Harriet.

'Ah Daniel, yes, I remember now,' recalled Mr. Sanderson as he shot a glance of impatience at Harriet. 'Our new milk monitor.'

'We done 'ave milk in this class 'cos I'm too big now! Miss is making me be register monster and I done wanna be.' He burst into tears and then started bawling. 'She's 'urt me arm. I'm gonna tell me Mum of you Miss.'

'Come now, come with me. Let's see if she's still around,' consoled Mr. Sanderson, 'I've only just finished talking to her.'

'I thought I could 'ear our Dannybabes cryin`, I'd know that cry anywhere! What's 'appened to yer babes?'

Mr. Sanderson ushered them both outside as quickly as he could and closed the door behind him leaving Harriet to pick herself up as she attempted to gain some control over the class. The door swung open again. It was Mr. Sanderson.

'She's taken him, Miss Glover. She's on her way to the doctor's to get him checked out. See me at break will you.'

This wasn't the start to the New Year that Harriet had hoped for. She knocked on his door and went in.

'Take a seat Miss Glover,' he said, pointing to the office chair strategically placed in front of his desk. 'Have you any, presumably self-inflicted, injuries?'

'No, just a bit shaken. I'm terribly sorry Mr. Sanderson, I was only trying to get Daniel to come out of the house.' Harriet was so embarrassed. She looked down, and then looked across at him.

'She's been on the phone, Miss Glover, threatening to sue us!'

'Why, was Daniel hurt?' quivered Harriet.

'Probably not, we'll just have to see. She was too outraged to listen to the question, let alone give me an answer. We've lost all threads of cooperation for the time being, I think!'

Harriet left the office feeling dreadful. She'd always had a penchant for tripping over, but lately it seemed to be getting worse. Harriet was forty now and she just wasn't feeling her old self anymore. She had been told many times that she didn't look her age and she considered herself well blessed to have inherited her mother's naturally blonde hair and maybe some age-resilient genes. But she was definitely getting fatter! It seemed to Harriet that however hard she tried she just couldn't get on top of those extra little pouches of flab that threatened to wobble her into middle age. These unfriendly blobs were well hidden under her clothes. She blamed them for her increasing clumsiness and was just thankful that Mr. Sanderson didn't know of them.

She'd hoped that Mark hadn't noticed either, but she tormented herself with Tricia's lean frame and felt very vulnerable especially as Tricia was quite a few years younger than her.

'Had a good day, Harriet?' said Mark as he came in from work.

'No,' said Harriet and she poured out the whole sorry tale before he was hardly through the door.

'Oh poor old Glover,' Mark sympathised, giving her a hug. That made Harriet feel much better. She knew she really did love him. He couldn't help his gross fear of commitment!

'Tell you what, Hat. It's Friday, let's get a take-away and a bottle of wine. We deserve it!'

Harriet lit the fire, put the plates to warm and changed into her jumper and jeans. 'No,' she thought, 'not this one. I'll go and find the skinny blue top that Mark likes.' She pulled it over her head only to find in places the 2x2 rib lifted as it gave up the struggle to sit neatly on her waistline. She looked at herself, full length in the mirror. 'Ugh!' she exclaimed. She didn't know how anyone could ever find her in the least bit attractive, let alone want to marry her!

In actual fact Harriet was considered by Mark to be very attractive. He could see no change in her over the years. He always said what a fine looking Hat and pair of gloves they were!

'Fancy another glass Hat?'

Harriet stretched her arms and legs to the luxurious warmth of the blaze in the hearth.

'Shouldn't really. Oh go on then!' She smiled and listened to the comforting glugs as they predictably effected the transition of rich red shiraz from bottle to glass. Mark put his arm around her and slid his hand down to allow her to lift her drink.

'This is comfy, Hat,' he murmured as he fondled her waist. Harriet attempted a speedy diversion.

'That's why we chose it, remember? From that place where you have to hurry because the sale ends on Sunday and starts again on Monday!' They started laughing. Mark had been talking about the sofa after all. Harriet buried her head in his shoulder and watched the cat lazily stretching to the full warmth of the fire. She vowed to herself to keep school out of their weekend.

Chapter 5

'Who's that?' whispered Mark as he came down the stairs the next morning.

'It's Mummy, she wants to know....'

'Are you listening Harriet?' came the voice down the phone. 'I asked how are you getting on with those bridesmaid's dresses? Only Geraldine's been on the phone. She's starting to get a bit panicky. Shall I tell her they're nearly finished?'

'No, definitely not,' said Harriet.

'I know she's being a bit of a nuisance Harriet, the wedding isn't 'til August for goodness sake, but I don't want to get on the wrong side of her again. She took it totally the wrong way when I told her Clarissa would need plenty of yardage in her wedding dress. I still think she's taking it out on poor James, though. He looked so miserable when he called in last night. Wouldn't say anything to us, of course, but she certainly rules the roost!'

'Leave it with me,' promised Harriet and her heart sank at yet more fittings with those two plummy girls.

'Rachael's just arrived!' shouted Mark in astonishment. 'We weren't expecting her this weekend, were we?'

'She must have been driving half the night, why didn't she let us know?'

Harriet was becoming increasingly alarmed. It was only the day before yesterday she'd had a furious phone call from Clare. 'Whatever could it be?' she said.

Rachael flounced through the door, the tears welling in her eyes. 'Ben and I are finished!'

'Oh no!' Harriet exclaimed 'Not finished!'

Rachael brushed the mop of dark curly hair away from her eyes to allow the tears to flow freely. 'That's the third time he's backed off a date blaming work. I know, I just know he's got someone else!' Rachael sobbed uncontrollably and Harriet scooped her baby into her arms.

'Now, you don't know anything of the sort Rachael! Come on, let's make a coffee and you tell me all about it.' Mark scurried off to the shed.

'There's nothing to tell,' sobbed Rachael. 'I haven't seen him for two weeks. I just don't believe him anymore.'

Harriet looked and felt quite helpless. Her thoughts were raging. 'How dare this jumped-up little city… city.' Harriet was having difficulty summoning up the right word. 'City dweller, no that's no good.'

'How dare he do that to my baby!' she exploded. 'He's not coming into this house ever again!'

Rachael looked at her mother, grateful for the unconditional support, but somehow hadn't meant to send her so completely over the top.

'He's not worth the breath,' declared a sniffling Rachael. 'Anyway, how's Clare? You wouldn't catch Rod ever doing that to her!'

'Hasn't she called you yet?' Harriet asked in surprise. 'She phoned a couple of days ago. Apparently they finished last week! She was livid with him! He blamed work as well but Clare wasn't having any of it. You'll hear all about it, she did say she wanted to tell you herself.' Rachael's recovery took a dramatic turn for the better. 'Well, that's men for you!' she exclaimed and settled down looking forward to commiserating with Clare just as soon as she got back.

Harriet began to wish the last few days hadn't happened. The phone rang and Harriet immediately thought of Mr. Sanderson. 'No, it won't be him, it can't be him,' she thought. She felt a cloud of apprehension engulf her as she picked it up. 'Oh it's you, Clare,' she said. 'How are you feeling now?'

'Don't ask,' came the reply. Harriet sensed that Clare's anger had given way to depression.

'I've been trying to get hold of Rachael…'

Before she could finish Harriet told her the story.

'I'm on my way Mum, see you some time this afternoon.' Harriet told her to take care and replaced the receiver to see a delighted Rachael who'd been listening over her shoulder.

Rachael thought for a moment and said, 'anything on at the sailing club tonight? Let's go out and drown our sorrows! You and Dad look as though you could do with a night out! By the way, how did New Year's eve go?'

Harriet looked at her shrugging her shoulders. 'I think it's the Burns' night bash tonight,' she said.

'That's it then,' announced Rachael. 'Men in kilts! We'll definitely treat you both to a good night out!'

Clare was certainly up for it! After a quick call from Rachael she'd searched the wardrobe for both her kilts before leaving and then hammered her way up the M40 pushing the Mazda MX5 for all it was worth. Eventually it parked very comfortably alongside Rachel's MG TF.

Harriet looked out of the window, feeling a great sense of pride at her babies' achievements.

'She's here!' shouted Harriet but Rachael was already out of the front door.

In different circumstances Harriet and Mark would have delighted in the opportunity for another family weekend but they were still recovering from a house full at Christmas. Certainly they had all enjoyed it and considered their expended energy well worthwhile for the sake of nurturing along their girls' relationships. Now they couldn't quite believe it was all to no avail.

'There's Clarissa on the threshold of marriage,' Harriet moaned to Mark, 'and our two…'

'Don't worry Hat,' he said as he disappeared into the bathroom.

'They won't even end up like me,' she mumbled to herself as she scrambled through the wardrobe for something to wear. Reluctantly she wrapped her much treasured but very old kilt around her waist. It hadn't seen the light of day for many years. Harriet nearly cut herself in two trying to coax the big black button into the buttonhole. She could feel it loosening. The kilt pin caught between her knees and laddered her tights just as the button spat through the air catching Mark as he innocently opened the bedroom door.

'Steady on Hat,' he winced and he shot back into the bathroom clutching at his eye.

'I'd better try this on,' she thought, anxious to get dressed before Mark could witness the offending pink fleshy wobbles and she slipped her head and arms into the rich burgundy velvet dress that had been promised an airing on New Year's eve. The deep pile hit the light at her waist and again at her hips. She turned three-quarters into the mirror and saw what she considered to be something very near to a hippopotamus in drag.

'Better try the silver one,' she despaired. 'Two piece should be better!'

She found it dangling from a thread in a suicidal threat as it tried to divorce itself from the tilting coat hanger. Skirt on, top pulled down, 'That'll do,' she thought. Quick glance in the mirror; this time she was unmistakably met with the image of a huge silvery grey whale!

She fell back onto the bed in disbelief. She didn't need this. When was life going to get better? She rummaged in the drawer for something she bought years ago after having the children. Her hands met with the shiny black rubbery girdle sporting its provocative dangly suspenders. She forced herself into its elasticised tomb and returned to the velvet.

'That's better,' she said to herself, trying to ignore the cramps as she looked for another pair of tights. 'Funny how we don't wear stockings any more.' Her mind wandered. 'Must get Mark to do the lottery before we go.'

'We'll need to win it to pay for eye surgery,' Mark retorted from the bathroom. Harriet felt awful. How could she be so engrossed in her blobs of fat to want to take such swift advantage of Mark's unfortunate exit?

'Are you OK?' she called.

'Just find me the eye patch Harriet and I'll go as a Celtic pirate!'

Chapter 6

The four of them arrived to Tricia guarding a clutch of tables in eager anticipation of all her personally invited guests arriving at once.

'You've brought your girls!' she shrieked in utter disbelief. 'Fancy them both coming all this way just for my haggis!' She launched herself at them in eternal gratitude.

'Well, it, er…' began Harriet.

Mark nudged her and she immediately withdrew.

Tricia continued, 'Mark! What have you done to your eye? Has `arriet landed you one? Poor Mark!'

With that she spotted further success coming towards her and charged off to secure their intention of haggis consumption. Harriet couldn't believe it. She had hardly recovered from Mark's intervention only to be attacked again. Her irritation bubbled over into annoyance. She was already feeling those blobs of flesh trying to escape from their uninvited encasement which was making her feel very hot and itchy, not to mention the increasingly sharp needles of pain now meeting in menacing clusters of four as her tights firmly buttoned the suspenders to her thighs.

'Are you OK Harriet?' enquired Mark, rather gingerly.

'Will be in a minute,' she grimaced, and shot off to the loo leaving Mark and the girls to catch the draught.

'That's better,' Harriet muttered to herself in great relief. She'd just managed to roll the girdle over her grateful stomach when Tricia shouted over the top of the loo door. '`arriet, Greg and Melanie are here and Pete and Andrea have arrived with two smashing young men! Don't know why Ben and Rod are missing, but your girls might enjoy a bit of a change, `arriet. Shall we pull the tables together then and make a night of it?'

'Sounds good to me,' said Harriet who'd stopped her activity abruptly, irrationally convinced that Tricia could see through the loo door. She heard Tricia rapidly mincing her way back, heaved a sigh of relief and rolled the black rubbery elasticised killer into as tight a bundle as she could manage before poking it into the corner of her handbag. She smoothed her dress down over the very relieved blobs of fat and trusted that the dimmed lights and the rapidly crowding room would disguise the worst.

With great caution Harriet opened the loo door. She half expected to see Tricia back again! She proceeded to the Powder Room door, pulled it slightly open and like the parting of the waves everyone suddenly lined the bar counters leaving a wide clear aisle to Harriet's table at the far end of the room. Harriet thought she might just as well be on the catwalk! Instinctively she retreated, waited a few moments and peered round again. 'Good,' she thought, 'they're starting to go back to their tables.' She judged another few seconds would do it, and she peeped round again.

'What's Mum up to now?' Clare whispered to Rachael. 'She's been popping in and out from behind that door like a yo-yo for the last five minutes!'

'Perhaps she's hiding from someone?' replied Clare, 'I know she can`t stand that Commodore chap Tarquin Bridgewater.' 'It's OK she's coming now: round the back of the tables. She certainly doesn't want to bump into *him*!

During Harriet's absence Tricia organised the three tables to be pushed together but was somewhat disconcerted to see the curvy triangular hole left in the middle. 'Oh well, the cloths will cover that!' she pointed out and then carefully placed the three green circular covers to grace the creatively enlarged surface. It distinctly resembled a huge three-leaf clover.

'There!' she said to Harriet as Harriet was struggling to find a place for her knees underneath it all, 'Couldn't be better! A shamrock! Most appropriate for Burns' night!'

Harriet watched her black diamond etched legs strutting away as the pleats on her kilt rhythmically rose and fell to the determined gait of her walk. Harriet was pleased that Mark was still at the bar. That kilt was far too short!

'Wasn't Robbie Burns Scottish?' Rachael whispered to Clare.

'I used to think so,' replied Clare and they both broke out into fits of giggles.

At an appropriate pause in her chatter to Melanie and Andrea, Harriet, now truly relieved of her constrictor, smiled across. She was so pleased to see her babies enjoying themselves. This was just what they needed!

'Make way for the chaps, guys!' said Mark as he led the group, glasses in hand. Pete ushered his smartly attired guests towards the girls.

'Ah, Rachael and Clare meet Tristan and Sebastian. Keen sailors from the green Surrey countryside!'

Both girls pricked their ears up. What potential!

Pete continued. 'Up here on business, dealing with one of our directors. Shown them how the really big propellers get made, a couple of times. Isn't that right lads?'

More interested in the girls, they both nodded briefly to Pete.

'Something to do with sailing this time: ah, Starboard Marine North West. I remember now,' he continued. 'That's a stroke of luck eh, didn't think you two would be here tonight.' He beamed at the girls and then at the lads. 'Far better than kicking your heels in that plastic hotel all evening chaps.'

Again, the young men nodded politely at Pete in agreement. The girls smiled and renegotiated the peculiarities of the reconstructed table to allow them both to sit down.

Harriet was so pleased for the girls as she watched the four of them exchanging glances, conversation, laughter and all those non-verbal gestures that indicated to her they were having a jolly good time.

'There,' said Tricia, 'will you pass the cutlery round the table `arriet, while I bring ours over?'

As Club Refreshment Co-ordinator, Tricia took her responsibilities very seriously. She had co-opted a couple of other unsuspecting members as well as

Bob to assist, and to her credit the evening was going superbly.

'There's plenty of room for us all,' she called as she teetered towards the kitchen. 'Sorry ours is the last, but that's the way you `ave to do it!'

'Quite right Tricia,' chorused the men and everyone eagerly awaited the evening feast.

Twelve seafood cocktails duly arrived and Tricia finally sat down squeezing herself between Bob and Mark.

'I don't like the look of that one, it's staring at me,' she announced to Mark, pointing at the large tiger prawn gracing the summit in the bowl, 'and those, those white things, they're going yellow round the edges. Ooh, I hope they're not off!'

'Mussels are supposed to look like that!' remarked Bob, trying to regain Tricia's attention.

Harriet watched her scanning the table. She eyed each pair of hands as they coped magnificently with extricating the prawn from its horny shell.

'She's going for it,' thought Harriet just as Tricia cracked it with the force of a sledgehammer. With great relief Harriet continued eating. She could only take so much of Tricia making a fool of herself in company. Sometimes Tricia got too close too home!

'Chat among yourselves,' she declared as she scooped the bowls from the table. 'Bob and I won't keep you waiting too long for the haggis!'

The wine was flowing and nobody really paid too much attention to her. They were already chatting among themselves. The room was packed, the bagpipes were struggling, the noise was rising with the laughter and it was difficult to make oneself heard.

'Having a good time Hat?' said Mark, placing his hand over his bad eye.

She squeezed his other hand under the table; school was a million miles away.

'Sorry about that,' she said, 'it just happened!'

'Like us,' said Mark, and Harriet couldn't disagree.

'Ooh, ooh, it's coming,' said Greg. Andrea turned round.

'Clear the way,' she said. The rest of the table looked across at three huge steaming haggis perched on a round silver tray.

'Pray, be silent for the ode, "Address to a Haggis", ' boomed Tarquin Bridgewater.

Tricia spindled her way in rapid bursts across the floor.

'I'll just put them in the middle, `ere,' she whispered as she stretched herself almost full length over the cacophony of tables. Legs up, revealing black diamond etched tights and red knickers, she stretched between Bob and Mark. The inoffensive trio of haggis leapt in surprise and then plummeted to the floor through the precarious layers of green cloth that had once disguised the hole left in the middle of the rearranged tables. The remaining cutlery followed suit until the green cloths and all they'd held clattered to the floor. Like a sparrow to the ground Tricia was under the table and up again in a flash.

'No 'arm done!' she said.

Tarquin Bridgewater attempted to regain the floor. To those steeped in the tradition of Burns' night there could be no humour in such an ill-timed interruption. Harriet glanced across to her girls and shook her shoulders to the rhythm of theirs as they writhed in the agony of stifled laughter, through the rest of the poem.

Harriet hadn't enjoyed herself so much in years! She was happy to stay put especially as it seemed to be the younger ones, amidst much laughter, indulging in the Scottish Reel and the Highland Fling. Mark was still holding her hand under the table and Tricia was so intent on hosting to perfection that Harriet felt no threat. The girls had ordered them yet another bottle of sauvignon blanc and Harriet was beginning to feel like the slimmest, most attractive girl in the world! The man of her dreams was right there nudging closer towards her. She didn't give a toss about school, and Mr. Sanderson had long since vanished from her mind!

'Drink up Hat,' said Mark, 'I think this is a different one,' and he held the bottle towards the flickering lights to catch the label before he filled Harriet's glass again. Harriet put it to her lips. 'Ah, a hint of sweet honey struggling through an orangey zest embracing the tangy threads of dry grape! It's the same one Mark,' she hummed.

'Well spotted Hat, just testing your grasp on reality,' and he hugged her.

'That's long since gone,' she mused contentedly. 'That's the way I like it!'

Harriet had lost all sense of time and it seemed to her that Tarquin Bridgewater was all of a sudden trying to wind up the evening far too quickly. She looked around to see the empty chairs now fully requisitioned. The music had stopped and there were intermittent bursts of clapping as skilled yachtsmen from their differing classes went up to collect their well earned awards.

'And now,' she heard him say, 'I have one final announcement. This has just been handed in to me. It was found behind the entrance door to the ladies Powder Room.' Harriet checked the floor.

'It's mine!' she panicked to Mark as Tarquin Bridgewater swung the open flapped black bag into the air by its loopy strap.

'Get it!' prompted Mark, 'now!'

As Harriet reached the platform the shiny rubbery black girdle hurtled straight into Tarquin Bridgewater's hands. He held it up. Suspenders dangling!

'Couldn't wait I see! Been eating your haggis in the loo, Harriet?! Not much left! Just the skin, oh, and these, the feet!' He poked at the dangling suspenders. Harriet grabbed the offending girdle and rushed off the platform to howls of shrieking laughter.

'Good job I'm just a bit tipsy,' she thought, 'otherwise this could be horrendous. So glad Mr. Sanderson isn't here though. That would be a different matter!'

She felt she was sobering up rapidly to have even had such a thought. She glanced back to the platform. A tall blonde gentleman lifted his hand and with a satisfied toss of hair strode to the exit.

'Oh no, that wasn't him, it couldn't be him! Whatever could he be doing here? No of course it wasn't him.' Harriet couldn't trust her judgement. She was feeling decidedly squiffy again.

'Goodnight!' 'Goodnight!' all the reciprocal goodnights resounded through the late night air.

'Goodnight `arriet,' chortled Tricia. 'That was the best laugh ever! By the way I'm sure I caught a glimpse of that gorgeous hunk from your school. You know, the one that smiled at me the other night at yours. Did you see `im? I'm sure it was `im, `arriet!'

'Can't say I did,' said Harriet trying to sound casual and so glad that they were well out of earshot of Mark.

'Night Tricia, thanks for a smashing evening!' Harriet, unable to ascertain the stability of her thoughts, made for the chattering group awaiting the taxi. She grabbed Mark's hand and just wanted to go home.

Chapter 7

'It was a good weekend though,' thought Harriet as she loaded the car up on Monday morning. 'The girls did enjoy themselves. I do hope they all meet up again down there; such nice lads! Where did Pete say they came from? …Something Marine, anyway it was definitely to do with sailing.'

Harriet already knew that Pete had something to do with manufacturing propellers though she thought his company was making rather bigger ones than that, more the size that go on the back of container ships. She wondered why the lads were involved with one of his directors; unless this chap was some way involved in this Starboard Marine place, which she'd never heard of. Anyway she refused to let any uninformed assumption negate Pete's inspired decision to invite them. She wanted it to work from both ends though. She wanted the lads to have to come back again. She wanted to see more of her girls.

As Harriet drove along she even managed a little giggle to herself about the girdle. How the four of them had laughed and laughed about it yesterday. It was such a relief to her that Mark had found it so funny. Not a mention of her necessity to wear it!

'Of course Mr. Sanderson wasn't there,' she went on to reassure herself. 'There were so many people, so many guests and we were all squiffy, especially Tricia. Anyway they'd only caught sight of him, …"that chap" she corrected herself, from behind, leaving in a hurry.'

She drove up to the lights and stopped at red. She glanced across the road to the empty showrooms on the corner as she usually did. 'SOLD subject to contract'. The board proudly presented its newly acquired status for all to see. 'Well, well,' thought Harriet, 'Bryce Rae Roberts have managed it at last! Must give them a ring while they're still in the full flush of success. It's about time they got ours on the move.'

Harriet drove through the opened gates and parked her car alongside Mr. Sanderson's. The silver Mercedes sporting his personal number plate, personified his style, his charisma, his charm and on the brink of meltdown, Harriet's excitement mingled with fear at the thought of seeing him again.

Alice Atkinson, the school secretary, very kindly opened the door as Harriet stumbled through, laden with schoolbooks secured by her chin, precariously balanced on top of an ageing brown leather bag choking with art materials. She clutched at her handbag sat on top of the pile, its long black strap falling over her shoulder looking for somewhere else to rest.

'Ah, Harriet,' said Alice earnestly, 'Mr. Sanderson wants to see you immediately. Don't worry about your class, Enid Frost will do the register and then take yours and hers down to assembly. The Deputy's doing it this morning.'

'Oh, OK,' said Harriet a bit more than taken aback. 'I'll just….' She stepped forward and found she couldn't move.

'Er, I think *this* is the problem Miss Glover.'

She turned her head round to see Mr. Sanderson unhooking the long black strap from its determined embrace with the door-handle.

'Having a bit of trouble with this thing, lately, Miss Glover?' he said before disappearing into his office.

'Oh no! What on earth did he mean?' She threw the bags and books down to hang up her coat. She racked her brains to imply a meaning other than Burns' night. She closed her classroom door behind her and scurried up the corridor to Mr. Sanderson's room. Then it clicked as she knocked on the door. Of course, it was on the top of the heap in the hall at home. He'd appeared to be almost scared of it. Great relief flooded through her as she entered his room.

'Take a seat Miss Glover, we've got ten minutes to go through this before Mrs. Bustard arrives. Tell me exactly what happened to Nathan.' Harriet didn't dare correct him. She recalled every cringing moment for him.

'Right, so as far as we can ascertain we carry no liability,' he stated.

'Well, it was an accident,' insisted Harriet.

'Did you call the boy Daniel, Miss Glover? I thought it was Nathan. Don't want to get off to a bad start with the woman!'

There was a short knock on the door.

'In,' boomed Joris Sanderson.

Alice Atkinson ushered Mrs. Bustard in and disappeared to scoop up Daniel who'd decided it was going to be more fun poking soil out of the much prized plant display in the foyer.

'Err, good morning Mrs. Bustard, where's Nathan? We trust he's feeling better.' charmed Mr. Sanderson.

Mrs. Bustard glowered at him. She didn't answer. 'Daniel, get in `ere now! Leave those plants alone will yer?'

'Ah Daniel, yes Daniel of course,' redressed Mr. Sanderson. 'How are you today?' 'I'm not bein` in `er class, anymore,' he spurted pointing a soily finger at Harriet. 'Me arm's got black all over it and it `urts.'

'Oh dear,' said Mr. Sanderson turning to his mother. 'What did the doctor say?' 'Said `es lucky to be alive! With that lot goin` on top of `im he could have bin dead!' Harriet panicked at the thought of being charged with murder.

'Are you sure?' said Mr. Sanderson suspecting they weren't hitting the truth.

'Yes I fuckin` am! Don't believe me now?! Our Bert'll sort you two out! Says there's a place up the road that will do *no sale, no fee.*'

Joris Sanderson looked puzzled.

Harriet intervened, 'You mean 'no *win*, no fee'.' Then she wished she hadn't. There she was putting words into this woman's mouth.

'Yes, that's it, that's the one! It's when you can get condensation for being injured.'

'You mean compensation Mrs. Bustard.' Harriet interrupted.

Mr. Sanderson shot her a glance.

Mrs. Bustard continued, unperturbed. 'Our Matilda punched her `erbert in the eye once, he blamed someone at work, they were always fightin' down there and he got a thousand pounds. They went to Majorca on it! I've got the name of the place right 'ere. Sounds like one of them places to me.' Mrs. Bustard finished with a grin and a whisper. She rummaged in her pocket to release a scrappy bit of paper into her hand.

'There!' she triumphed and punched it with great force towards his face. 'Broadbed, Rudey, Sex & Co Solicitors.'

'Err, I think you'll find that's *Broadbent* and the last name is *Essex* Mrs. Bustard,' corrected Mr. Sanderson.

'Well how do I know when the fuckin` letters keep fallin` off! Cum'n Daniel we're going there, straight now. We'll get a Butlins out of this!' The door closed behind them.

Harriet and Mr. Sanderson looked at each other.

'We'll just have to let it take its course Harriet. There's nothing you can do once these people make up their minds to sue. She doesn't stand a chance anyway. At least the boy's not had anything broken. I thought she was going to land me one for a minute!' He smiled and Harriet, transported by his return to the use of her Christian name found herself in a precarious kind of heaven.

'That's funny,' he continued. 'A colleague of mine was telling me about another awful woman who punched her husband in the eye at the weekend. Just about to go out for the night as well! Poor chap could hardly see, apparently.'

'Will that be all, Mr. Sanderson?' said Harriet and hurried out.

'Oh no! Surely he's not referring to Mark and me,' she thought, starting to feel highly uncomfortable.

'No, don't do this to yourself Harriet! It just couldn't have been him at the bash on Saturday night.'

She hurried along the corridor, vowing not to let this thing take her over.

'Thanks, Mrs. Frost,' said Harriet as she beckoned the last of her class through the door.

'Will you mind this Miss?' said Kevin thrusting his perennial banana at her.

'Won't it fit in your lunch box, Kevin?' enquired Harriet who was getting very fed up with Kevin constantly losing them.

'I'll go an` see,' said Kevin as he galloped towards the lunch box trolley making a grab for the dark blue one with lime green handles.

'Careful Kevin,' called Harriet. She didn't want another hazardous mountain created on the classroom floor!

'Found it, Miss!' triumphed Kevin and Harriet sprinted over just in time to stabilise the angular plastic mountain as Kevin tugged for all he was worth. Without warning, Kevin descended to the floor.

'They've all fallen out Miss!'

Harriet looked down to see Kevin with the upside down lunch box resting on his knees and a cluster of crusty, curling sandwiches peering from under his legs. The room filled with the smell of fish and the gleeful laughter of children enjoying an unscheduled diversion from the class routine.

'Simon Clarke put those scissors down now! Take them away from Melanie's hair this minute!'

Harriet leapt over Kevin and his escaped sandwiches to grab the scissors from Simon as he let go of a bunch of Melanie's hair.

'Get those picked up!' she shouted to Kevin. 'And come out of that water Andrew. No Andrew, don't pull the plug out!' But it was too late. The water table was rapidly emptying as its contents oozed and splashed the classroom floor in unpredictable bursts. Harriet grabbed a bucket and struggled to replace the plug. 'Right, everyone to the story corner,' she demanded. 'Helen and Lucy go and get the caretaker.'

Harriet managed to make 'news time' last until break, when, with great relief, she ushered them all out into the playground.

'I don't think I want to do this any more,' she said half aloud in the silence of the now dead chaos.

Mr. Sanderson suddenly shot the door open, sharply disturbing her thoughts. 'Harriet, you've got a boat. Where do you go for your spares, bits and pieces, maintenance and things like that?'

'Out of town, really,' said Harriet, trying not to look too surprised. 'That's the trouble, there's only one place round here and it hardly ever opens. It's a wonder somebody hasn't seen the need.'

Mr. Sanderson shot her an appreciative smile as he stroked his nose.

'Thanks Harriet,' he enthused and turned on his heel.

She watched his tall masculine frame head to the door by the lunch trolley where he briefly turned to smile again

'He is *gorgeous*,' she declared to herself, '*Absolutely gorgeous*!'

Harriet couldn't leave it there. She peered round the door just to catch a final glimpse of him marching up the corridor. She absorbed him head to toe, then, to her horror, looked down to see one of Kevin Connolly's chunky white bread bloater paste sandwiches stuck to the right heel of his highly polished shoe. Harriet's ecstasy dissolved into disbelief. This she just did not need.

Harriet spent the rest of the school day studiously avoiding Mr. Sanderson. She consoled herself with the thought that once he'd discovered it he wouldn't really know how it had arrived. After all there was no trace of lunch left on her classroom floor. She acknowledged that Kevin had made a jolly good job of picking everything up but wasn't too sure how he could have missed that one.

'It was probably when I had to leap over him to abort Melanie's no. 2,' she thought as she packed her bags for home. 'No good mulling over this all night, I'll pop into the estate agents on the way home and see if there's any sign of activity.'

It was only a short detour for Harriet and renewed by the sight of the 'sold' sign at the showrooms by the traffic lights she took a left turn and headed towards Bryce Rae Roberts.

In anticipation of ensnaring a potential buyer, Harriet was greeted with the kind of enthusiasm normally reserved for royalty.

'Er, no,' said Harriet beginning to feel a little uncomfortable. 'I'm Ms Glover. 4 The Willows. We are up for sale with you. It's been on the market for months and we haven't had a single viewing yet!'

'I came to see it only last week,' came a very familiar sounding voice from behind. Harriet jumped and turned round to see Mr. Sanderson standing within inches of her. She could feel herself colouring from head to toe.

'All viewings are supposed to be conducted through us Mrs. Glover,' came the semi-offended voice of the immaculate looking estate agent. 'You do realise that you are contracted to us and any sale achieved during this period will be assumed to have been so as a result of our endeavours.'

Mr. Sanderson laughed, 'Only joking,' he said. 'No one would want to buy Harriet's house anyway, its too untidy. I nearly broke my neck going in!'

'Well, there's your answer Mrs. Glover,' triumphed the smug estate agent. 'Go and tidy it up and then we'll look into it.'

Harriet flounced out of the door, just recovering enough equilibrium to peer through the glass at Mr. Sanderson's right shoe.

'Must be like glue that bloater paste,' she flustered to herself. He'd lost the sandwich but she considered the descending brown mound could well evacuate to the estate agent's carpet. 'With a bit of luck,' she thought.

In a daze Harriet got into her car and headed for home. She began to think she was hallucinating. Was Mr. Sanderson destined to present like some ubiquitous apparition wherever she went?

'What on earth was he doing in there?' She tossed and turned it in her head but couldn't find an answer. 'Come to think of it, why did he suddenly decide to ask about the boat?' Harriet had been too distracted to even consider asking herself the question at school. She gave up trying to fathom it all out. 'Oh that gorgeous, gorgeous man. None of it matters, just as long as I get to see him!'

She decided not to tell Mark. She didn't want to arouse his suspicions. Anyway the girls were phoning. They'd have enough to talk about once she knew how they'd got on with those boys.

Chapter 8

'Had a good day Mark?' asked Harriet as he came through the doorway.

'Not bad, not bad,' said Mark in predictable response.

'What about you, Harriet? That woman done any more about suing you?'

'Don't mention it. I think I've had enough of that place!'

'Maybe you could pack it in Hat,' began Mark constructively. 'Once we've downsized and got rid of the mortgage we should be able to manage.'

'Oh and that's another thing,' said Harriet, 'I've just called in there. Most unprofessional they were, said they would look into our lack of viewings.'

Harriet stopped fully aware that she'd only told half the story.

The phone rang and they both rushed to answer it. Mark just made it.

'It's the estate agents,' he mouthed to Harriet, 'want to take it?'

Harriet took over the call. 'Well that is a coincidence,' she said, 'viewing on Saturday 10 a.m. That shouldn't be a problem. Thanks a lot.' She put the phone down. 'We've got a viewer on Saturday morning, would you believe?'

Mark groaned. 'Oh no! I'm supposed to be helping Bob at the club, Harriet. You might have asked me first. Can't you see to it without me?'

'No,' insisted Harriet. 'It's the first flicker of interest and you can jolly well be there to answer any awkward questions!'

'What awkward questions?'

'Anyway,' continued Harriet promptly ignoring his last comment, 'There's all sorts of touching up to do and no one will ever want to buy it if you don't get rid of that mould round the bath.'

'What do you mean, *touching up*? I thought we'd just done it up! We've certainly spent the money.'

Harriet looked around. 'After a fashion.'

'OK Harriet, you win. I'll have to let Bob know though,' mumbled Mark as he went upstairs.

Harriet was just coming to terms with the amazing change of fortune when the phone rang again. 'Ah, this'll be one of the girls,' she thought as she went to answer it. 'Hello, Mark?' came the girlish voice on the other end.

'Oh, Mark,' said Harriet in surprise, 'who's speaking please?'

'Melissa Scott, Mark's secretary. Could I possibly have a word with him?'

'Er yes, I'll just get him.'

'I'll take it up here, Harriet,' he called.

With great reluctance Harriet replaced the receiver. Harriet was quite shaken. She didn't even know Mark *had* a secretary. Harriet just waited and waited. It seemed an eternity before Mark came down stairs again.

'You didn't tell me you'd been given a secretary,' said Harriet trying to look nonchalant.

'I haven't,' said Mark, a bit taken aback, 'is that what she said?'

'I think she did,' said Harriet.

'We share her Hat, she works for eight of us in the department. I should be so lucky to have my own PA. Anyway she needed to know where the RB2 file is for Marcus Cooper. They're up for a board meeting tomorrow.'

Harriet breathed a sigh of relief. She had enough on her plate trying to second-guess the significance of Tricia in his life without any new chicks coming into the frame! She went to the kitchen to prepare the meal.

'Curry OK for tonight Mark?' she called.

'That's fine Hat,' he said. 'I'm just going to give Bob a call.'

Harriet was fully aware that Bob might not yet be home, so she turned the radio down a little and moved to the end worktop where she felt she might hear just a little better.

'Hi Tricia, you both OK?'

Long pause. Harriet hated long pauses.

'Oh, sorry to hear that Tricia, anything we can do?'

'No, there bloody isn't,' an infuriated Harriet said to herself.

Another long pause.

'Ah, I see,' came Mark's best understanding voice. Silence again.

'Whatever's the matter with her now?' thought Harriet impatiently. Tricia was always having one crisis or another!

'Right then Tricia, try not to worry too much, these things have a habit of sorting themselves out. Anyway if you can pass the message on to Bob that I can't manage Saturday morning after all, I'd appreciate that. I'll catch him again.'

With that Harriet scuttled back to the sink and promptly turned the radio off as Mark came in.

'Everything OK?' enquired Harriet with as much disinterest as she could manage. 'Tricia's a bit upset.' Mark hardly had time to finish his sentence when the phone rang again.

'I'll get that,' said Harriet, 'it's probably one of the girls.'

'Hi Mum!' enthused Clare down the phone. 'Thanks for a cool weekend, it was brilliant!'

'That's good,' said Harriet, feeling the annoyance Tricia had encircled her in rapidly dissipating.

'Well, thank you and Rachael. You treated us, remember? We enjoyed it too, very much.'

'Oh Mum,' swooned Clare, 'he's such a dish!'

'Who?' questioned Harriet, wanting to be sure her response was rooted in firm ground.

'Ooh Sebastian of course, and would you believe it, Rod phoned, said he'd been sent to the States on business and wants to see me again! Well, I said I'd let him know. I'm not rushing back to him whilst I'm waiting for a call from Sebastian! Guess what? They're both coming up again soon and want to know if Rachael and I will be around.'

Just what Harriet wanted to hear.

'Rachael phoned last night,' Clare continued. 'She still hasn't heard from Ben, but Tristan phoned her! He said that he and Sebastian want to meet up with us at the weekend. Wow Mum, would you believe it!'

Harriet was almost as thrilled as the girls, and having established that this foursome was off the ground she swiftly moved to more practical matters.

'What exactly did they say they were doing in this area, Clare?'

'They didn't really say. Something to do with a new business partnership. It's obviously to do with Pete's work, boats and propellers. Still I expect we'll find out one of these days. Must go Mum, love to you and Dad. I promised to give Rachael a quick ring.'

'Give her our love,' said Harriet, 'talk to you soon and mind how you go.'

Harriet returned to the kitchen. 'Well,' she thought, 'Who would have guessed things could have changed so rapidly for the girls?'

'Dinner's ready,' she called to Mark. 'Hurry up, I want to tell you all about the girls and those boys.'

Harriet and Mark finally sat down after finishing their meal.

'Come on Hat, give us a cuddle.'

Harriet moved along, 'You never did tell me what the matter was with Tricia.'

'Can`t even remember, she didn't really say,' murmured Mark as he stroked her hair back and lightly kissed her cheek.

'That's good,' Harriet said to herself and her thoughts returned to the girls and the ultimate joy of them both coming back home. 'A double wedding,' she mused and then 'grandchildren' she triumphed to herself.

Harriet loved babies. She was always sorry not to have had more. She was only too aware of the regular monthly flirting with the possibility, but somehow she had never quite had the courage to take the plunge, completely. Mark was quite laid back about it but he couldn't understand Harriet's fluctuations. 'If you want one Hat,' he would say, 'why don't we just go for it?!'

'A penny for your thoughts, Hat,' Mark whispered.

'Just thinking of grandchildren, really.'

'Just thinking of babies you mean,' nuzzled Mark into her ear drawing her very close.

Chapter 9

Harriet greeted the morning in a surge of unsurpassed panic.

'What have I done?' she uttered to herself as she faltered to the bathroom. She could feel the well of anxiety washing her strength away as she attempted to struggle with her optimum fertility countdown. Her mind couldn't cope. She was hopeless with dates. She swung violently from the impossible to being 100% pregnant. She'd have to give up her job and what would the girls say? And her mother, what would she say? She still wasn't married. She wouldn't approve. And Mr. Sanderson! Oh no! Harriet still hadn't worked that one through. Harriet thought it better not to confide in Mark. She glanced at him across the breakfast table and recalled all her previous panics.

'Of course I'll be all right,' she reassured herself, 'must get this place sorted out for that viewing tomorrow! I wonder what Mr. Sanderson was doing in the estate agents though?' Harriet's thoughts had swiftly returned to default. 'What was he doing in there?'

Harriet was none the wiser when she returned home. Mr. Sanderson and the Governors had been interviewing all day and apart from Danny's uncontrollable desire to broadcast his mum's threat to get her and Mr. Sandcastles for the house breaking his arm, Harriet was otherwise thankful for the non-eventful day.

'Can you do the mould round the bath Mark?' came Harriet's voice from the kitchen as soon as she heard the front door close. 'We haven't got much time to get sorted in the morning.'

'Let's get in first Hat,' he pleaded trying to avoid the cat who'd wrapped its tail around his right leg. 'You could do with de-moulding too!' he teased.

'Well, that's not very nice,' thought Harriet defensively, 'especially after last night, especially after getting me into trouble last night!' And she threw Mark a steely glance.

'Not you, the cat! Daft Hat! Come here.' He gave her a hug.

'Not surprised I'm so sensitive,' she thought to herself and the remnants of annoyance that wouldn't go away became coated in renewed fear.

Chapter 10

Early morning found Harriet cramming the already groaning cupboards with everything in sight. 'Mark, can you close this door while I lean on it?' she called in desperation. 'And you've left all your tools in the porch. We don't want her to go flying before she gets in. We do enough of that in this house!'

'House? It smells more like a brothel! What on earth have you sprayed in the bathroom?'

Harriet had to admit to straining her meagre atomiser to its limits forcing it to shoot millions of droplets of her favourite perfume at the ceiling in an attempt to drench the disgusting smell of mould remover.

'Oh I'll put the coffee pot on then,' she panicked. 'It'll mask it. Leave the bathroom door open, Mark.'

'What else can I do?' Harriet, by swift association suddenly remembered the smell of baking. 'I'll just pop the rest of that French loaf into the oven on low and that's us sold!' she thought.

'By the way, Hat, who did you say was coming?'

'Er, I think it was someone on her own, a Ms Oxford, or Cambridge or something like that.'

'That's the doorbell Mark!' screeched Harriet. 'Quick, hide the cat's food in the cupboard under the sink while I answer it.'

Mark quickly grabbed the cat's bowl as Harriet straightened her jumper and smoothed her hair, glancing briefly in the hall mirror as she went to open the door.

'Get out of it!' she heard Mark bellow. 'You didn't want the bloody stuff half-an-hour ago,' and she opened the door to the sound of a resounding bang from the kitchen that seemed to shake the whole house.

'Er, sorry about that,' greeted Harriet, noting that Mark still hadn't moved the magnifying glass from the window sill. 'The wind must have caught the back door.' 'Really?' sported the astonished and very cultured voice from this gorgeous streak of leggy blonde. An equally leggy arm outstretched to Harriet, extending a white, swanlike, graceful hand. Harriet instantly became transfixed by the huge, glinting, brilliantly cut diamond on the engagement finger of her left hand as it clutched a petite but expensive leather bag to her side.

'Mrs. Glover?' She raised her finely manicured brows and smiled to reveal the most beautifully even teeth Harriet had ever seen. 'Belinda Oxfordshire, frightfully pleased to meet you.'

'And you,' responded Harriet, determined not to feel fat and very ordinary alongside this creature who'd obviously escaped from a magazine cover. 'I'll take you through. Er, Mark will answer any technical questions you may have about the house later. Are you from this area?'

'Good heavens, no! Down south, actually. My fiancé…' Harriet held her breath. She was about to have a very irrational moment. 'Not Mr. Sanderson,' she thought. 'Oh no!'

'My fiancé, Ted, and I are relocating for business reasons. He's frightfully busy just now, so I've got the job of house hunting. Of course it's not a long-term move for us, we're a rapidly growing company and we'll be moving around until our expansion targets have been met. Then we'll float on the Stock Exchange to become a public company. Not an inappropriate metaphor actually. Jolly exciting!'

Harriet had long since lost track, she was still basking in relief that Mr. Sanderson hadn't been in some way responsible for this viewing. Enthused by the prospect of serious buyers at last, she proceeded with renewed determination to make a sale. Taking great care not to be followed (bottom too large) Harriet ushered Belinda Oxfordshire up the stairs.

'Nice big bedrooms,' she heard herself say, but no matter how hard Harriet tried to coax her to enter, Belinda Oxfordshire insisted on peering from each doorway, until they reached the bathroom at which point she suddenly strode right in.

'The most important room in the house,' she announced.

'Ah! Right! Yes!' said Harriet who thought she could hear the cat come in and cursed herself for not remembering to lock the cat flap.

'Not exactly large enough for two,' mused Belinda as she scanned the bath. 'We always double with the bubble as we say, or rather with the bubbly! Still, it's a largish room, maybe a corner bath here.' Her long creamy white finger flicked its imaginary beam across the taps and pointed to the corner. Harriet's eyes immediately obeyed and stopped in horror as it sketched the mass of green mould still legging its way up the wall.

'Where's Mark?' she snapped to herself, hearing the cat meowing.

'Shall we go down now?' Harriet demanded as she ushered her towards the stairs.

'I say,' said Belinda, 'what a wonderful smell of baking. Compliments the coffee superbly!'

'Glad you like something,' thought Harriet crossly suddenly remembering she was pregnant. By now her fear had transposed itself into complete rage with Mark. 'That's the only thing he is good at,' she stormed to herself as she opened the lounge door.

'You have a cat?' queried a very puzzled sounding Belinda.

'Oh, it's somewhere,' muttered Harriet, trying to play it down. 'Er, that's a real fire,' announced Harriet, proudly. 'So nice for cosy evenings together.'

'Oh, a working fire. Can't be doing with them myself. Is there a gas point around?' 'Not sure really, a technical question,' said Harriet, 'better ask Mark. Anyway do feel free to have a good look around,' continued Harriet who was now feeling infuriated at Belinda's insistence on framing herself into every doorway.

'And this is the dining room, south facing so it catches most of the day's sun,' said Harriet rather briskly.

'Ah, I see what you mean,' said Belinda as the sun obligingly shone in. 'Such a pain for the domestic, though. Now I won't take anybody on until they've done the window test. My last one couldn't cope with streaks.' Belinda said in a voice as critical as her eye. 'Is the cat in here? One can hear it meowing rather loudly.'

'Er, shouldn't think so,' retorted Harriet, now feeling extremely irritated at having to cope with further disapproval. 'Shall we go into the kitchen?'

Belinda Oxfordshire twitched her classically grafted nostrils as she followed Harriet in.

'The cat's in here!' she triumphed.

'I don't think so. No sign of it in here, she's probably on the step wanting some attention. She's always doing that.'

Belinda Oxfordshire waltzed straight to the window, pinned her legs to the gap between the doors of the cupboard and stretched over the sink and taps pressing her nose against the glass in an attempt to see it. Then she leapt back drawing her hands to her face in horror. 'You've got a mouse! I felt it run up my leg! Oh! Let me sit down!' She pulled a chair towards the oven as the colour drained from her face turning it to white porcelain. At that point Mark opened the back door carrying a bucket of water.

'Good morning Miss Cambridge,' he said, standing to impress. 'Just off to wash the car!'

Harriet scowled.

'Oxfordshire, actuall…' Belinda, unable to finish her words, promptly went into a spin. 'What's that?' she screeched pointing to the cupboard door. 'It's that mouse, it's dying!'

All three stared at the clutch of fur limply clinging to the last shreds of life as it slowly swung from side to side.

'The cat! Where's it gone? How did it manage to trap it like that? Just leaving it hanging there! You didn't say you had mice, Mrs. Glover.' With that she fainted. Mark just managed to save her from falling off the chair.

'Let the cat out of the cupboard, quick,' whispered Mark, grinning, not anxious to let go of the gorgeous creature now cradled in his arm.

'You what?' Harriet couldn't believe her ears. She opened the cupboard door and the cat shot out. It flew to the cat flap trailing a limp tail behind it, leaving its bowl clattering as it curled its way noisily round the ceramic tiled floor.

'Something's burning! I can smell smoke!' Harriet and Mark jumped at Belinda's rapid recovery. Mark let go of her and immediately turned off the switch. The smoke was starting to seep from the oven door.

Harriet spotted the bucket of water. 'Right!' she said. 'It's coming!' Harriet grabbed it. She swiftly turned towards them. 'You've asked for it!' she fumed to herself. With every intention of drowning Mark in one good douse, he shot past to open the back door leaving Belinda Oxfordshire to cop the lot. If she hadn't quite come to, she was now most certainly fully conscious. She retrieved her car keys from her once beautiful, but now drenched bag and stared at them both.

'You'll be hearing from my solicitor,' she snapped, and dripping wet stormed out.

'No technical questions, then?' managed Mark to the sound of the revving engine, before he collapsed in a heap on the floor, but she was gone.

Of all the emotions that flooded Harriet's mind, try as she may, laughter was the one she just couldn't contain. Mark pulled her down and they ached as they rolled round laughing, oblivious to the wet, cold tiles.

Chapter 11

Monday morning found Harriet quite dazed from the emotional mix traumatising her life. The humour of Saturday had long since dispersed as she tried to cope with two impending court cases, being pregnant and a hormonally linked rapidly developing spot on her left cheek. She'd fully expected a call from Bryce Rae Roberts confirming her worst fears but, as yet, all was silent.

Harriet, narrowly avoiding their boat, drove out of the gateway wondering how she was going to cope with calling the register, never mind the school day. 'Two good things, anyway,' she consoled herself, 'Mr. Sanderson doesn't know I'm pregnant and he'll never know about the viewing fiasco, however many times I see him in the estate agents. Come to think of it,' she continued, grateful for the impending deviation, 'what was he doing in there?'

Harriet approached the traffic lights as they turned amber and promptly screeched to a halt. She took her customary glance at the recently sold showroom premises on the opposite corner. Above the whitewashed windows a deep Oxford blue border sported an expensive set of gold leaf lettering: STARBOARD MARINE NORTH WEST. 'That rings a bell,' she thought, but couldn't think why. The blast of a million horns finally spurred her on her way. She drove on feeling a little unnerved and finally gave up all attempts at recall as she entered the school gateway.

'Good morning Harriet!' beamed Mr. Sanderson as he passed her in the corridor. 'Spare me a few minutes at break will you? We've had a letter from that woman's solicitor.'

Harriet drained.

'Are you feeling all right Miss Glover? Don't worry, at least we'll go down together!' He shot her a look of humorous concern and Harriet forced a brief smile. Not that Harriet would have minded going down with Mr. Sanderson, but he didn't realise she'd get double time for soaking Belinda Oxfordshire and now pregnant as well! How could she cope with giving birth in jail. Harriet pushed all these ridiculous thoughts to the back of her mind as she felt a tug on her skirt.

'My Mum's gonna get a case,' came the excited shriek from Danny Bustard.

'A case?' puzzled Harriet.

'Yeah! Not one you put your bananas in like mine. That man is gonna make her a real one. My mum says we'll be able to go to Butlins now! He's making us a big case for all our things so they won't fall out.'

Harriet went sick again.

'No Danny babes,' came a shrill from his mother, 'it's not that kind'a case. She'll know soon enough without you tellin` `er. Cum'n get this coat off!'

Harriet escaped into the classroom leaving the escalation of familiar voices behind as the arrivals gathered pace.

'Deep breath Harriet,' she instructed herself, 'it will soon be break time.'

But Harriet knew she was kidding herself. Each minute became so elongated she was convinced she'd been caught in a horrendous universal net of extinguished time. At last the bell rang. She headed for Mr. Sanderson's office.

Harriet took a deep breath and knocked gingerly on Mr. Sanderson's door.

'In!' he commanded.

She entered, feeling like one of the many deviant children.

'Take a seat Harriet,' he smiled.

The knot in her stomach loosened as he spoke her name.

'Let's see what they've got to say, shall we?' He stretched forward and his strong hand reached from its immaculate, white cuff for the letter from Broadbent, Rudey, Essex & Co. Solicitors.

His face, now serious, 'seriously handsome,' thought Harriet, levelled with the paper, his blue eyes scanning the print as he ran his fingers through his thick blonde hair. Harriet noticed it just starting to curl against his pristine white collar. 'This man just shouldn't be allowed,' she thought as she felt every cell in her body collapsing in utter surrender.

'I don't remember calling her that, Harriet!' He shifted the paper and swept at the print with a very determined hand, fixing his gaze at her. Harriet immediately reached for the uninvited protrusion on her face, now basking in awkward exposure. She smoothed her hair and moved her finger along pressing firmly against it.

'Here, read this,' he ordered. No good, both hands required. Harriet, now vulnerable, tried to concentrate on the text as she sensed he'd firmly established a magnetic relationship with this undesired eruption.

'Slander and post-traumatic stress. I never heard the like!' Mr. Sanderson was absolutely fizzing. 'Have you ever heard me call her Mrs. Bastard, Harriet?' Fortunately he didn't wait for the reply. 'Bed-wetting, the boy's reverted to bed-wetting. I'll show her what "pissed off" really means!' Harriet felt the colour flood to her cheeks as she handed the letter back.

He read on:

'I have advised my client that it would be in her best interests to settle out of court for the undisclosed sum of £3000. Your early attention to this matter is advisable.' 'Three thousand pounds!' exclaimed Mr. Sanderson as he flung the letter to the desk. 'The Governors will never wear it. Where's that Broadbent fellow coming from?!' Harriet lost all ability to respond. She looked up at him as he paced the floor wondering why trouble followed her as naturally as a river to the sea.

Harriet lifted herself from the chair, as Mr. Sanderson moved towards her. 'I'm terribly sor...,' she began, very conscious of his proximity. Then she felt herself being drawn into his arms and he held her very close. Her feet almost left the ground as she finished the words into his lapel. She felt his chest pressing into her and the weight of his body against hers sent intoxicating waves through her whole being. She felt his lips resting on her hair and in all her life she had never been to this kind of heaven.

'Go, Harriet,' he ordered, 'my life's already too complicated.'

Harriet went, but she didn't know to where. It was sheer instinct that got her back to the classroom. Her mind danced with this new infusion of delight as it filtered through all her senses. The taste from his jacket was still on her lips. She was still pressed tightly to his chest and the warmth of his mouth was still in her hair. She called the children in and floated through the day. Everything she saw, heard and touched intensified the magical world she'd now entered. There was no going back. This was hers to keep, forever!

Chapter 12

'Had a good day Hat?' enquired Mark as he closed the door behind him. 'Any messages from the estate agents?'

'Oh, I haven't looked yet,' said Harriet, leaning over to give him his customary kiss.

'You haven't? I thought that would be the first thing you'd do.'

Harriet shot to the answer machine, wanting to appear normal. 'There's three messages.'

'Well play them then, Hat! That's what we do. Press the button. Remember?' Harriet duly obeyed.

'Hello Harriet, it's Mummy!' came the short impatient bursts. 'Just a quick call to see how those bridesmaids' dresses are coming along. Only Geraldine's been on the phone again and she's getting a bit twitchy about them. Clarissa's invited those delightful girls round on Sunday and wants to know if you need them for another fitting. By the way, must tell you the good news. We were right Harriet. Susan is expecting again! Baby's due in August. Do phone back darling! Love to all.'

'Mightn't be the only one, Hat,' grinned Mark.

'Oh I shouldn't think so,' replied a still dazed Harriet.

'You mean we've got to do it all again?' came Mark's eager response.

Harriet went very quiet.

'Haven't changed your mind already, have you, Hat?' said Mark now anxious to escape up the stairs.

'But Susan isn't ripped by the pain of passion for the most gorgeous man in the world,' she half-whispered, pressing the button for the next message, knowing Mark was safely out of earshot.

The green light flashed again: 'Hi Harriet,' bounced Tricia, 'got some really exciting news! Well apart from being re-elected Refreshments Officer at the AGM last night! Why didn't you and Mark go 'arriet? I was looking for you both. Anyway, remember when I spoke to Mark, when I was really miserable the other day and didn't want to talk about it. Well, I didn't get that job, but I've applied for another one and I've been short listed. See you soon.' With that she was gone. Tricia had been job-hunting on and off for years but it never came to anything very much.

Harriet paid it scant attention and waited for the final message.

'Good afternoon, Bryce Rae Roberts here, a message for Mr. and Mrs. Glover. Please would you phone the office as soon as possible. Thank you.'

Harriet thought of Belinda Oxfordshire. She definitely needed Mark for this one.

He came down. 'What else was on there, Hat?' His face straightened as Harriet swiftly moved on from Tricia to Bryce Rae Roberts.

'Hmm,' he said, placing his hand over his mouth. 'I think we'll let that one ride for a few days.'

'Can we do that?' said Harriet, looking alarmed.
'Course we can Hat! It'll blow over. You see.'
Harriet wasn't so sure.

Chapter 13

Not having seen him, to her deep disappointment, Harriet had to make do with the occasional sightings of Mr. Sanderson's car for the rest of the week and on the days she knew he was in, Amanda Woods, his deputy, took assembly. Harriet, feeling utterly miserable, was convinced he was avoiding her and by Friday had decided to put him out of her life forever.

On her way home she stopped at the lights, glanced at the showroom on the opposite corner. There were no bells ringing for her now. She eyed the depressingly silent gold leaf lettering of STARBOARD MARINE NORTH WEST and drove off glancing into her rear mirror. Suddenly she jumped.

'Was that *his* car parked on the corner?' She caught a glimpse of a silver Mercedes and Harriet felt herself coming back to life. In a flash she turned left. 'I've got to go back, got to make sure,' she gasped to herself. A curiously excited Harriet drove round the block only to have a huge truck keep pace with her, completely obliterating her view.

'Sod off!' Harriet hissed, and promptly realised she was in the wrong lane anyway. Without too much thought she did a swift swerve to the left, just pulling in behind it to the screech of brakes from her rear. The lights changed to red.

'I'm terribly sorry,' she heard herself saying to a twitchy, thin looking bespectacled man who'd just thumped on the window, forcing her to wind it down.

'So you bloody should be! Could've been up your backside then.' Sensing the traffic was about to move on he shot back to his car leaving Harriet, nerves in shreds, to falter left, completely forgetting her mission.

'Concentrate Harriet! Round just once more. Stay in the left lane, idiot!' And she did. The lights were on green and realising she'd have to do it all again in order to get home, skirted past Mr. Sanderson's car on the corner to see the shop door ajar. Round the block again but the fear of spending the rest of her life encircling this stupid shop panicked Harriet into the right lane. She drove past just in time to see Mr. Sanderson closing the door behind him.

'Wow!' Harriet exclaimed to herself. 'So that's where he's been all week!' She drove home, desperately trying to put him to the back of her mind.

She followed Mark into the driveway.

'You're a bit late tonight, Hat,' he greeted.

'Oh! Got stuck in traffic.' Mark thought nothing more of it.

'Must get this down to the club tomorrow,' he said, thumping the boat. 'I'll give Bob a ring. He'll give me a hand.'

'Oh no!' thought Harriet, 'I'm just not in the mood for Tricia or any of that lot.' Then salvation. Harriet suddenly remembered the bridesmaids' dresses.

'You suit yourself Mark. I've got an appointment with the sewing machine.'

Harriet opened the front door to the sound of the phone ringing. Her heart leapt, 'It's him,' she thought.

'Aha! Good afternoon, Bryce Rae Roberts here. Mrs. Glover?'

'Err, yes,' said Harriet cautiously, 'I'll just get my husband.'

'Since when?' Mark queried as he came to the phone.

'Since bloody never!' stormed Harriet and she thundered her way up the stairs. 'Men,' she fumed, 'who bloody needs them?' But Harriet certainly did!

'Only joking Hat,' his voice synchronising with his heavy strides as he mounted the stairs in pairs behind her. 'They've had a complaint from a Miss Oxfordshire.' Harriet's heart sank.

'Seems she got caught up in a domestic squabble, Hat, and was the unwitting victim of a bucket of water thrown in rage! Whilst they appreciate it wasn't my fault, Hat,' continued Mark grinning, 'they feel you owe her a personal apology especially as she actually expressed some interest in the property.'

Harriet was speechless. Then the full flood of anger released her vocal chords. 'It was *you* who trapped the cat's tail in the door. I'm not bloody apologising!' she stormed. 'If she does come to see it again, she won't catch *me* in.' Harriet was as good as her word.

Chapter 14

Saturday morning saw Harriet determined to move the sewing along. She heard Bob's voice from outside and then the slam of a car door.

'On the dining room table, please, Mark,' she said, peering over his shoulder as he struggled with the ancient, faulty machine. He finally emerged from the cavernous hole.

'It's a bloody shambles in there. You would insist on jamming it up with that filing cabinet of yours!' he exclaimed. 'And that old holdall! Does the cat have to sleep in it under there? "Useful under stairs storage space". I don't think Mzz Cambridgeshire would think so.'

'Sod Mzz Oxfordshire, just get on with it,' ordered Harriet and went to answer the doorbell.

'Hi Bob, alright?' she asked as pleasantly as she could manage.

'Oh fine, and you Harriet?'

'Definitely not,' she said to herself as she saw Tricia's head bobbing over the hedge. She wondered why Tricia had come.

'Hi Harriet,' bounced Tricia, 'coming to give the lads a hand?'

Before Harriet could answer they were both inside.

'Well!' chortled Tricia, 'It was more an excuse to come and tell you my exciting news! Remember my message? Well, I only found out last night! By the way `arriet, what were you doing driving round and round our showroom like that? Mr. Sanderson, my new boss; well as from Monday he will be, no, Joris, he told me I must call him Joris, thought it was really funny. Said something about you being…oh, I've forgotten now!'

'Forgotten what!' sparked Harriet, 'What did he say about me?'

'Oh it'll come back, I'm sure,' she smirked at Harriet. 'No offence guys, but oh what a dish!'

Harriet feeling outraged took a deep breath and looked down at the floor.

'It was all my experience at the club that got me the job. Joris said as well as the office work and selling I'd also be doing some hostessing.'

'It's pronounced *Yoris*,' Harriet interrupted. 'It's spelt Joris, but it's pronounced *Yoris!*'

'Cor, what's in a name, eh!' replied Tricia, refusing to be put off her stride. 'Call `im what you like. I'd hostess for him any day, or night.'

Harriet glanced at Mark who was beginning to look somewhat deflated.

'OK, Tricia,' chastened Bob, 'give them a chance to congratulate you.'

Mark and Harriet duly obliged.

'So we've both got the same boss now `arriet! I bet you `aven't got a two-way mirror by your door though `arriet. Ooh I'll be able to see `im coming and going all the time.'

She seemed incapable of shutting up. Mark looked at Harriet, his expression perplexed.

Harriet whipped her off the subject. 'Well, sorry and all that, but I must get those bridesmaids' dresses finished. Mark's just got the sewing machine out.' She left the three of them to get the boat off the drive.

With great reluctance Harriet fished for the bag of purple silk, an unfinished, demanding heap. Spilling from her arms it trailed behind her in its eagerness to escape. The long raw threads tickled at her ankles. Harriet felt itchy and irritable. She glanced at the phone pleading with it to ring. She wanted some answers to make her feel better.

No such luck. Harriet plonked the unfinished dresses down on the table next to the sewing machine and sat down. She struggled with the resistant curl of purple polyester thread that refused to enter the needle's eye. The needle stood defiant in its ancient black and gold carcass.

'Oh sod!' she exclaimed. Her concentration had gone. Her mind was battling with the tortuous convolutions of her dilemma. She felt the tears well up in her eyes. She blinked rapidly and continuously to hold them back. She swallowed hard to force the lump in her throat down. Her finger just missed catching the first tear gliding along the hard black metal surface of the sewing machine. 'Get on with them, Harriet,' she ordered. 'Just get these bloody awful heaps of purple out of the way. Sew! Sew! Sew!'

She swore and coaxed the rattling old machine into as much cooperation as it would reluctantly give. She drove the foot pedal as hard as she could as she tossed and turned the silk between her fingers. Harriet began to feel better and with a determined effort tried to rationalise the emotional mix within her. She trawled her mind for consolation. Suddenly she was able to think of her pregnancy without fear. 'Tomorrow I'll know,' she comforted herself , 'I want my baby, now.'

Chapter 15

Harriet woke to the familiar dull ache that would eventually drag her into another month of lost fertility.

'Not this time Mark,' she announced after she'd thanked him for the morning tea.

'Not what time Hat?' said Mark, getting back into bed sounding increasingly puzzled. 'It's not exactly early Hat.'

'No, not this time, no baby this time.'

'Never mind Hat,' said Mark, somewhat relieved. He wasn't sure if Harriet really knew what she wanted. 'There's always next month.' He pulled her very close in an attempt to nurse her disappointment away.

'Tricia was saying something about a celebration opening for that new marine centre, Hat.'

'What new marine centre?' queried Harriet trying to feign amnesia.

'Come off it Hat!' declared Mark. 'You couldn't stop yourself from driving round it, according to Tricia. And not just once, by the sound of it.'

'She was obviously mistaken,' Harriet snapped.

'Well if she was, *he* certainly wasn't! Got stuck in traffic, eh Harriet? You usually do if you put yourself in the way of it.'

Harriet didn't answer.

'You didn't tell me that Joris fellow had such diverse talents,' Mark continued. 'I don't know how he's going to run the school and manage that lot, given he's already on the board of directors at Pete's place.'

Harriet pricked her ears. 'Heaven only knows,' she retorted, grateful he'd moved the conversation along. She didn't want to talk about it.

She reached for her cup and jumped at the ring of the phone. Suddenly she was splattered with brown blobs of hot tea.

'Steady on Harriet,' uttered Mark, dodging the spray as he reached across to answer it.

'It's all over the pillowcase now and I'm not in the mood for washing them.'

'Are you ever?'

'Don't worry about me, that was hot!'

'Hello, you're early!' exclaimed Mark, 'We're still in bed!' "Rachael" Mark mouthed to Harriet. 'Coming today with Clare, Tristan and Sebastian. Oh....all bung up here?! I'll pass you over to your Mother.' Mark grimaced at Harriet, all too aware that his anticipated weekend of peace was about to melt into oblivion. 'Coming to help organise the grand opening,' repeated Mark to Harriet as he handed her the phone.

'What grand opening?' asked Harriet, still in denial. 'Remember Mum? Burns' night. Tristan and Sebastian from Starboard Marine North West,' came Rachael's voice sporting a note of impatience. 'They've opened a new branch near you. Is it OK? Should be there shortly after lunch.'

Harriet handed the receiver back to Mark who replaced it with a groan. Now united in their mutual disappointment at the prospect of a lost weekend, she returned to the warm comfort of his arms. She scolded herself for her inability to associate the newly sold shop with the lads from the south they'd met at the sailing club. She cringed in the knowledge that it must have been Mr. Sanderson she saw leaving there that night and every time she'd spoken to him since he would surely see her face framed in that black girdle!

With too many uncomfortable thoughts swirling around Mr. Sanderson, Harriet nudged closer to Mark.

'Mark, what do you really think about me packing in work? Do you think we could manage?'

'If we could get this place sold, Hat. Where are you Mzzz Cambridgeshire?'

Harriet could feel the flush of irritation gaining hold at his inability to take her seriously.

'Unless we win the lottery of course!' championed Mark.

'Fat chance,' retorted Harriet who decided the conversation wasn't going anywhere. She now deeply regretted re-mortgaging to fund the home improvements, the boat, the cars and various expensive holidays. Her thoughts returned to her baby. She felt a strange mix of intense disappointment couched in relief. 'When would it have been born?' she mused to herself. 'November, let's see..., November 15, 16, 17. Yes, November 17th, probably around 10.30 p.m.'

'Better get up Harriet,' interrupted Mark, briskly, 'before we're inundated!'

Harriet agreed. She knew her thoughts were starting to get silly.

Chapter 16

In one huge gust of enthusiasm the four of them arrived before Harriet had hardly had time to wash the lunch dishes.

'Mum, do you mind if we hold the meeting here?' asked Rachael. 'It's just that there's another chap and his secretary as well. With six of us and the decorators at the new centre it's not going to work.'

'That's no problem, is it Hat?' said Mark, just a bit too quickly for Harriet's liking. 'They can use the dining room.'

In a flash Tristan was on his mobile. 'Half an hour, is that OK?' He looked for the nod from Mark and Harriet. 'Fine, I'll just hand you over to Clare, she'll give you the address.'

Harriet decided it was time to disappear. This was all too close for comfort! She didn't dare enquire as to whom this other chap was. She would make her excuses, go and see her mother, take the cat to the vet, do the lottery, yes, and maybe an extra line. Anything to escape!

'That's a bit off Hat,' grumbled Mark when she told him she was going out.

'Well you go too, go to the club or something. Better still, take the cat to the vet. She still needs that vaccination. Oh and while you're there get him to look at her tail. It's your fault she got it trapped in the door like that.'

'Your turn Hat,' replied Mark, ignoring the comment. 'Anyway, I refuse to carry it in that old bag again.'

'You know she won't go in anything else. Oh just forget it! Let's get out before they all land. They don't need us,' Harriet retorted.

Without waiting for a reply Harriet was gone. She drove out of the gates in a panic. 'Lottery and then Mum's,' she told herself. 'No Mum's and then lottery.' Harriet had to concentrate very hard indeed. She finally arrived to see Clarissa's baby Jag on the drive. Too late! Her dad, garden fork in hand, popped up from behind the rhododendron bush, then he started waving it vigorously at her car. He beamed. He was always pleased to see her.

'Well, that's a nice surprise! Come on in love, we've got Clarissa here.' He tossed his head towards the house. 'Weddings, that's all they can talk about! I came out here to escape. As long as the rain keeps off,' he continued.

'Me too,' said Harriet, looking at the sky and deciding that it wasn't one of the best times to make a run for it.

'Harriet darling! What a lovely surprise. Clarissa's here, just popped off to the bathroom.' Harriet noted her mother's whispered tones. 'It's such a coincidence. Clarissa popped in to see how those bridesmaids' dresses are coming along, Harriet. It'll save me phoning you later. She wants to know if you can see the girls tomorrow. Do say "yes" Harriet.' Her voice, again, quickly reduced to a whisper. 'Quite frankly she's getting me down.'

Harriet felt a surge of sympathy and hugged her. 'OK Mummy, don't worry. They're nearly ready, just need to fit the bustles. Tell her I'll see them at four tomorrow. I must go and get on with them.'

'But you've only just...' Harriet waved both her hands over her face, stunning her mother into silence as she heard the flush of the loo from upstairs. She kissed her mother quickly.

'Must go, thought you and Daddy were on your own. Was only popping in for a tick.'

'Gotta go,' Harriet whispered to her father now on his knees again. He winked at her. Theirs was a mutual understanding.

Harriet, after a brief wave, zoomed off. 'There's no escape,' she thought, 'I've got to get away on my own. Ah, travel agents. That's what I'll do. Maybe check out a city break.' With that, she headed towards town, feeling quite uplifted at having regained her composure.

Armed with a handful of brochures she felt the first drops of heavy rain on her face. She held them inside her jacket to keep them dry as she approached the wine shop. 'I'll spend some time in there, deliberating,' she thought. Harriet definitely knew her reds from her reds! She leaned against the door with her back straining to take its weight whilst desperately clinging to the mass of shiny paper now slipping uncontrollably to the floor. She finally forced it ajar.

'Oops! Sorry!' she mumbled to a pair of black shoes. 'Excuse me. You're treading on my brochures!'

'Going somewhere Harriet?'

Harriet, dumbfounded, looked up to the familiar smile of Mr. Sanderson.

'Er, just to get some wine and then do the lottery.'

'Cum on, shuv out the way. We wonna get out!'

Harriet now gazing at two pairs of bovver boots, one pair of scruffy trainers and Mr. Sanderson's rapidly moving immaculate black shoes, scrambled to her feet just saving herself from an unscheduled collision with the revolving wine rack.

'Stupid place to put it, right by the door,' she thought.

She felt the need to escape.

Too flustered to be in any way selective she grabbed two bottles of red off the stand and plonked them on the counter.

'Have you a carrier bag, please?' she enquired as she took her change.

With great relief Harriet sat her brochures between the two bottles and hurried off to Whellred's the newsagent. She mused for a moment at the appropriateness of his name and then, wiser now, front facing, pushed the door open with a determined shove.

'Steady on love,' came Mr. Whellred's stern but amiable warning. 'Don't want Health & Safety after us for broken hinges, do we?!'

'Sorry,' apologised Harriet, 'I was expecting it to be a bit harder than that.' Mr. Whellred was far too absorbed with his next customer to be bothered about Harriet's reply. She moved quickly to the lottery stand and pushed her slip at an obliging assistant.

'Harder than what?' came an all too familiar voice from behind. 'Is that what you've been tellin` `im? So that's why we `aven't seen him all week! We're still waiting for our trip to Butlins, aren't we Danny Babes?' Harriet's heart sank.

'Oh, hello Mrs. Bustard, Danny. Must go!' This felt like Harriet's theme for the day. She shoved the lottery slips into her pocket and dashed out of the shop heading straight for her car.

Twenty metres down the road she heard a familiar cry.

'Miss, Miss, you dropped this. Me Mum said keep it, but its yours Miss init?!'

He shoved the ticket into her hand. Harriet was impressed by such righteous indignation on her account. She watched Danny panting his way back to a screeching Mrs. Bustard. 'Wait till I get yer `ome!'

Harriet hoped she hadn't landed him trouble.

She hurried to her car. Someone had parked just inches away from her. She cursed as she squeezed her way into the driving seat. She hurled her bag of bottles on to the empty seat along side her. She was still thrown from meeting Mr. Sanderson. It was too much of a coincidence.

'He's got to be on his way to ours. Surely he's not going to get there first?' she panicked. 'What to do? Nothing for it but the shed!'

She didn't remember driving home only that she had had to park three houses back. After making sure no one was looking she'd half stooped her way past Mr. Sanderson's car, carrier bag in tow, to the garden shed.

'How long have I got to sit here,' Harriet asked herself as she scrambled her way past the bikes, the plant pots and various bits and bobs of miscellaneous equipment to the army of folded chairs.

'Oh sod it!' she blurted out aloud. 'Fancy leaving a bottle of methylated spirit there!'

The glass bottle shattered and she watched the purple liquid drain down the wooden slats as it journeyed behind the junk along the concrete floor.

Harriet pulled at the chair, which in an unprecedented bout of stubbornness refused to move. She heaved again and released it only to be trapped by the fury of an uncontrollably aggressive bike. 'Sod, sod, sod!' An outraged Harriet unwound herself from her metal encumbrance, unhooked the chair from the pedal and banged it down by the open door.

Although not averse to the smell of meths, she considered it to be safer to sit there. She reached for the carrier bag and the holiday brochures that had obligingly propped up the wine bottles. They jarred as their support disappeared. 'Don't you fall over as well,' she growled. 'If you can't get on together then one of you will have to go!' Harriet noticed that she'd picked up screw top bottles more by good fortune than good judgement and without a second thought she was slugging her way through the offending bottle, transported to Paris, Venice and Rome. As she neared the end of the bottle, Harriet considered that she hadn't felt this good for some time.

'No more Harriet!' she said to herself, 'Well not until you've had just a tiny peep through the dining room window. They might have gone long since.' She faltered as she raised herself from the chair. 'Mustn't let them see me. Just crawl

Harriet. Keep this side of the rose bushes and crawl along the back of the house and then just a tiny peep. Only a tiny, teeny, tiny peep Harriet!'

Harriet cautiously left the shed, scrambling on hands and knees following the line of rose bushes. 'Suppose they see me?' she thought. 'Just suppose they see me. No, can't do it. Another little sip, then I'll do it!' She scrambled back to the shed and with some difficulty unscrewed the top from the other bottle of wine. 'I'll just take you with me,' she hiccupped at it as she slurped her way round the rose bushes and along the back of the house. Now firmly placed under the dining room window, half empty bottle in one hand, her other reached very precariously for the window sill. She heaved herself to eye-level just in time to see them pointing towards the far end of the garden, having just risen from their seats.

'Oh no! They're all coming out the back way!' Harriet panicked. She jogged her bottle and now splashed with red wine hid behind the lilac bush just to the side of the window. She watched them wander down the garden and back. She heaved a sigh of relief that shook the delicate populations of flowers to their core. 'They haven't seen me and they're going, going, gone,' Harriet said out loud from under the bush. 'Not quite Harriet,' came a voice from far higher than the pair of shiny black shoes firmly planted in the soil next to her.

Harriet, having déjà vu, convinced herself she was hallucinating. She looked up. 'Er, shorry Mr. Shanderson, just....'

'Just what Harriet?'

'Just don't tell anyone.'

With the rest of the party well ahead, he carried her into the house, took her upstairs and laid her on the bed. He bent over and kissed her cheek.

'I won't, if you won't Harriet.' Quietly, he closed the bedroom door behind him and went to join the others as they congregated on the drive.

Chapter 17

'Bye, Mum, hope you're feeling better soon.' Harriet half dazed awoke to her girls rushing off.

'Can't stop! We've all got to get back, but thanks for putting us up!'

Harriet managed to kiss them goodbye through an apologetic outburst.

'No Mum, don't worry about it. We do it all the time. It's cool to chill out!'

'You think so do you?' came Mark's voice from the landing.

'Oh don't be too hard on her,' chorused the girls. 'Just find out how she managed to climb the stairs! Bye Dad, see you both soon.'

The door banged behind them as Harriet struggled to the window to wave them off.

'You've got some explaining to do Hat,' said Mark, as he helped her back to bed. 'Explaining!' retorted Harriet, 'Where did *you* go, anyway?'

'Where you told me to go Hat! Bob's my witness!'

'Was Tricia there?' asked Harriet, trying to gather her senses from the pain and fragility that had overtaken her head.

'No, Hat, Tricia was going to be here, remember? Wasn't she coming round with that ubiquitous lump of lard that's supposed to run your school?'

Harriet let that one go. She forced every brain cell into aiding her recall but to no avail. She just couldn't remember whose faces were looking out of the dining room window late yesterday afternoon apart from one, of course.

'Well, go on,' insisted Mark.

'Came back too soon,' Harriet looked crestfallen as she mumbled the words. 'I just didn't feel up to it.'

'Well, you might have saved a bottle for me Hat. A bit much whacking your way through both of them.'

Harriet looked up and caught the smile in his eyes. He propped himself against the pillows behind her.

'Not washed this pillowcase yet?' he remarked to a most indignant Harriet. She hoped Mr. Sanderson hadn't noticed the tea stain.

'Anyway, how did you manage the stairs?'

'Can't remember!' came Harriet's reply as she felt the colour rushing to her cheeks.

'You alright, Hat? You look very warm. You didn't polish off the meths as well, did you?'

'With that Harriet attempted to flounce out of bed.

'Steady on Hat! What's the panic?' said Mark as Harriet staggered to the bathroom. 'I've got those girls coming at four o'clock!'

'Which girls?' shouted Mark.

'The bridesmaids, I've got to fit the bustles!'

'You'll find me in the shed!'

It was some time before Harriet started to feel half-human again. After phoning the girls to offer yet more apologies it would seem that nothing short of her presence at the official opening of Starboard Marine North West would placate them.

'Oh, I suppose so,' agreed a most reluctant Harriet. 'By the way,' she enquired as casually as she could. 'Was Tricia at the meeting yesterday?'

Clare's voice faded and returned. 'Bad signal Mum, sorr…' The conversation ended and Harriet was left to wonder.

The minutes ticked by gathering pace to the dreaded four o'clock. Harriet's recovery was almost complete. This was the only compensation for having to tussle with two large girls and their purple silk bustles. This she did not want to do but consoled herself in the knowledge it would be the final fitting.

Mark, as good as his word, disappeared into the shed.

'What a mess Hat,' he called as he opened the door. 'Do we want these old holiday brochures? I don't know what they're doing in here.'

'No,' she called to the sound of the doorbell. Harriet knew just where she was going.

'Must answer the door.' She looked at her watch. 'They're early!'

'Hi Harriet,' came the chorus, 'Hope we're not too early?'

'No, not at all,' said Harriet politely. 'Come on in. Shouldn't take long actually. Both of you pop upstairs and change into the dresses. Then I'll fit the bustles.'

Samantha and Gabriella heaved their way upstairs like a couple of ugly sisters. Harriet could hear their theatrically rounded vowels resounding along the landing and eventually down the stairs, momentarily reminding her of Belinda Oxfordshire.

'Ah, you're ready,' smiled Harriet as they came into the dining room.

'Don't we look gorgeous!' demanded Gabriella.

'We do!' agreed Samantha. 'I wonder which one of us will get Prince Charming?' 'Most appropriate,' mused Harriet to herself as she smiled at them.

'We're not joking Harriet!' exclaimed Samantha. 'Apparently that gorgeous blonde chap's been invited. The one we saw coming out of Clarissa's. A real hunk! Clarissa said her daddy met him at the golf club. Isn't he called Maurice or Boris, or something, Gabriella? Anyway he's jolly well single, we asked Clarissa's daddy. What a smile. Can't wait for the wedding!'

Harriet couldn't believe her ears! 'Just turn this way a little,' ordered Harriet, poised with pin in hand. She slapped the bustle on to her overly large backside and fed the pin into the swathes of purple silk.

'Ouch!' screeched Samantha, 'that went straight into my arse.'

'Terribly sorry Samantha, it's so slippery this fabric,' apologised Harriet, shocked that refinement could produce such coarse language. Then uncontrollable mirth set in. Harriet holding her breath to suppress it shot out of the room and returned with one of Mark's large white handkerchiefs over her nose and mouth.

'Sorry girls. I think I'm about to sneeze!' She fled the room again, shoulders shaking from the hysterics rapidly overtaking her. She flew out of the kitchen.

'What's the matter with you?' asked Mark as she made her way into the shed.

'Tell them I can't stop sneezing, or I'm ill or something, but get rid of them, please Mark,' she gasped. Harriet could hardly get the words out. Mark not wishing to become infected with Harriet's absurd condition rapidly vacated to the house to be met with the sound of heavy thuds upstairs.

'We're just getting changed,' one of them called. 'We assume you've finished now. Gabriella and I don't want to catch a cold, Harriet.'

'It's not Harriet, it's me,' called Mark. 'Harriet's come down with an uncontrollable sneezing fit. Do you mind seeing yourselves out?'

'Not at all,' they chorused, 'we'll close the door behind us.'

Harriet limped out of the shed as she heard the revving of the engine. Her sides were aching and her eyes were still streaming.

'Come on Hat, share the joke,' demanded Mark impatiently; but every time she tried to tell the tale the onset of laughter aborted it. Mark looked at his helpless Harriet. The more she laughed, the more irritated he became. He didn't like the esoteric air that had overtaken her. He shrugged his shoulders and went off quite huffily back to the shed.

Harriet, fearing the very real possibility of spending the rest of her life in uncontrollable hysterical fits sought a distraction. She opened the Sunday paper and leafed through the pages in an attempt to find last night's drawn lottery numbers. Her mind rapidly returned to default. This time Harriet was grateful for the calming effect the customary lack of expectation was having on her. 'That's better,' she thought as she finally found the page. 'As predicted.' Her eyes barely scanned the line. 'Not even a tenner!' Then she remembered her extra line. Her baby's line! Seventeen. Eleven, Twenty '0' Four, Ten Thirty. Some of those numbers were there. Harriet could see that some of those numbers were most definitely there.

4 10 11 17 20 31 BONUS 38. Harriet could hardly believe it. She checked the numbers over and over again and finally convinced herself she'd managed five! She turned the television on for the Teletext to see how much she'd get. She waited an eternity for the page number to appear after a never ending scroll down. Ah this was it. Saturday night's lotto draw:

One lucky winner scooping 2.9 million,

four lucky winners for five numbers and the bonus ball, one hundred and two thousand pounds each.

'Oh, just one more number. I could've paid the mortgage and given up work. Sod!!!' she exasperated to herself. Her eyes went to the line below:

thirty seven lucky winners with five numbers each receive three thousand one hundred and forty nine pounds. It could have been worse. Then she remembered little Danny Bustard panting his way to her with the ticket. She smiled to herself, 'You'll be off to Butlins Danny. Don't worry.' Harriet decided not to tell Mark.

Chapter 18

Monday morning again. Harriet couldn't believe how quickly it came round and even the thought of the half term break next week couldn't dispel the inevitable gloom it cast. It did the trick though, it had a hugely sobering effect on her. Much to Mark's annoyance she'd kept them both awake with uncontrollable outbursts of stifled laughter from under the duvet. It was only when she awoke that the full force of Samantha's comments really hit her. 'How long have James and Geraldine known Mr. Sanderson? Does he know James is my brother? Surely he's mentioned his headship, his school? Oh no,' thought Harriet, 'I hope he hasn't, I hope he hasn't mentioned me!' Harriet couldn't face the thought of him turning up at the wedding and deliberately switched her mind to more pressing things. 'Must try to catch Danny's Mum if I can this morning, with a bit of luck we'll all be off the hook!'

Harriet arrived at school, hoping against hope she wouldn't see Mr. Sanderson. 'At least his car's not there,' she consoled herself as she struggled through the door. 'Good morning Harriet,' greeted Amanda as she breezed her way into Mr. Sanderson's office. 'Assembly again! You don't need it first thing on a Monday morning, do you?'

'Certainly not, Amanda! Mr. Sanderson not in?'

'Not as far as I know.'

Harriet relaxed in instant relief. She continued down the corridor in search of Mrs. Bustard.

'Ah!' said Harriet, 'Just the person I want to see. Where's Danny?'

'He's out there playin` with Kevin and Sabaru. Why, anyway, what's `e dun now?' 'Nothing, nothing at all,' began Harriet. 'Would you pop inside for a moment? I'd just like a quick word.' Mrs. Bustard followed Harriet into the classroom.

'Mrs. Bustard,' began Harriet. 'This out of court settlement…'

'Oh yea,' interrupted Mrs. Bustard, 'you `urt our Danny and yer needn't think yer gettin` away with it!'

'Er, no, Mrs. Bustard, I've thought of a way you can get the money more quickly.'

'More quickly! What were yer thinkin` of, robbin` a bank, or doin` a few rounds with `im now `e`s hardened off?' Harriet was shocked.

'I think you'd better find Danny Mrs. Bustard, the bell's about to go. Please forget I ever mentioned it.' Mrs. Bustard turned on her heel, leaving Harriet in a bright pink fluster. 'Oh no! What a start to Monday morning,' she thought.

Harriet called the register and then trooped the children down to assembly. She was grateful for the chill in the large hall, at least it would help restore her normal colour. She directed her class into their usual two lines and watched them struggling to sit cross-legged on the cold parquet floor. She moved a chair towards them. Her bottom landing just a bit too quickly on the hard seat forcing its legs to screech along the aging wood. It disturbed her children who'd only just finished wrestling with the contortions demanded of them. She glanced along the line to see two bobbing heads joined in unmistakable sniggers. She had to get to Danny and Kevin before they disrupted the whole class. She inched her way between all the pairs of little feet, trying to avoid their upturned toes.

'Quiet,' she whispered, 'or you'll have to go outside.'

She wound her way along the line and back to her chair. Mrs. Lacey struck the first piano chord and Harriet was relieved the silence of the now packed hall had been broken. Harriet glanced out of the window just as Mr. Sanderson drove in. Her heart leapt! She turned to her class. Danny and Kevin had somehow been overtaken by the impelling need to conform to the 'hush consensus' now pervading the chilly air.

'Just get through the day Harriet,' she told herself, 'and put that man out of your mind for good!' With assembly over and filled with new resolve she marched her children back to the classroom, functioned on automatic and waited for home time.

The three-thirty stampede came and went. Harriet was just putting her jacket on when Mrs. Bustard burst open the door with Danny in tow.

'She nearly fell off `er chair this mornin`,' Danny announced, grinning all over his face.

'Shush, Danny! Don't yer be so rude to `er,' she scolded. 'Ave bin thinkin` `bout what you said this mornin` Miss. What did yer mean, get the money quicker?' Harriet was taken aback. She'd long since decided it probably wasn't a good idea anyway but should have realised Mrs. Bustard wouldn't leave it there.

'It was just a thought,' began Harriet, 'it'll probably take some time for this payment to be approved by the school governors, that's assuming of course, it is. They might choose to contest it.'

'Oh yeh,' replied Mrs. Bustard somewhat suspiciously, 'and what does that mean?'

'Well, they could decide to make a case against your claim, rather than settle out of court and if they won you might end up having to pay all the court costs.' Harriet felt a bit uncomfortable. She wasn't sure of her facts here, but justified any alarm she might be causing Mrs. Bustard on the grounds that at least she would be sure of the money.

'Ooo I see,' replied Mrs. Bustard, moving a bit closer to Harriet.

'Look, if you tell your solicitor that you've changed your mind about the whole thing, I'll write you a cheque for all the money.' Harriet began to feel like she was proposing a most dreadfully dodgy deal. 'Do you have a bank account?'

'Course we do, can't get yer benefits without one these days!'

'Yes of course, sorry,' said Harriet.

'Yeah sounds good to me! Is this goin` to be our secret, then?'

Mrs. Bustard was sharper than Harriet had given her credit for. Danny was clattering around in the play corner.

'Don't worry `bout `im,' she said, catching the look on Harriet's face, 'He `asn`t `erd a thing!'

'Once you've spoken to your solicitor he'll write to Mr. Sanderson informing him that you've decided against an out of court settlement and you wish to drop the case.' explained Harriet.

Mrs. Bustard inched closer to her. 'Then what?'

'As soon as I've seen the letter I'll give you the cheque for three thousand pounds.' Harriet put her finger to her lips. 'Shush,' she whispered. 'We're not actually doing anything wrong, we're just making life a little less complicated, that's all.'

Mrs. Bustard took hold of Harriet's arm and something clicked between them.

'You don` know what this means to Danny an` me. You're a good`n you! Wait `till I tell our Bert. It's our lucky week Dannybabes!'

Harriet breathed a sigh of relief. Mrs. Bustard ushered Danny out and closed the door behind her. She ran her fingers through her hair as she tried to convince herself this was the right thing to do. She didn't doubt Mrs. Bustard's integrity as far as this was concerned. Harriet knew once trust had been established loyalty was the hallmark of such people. 'Must get the lottery claim in,' she thought, 'and then it's just a question of waiting for the solicitor's letter.'

Her thoughts were interrupted as the door swung open. 'Been having words with that Bastard er Bustard woman, Harriet?' came Mr. Sanderson's enquiring voice.

'Mrs. Bustard you mean,' corrected Harriet looking up at him yet again feeling all her resolve draining away. She tussled with herself, her discomfort momentarily masked by her smile. 'No,' she thought, 'he should have more respect, really he should!' Mr. Sanderson sensed her unease.

'You haven't changed sides, have you Harriet? Not after all the bother that woman`s heaped on us!'

'No, of course not,' said Harriet, 'it's just that…' Harriet didn't have time to finish. 'Look Harriet, it only takes one in a pack to turn the rest. We haven't even touched the parenting classes yet. Amanda's been sounding out as many parents as she could since term started and has drawn an absolute blank. They don't want to know!'

'OK,' said Harriet, 'I take your point but maybe we're going about it the wrong way.' Harriet couldn't believe she was talking to him like this. Harriet was still very moved by Mrs. Bustard's reaction which had made her so aware of the struggle she must be having trying to pay for a holiday for Danny.

'Sit down Harriet,' ordered Mr. Sanderson as he eased his way into the chair at her table. Harriet sat down beside him. 'Well, go on.'

'We need to get them on our side,' began Harriet.

'Aren't we trying to do that, day in, day out Harriet?'

'Yes, of course we all are,' continued Harriet, now feeling a sense of betrayal. She hadn't meant to sound critical. 'It's just that, as you've just said, we're not succeeding, are we?'

'Well, no,' agreed Mr. Sanderson, 'What do you suggest?' Mr. Sanderson drummed his fingers on the grey, unyielding metal tabletop. This was becoming very difficult for Harriet.

She hesitated, 'Perhaps we can learn far more from them than they can from us.'

'In what way Harriet?'

She noticed his smile just starting to complement the twinkle in his eyes.

'Think about it,' she said. 'They're always in poverty, in real terms, the next generation is barely better off than the last. They inherit the ability to survive by whatever means they can so their values are bound to be different. They're very intelligent, most of our parents and they push very hard for their kids. They work hard. They struggle. They do their very best for them in their own way. They think there are better things out there for their children and education is the way in. They march them through the gates placing all their trust in us to give them the chance of a better future and what do we do? We patronise them. Let's get them together, let's establish some common ground and build on it. Let's find out what they really want for their children. We want them to go to university, ultimately, and after all that pushing, they don't. Even our "best" parents can't make that final shove. How many bright kids take their A-levels into insurance offices? It's very complex. Maybe there isn't anything wrong with that anyway. We send out signals that our lifestyles are better, more desirable, *superior*. It feeds our own egos, doesn't it?'

'Well, aren't they, Harriet?' enquired Mr. Sanderson.

'We shouldn't make value judgements. If we ask them about their leisure time and what they like to do...'

'Drinking, most probably,' interrupted Mr. Sanderson, 'but then you like to do that too, don't you Harriet?' he enquired with a broad smile.

Harriet looked down. 'Well yes, sometimes,' she hesitated, 'but what's the difference between their drinking and our drinking?'

Mr. Sanderson thought for a moment. 'Probably none,' he agreed. 'It's all alcohol, isn't it?'

'Precisely!' triumphed Harriet. 'And why should playing darts or bingo be any less enjoyable than sailing or golf? Pleasure is a very subjective thing.'

'It certainly is Harriet. You are lovely!'

Harriet looked into his eyes. She became transfixed by their colour. 'Just never ending blue,' she thought. He looked at her with an intensity she found quite irresistible, though she tried so very hard to resist.

'This is a *serious* conversation Mr. Sanderson,' she said, taking a deep breath as she attempted an equally serious tone.

'It's very serious Harriet,' he whispered as he drew her close. 'I've never been more serious in my life.'

The door handle rattled to the sound of a clanging bucket. Mr. Sanderson and Harriet swiftly moved apart.

'Oh sorry!' came the very apologetic mumble of the cleaning lady, 'thought everyone would have gone `ome by now.'

'Quite right, too,' smiled Mr. Sanderson, 'Miss Glover and I were just leaving!'

Chapter 19

Harriet drove home with her head in a spin. 'No mention of Saturday afternoon,' she thought, 'just an oblique reference.'

She recalled, but only just, how he'd laid her on the bed and kissed her cheek. She flushed at the thought of being so close to him, yet again. 'What did he mean, he'd never been more serious?' Harriet oscillated like a bubble in a spirit level desperately seeking even ground. 'Switch off Harriet,' she warned herself, 'this is rapidly becoming dangerous.'

She turned the car into the drive. Mark was already home.

'Late tonight, Hat,' he said as she opened the door.

'Trying to get some ideas off the ground for the parenting classes.' She answered as truthfully as she could.

Mark threw her a glance. 'Hope that lard ball hasn't been melting all over you Harriet.'

Harriet didn't answer. She went upstairs to get changed.

'Harriet, I've got to go away for a couple of days,' Mark announced as she came downstairs.

'Away?' Harriet questioned. All of a sudden her suspicions were aroused. 'Who with and what for?'

'We've got a meeting in Basingstoke. We're trying to pull together the various strands of this project.'

'Oh,' said Harriet, 'and who'll be going?'

'Kevin and Nigel, I should think and probably Paul Meadows.'

'When is it, then?' asked Harriet.

'Next Monday, but we'll be leaving Sunday morning. Should be back on Thursday at the latest.'

'I'll miss you,' said Harriet, burying herself in his chest.

'I'll miss you too, Hat. Still, it won't be for long.'

'Good,' said Harriet, 'now where can *I* go?'

'You can go and get the tea,' replied Mark with a broad grin.

Harriet drowned the rice in water. She usually did. Her brain never seemed to get the message. She popped the remains of last night's chilli into the oven and before she'd closed the door she decided this was her perfect opportunity for that short break away.

'Not much time though,' she mused. Her thoughts turned to Mr. Sanderson. 'I need a chance to sort myself out. I follow my heart and live my dreams, or I just stay like this, nobody's wife, nobody's lover. I just have to get away. Get away.' Harriet's thoughts now turned to Danny and his mother. 'Must phone that lottery place. I'll do it now whilst Mark's outside.'

Harriet knew he'd be ages having heard the shed door bang. She rummaged in her bag for the lottery tickets. 'No, its not that one,' she mumbled impatiently to herself as the familiar birth dates jumped out at her. 'Ah! This is the one.' She grabbed the ticket flipping it over for the phone number without reading the instructions properly. She glanced at the winning row of numbers while she waited to be connected. 'Just a minute,' she said out loud, 'that's not my line!' Harriet looked across to see all thirties and forties. She knew these weren't her baby's dates. She replaced the receiver. She studied the line again and then turned the ticket over. 'I needn't have bothered with the phone call either, for that amount it would have been collection from the post office, anyway.' She shrugged her shoulders as Mrs. Bustard's words came to her, ..."It's our lucky week Dannybabes!"

Then the reality sank in. She'd already promised her the money. Mrs. Bustard already had the winning ticket, her ticket. 'Had Danny snatched the wrong one back before his mum could stop him?' How ever it had happened, Harriet certainly wasn't the winner.

She went back to the kitchen, rescued the now soggy heap of rice just as it began to bond irretrievably with the singeing base of the saucepan. She ran her fingers through her hair. 'Where, oh where am I going to find three thousand pounds to pay her now? No, no, I'm just going to have to pull out, but how?' She lifted the newly moulded cradle of burnt rice from the pan. She lobbed the lot into a well-used Pyrex dish and stirred vigorously scattering the saturated, swollen grains into the unyielding black chips of incinerated starch. 'The chilli will hide this,' she thought as she became transfixed by the horrendous spectacle she had just created. She stirred it again as if a solution would emerge from the rapidly browning sludge. Then the phone rang.

'HELLO,' blurted Harriet. Someone put the receiver down. She stormed into the kitchen as Mark opened the back door.

'Thought I heard the phone Hat. Was it for me?' he enquired pointing to Harriet's latest culinary disaster with a grin.

'No,' she announced curtly. 'They hung up.'

It rang again and Mark shot to answer it with Harriet close behind.

'Ah, Melissa,' oozed Mark. 'Yes sure we can manage that. No, no, of course not. No point at all.' He caught Harriet's steely gaze. 'Just our contribution to saving the planet. Think nothing of it!' Down went the receiver.

Harriet couldn't believe her ears. 'What was that all about?' she demanded.

'Just a bit of car sharing Hat. Seems a bit daft not to when we're all going to the same place. Melissa's very conscious of global warming.'

'Oh is she?' replied Harriet trying very hard to be restrained. 'You didn't say *she* was going.'

'Didn't I? I thought I had. Still it doesn't much matter to you either way, Hat. Or does it?'

'Certainly not!' snapped Harriet anxious to relinquish her position. She marched to the kitchen in a frenzy of renewed determination. She tugged at the calendar sending the drawing pin spinning over her shoulder. 'This is where *he* goes,' she reminded herself as she gazed at the snow capped mountain peaks etched against the clear blue sky. She scanned the valley of green adorned with copious sprays of white and yellow buds. She could almost smell the scent of the red and blue taller flowers speckling their way through the sweet meadow grass. 'I want to go there,' she decided.

She leafed through the pages offering a variety of scenes appropriate to the months. She hovered over Paris, Bergen, Venice and stopped at Bruges before returning to her favourite picture. 'Switzerland,' she reminded herself, 'that's where *he* goes.' For a moment she lay on the grass beside him feeling the soft warmth of his lips on hers as he scattered her dress with spring flowers. She smiled at the thought. Harriet knew it was only a thought. She decided this was definitely for her.

'Dinner ready yet Hat,' shouted Mark, 'or have you managed to annihilate it completely?'

Harriet tried to pull herself together. She'd almost forgotten about the tea.

'Mark,' said Harriet in a very determined tone, once they had started eating.

'Yes Hat,' replied Mark rather curtly.

'Mark, as you are off on a jolly, I've decided to have one too.'

'Mine's work Hat!' exclaimed Mark indignantly. He piled the mix of chilli and burnt rice on to his fork. He peered at it suspiciously for a closer inspection and started poking it with his finger.

'Mark that's gross! Anyway I'm going.'

'Ouch!' squealed Mark, 'What was that?' He rummaged further into the cascading heap. 'OK Hat anything you say,' he declared as he rolled the chilli laden drawing pin in the palm of his hand. 'No need to go to such lengths to get your own way.'

Harriet felt dreadful.

'That's where it went!' she gasped. 'It shot over my shoulder when I took the calendar off the wall. Go and see for yourself.'

He stood up with pin in hand, raised his arm and dropped it from a great height back on to the plate. 'I'll get some fish and chips, Hat.' Without waiting for a reply he disappeared.

Harriet seized the moment. She looked at her watch and grabbed the phone book. 'If I'm quick I might just catch the travel agents,' she thought.

'Flights to Switzerland, er, cheap flights to Switzerland. Let's see...'

Harriet waited whilst her request was being attended to. 'Should have gone on-line, I'd have been quicker doing it myself,' she muttered impatiently.

'Ah sorry, we can't do cheap and cheerful on that one for next week. Let's see what other offers we've got on. Ah! We've a brilliant deal to Nice, £12.00 outward.'

'I'd rather like to return as well,' replied Harriet somewhat frostily.

'Have you thought about a mini-cruise at all?' came the unruffled voice from the other end. 'Three nights to Bruges on the "Christiana" sailing next Monday, we've a fantastic offer on balcony cabins. We've a whole deck's worth at less than half price! Free return coach to Southampton as well.'

'I'll go for that,' replied Harriet, astounded at her ability to make such a snap decision.

'I'll just take your card details. Er, how many for, …just you? Well you'll have the luxury of a double cabin with balcony anyway for a small single's surcharge. We only received this instruction from the shipping line an hour or so ago. It's your lucky day!'

Harriet replaced the receiver feeling very pleased with herself. 'What a brilliant way to relax,' she thought, 'I might even find a solution to dealing with Mrs. Bustard whilst I'm stretched out on my very own balcony.' She could hardly wait to pick up a brochure.

The phone rang and her heart leapt. 'It's him!' she panicked briefly, then intense disappointment set in.

'Oh, Hi `arriet, Tricia here. Oooh `ave I got some news for you!'

'News?' queried Harriet, 'What kind of news?'

'Well, our boss, but not your boss on this occasion, if you see what I mean. Well, my boss Joris, would you believe it is off to Switzerland on Monday. `e does have to go from time to time, you know.' Of course Harriet knew and she was beginning to feel very irritated.

'Oh, that's nice for him! Is that it, Tricia?'

'Oooh no! The best bit's yet to come. It's even better than sitting next to `im in your house `arriet.'

By now Harriet was blazing. 'Go on then, don't keep me in suspense.'

'`e, `e wants me to go with `im. Said `e would need some secretarial assistance. Something to do with `is banking over there. Anyway I've told you now. Isn't that just the most exciting news of all?'

Harriet didn't think so. 'Well I'm very pleased for you Tricia. Actually I'm going away on Monday too,' she continued defensively.

'That's you and Mark you mean don't you `arriet?'

'No, Tricia, just me. Mark's in Basingstoke next week and as it's half term I thought I would take the opportunity.' Harriet knew she was saying far too much but somehow just couldn't help herself. 'I'm spoiling myself with a luxury cruise on the "Christiana". She sails from Southampton on Monday. Free coach from Liverpool, so I'm just going to sit back and enjoy it!'

'Ooh, very nice `arriet,' replied Tricia. 'It's a shame you'll be on your own though. Where did you say you were going?'

'Bruges,' said Harriet.

'Where's that then?'

Harriet was tempted to say the Bahamas, but refrained. 'It's in Belgium, Tricia. It's a beautiful medieval town laced with canals. They call it the Venice of the north.' That was it. That was the best Harriet could do to redress the balance.

'Ooh Bob and I went to Belgium once. It was alright, nothing special. Well not for us if you see what I mean. A bit too flat for Bob and me. We like the mountains. Ooh I've never been to Switzerland before. I can't wait! Well fancy that `arriet you wouldn't believe it, would you? We're all going away together.

Well not together, of course, if you see what I mean! I'm sorry you can't come with us, but three might be a crowd, as they say. Only joking `arriet. If you see `im in school don't tell `im I told you, promise?'

Harriet promised but she forgot to ask the same of Tricia.

Chapter 20

Harriet was used to 'bubble-burst'. It was her own little phrase to describe how the ultimate state of euphoric delight could suddenly come crashing in on her whole world.

'What an absolute toad he is,' she said out loud on the way to work the next morning. She vowed not to glance over at Starboard Marine North West when she got to the lights. She recalled yet again how they had almost kissed the evening before. She had almost surrendered herself at the very desk she was having to return to. She didn't want to see him. Oh no, she didn't want to see him today, or tomorrow, or any other day in her life!

She drove through the school gateway. She didn't want to see the silver Mercedes sat beneath his office window, either. She parked as far away from him as was physically possible.

'Eh mind the flower bed there, will you, 'arriet. We don't want you squashing me best geraniums do we?' came the voice of the school caretaker through the open window of her car.

'If I'm going to squash anything, it won't be one of your geraniums Mr. Brown.' Harriet fumed.

'Alright, keep your 'air on,' came the humourless reply. 'Only the boss always passes me a complement in respect of them and I wouldn't want to 'ave to tell him you ran 'em over!'

'Oh sod,' muttered Harriet getting out of the car. She tugged relentlessly at her handbag not realising the strap had looped itself round the gear lever as she tried to slam the car door.

'And you can sod off, too as well as that Mrs. Bustard,' she declared as she saw Mr. Brown turn on his heels. She grabbed her bag and marched towards the school building.

Harriet, not looking back pushed open the old, heavy entrance door and headed straight for the classroom. She slung her bag onto the desk and attempted to calm down. 'Right,' she said to herself, 'I'll ask Mrs. Bustard to see me this evening and I'll get that money thing sorted out once and for all. No lottery ticket! No money!'

But it was not to be. Danny never arrived.

By the end of the day Harriet felt very fortunate not to have seen Mr. Sanderson. 'No doubt polishing his patter for the trip to Switzerland,' she thought. She'd noticed his car had disappeared at lunch time. She'd tried not to let it bother her. 'Mark can have green Melissa and Tricia can have *him*,' she snapped to herself. 'Who knows what talent will be on that cruise. I might just meet Mr. Right!'

As it is frequently given to do, the door suddenly shot open, jolting Harriet from her less than consoling thoughts. She turned round to see Mr. Sanderson standing tall in the doorway, his face serious, his demeanour correct.

'Miss Glover, just a quick word.' He beckoned her over, stepping back as she approached. 'I've received a complaint today from Mr. Brown the school caretaker. He said you were most rude to him this morning.'

Harriet, her face flushing, looked up at him. She searched for the twinkle in his eye but it wasn't there. His expression was set and she grappled with the opposing mix of emotion flooding her mind.

'I got annoyed with my bag,' she said, 'the handle got stuck round...'

'Miss Glover,' he interrupted, 'I don`t want to know the ins and outs of it but I suggest you apologise to Mr. Brown straight away. The last thing we need is a truculent teacher rocking the boat. We all get stressed Miss Glover, but try to retain a modicum of professionalism whilst you are here.'

He turned to go. 'Ah!' he recalled, 'did Alice tell you we're running the parenting class an hour earlier tomorrow evening with it being half term?'

'I've just given all the letters out Mr. Sanderson,' Harriet replied, trying to suppress her fury.

'Yes, of course!' came the response and he marched up the corridor.

'Him and his bloody parenting classes!' Harriet stormed to herself. She couldn't believe her ears. 'Retain a modicum of professionalism! Does he know what the word means?' She recalled the near kiss of the evening before and dismissed it in utter disgust.

'Well, he's done me a real favour this time,' she fumed to herself. 'Didn't I just need this to make me see sense. He's out of my life forever!' She stomped off to try to find the caretaker, furiously working out just how quickly she could hand in her notice.

Of course the caretaker was nowhere to be found. Harriet enquired as to his whereabouts of the half-dozen or so cleaning ladies busily squiggling their moulting cotton headed mops into the swirls of grey water. 'Try his room,' came the repetitive response. 'He's never there!' retorted Harriet as many times as there were cleaners.

In the end there was nowhere else to go. It was a bit too close to his office for her liking, but she checked to see if the coast was clear and arrived in three sharp strides. She knocked on the door and as there was no reply she went in.

'The trouble with caretaker's rooms,' thought Harriet as she eyed the variety of ladders, buckets and tins, is that they're dark, cold and still have all sorts of doors going off them.

'Mr. Brown,' she called trying to close her nostrils to the undiluted smell of school. No reply but Harriet thought she could hear a shuffle coming from his office door at the far end of the room.

She knocked louder this time, pushing the door open as she did so.

'Watch it! Ooo! Oooh! Aaarh!' came the rapidly disintegrating voice of Mr. Brown as he clung helplessly to the side of the ladder and the top of the door frame. Harriet shot in and with her right arm and left shoulder just managed to save him from tumbling to the ground.

'I sent you to apologise to him Miss Glover, not to compromise him.'

Harriet peered over Mr. Brown's left shoulder at Mr. Sanderson's stern face. She knew if she moved, the ladder would come crashing down. The rungs were wedging her rear end like a toast rack and for a moment she was devoid of all mobility.

'May I release you Mr. Brown?' he queried with polite precision and stepping forward to separate them sent Mr. Brown, Harriet and the ladder clattering to the floor.

'I'm ever so sorry Mr. Brown. Are you alright?' he enquired.

'Bit of a shock Mr. Sanderson, but no `arm done! Not been one of my better days today.' he complained glaring at Harriet as she heaved herself up from her prison of wooden rungs. He nodded to Mr. Sanderson before limping away.

'Any damage?' barked Mr. Sanderson.

'No, I think I'm alright, thank you,' replied Harriet very shakily.

'I meant the ladder, Miss Glover. Are you making it your life's work to keep the legal profession in business? We haven't sorted that Bastard woman out yet!'

With that he strode off.

Harriet couldn't believe her ears! He'd just turned from a toad to a swine! Shaking, she went back to her classroom, gathered her things and drove out of the open gates vowing never to return!

Chapter 21

Of course Harriet had to return. As she drove to school the next morning she remembered Mark's fury. 'I'll go and see the so and so!' he'd said.

Of course Harriet had to talk him out of it. She considered it a far better option to just quietly resign.

'Just coast it then Hat. We'll work something out when we're both back at the weekend. We'll manage. We've managed before.'

That made Harriet feel so much better. In all the world there was nobody like Mark. How could she have been so stupid? She approached the traffic lights and again refused to look across to Starboard Marine North West. 'They'll be having their grand opening soon,' she thought, 'I'll have to make an excuse to the girls. I *definitely* won't be going.'

It was only the thought of breaking up for half term that kept Harriet driving along. 'I wish I didn't have to go to that parenting meeting tonight,' she said to herself. 'If he gets any cooperation from the parents he won't be getting any from me, that's for sure.' She wondered if Danny would be back in.

* * *

Harriet, who'd spent the day in the grip of regenerated fury made her way to the school hall promptly at six o'clock that evening. She hadn't thought it worthwhile to go home and then come back again so she'd swallowed a hasty sandwich, borrowed the kettle and brewed a cup of tea in the classroom. She wasn't feeling at all sociable. In fact Harriet was feeling downright antisocial. She decided to sit as inconspicuously as possible in the far corner at the back of the hall. 'As Mr. Sanderson likes staff to mingle with parents on such occasions, he can have no objection,' she thought.

She tried very hard not to watch him take command of the meeting. He marched into the packed hall. 'No doubt he's pleased at the level of interest. It's a pity anyone turned up,' she muttered to herself. After the initial lack of interest Harriet was very surprised to see so many parents, now chattering loudly as they eyed up the agenda on the pink and yellow cards Alice Atkins had thrust at them in the doorway.

'Good evening to you all,' he smiled and the hall fell instantly silent.

Harriet, still drawn to him against her better judgement, couldn't resist gazing across to watch this hunk of a man perform.

'I'm delighted to see so many of you here.' Mr. Sanderson beamed at his audience. 'I hope you're not all going to be in my class, though!'

'So do we!' came a strident voice from someone in the middle of the hall.

There followed an instantaneous burst of laughter.

'Hmm, quite,' muttered Mr. Sanderson, looking considerably dampened.

'Anyway, to serious matters. We are here this evening largely for the ultimate benefit of your children and the time you spend during the course of the next six weeks with us will probably be the most worthwhile thing you have ever done for them.'

'Ouch!' thought Harriet as she sensed a shuffling and murmuring all around her.

'In fact, I can promise by the end of that time your new found parenting skills will be second nature to you all!' he continued.

'Ouch again!' she cringed as she noticed the door slowly opening. 'It's Mrs. Bustard!' observed a surprised Harriet as she tried to shrink herself further into the corner.

Too late! Harriet had been spotted! Mrs. Bustard pushed noisily past everyone seated in the back row, waving and winking at Harriet as she went.

'Don't worry Miss Glover, I'll sit on the window ledge,' she whispered loudly, 'Only our Dannybabes has been really poorly, but I wasn't going to miss this one!' she grinned. 'Oh I've still got `is banana in me bag! `e's really taken to them since `e's decided `e wants to be like that boy Kevin.' She pulled it out, winked at Harriet and then pointed it like a gun towards Mr. Sanderson.

'He's only just started,' whispered Harriet studiously ignoring the banana, wondering how she could possibly extricate herself from this evolving nightmare.

'Let me explain a little of how we plan to set this thing up. If you look at your pink card,...'

'I `aven't got one!' shouted Mrs. Bustard pointing her banana in the air, interrupting Mr. Sanderson without compunction.

The hall rocked with laughter.

'Have this one Beattie. It's a load of rubbish anyway,' shouted another woman with a luminous orange jacket slung over the back of her chair.

'As I was saying,' snapped Mr. Sanderson, trying to gain control, 'you will see that we are placing you into groups of twelve and each group will be supervised by a member of my teaching staff. Each week a different aspect of the socialisation process will be covered and you will notice the emphasis will be on your behaviour. You will have the opportunity to examine your own attitude to school and the wider world. You will see how your thoughts and feelings are readily transferred to your children, who in turn may have difficulties in understanding and accepting the values of the school.'

'Oh, no!' squirmed Harriet. 'Hasn't he thought this one through?'

'Now!' he ordered, 'Turn to your yellow card!'

'I bet Beattie Bustard `asn`t got one of them either!' came the shrill voice of another woman, her bleached blonde hair trailing the worn black leather coat in brittle, long tails.

'She's got a banana though! Aven't you `ad yer tea yet Beattie?'

'She's keepin` it for later!' came a raucous voice with a laugh to match. 'Better than anything your Bert could come up with, eh Beattie?'

'`im, `ee `asn`t `ardly got one anymore!' laughed Mrs. Bustard, 'anyway it's me yellow card I'm talkin` about. I `aven't got one!'

'Ere, Beattie, `ave mine.' In an instant it shot over the heads of the crowd in the form of a small but stout aeroplane.

'Eh! That's a good idea!' came an excited shrill from the front row and within seconds the hall was filled with pink and yellow flying missiles. Mrs. Bustard nudged Harriet. 'Just look at `is face!' she smirked. Harriet didn't dare.

On impulse Harriet stood up. 'Right!' she said as she straightened her jumper. Everyone turned in their chairs and the hall fell silent. 'What do you think of it so far?'

'Rubbish!' came the unanimous response.

'You're absolutely right!' replied Harriet, smiling at everyone. Out of the corner of her eye she caught the bemused Mr. Sanderson scratching his head as he seated himself on the piano stool.

'You expected such an introduction from us and we expected a bit of a reaction from you. Well, if we're truthful, maybe not such a colourful one!' The sound of laughter filled Harriet's ears. Then a further hush descended, a respectful silence in anticipation of Harriet's next words.

'Sorry! We didn't feel too good about setting you up but we wanted to take you from your expectation of what this is all about to the reality of how we want it to be, with all of us listening to each other, contributing and working together for the benefit of the children.' There was a huge round of applause.

'She's a good'n, she is!' shouted Mrs. Bustard pointing her finger at Harriet.

'Not for long,' thought Harriet, suddenly remembering she still had to face her over the money.

'If Beattie Bustard says she's a good'n, then she is!' came another loud voice from a very large woman in the back row. The clapping was now accompanied by loud cheers.

'So, you don't like the idea of being placed in groups?' Harriet continued.

'No, just like school that is. We don'wanna be treated like your kids!' croaked the gruff voice of a woman in a purple and yellow striped headscarf who, desperate for a fag, was wobbling into the aisle.

'Precisely!' retorted Harriet, now getting into her stride. 'Mr. Sanderson wanted to get you all thinking about how you would like it to take shape. Have a chat among yourselves. How long did you want to give it Mr. Sanderson?' she called across the hall. He stood up, smiled and opened his fingers and thumbs on both hands to indicate ten minutes and then sat down again.

'Right,' said Harriet, in a very determined voice. 'you've got ten minutes. Move around the hall, exchange ideas, decide which of you are going to speak out for the majority views. Give us a few lessons in how to get organised quickly. Feel free to ask any questions as we walk about.' Harriet nodded to the rest of the teaching staff who obediently vacated their seats and started talking to the parents.

In the noise and activity that followed Harriet inconspicuously made her way to Alice Atkins who was still guarding the door.

'Alice, pass the message on to Mr. Sanderson will you please that I've got the most dreadful migraine coming on. I'm off home, whilst I can still see to drive.'

'I spoke for the things I believe in,' she told herself as she was driving home. 'If he didn't like it, too bad! I'm leaving anyway.'

Harriet's fury was interspersed with uncontrollable bouts of amusement as she recalled the farce of the meeting, though for the life of her she could not think why she'd tried to bail that despicable man out.

'How did it go Hat?' greeted Mark as Harriet let herself in. 'I thought you'd be later home than this.'

'Horrendous! Funny, but horrendous!'

'Can it be both?' enquired Mark somewhat puzzled. Harriet ignored it.

'That place has given me such a bad head,' complained Harriet placing her hand just above her eyebrows. 'I've finished with it all, Mark. Thank goodness it's half term.'

'Don't give *him* a second thought,' said Mark putting his arm round her. 'How about we do that cruise of yours together?'

'Wish we could, but you're already going to be away, remember?'

'Oh Hat, I'll take a few sickies, no one will know.'

'And what about your contribution to the research? There's no point in anyone going if you're not going to be there,' Harriet said.

Mark was suitably flattered. 'Dear Hat,' he replied, as he tightened his arm around her, 'I don't think anyone would miss me.'

This was definitely the best part of the day for Harriet. He'd forgo the trip for her! She'd just discovered that Melissa Scott couldn't possibly figure in his life after all. Brimming with confidence, Harriet now knew she was the love of his life and there could be no competition from anyone. 'Well maybe Tricia,' she couldn't quite sit on the thought. It was the perfect opportunity to tell Mark about her trip with Mr. Sanderson.

'I told you he was a lard ball, Hat!' Mark triumphed, 'and she's no better than she ought to be either! Mind you, Bob's no fool, he'll soon put a stop to that job of hers if he thinks anything's going on.'

'Oh, please don't tell him,' pleaded Harriet. 'It's probably only business anyway. You can never tell when Tricia's just joking.'

'Of course I won't tell him. What do you take me for, Hat? He'll draw his own conclusions if he hasn't already done so. I can't think why he let her work for him in the first place.'

'But you let me work for him,' said Harriet suddenly beginning to feel she was losing ground.

'Harriet, neither of us knew what he was like when you got that job, remember? Anyway there's a world of difference between you and Tricia. She's just plain flighty! The joke of the sailing club. But you, Hat, you're different. You are 100% mine, always were and always will be. I'd trust you even if you shared the same bed as him. I don`t think Bob could say that of Tricia!'

'Well, as far as I'm concerned that's one theory that's not about to be tested,' retorted Harriet.

'Jolly good Hat,' chivvied Mark, 'let's open that bottle of wine!'

Chapter 22

'How many bottles do you reckon we got through last night, Hat?' Mark smiled as he cuddled up close.

'Don't know and don't care,' yawned Harriet delighting in the warmth and security such proximity brings. She could just see the sharp blade of daylight slicing through the top of the curtain. 'What time is it, anyway?' she murmured. 'I think I'll just stay here today.'

'I don't have a problem with that, Hat,' declared Mark as he slipped her narrow silk nightdress strap over her shoulder. Harriet snuggled closer, 'Good, what time did you say it was, again?'

'Time for us Hat,' he whispered, 'all day, just time for us.'

The love nest that had just been created in the front bedroom of 4 The Willows suddenly disintegrated as the brash, demanding, unrelenting rings of the phone charged the atmosphere.

'You'd better get it Mark, it might be one of the girls.'

'Yes?' shouted Mark as he lifted the receiver, determined to make his displeasure felt. 'Oh, good morning... You've apologised profusely to Ms Oxfordshire on our behalf...right, oh right.......yeah, yeah, yes, OK. Afraid we're both away next week. Oh right, Ms Oxfordshire very keen. Ask Mrs. Glover, did you say? Just a minute then, I'll have a word with my wife.'

'Wife!' exploded Harriet, 'Since when?'

'Shush Hat,' chastened Mark as he placed his hand over the receiver. 'It's that woman, very serious about the house and wants a second viewing next week.'

'Better ask your wife,' muttered Harriet feeling the onset of a very childish moment as she slipped her arm back into her nightdress.

'OK Hat, you talk to him,' said Mark pushing the receiver into her hand.

'Er, yes,' said Harriet, 'we are both away I'm afraid. Pardon, sorry I didn't quite hear you. Oh sorry, yes certainly that would be alright. I'll drop the keys in to you. Thanks a lot.' Harriet passed the receiver back to Mark. 'Bloody cheek, apologising to her on our behalf,' she fumed.

'So they're going to do the viewing for us, are they?' said Mark, ignoring her comment. 'Better get some cleaning up done before you start packing.'

'Huh!' exclaimed Harriet, 'what a cheek! You're the one who left all that rope in the hall for everyone to trip over. Your jumpers are all over the place and I'm sick of moving your shoes from the kitchen doorway. And I can't remember how many times I've asked you to put that magnifying glass away. I don't know what it's doing on the hall window sill anyway. *I'm* not moving it! You're the untidiest person on the planet. Better ask your wife to clean up for Belinda Oxfordshire. I'm not touching a thing!'

'Well I'm certainly not!' replied Mark and both were as good as their word.

Chapter 23

'Get out will you!' Harriet ordered the cat for the fourth time as it tried to curl up on her neatly folded clothes. 'It's bad enough having to use this smelly old thing! You'll just have to find somewhere else to sleep while I'm away.' She went to get her black mohair jumper and popped it into the holdall just as the doorbell rang. 'Plenty of room left for any bargain bottles,' she thought as she descended the stairs. 'Why do milkmen always want paying when you're in the middle of doing something, especially something awful that you don`t want to go back to?' she asked herself on the way back up.

Harriet hated packing, besides she was still smarting from yesterday and didn't see why she was expected to pack Mark's stuff as well. She was annoyed that he'd insisted on having the only decent suitcase she could find.

'His wife can do it!' she muttered to herself. 'I'm not his wife and I don't now wish to be. In fact, I don't wish to be anyone's wife or anyone's lover! If Belinda Oxfordshire so chooses to buy the house we'll split the proceeds and I'll get an apartment. I've had it with men!'

The phone rang. 'Oh, hi Tricia,' said Harriet trying to sound light-hearted. 'Well, that's very nice of you and you have a good time too. You're meeting him where? Oh, at the airport. That'll be an early start! At least I'll have time to collect myself before I get to the coach station. Mark? Yes, Mark's off this afternoon. They're going by car. They're picking up Melissa Scott on the way.'

'Who's that?' came Tricia's intrigued voice from down the phone.

'Why did I go and say that?' Harriet thought. 'Oh just a secretary I think,' replied Harriet trying to play it down.

'Not Mark's I `ope! Looks like we might all be going to have some fun! Hope you enjoy all that culture `arriet, as long as you don't end up making lace. That's what they do over there don`t they or is it chocolates? I can't remember.'

'Both actually, Tricia. Don't let him work you too hard!'

'Depends what you mean by work,' came the giggly response. 'Actually, well I shouldn't be telling you really but he's given me this suitcase, locked of course, to carry for `im. First of all I thought why couldn't he carry it `imself and then I thought well there must be something very special in it. It might be for me, `arriet! I'm so excited as to what he's got me! Men are so funny about carrying presents, aren't they?'

'Well, I suppose they can be. I do hope it's something nice Tricia. I'll be interested to hear all about it,' Harriet said stiffly, forcing politeness.

'Me too about yours, but I don't expect it will be half so exciting for you. Still you never know! Bye `arriet.'

'Bye Tricia, take care.'

Harriet put the phone down somewhat surprised at the concern mounting within her. 'Why on earth would he give her a suitcase to carry? Pretty large present! I'd say that was most unlikely. I really should have warned Tricia about that toad of a man.' She suddenly felt guilty and then remembered Tricia hadn't been that nice to her!

Chapter 24

Monday at last! Harriet couldn't wait to escape. She recalled the somewhat reluctant kiss she'd given Mark yesterday afternoon before he'd dashed out to greet the car full of merriment. 'Huh, anyone would think he was off to a Christmas party,' she'd thought as she remembered all the laughter escaping through the car door as he got into the back seat. She wasn't too pleased that that Melissa woman would inevitably be squashed alongside him either. She knew it would be Mark who'd move along and sit the whole journey like an octopus in a matchbox, in the middle!

She'd been pleased to hear from her babies, though. Tristan and Sebastian seemed to be very much at the forefront of their lives and oh how much they were all looking forward to the grand opening of Starboard Marine North West. Harriet had tried to play it down.

She zipped her holdall closed and tried to empty her head to allow herself to concentrate on getting to the coach station. She struggled downstairs with her luggage, took a deep breath, and closed the front door behind her. 'Time to go! I wonder what's in store?' she thought, pushing everything into the car boot.

'Just take one thing at a time,' she told herself as she drove along. Then her mind switched as she tried to think if she'd forgotten anything. 'Passport? Yes. Tickets? Yes. Money and cards? Yes. Keys to the estate agents? Yes. Cancelled the milk and papers? Yes. The cat? No! Oh no I've forgotten about the cat!' Harriet was mortified. 'No food, no milk!' she panicked and glanced at her watch. 'No time to go back, I'll miss the coach,' she said out loud. 'Oh sod, sod, sod! If it hasn't got the gumption to find some puddles and catch a few mice it deserves to be dead on the kitchen floor when I get back.' Harriet made a swift decision. 'No, it's got a better life than me at the moment. I'm not giving up on this cruise.'

Harriet drove into the coach station car park, suddenly cheered by the unexpected greenery and the rustle of leaves. She looked up to see the wind bending the tall trees against the fluffy white clouds as they scooted their way across the blue sky. She spotted a really good slot right on the end of the first row in. 'That's lucky,' she thought, noting how packed everywhere was. As she glanced around she suddenly stiffened. She thought she saw Mr. Sanderson just disappearing behind the kiosk. 'No, it couldn't have been. For heaven's sake Harriet forget about him. Of course it wasn't him! How could it be him when he's on his way to Zurich with Tricia?' Annoyingly Harriet's hair blew over her face as she slammed the car door and opened the boot to get her luggage. The more she held on to her hair the stronger the wind blew and she was finding it difficult to look without making it obvious. She could feel the fury starting to burn within her. She grabbed the bag. 'Of course I'm not jealous of Tricia,' she told herself. 'Why should I be? Who'd want to be with such a double crossing two-timer anyway?' Deep in thought she headed for the smart, newly refurbished reception centre but her anger couldn't win out to the emotional pain physically stabbing her consciousness. She pushed against the door, hair in a complete tangle, only to feel the weight being lifted from behind.

'That's better,' she thought as she smoothed her hair down. Then she looked behind to say thank you.

'Can I offer you a lift, Harriet? I think we're both going in the same direction.'

Harriet was stunned into complete silence.

'A lift Harriet,' repeated Mr. Sanderson with just a hint of impatience in his tone.

'Er, I don't think so, thank you, Mr. Sanderson,' replied Harriet starting to feel just a little dazed.

'Next please,' came a no-nonsense voice from behind the desk, obviously aimed at both of them.

'Er not us, thank you,' said Mr. Sanderson moving Harriet back towards the doorway. 'Come now, why sit on one of those bone rattlers when we can both go down together?'

'But you're supposed to be going to Switzerland with Tricia, aren't you?' exploded Harriet.

'Next please! We are now into boarding time,' came the same insistent voice.

'Not your concern Harriet. Let me take your holdall.'

'No thank you, thank you very much,' Harriet spluttered, and in a state of shock walked away from him. She placed her boarding ticket on the counter much to the satisfaction of the clerk and turned to see Mr. Sanderson making his way towards the kiosk.

'What have I done?' she asked herself, her trembling legs hardly supporting her body as she stumbled to the coach trying to make sense of it all.

'No Miss, bags and cases go in the big boot at the back of the coach,' called the driver. 'Just hand luggage on the top racks.'

'I think he means you dear!' came a very refined voice into Harriet's ear from behind.

'Oh!' said Harriet now feeling very flustered. She hadn't realised a queue had formed whilst she tried to turn on the steep steel steps without prodding the rotund lady who'd kindly enlightened her.

'Pass it down!' ordered a trim, moustached sergeant major of a gentleman from the bottom.

Harriet obeyed. She sent her thanks down the descending line of impatient shoulders and continued her struggle to the narrow platform behind the driver's seat feeling a little uneasy at not handing it over herself.

'Seat number 48. That's got to be right at the very back,' Harriet deduced. All eyes were on her as she walked the narrow aisle. She tried to shrug off the uninvited celebrity status the seating layout unwittingly produced and was relieved to sink into the corner window seat on the back row.

After a quick head count the driver pulled away and Harriet was relieved to be on her way at last. She took a deep breath, grateful for the grey and blue upholstered seat supporting her completely redundant legs. She looked out of the window but her mind didn't want to see. 'How did he know I was going to be there?' she puzzled. Then she suddenly remembered she'd told Tricia all about her trip. 'That's it! It must have been her,' she concluded. 'Why, oh why did I open my mouth?' Then she was glad she did. Then she wasn't. Then she was. This was no good! She forced herself to move on. She thought about the cat, Mark, her babies and then had a little worry about her luggage. 'That's irrational! Tricia's got more reason to worry about that suitcase. What on earth is he playing at?' Harriet could find no answers. She looked around the coach, weighing up her fellow passengers most of whom looked like couples. Not the woman in front, though. Harriet had only just noticed the rotund lady must have followed her down the aisle to the seat directly ahead. At that moment she turned round. 'Hello again!' she said pleasantly, 'are you on your own, too?'

'Well, yes, just taking the opportunity to get away from it all for a few days.'

'Me too, my name's Molly, Molly Potter, and you…?'

'Harriet Glover,' smiled Harriet as she leant forward to shake hands.

'Would you like to join me in a coffee when we do our comfort stop?' whispered Molly suddenly aware of her fellow passengers.

'Yes, thank you,' said Harriet, 'that would be very nice!' Molly beamed and her stout middle-aged face creased to the lines that penned her once good looks.

Harriet settled back feeling a little easier now. She stretched her legs as far as it was possible and wriggled her feet under Molly's seat. They were starting to feel as though they belonged to her again. The onset of renewed energy enabled her curiosity to release itself from the surge of adrenaline that had reduced her to a legless quiver but however hard she tried Harriet couldn't rationalise Mr. Sanderson's appearance. She wasn't sufficiently recovered to take on the many questions and anyway she knew all the speculation in the world wouldn't produce the right answers. She recalled him standing in the doorway. Hair blown, eyes twinkling, commanding, demanding.

'Oh I wish I'd gone with him now, I really do.' She tried to remind herself of how despicable he was over the fracas with the caretaker but it didn't work. She could feel the power of attraction overtaking every shred of common sense. 'It's got to be like a drug. I'm utterly and completely addicted to him!' If it had been possible, Harriet would have allowed herself to bask in the delicious glow of his offer for the whole journey but increasingly she became more and more annoyed with herself at turning it down. 'For goodness sake Harriet grow up,' she told herself sharply. 'Distraction, just try distraction!'

So Harriet seized her imagination and looked out of the wide panoramic window onto the traffic. She was amazed at the different perspective the height of the coach offered. Cars, vans and lorries, nose to tail, all crawling their way in and out of the city, yielding only to traffic lights standing guard at the entrances to yet more one-way systems. Harriet told herself to try harder. She could still feel the deep regret of refusal. With the coach responding to the full force of its brakes she watched intently as the lights shining from the three vertically placed giant boiled sweets changed from red to orange to green. Harriet looked at the massive dinosaur headed cranes dominating the sky line. She watched them shift backwards and forwards behind the traffic lights, now nothing more than midget gems to these metal monsters. Calmer now she found herself admiring the beautiful buildings that graced the route and thought of Bruges. Harriet liked cities. She loved all the hustle and bustle. 'They must have been just as vibrant in medieval times,' she thought. She would concentrate on the cruise and all there was to look forward to.

They were soon out of the city and heading for the motorway. The coach veered its way through leafy lanes and Harriet glanced across to see the cream woolly sheep set like fair aisle in the rich blanket of green. The white clouds were still scooting endlessly across the blue sky. She stayed with them as their ever-changing edges made new images and she thought of James and Paul and of how they would all lie on the grass as children looking up to the clouds, pointing and shouting as the wind constantly etched new pictures. There was always so much rivalry between her two brothers. Paul on the creative side always managed to outdo James, who, even as a child was sharp and convergent in his thinking. But then it was that unemotive analytical ability that eventually earned him his place at Cambridge where he had met Geraldine. Harriet wished he hadn't. Her thoughts turned to the wedding. 'Not too long now before the big day,' she said to herself. Then she suddenly remembered Mr. Sanderson's invitation. In all the chaos of her life she had completely forgotten his circuitous invite. She deliberately clicked 'delete'. 'Not long after that Susan's baby will be due.' She felt a twinge of jealousy, disappointment. She tried to put it out of her mind and went back to the clouds.

'I do hope the wind dies down,' she thought and then she remembered with dismay it might be nearing the equinox. She racked her brains trying to remember when it was. 'No wonder they had so many cabins left,' she panicked. The coach suddenly veered off the motorway towards the services. Harriet so deep in thought hadn't even noticed they had left the lanes. Molly turned round in her seat and gave Harriet the nod. Harriet reciprocated, glad of the opportunity to glean Molly's opinion on the likelihood of a stormy passage.

'Oh no dear,' reassured Molly as she peered over her tea cup, her eyes twinkling from the wisdom of her years. 'Just don't you worry about that. These ships are so large and so well stabilised there would have to be a hurricane out there to even notice the slightest ripple!'

'Point taken,' smiled Harriet who was more than prepared to go along with the exaggeration simply for the pleasure of being in the company of such a comforting woman.

'Anyway dear, where's your cabin? I got such a bargain you know! Balcony, bathroom, queen sized bed; I believe they had a whole deck-full to dispose of!'

Harriet didn't get chance to answer.

'Just a minute dear, I need to have a quick word with Mr. Fishwick. I'll be back in a tick!'

Harriet glanced over to see her chatting and laughing into the immaculately framed ear of the sergeant major gentleman who was sitting on his own.

'Sorry about that dear. Such a nice man, recently lost his wife. Don't wish to intrude of course but I can't bear to think of him on his own. A cheery word now and then might keep his spirits up!'

'That's so very kind,' said Harriet, 'would you like him to join us?'

'Good heavens no, dear!' replied the astonished Molly. 'A friendly eye will do.'

'Ah cabins that's what we were talking about. Where are you again?'

Harriet was about to reply when the five minute call came.

'Ah, just time to visit the ladies. See you back on the coach, dear.'

Harriet returned to her seat pleased and amused by her newfound companion but somewhat relieved that she wasn't to be the entire focus of her obvious kindness. She rested her head, briefly wondered how Mark was getting on, then closed her eyes giving over all responsibility to the driver as the engine powered the wheels along miles and miles of unrelenting motorway.

'It's lunch time dear,' whispered Molly very courteously as she turned her head to see Harriet fast asleep behind her. 'Are you taking lunch with me, Harriet?' This time her voice was a little louder.

Harriet came to with a jump.

'So sorry dear, I didn't mean to startle you.'

'Oh not at all,' said Harriet rubbing her eyes. 'I didn't mean to doze off like that!'

'I'm sure it will do you good dear. No panic, we'll wait for everyone else to get off the coach. This is just a short stop I think.' Molly looked at her watch. 'Yes it's a quarter to one. We have to be at the port for two o'clock and we are just about a half-hour's drive from Southampton now.'

Harriet couldn't believe her ears. 'Have we come this far already?'

'Oh they don't hang about dear, especially when they've got deadlines to meet. Sometimes it can take a while to go through boarding procedure on these shorter cruises so they like to make sure we've all eaten before we queue.'

'Oh right, well that's very nice of them,' said Harriet trying to grapple with the concept of queuing. 'Surely you just show your passport and get on?' she said to herself. She'd just been asleep and was most anxious to return to that pleasant state of oblivion.

Good as her word Molly waited until all the seats had emptied before ushering Harriet down the aisle towards the services. They were met with Mr. Fishwick at the entrance. 'Do you mind if I join you two delightful ladies?' he enquired.

Molly and Harriet looked at one another. 'Not at all,' they said almost simultaneously, to which Mr. Fishwick touched his hat taking his turn behind them in the queue at the self-service counter.

Harriet eyed the dwindling potato mash looking stale and depleted in its large steel container. The limited selection of drying vegetables alongside the fish and brown stew looked even less appetising. She decided on a sandwich together with Molly and Mr. Fishwick.

'It'll leave us plenty of room for the five course meal onboard this evening,' Molly said. 'Tea everybody?'

The large room was noisy and very crowded and an empty table, even one drowning in tea-slops and bits of used sugar paper, was not to be found. Eventually Mr. Fishwick spotted three available bar stools right at the far end of the room.

'Over here!' he commanded.

Harriet and Molly immediately responded, marching over with tea-cups rattling in their saucers and their sandwiches just clinging to the plates. They finally perched themselves on the very high stools with a smile.

'Well done Mr. Fishwick!' praised Molly.

Mr. Fishwick beamed and touched his hat before removing it. He popped it down on the red vinyl seat, then with one supreme effort he placed his right foot on the stool's lower supporting ring, and with both hands heaved himself up. He suddenly vanished straight over the top, shooting his hat into a passing bowl of tomato soup! It splashed a shower of orange rain everywhere as it smashed into the hard floor.

Harriet and Molly were creased double. They could hear his apologetic bursts from the floor and looked up to see the soup-drenched hat being placed firmly on his head by an angry girl whose tattooed hand now strangely matched her orange splattered black leather jacket.

'Ger off with yer, yer clumsy 'ol geezer!' came the shrill voice. 'No I done wanna nutha one off yer!'

Harriet and Molly looked at each other and tried to stifle their laughter. They each took a deep breath in an attempt to regain their composure. Molly who was having the most success, struggled to bring Mr. Fishwick to his feet. Harriet, almost legless by now, could do little more than offer a gentle push from behind.

'I'm quite alright, really I am,' said Mr. Fishwick peering up through his soup laden eyebrows. Harriet took another deep breath trying to seal the erupting explosion of giggles from within. She had to get away.

'Can you manage there, Molly, with Mr. Fishwick? I'll go and see if I can get a few cloths.' Harriet just about got the words out. Tears streaming down her face and shaking she made towards the door by the till marked 'Staff Only'. She kept her head down. Out of the corner of her eye she could just see the till approaching. It was too close, she was still uncontrollable when she arrived. She found herself in the queue. She tried to lower her shoulders. She thought it might stop them from shaking. She didn't dare look up!

'Your change sir,' she heard the dark haired girl from behind the till say to the person in front.

'Ah, thank you indeed,' came the reply. Harriet jumped. Suddenly she felt the man's arm enclosing her as he took the money.

'Those tears for me Harriet?' Mr. Sanderson squeezed her shoulder and raised her chin.

'Evidently *not* Miss Glover. I don't go much on being made to look a fool.'

He didn't wait for a reply. He stormed off leaving a dazed Harriet not knowing now whether to laugh or cry.

Harriet was relieved to rejoin the coach. She gazed and gazed out of the window in the hope of seeing Mr. Sanderson's car overtake them but she knew it wouldn't. She took her diary out of her bag and turned to the map at the back. 'He'll be heading for the M3 now.' She could hardly bear to hold the thought. 'Then Heathrow to board his flight to Zurich.' She wondered why he hadn't just gone from Manchester. 'Why did he want to go so much out of his way for her?'

Molly turned in her seat. It distracted her from the ache that was beginning to materialise into a huge lump in her throat.

'Mr. Fishwick's promised to find our cases as he's first off the coach,' whispered Molly.

'That's kind of him,' said Harriet, wondering why she'd ever worried about it. She had far more to concern her now!

Chapter 25

Molly wasn't wrong in her anticipation of a long, tedious wait to board the ship. It certainly gave Harriet plenty of time to descend into the depths of utter despair. She couldn't believe that Mr. Sanderson had followed the coach to be with her. She couldn't believe that he'd actually left Tricia to go it alone to Switzerland just so he could give her a lift to the port. None of it made any sense. 'There's only one answer,' Harriet said to herself. 'Could it just be he's fallen in love with me?'

'Harriet, you need to move along now dear!' reminded Molly as a considerable gap had formed in the snaking queue.

'Oh!' said Harriet, shaken from her thoughts. She lifted her holdall and hurriedly joined Molly and Mr. Fishwick. The long line behind her gradually shuffled forward to close the gap.

Harriet thanked Molly. Mr. Fishwick, propped up by his golf club, smiled at her. She noticed he was holding his coat rolled inside out but his hat was nowhere to be seen. She was drawn to the faint traces of tomato soup remaining on his once white eyebrows and she smiled back at him. The humour had gone. 'That was an awful thing to happen Mr. Fishwick. Are you sure you're alright?'

'Just fine my dear!'

Harriet returned to her thoughts. Oh how her heart was aching. How could she have blown it all as easily as that? She tried very hard to concentrate on Mark but it wasn't working. She tried a different tack. 'The cat, the poor cat! How could I do that to the poor cat?' But at that moment Harriet didn't give a toss.

Are you alright Harriet?' enquired Molly. 'You've been very quiet since you came back with those wet cloths.'

'It's my most unfortunate accident,' piped up Mr. Fishwick. 'Don't be upset my dear, I'm quite alright now. Molly made a spanking good job of cleaning me up, for which I'm very grateful to you.' He pointed towards Molly with his golf club and winked at Harriet, stepping just that little bit too close to her. Harriet stepped back to retrieve her much needed space. Mr. Fishwick just gazed at her and Harriet switched off.

'I appreciate the praise Mr. Fishwick,' chimed in Molly. 'But I think you'll find there's plenty of soup stains left. You certainly won't be helping the matter wrapping that hat in your jacket like that. They'll never dry! I think they're most likely ruined, anyway. You're probably going to need some new ones. We're bound to find a gentlemen's outfitters on board.'

'Never!' retorted Mr. Fishwick. 'My dear wife bought me these. They were the last things she got me. I'll wear them until the day I die!'

An exasperated Molly turned towards Harriet. She could see Harriet was miles away so she let it ride.

'He'll be well on his way to the airport now to join Tricia in Switzerland,' Harriet bemoaned to herself. 'She won't even mind not flying with him once she's opened her present. He's probably bought her something absolutely gorgeous and it's in that suitcase!' She suddenly envied Tricia. 'So he can't be in love with me then if he's fallen for her.'

The more Harriet shuffled her way along the never-ending queue the more she oscillated in trying to rationalise the situation. She was consumed with regret, jealously and desire. She totally ached for him as she constantly turned around to see if she could see his car. Eventually they snaked with the queue into the checkout where, to her frustration, she could no longer see the stream of traffic moving slowly along the dockside.

'We'll need our tickets and passports,' Molly said. 'Come Mr. Fishwick, it's best to have them ready. Harriet, have you got yours dear?'

Harriet and Mr. Fishwick placed their luggage on the floor and immediately started searching. Molly looked down to see Harriet's green Deck C luggage label. 'We're on the same deck, dear,' she said to Harriet, looking very pleased. 'What deck are you on Mr. Fishwick?'

'Not too sure, now. Just a minute,' he said. Mr. Fishwick clicked open his case and pulled out his label which was attached to a very long string. 'I do this to protect it and it affords a certain amount of privacy of course!'

'Of course,' said Molly, feeling she'd been a little intrusive. She noticed with a little disappointment that his ticket was pink and not green.

'Deck B,' declared Mr. Fishwick. 'One higher than you two. Still there's always the lift!' He nudged Harriet and winked. Molly looked surprised, not as surprised as Harriet though.

'Just trying to cheer her up,' he said to Molly. 'I'm so taken with her lasting concern for me.'

'Well I'm concerned too, you know,' Molly reassured him.

'How lovely, two caring companions. Not like that rude and vulgar young lady.' Then he knelt down and started shoving the luggage label back into his case.

'Well she was covered in soup,' Harriet thought and for a moment it brought the smile back to her face.

At last it was their turn to check in and after parting company briefly for each to pass through checkout, they left the long row of desks and arrived at the bottom of the walking stairway to be met by a group of security officers.

'It's always a relief to be waved through,' Molly said to Harriet. 'We'd better wait for Mr. Fishwick though. I think it's that golf club that's causing the problem.'

'Whatever has he brought that for?' asked Harriet, completely puzzled.

'Unless there's a chance of a round onboard ship, I really don't know. Still, it's keeping him upright. He'll need it to get up there!'

They both looked up at the long, narrow, moving platform ahead.

At last a much relieved Mr. Fishwick was allowed through and the three of them moved upward and forward, intent on enjoying their holiday.

Chapter 26

'You a threesome?' greeted the ship's photographer as they finally reached the end of the steeply rising walkway.

'We most certainly are!' sported Mr. Fishwick.

'Closer ladies, move right in close to the gentleman.'

Harriet and Molly did just as they were told.

'All smiling please!' continued the photographer.

With a click and a flash it was done and the three of them moved towards the uniformed officers waiting to greet them at the ship's entrance.

'This is nice,' thought Harriet as she returned the smile to a tall, dark-haired man with a very strong handshake.

'Onward and forward I think,' Mr. Fishwick advised.

'But it's so big!' exclaimed Harriet who'd snatched a passing glimpse from each of the walkway windows and could hardly believe that the ship was at least as long as her road.

They walked towards the reception area just behind the atrium. Its magnificent waterfall cascaded down the awe-inspiring chasm flanked either side by staircase upon staircase to almost the top deck of the ship. She luxuriated in the carpet underfoot. Her eyes followed it up along the stairs. The rich deep pile struggling in its folds. She noted how well the shiny brass banisters painted their importance in the fight for opulence that was everywhere.

Mr. Fishwick touched his forehead to the girl at the desk then steered them towards the glass faced lift at the stern of the ship.

Harriet wasn't prepared for the endless miles of corridors and cabins. In spite of his irritations she felt very grateful to Mr. Fishwick for his guidance.

They entered the glass-sided lift which framed the eastern end of the dock and in one long rise they saw ships, tiny cranes and miniature buildings alongside acres of cars now looking like tiny coloured mosaics in their even lines. Harriet felt a bit nervous. A tall thin young man languished in the corner with his suitcase at his feet. She was just able to read the name on the pink luggage label stuck to the top. Mr. H. Walker. He picked it up. She noticed it had HW embossed in gold on the side.

'Could be Harry or Henry or Horace,' Harriet thought. She had a thing about names.

'Is this your stop young man?' enquired Mr. Fishwick.

'No, I'm a bit higher, thank you,' he replied politely.

Harriet smiled across at him. 'Mr. Fishwick wouldn't have noticed they were going to be on the same deck.'

'Deck C coming up ladies. I'll join you later!' Mr. Fishwick guided them out of the doors.

'What's your cabin number dear?' Molly enquired of Harriet as they marvelled at their surroundings.

Harriet fished in her handbag and pulled out her ticket. '347,' she replied.

'Ah, what a shame, mine's 341. It would have been nice if we'd been next door to each other. Still we're not too far away.'

They continued their march up the long corridor, which suddenly took a sharp right hand turn.

'Wait a minute now, I think these are the 34's,' said Molly. 'Ah yes 341, that's mine. Now let's find yours dear so we can get our bearings.'

'It's right next door!' exclaimed Harriet. 'What a coincidence!'

At that moment a young steward came up behind them.

'Just slide your key card into the slot on the top, push the handle down and the cabin door will open.' He smiled and Harriet couldn't help but admire his broad, even teeth set pure white against the rich brown shade of his skin. Harriet thought he was very good looking.

'I'm Charles,' he said and shook hands with them both. 'I'll be looking after you both during your stay onboard. Just dial 101 and I'll be of help to you.'

'Thank you so much,' smiled Harriet in return and Molly nodded in agreement.

'Oh! Just one more thing,' he reminded them. Harriet became fascinated with the unmistakable lilt that people from other parts of the world sometimes give to spoken English. 'It is most important to watch the TV video that's now running in your cabin before the emergency drill at 3.30pm. Then you'll know what to do if we sink!' His broad smile burst into a huge grin and he went off down the corridor chuckling away to himself.

Harriet looked at Molly. She knew he'd just been joking but an uneasy wave of concern went through her.

'Oh you get used to these drills,' said Molly. 'All we have to do is listen carefully for twenty minutes or so and then forget all about it. Anyway Mr. Fishwick is sure to bail us out if we need it!'

'As long as he doesn't use his hat!' laughed Harriet as she slipped her card into the slot. 'See you shortly, Molly.'

Harriet's cabin door swung closed behind her and she made for the huge, beautifully presented, queen-size bed. She flopped onto the edge and then rolled into the middle, kicking off her shoes as she did so. She stretched full length and just lay there, completely motionless with both hands resting on top of her head. She looked around her cabin delighting in the space, the beautiful drapes, the pictures. It was all so lavishly furnished. She stretched out again and decided not to move until she'd watched the lifeboat drill instructions being pumped out of the cabin's television. With some reluctance she tried to take it all in but it wasn't easy. Harriet's thoughts turned to Mr. Sanderson. 'Just as well we parted company.' She tried hard to concentrate on the life saving drill but needed a second run to erase Mr. Sanderson from her mind. Once over she switched the television off and lay on the bed. Her thoughts returned to Mr. Sanderson before drifting off into a delicious, delirious sleep.

Chapter 27

Harriet awoke to a loud knock on the door. She could hear someone shouting. 'Harriet!' said Molly, panicking.

Harriet shot off the bed and quickly opened the door.

'The alarm's gone and we're supposed to be on our way to the Neptune restaurant for lifeboat drill!' said Molly grabbing the cabin door before it banged itself shut.

'Oh dear!' exclaimed Harriet slipping her shoes back on and snatching her lifejacket. 'Thanks Molly! We're on our way.'

'We should meet up with Mr. Fishwick again,' said Molly as they marched along the corridor following the continuous ribbon of little green lights that skirted the joint between the wall and the floor. They came to a sharp left turn just in time to see someone crawling on their hands and knees at the end of the long corridor ahead.

'What on earth is he doing?' queried Harriet.

'I can't think!' replied Molly, astounded. 'Come on Harriet, let's run and see. We're late anyway.'

Harriet and Molly put a huge spurt on and turned the corner at the end of the corridor very short of breath only to see Mr. Fishwick collapsed in a heap near the lift doors.

'Mr. Fishwick! What on earth are you doing?' panted Molly.

Mr. Fishwick touched his forehead. 'I must admit I was having forty winks when that pesky alarm woke me up just in time to hear those instructions "...crawl along the corridors and the green lights will take you to your lifeboat station." '

Mr. Fishwick, eyes wide, looked at Molly. 'You've been struggling along there too, haven't you my dear and you?' He nodded at Harriet, 'I can see you are both out of breath.'

'No of course we haven't Mr. Fishwick. You're only supposed to do that if the place is filled with smoke!'

'Poor Mr. Fishwick,' joined in Harriet catching her breath as she helped Molly bring him to his feet. 'You only saw a snatch of that killjoy programme. I fell asleep too after the second loop. It's a wonder though. It nearly frightened the life out of me!'

Mr. Fishwick smiled at Harriet. 'It's most probably intended to my dear. I'll watch it again later when I've had a stiff G&T.'

'No, no, Mr. Fishwick,' said Molly. 'You'll still be crawling along the corridors if you do that. You must join me in my cabin and we'll go through it together, then you will know exactly what to do.'

'That's most kind of you! Then we'll have that stiff G&T together when it's over and Harriet will come and join us.'

'I think we've one more flight of stairs before we get to the Neptune restaurant,' said Harriet studiously avoiding a reply.

Harriet and Molly linked arms with the hobbling Mr. Fishwick and eventually they arrived at the doors.

Harriet looked around. It was the most sumptuous restaurant she had ever seen and she and Mark, in the past, had certainly done themselves proud when it came to the eating out stakes.

She drooled over the huge chandeliers that lit the first floor with such grace. Then her eyes followed the sweeping curve of the staircase to the upper floor and saw a balcony of beautifully laid tables draped with starched white cloths, each one adorned with an exquisite central floral display. Her eyes came down past the bandstand, the beautiful grand piano luxuriating proudly in acres of deeply carpeted space.

Harriet felt herself being dragged along by Molly and Mr. Fishwick. They were the last ones in and were therefore obliged to troop across the floor and around the bandstand to find somewhere to sit.

'This will do,' whispered Molly and the three of them sat down to a large round table laying their hands on the pristine cloth.

'For the benefit of the three people who have just arrived, I'll repeat that again,' said one of the officers who had a lifejacket in one hand and a whistle in the other. 'Where's your lifejacket sir?' he said, pointing to Mr. Fishwick.

Mr. Fishwick blustered.

'Take this!' the officer ordered and he thrust the demonstration lifejacket into his hands.

As if by magic, by the time he'd returned to his position the same officer was sporting yet another and the three of them fell into the routine of listening and obeying.

'May I assist you sir?' the officer said, marching towards Mr. Fishwick again who was having some difficulty doing up his lifejacket.

'No Sir, I'm afraid not. There's something obstructing it around your middle!' insisted the officer.

Mr. Fishwick cautiously placed his hand inside his jacket and brought out a hefty dark green glass bottle filled with gin.

There was silent amusement from those around the nearby tables.

'Don't worry,' said Molly to the officer. 'He's coming back to my cabin for a lesson or two later.'

A roar broke out. Molly, delighted by her new audience smiled graciously. 'Without the gin bottle, I hasten to add!'

All the passengers were quickly brought back to the gravity of the drill and it was a good twenty minutes before they finally filed out of the Neptune restaurant.

'Give him his due,' said Molly on the way back to their cabins, 'that officer certainly made sure everyone knew exactly what they should be doing.' Harriet couldn't help but agree.

'I'm not so sure about that,' objected Mr. Fishwick. 'What's the most important thing you need in a lifeboat if it isn't a bottle of gin? I'm going to have to think of a better place for it!'

Harriet and Molly smiled at one another. 'Well, if you're thinking of crawling your way to the lifeboat station Mr. Fishwick, don't put it in your sock!' Molly winked at Harriet.

Chapter 28

'It says dining tonight is informal,' Harriet reminded herself as she replaced the various notices and cards into her information folder. She returned it to the dressing table and thought about what she might wear.

There was a knock on the cabin door and Harriet went over to open it, letting Molly and Mr. Fishwick in.

'We're off to find the purser fellow to see if we can rearrange our dining table allocations,' said Molly. 'Shall we all dine together, Harriet?' Harriet nodded in agreement. The three had become so bonded it would be unthinkable to do anything else.

'Mr. Fishwick says there's a pleasant young man called Horace on his own in the cabin opposite who might like to join us. Would that be alright with you Harriet?'

'Of course,' agreed Harriet without hesitation. 'We're more likely to get a table for four.'

'We'll trot off then. See you shortly,' said Molly.

Harriet closed the door behind them. 'An old man, a young man, all needing mothering. Well Molly and I are just the ones to look after them. Poor chap with a name like that, no wonder he's lonely,' she thought. Then she remembered the boy in the lift and the initials on his suitcase.

'Of course,' she said to herself as she opened her holdall. At that moment Harriet froze. To her absolute horror the cat jumped out!

Harriet couldn't believe her eyes. She felt sick. She was now guilty of smuggling a domestic pet onboard ship. She'd chased the cat out of her holdall so many times, how could she not have noticed it was still in there? She'd put her black mohair jumper in last of all. She would hardly have mistaken it for that. Had it got in while she was on the phone to Tricia, or when she was paying the milkman? Harriet just couldn't remember. She sat down in a state of shock. She didn't want to be arrested. If she confessed no one would believe it was an accident. What was she to do? 'Mark'll know,' she panicked. She took her mobile phone out of her handbag and rang his number. There was no signal. 'Oh no, I won't be able to tell him either. If I use the ship's phone and someone picks up the message I'll be caught!' Harriet went sick to the core.

The cat, looking very dishevelled, brushed its way around Harriet's legs, purring so loudly she feared the whole of the ship would hear.

Then there was a knock on the door. Harriet bundled the cat into the wardrobe, closed the door and turned the television on loudly. The knock came again. Harriet opened the door to see Charles beaming at her.

'Ah there you are!' he exclaimed in his rhythmical, soft tone. 'I just need to tell you, you know, that you must leave your card on the door knob outside for breakfast in your room.'

'Oh right,' said Harriet, 'what's being served?'

'Just continental in your room but if you want your full English then you go to the restaurant,' he replied, still smiling.

'Look, please could I possibly have cereal with milk as well as cooked meat and croissants? It's just that I'm on a special diet and I have to drink as much milk as possible. I forgot to include it on my booking form.' Harriet gave him a half-forlorn smile and she watched Charles first scratch his head and then stroke his chin.

'Oh dear. I see. I'll see what I can do for you,' he promised with a look of great concern spreading across his face.

'And by the way, I need to sleep a lot so I would rather not have my cabin cleaned if that's alright with you.'

'Oh that's fine,' agreed Charles, the smile returning to his face.

'I know it takes you ladies in different ways. My wife was about twelve weeks like that but by the end of the nine months she was blooming you know.'

Harriet smiled and nodded at him. 'Don't worry, I'll be fine now, thanks to you. Oh and I'll pass the breakfast message on to my friend Molly next door, if you like.'

'Ah, thank you very much indeed,' he said and went off to knock on the cabin door opposite.

Harriet, thinking fast on her feet, called him back. 'I don't suppose there's any chance of some milk and cold meat now, is there? It's just that I'm feeling terribly sick and it's the only thing that will stop it.'

'I'll certainly do my utmost to be of assistance to you,' he declared and marched off at top speed down the corridor.

All of a sudden Harriet was feeling just a little bit better. At least she would be able to feed the cat once a day. She decided she would line the bottom of the wardrobe with one of her laundry bags and fill another with torn newspaper. She reckoned the cat would soon get the message. Besides, that's where she intended to keep it for the next three days.

In a flummox, Harriet carried on unpacking. She felt her stomach starting to churn again and she went very hot. 'I'd better see if it's alright,' she thought. She gently turned the key in the wardrobe door. It was curled up on a spare pillow on the floor. 'I should bloody well think so!' She closed the door on it before flopping on the bed. The wave of panic subsided.

She lay bemused at the happenings. 'It doesn't really matter if Charles thinks I'm pregnant, as long as he doesn't tell anyone.' She took a deep breath. 'The most important thing is that no one finds out about the cat. Cat, damned cat! How could it be so thick? It never misses an opportunity to blow everything at the most critical times,' Harriet thought, remembering how it nearly finished Belinda Oxfordshire off. 'Oh well, at least she'll get her second viewing round the house without sight nor sign of it.'

Almost twenty minutes had passed since Charles had embarked on his mission to find her some food. She decided to just have a quick look out of the door to see if she could see him. 'No sign.' She suddenly pricked her ears to the sound of distant voices. 'Ah! That sounds like Molly and Mr. Fishwick coming back.' Quickly she popped her head back in and closed the door. She waited until she could hear them quite distinctly outside and then reopened the door not giving them a chance to knock.

'All sorted!' said Mr. Fishwick walking in with Molly in tow and once again feeling very pleased with himself. They sat down on the settee.

'Mr. Fishwick's managed to get us a table for four right by the window. Isn't he clever Harriet?'

'You certainly are Mr. Fishwick,' replied Harriet, nestling into the armchair. 'I love watching the water.'

'What would we girls do without you?' said Molly. Mr. Fishwick beamed at them both.

There was a sharp knock on the cabin door. Harriet jumped. She knew it would be Charles. She wasn't sure what to do. She felt herself freezing over.

'That was a knock Harriet,' Molly informed her. 'Shall I go?'

Before she had time to answer Mr. Fishwick had opened the door and let Charles and his white napkin covered silver tray in.

Charles beamed at Harriet. 'Yes you don't look too good you know. This will make you feel better.'

'Oh, thank you so very much.'

'It's my pleasure!' he exclaimed looking at the others. 'She's eating for two you know!'

He departed leaving Harriet to cope with the outburst of joyful concern from Molly and Mr. Fishwick.

Harriet knew she had to come clean. 'No, no! He's just assuming that!'

'Whatever do you mean dear?' queried Molly looking at the covered tray. 'You've no need to be shy with us.'

'Certainly not!' supported Mr. Fishwick. 'Anything we can do to help?'

'There could well be!' exclaimed Harriet, just at the same time as a loud meow could be heard, coming from the direction of the wardrobe.

'Do you know,' said Molly, 'I'm sure I heard a cat meowing then.'

'A cat!' exclaimed Mr. Fishwick. 'I didn't hear anything.'

'There, there it goes again. Oh dear, I'm not starting to hear things now, am I? Can you hear it Harriet?' Molly asked.

'Mr. Fishwick, why don't you go and look outside and see if there's one in the corridor?' suggested Molly. In an instant he disappeared. The door banged behind him.

'Molly, quick, it's in here!' said Harriet unlocking the key in the wardrobe door.

'In where? Whatever is a cat doing in your wardrobe, Harriet?'

As Harriet opened the door the cat shot out and started rubbing Molly's legs vigorously. 'It must have got into my holdall while I was packing. Well her holdall actually. It's where she usually sleeps. I had no idea I'd brought it with me!' Harriet gabbled. She went very pink. 'I couldn't find another case after packing Mark's. Poor thing, it must be starving,' she finished.

Molly's face crinkled into a kindly smile. 'So you meant what you said. You're not expecting then, Harriet?'

Harriet shook her head. She lifted the cloth off the tray and put the plate of cooked meats on the floor. The cat meowed loudly and nudged her hand with its wet nose.

'Please don't tell anyone,' she pleaded to Molly. 'If I can get it home the same way as it came, I'll just be so relieved.'

'Of course not. I'll help you with this one Harriet. It'll be alright, you see.' She took the glass of milk and poured some of it onto the licked clean plate.

'Oh thanks so much, Molly,' said Harriet.

'I think it better if we don't tell Mr. Fishwick though, Harriet. Oh there he is, back again! Just don't answer it.'

Harriet nodded in agreement.

'We'll need a plan if we're going to make this one work,' said Molly touching her forehead with her index finger. 'Now let me think. It's probably best to leave it here in your cabin but I'll come and sit with it from time to time.'

'You are kind, Molly, but I couldn't possibly let this stupid cat ruin your cruise, too.'

'No dear, it's quite alright, really it is, and it's not going to ruin yours, either.'

'I just can't thank you enough Molly. You've certainly made me feel a whole lot better!'

'Not at all Harriet! Now you go and have a wander round the ship to get your bearings. You haven't been anywhere yet.'

Harriet gladly took Molly's advice. 'I won't be long,' she promised and smiled at Molly who now had the cat purring on her lap. Harriet waved and closed the door behind her.

Her footsteps, sinking into the luxurious deep blue carpet, took her to the end of the corridor. She descended the staircase.

'Ah there you are,' said Mr. Fishwick. 'I've looked everywhere and no sign of a cat anywhere. Mind you I never heard one in the first place. No wonder you didn't answer the door. I didn't know you'd gone out. I knocked about five minutes ago. Has Molly gone looking in the other direction then?'

'Er yes,' said Harriet feeling uncomfortable. She scratched her head as people often do when their words are incompatible with the truth. 'I think we've just been hearing things. It's still very windy and I'm sure there's all kinds of things whining and rattling around out there,' she continued, gazing through the three sets of glass panelled double doors leading to the ship's rail.

'I'll go that way and take the fresh air,' she thought, changing direction.

'I'm just about to use the lift my dear. Will you join me?' he asked, glancing swiftly across to Harriet, his face breaking into a knowing smile. 'Best not to overtax yourself at this stage.'

'Oh!' said Harriet, desperately trying to work out what he meant. 'Oh, most thoughtful, Mr. Fishwick.' Curtailing her exploration, Harriet obeyed. It wasn't until she was on her way back to the cabin the penny suddenly dropped.

She called to Molly as she gave a light knock on the cabin door and Molly let her in.

'Oh I wouldn't worry about that dear,' said Molly gently stroking the cat. 'It's better he's got his own explanation for what's going on. I'll pass him the word not to mention it, though. It won't matter, we're only with him for a couple of days. Now off you go dear! Go and have a good look round. I'd try the other direction if I were you!'

Harriet went off heading straight for the glass lift at the stern of the ship. Nervous at first, she took it right to the very top, as high as it would go and watched the miniature world below with increasing fascination. Top deck. Out she came to see the swimming pools and jacuzzis, the softball court and the quoits run. She looked out up and over the water to the sea and took a deep breath. In spite of the cat, Harriet was glad she came.

Her descent revealed bars and shops, the beautifully furnished library, the theatre, the computer room, the gymnasium and so very much more. Harriet could hardly take it all in. She returned to her cabin.

'You know Molly, it really is a floating city. A spotlessly clean, luxurious floating city!' Harriet could hardly get the words out. She was so inspired. 'Thank you so much, Molly.'

'Now don't you thank me again. It's my pleasure to help if I can. Now, I think Pussbags, no Pepper! Sorry Pepper. I did hear you call her that didn't I Harriet?'

Harriet smiled and nodded.

'I think she'll be alright in the wardrobe over dinner, so I suggest we get ready. I'll just see if I can find Mr. Fishwick to ask for his discretion. We'll arrange to meet him and that young man at the Neptune restaurant door shall we?'

'Oh that will be just fine and thanks again Molly for everything.'

'Not a word of it!' replied Molly and out she went closing the door behind her.

Chapter 29

Harriet lay down on the bed for a few moments, the cat curled up at her feet. She was nervous that someone might see through the patio doors from her balcony but quickly reasoned there was no access. From that height there was certainly no access. Harriet felt as though she was on the top floor of a skyscraper. 'Poor Mr. Fishwick, he's even higher,' she thought. 'I wonder if Molly has managed to find him yet?' The cat nudged closer to her feet.

'It's time for you to disappear. You're an absolute pain.'

With that it jumped on to the duvet and curled up to her ear. 'No you're not getting round me like that. In, before I throw you overboard.'

The cat completely ignored her. Harriet returned to the bed. 'What to wear? I think I'll save the dress for tomorrow.'

Then she thought about Mark and Melissa Scott.

She thought about her babies and their excitement at the grand opening of Starboard Marine North West.

She thought about Mr. Sanderson and the dilemma she was in.

'He's probably with Tricia now in Switzerland. For some reason it obviously suited him to go south first before joining her.' Then Harriet reminded herself she'd come away precisely to forget all of that.

She jumped off the bed and changed into her brand new trouser suit, all gleaming white. She looked in the mirror and liked the way its clever lean cut disguised all those residues of fat she'd long since disowned. She loved her new shiny, silky red blouse. She'd picked it up and put it down so many times in the shop, wondering if it wasn't just a little too bold with that plunging neckline. Then she put on her special diamond pendant that Mark had bought her for her fortieth birthday and instantly felt more comfortable.

Time was ticking by.

'In you go NOW!' she ordered the cat as she pushed its backside into the wardrobe. 'Oops! Sorry, nearly caught your tail. No more than you deserve. I'll be back later.' She powdered her nose and quickly brushed her hair. She picked up her shiny red leather handbag, slipped on her matching shoes and made her way to Molly's cabin.

'Ready,' said Molly as she opened the door.

'You look lovely, Molly. That shade of blue really suits you.'

'And so do you dear. I like red. It used to be one of my favourite colours when I was younger. Now which one do we go for?' she asked, laughing. 'Do you fancy the toy boy, Harriet?'

'Might be preferable to Mr. Fishwick! Not that he isn't a very nice man.'

'You're right Harriet. He's a very nice person but perhaps we're in need of a change. Mind you, I'll not fight you for him. I'll give in graciously.'

'Most kind Molly, but with a name like Horace I think I'll pass!'

They made their way to the Neptune restaurant and were surprised to see Mr. Fishwick at the doors, standing alone.

'Oh, hello Mr. Fishwick,' said Molly, 'no sign of that young man Horace? We were so looking forward to meeting him.'

'Oh he was delayed, said he had to take a ship's call, but would be along shortly. Anyway, I think it's about time you two ladies called me Percival, or Percy if you prefer.'

'Percy it is then Mr. Fishwick,' replied Molly. Harriet and Mr. Fishwick laughed as the waiter guided them to their table.

'Same palatial surroundings,' thought Harriet, 'but how the atmosphere's changed from its earlier life as a muster station.'

Mr. Fishwick beckoned the ladies to sit next to the window and then placed himself alongside Harriet.

'Isn't this splendid,' he mused. 'It never fails to please me.'

Harriet and Molly agreed.

Harriet delighted in the gentle chatter interspersed with the bursts of occasional laughter set against the soft melodic tones from the grand piano.

She watched the waiters going back and forth, smiling, efficient, genteel.

She looked around and saw the millions of tiny chandelier lights glinting off the numerous wine glasses being lifted, held and replaced onto the starched white tablecloths.

'This is such a lovely thing to be doing,' she thought looking across the table smiling at Molly.

Molly returned the smile 'When's this young man coming, Percy? He needs to be here to place his order. Ah! There's someone just walked in now. No, that can't be him, not young enough or thin enough,' she finally decided.

Harriet didn't bother to look round. Head down, she returned to her menu just to delight in reading the elaborate choice again.

'Good evening!' she heard Mr. Fishwick say. 'Let me introduce you to my friends.'

Harriet, startled, looked up, feeling the colour flooding her cheeks and for a moment she couldn't move.

'Molly and Harriet this is Horace,' he continued. 'Horace may I introduce you to Molly, a very dear lady of recent acquaintance.'

Molly stood up and put her hand out.

'Now Harriet, also a newly acquired friend and such delightful company!'

Harriet recovered sufficiently to stand up and shake his hand. 'Good evening Horace,' she stumbled.

'It's a pleasure to meet you,' he beamed, 'but you must all call me Joris as that's my name. Joris Sanderson. I'm delighted to be in your company!'

They all returned to their sumptuously padded seats but no one needed to sit down more than Harriet!

Orders placed, they settled back in their foursome. Harriet couldn't bring herself to look at him. She stared out of the window gazing at the smaller boats in the distance, weaving their own patterns in the huge wake of their gigantic vessel. She became transfixed by the endless motion of the sea. She watched the sun trying again and again to paint its glorious crimson stripes across the heaving blue water only to have them fragment into thousands of red splinters soon lost in the white foaming waves.

She could vaguely hear Molly and Mr. Fishwick chattering to Mr. Sanderson. She knew she had to join in.

'Are you happy with this choice of wine, Harriet?' she heard Molly say. 'I think Percy's about to give the waiter the thumbs up.'

'Oh perfectly, thank you,' replied Harriet, without even reading the label on the bottle.

'Is this young lady always as quiet as this?' Joris Sanderson enquired.

Harriet looked up to see those intoxicating good looks now amplified by his dark, expensively cut suit, tailored self-striped shirt and black bow tie. She could barely look at the blonde soft curl of hair against his spotless white collar.

'Oh no!' exclaimed Molly. 'Harriet's very friendly, aren't you dear?'

'Good, glad to hear it!' came Mr. Sanderson's enthusiastic reply. 'And may I ask what you do for a living?'

'Most certainly, I'm a teacher.'

'Well, well! And what age of children are fortunate enough to be taught by you?'

'Well, I wouldn't exactly say fortunate,' replied Harriet going very red again, 'but I look after the juniors, seven and eight year olds.'

Harriet didn't know how long she would be able to keep up this charade. She was relieved to see the waiters heading for their table, plates across arms and napkins over wrists, smiling, beaming, anxious to serve.

'Very admirable!' piped up Mr. Fishwick. 'I used to teach languages, much older children of course. I never knew how teachers managed with the young ones though. Well done my dear.'

'Here, here!' agreed Molly lifting her wine glass. 'A toast to Harriet for doing one of the hardest jobs in the world.'

'I'll second that!' agreed Mr. Sanderson.

'Me too!' chimed Mr. Fishwick, not wanting to be left out.

They all clinked glasses to Harriet's utter embarrassment. She felt she'd been coerced into accepting the compliment.

'And what's your headteacher like, Harriet?' asked Mr. Sanderson mischievously. 'Is he worth toasting?'

'Burning at the stake, more like,' Harriet blurted out without looking up, to the great amusement of Molly and Mr. Fishwick. Then she glanced diagonally across the table straight into Mr. Sanderson's serious, blue eyes. 'But he's absolutely gorgeous!'

Chapter 30

Harriet couldn't remember how many more glasses of wine she'd had in an attempt to drown her naked revelation and reality was starting to come and go. She opened the cabin door to find the covered tray left on the dressing table. She lifted the napkin, removed the plate of cooked meats and placed it on the floor.

'Out you come, Pushbags, you load of trouble!' her tone softer now, as she turned the key in the wardrobe door. It shot out, just making it before the door swung back on itself. 'There, it'sh over there. Just give me my legs back, what'sh left of them and go and eat your shupper.' With that she flopped on the bed.

'Eaten it already?' she asked it as it leapt up to join her.

'Come on then, it'sh milk time. Gosh you remind me of one of my mosht fortunate pupils, well, not sho fortunate really.' Harriet was starting to feel confused. 'Poor Danny. You're sho lucky, he'sh too old for milk. Thatsh why I couldn't make him milk monitor. Shilly Mr. Shanderson!'

The cat sprayed the carpet with a shower of tiny white blobs as her little pink tongue got to work. Harriet watched in a semi-fascinated state feeling much more relaxed about her stowaway companion now.

'There's shtill a bit of a problem with you shomehow but I can't quite remember what. Shsurely I haven't had that much to drink? I hope it comesh to me in the morning.'

Harriet climbed back on to the bed and rolled her way to the middle. She gazed around the cabin not quite believing all that had gone before.

'He musht have been intending to do this cruishe all along but how on earth did he know I wash going?' she asked herself over and over again. With her brain saturated in alcohol she couldn't establish any connections.

'He'sh shupposed to be with Tricia in Shwitzerland. What ish he doing here?'

She concentrated very hard, then slowly but surely it started to dawn on her. 'Tricia! Of courshe Tricia! She must have told him and he'sh actually choshen to be with *me*!'

The realisation brought a temporary wave of clarity to Harriet's mind. She lay there, gazing at the joints in the cabin ceiling in utter disbelief. She slipped herself out of her jacket and went with the wave of desire that slowly, intensely moved through her whole body. She remembered Mark's words. ' "Even if you shared the same bed with him I would trust you completely." '

'But we're not married,' she answered him from the silent depths of her mind, knowing she was rapidly being overcome with an uncontrollable desire for this most gorgeous man to make love to her.

Still lying on her back she slipped the button from its buttonhole and undid the zip on her white trousers, wriggling, tussling herself out of them bringing her new lacy white panties down with them.

Slowly she undid the buttons one by one on her plunging silky red blouse and rolled from side to side slipping out each arm as she went. She lay still for a few seconds. 'I'm ready for him,' she murmured. Then she rested on her elbows before undoing the hooks on her matching skimpy bra. She tossed it across the bed and reached for her new silky red nightdress, which she'd left carefully folded on the duvet.

Then she waited for him.

There was a gentle tap on the door. She knew in her heart she was more than ready.

'Coming!' she called. Just at that moment the door opened.

'I just let myself in to save you bothering,' said Charles amiably. 'Good thing that I do! You are resting. I come for the tray and to see how you are, but I have the ship's doctor, at least I think it's the ship's doctor, man holding large black bag. You ask to see the ship doctor on account of your condition? Yes? No? Very urgent! You ask him to check you out at this time of night?' He smiled at her. His voice was sympathetic. 'Shall I tell him to come in?'

'What did you shay hish name wash?' asked Harriet, a bit taken aback.

He closed the door to and Harriet could just hear them both in quiet brief conversation.

'It's a Mr. Sanderson,' said Charles holding the door open. 'He Mr.! He not Doctor! My brother, he also a specialist. Why I not meet this specialist on my ship before?'

Then she saw Mr. Sanderson in the doorway and smiled.

'Shank you Charlesh. I'll shee you in the morning,' replied Harriet desperately trying not to slur her words.

Mr. Sanderson nodded at Charles and closed the door behind him. He walked in placing his bag on the floor by the bed, looking tall, handsome, intent.

'Well, well, Harriet,' he smiled, 'I didn't expect to see you looking like this!'

'An early night! I just thought I would have an early night,' replied Harriet trying to sober up rapidly.

She lay very still on the bed and in an attempt to hide any lurking, wobbly blobs, tugged her nightdress down towards her knees. Then she pulled at the top trying to reduce the extended plunge she'd just made.

'There's not a lot of that to go round Harriet! Just relax and leave it exactly where it is.'

Harriet lay quite still. She felt his serious blue eyes covering her body as he moved them slowly back and forth. Then he looked across to her scattered clothes. He smiled at her and she relaxed a little. He took off his bow tie and undid the button at the neck of his shirt.

'Harriet,' he said. 'There is something I would like you to do for me.'

'Yesh,' replied Harriet, 'anything at all.'

He walked round the bed, zipped open his bag and returned to sit alongside her.

'That woman, that Bustard woman. Can you persuade her to take the cash and drop the whole thing?'

'I'm sure I can,' replied Harriet desperately wishing all her clothes were back on instead of lying in exposed heaps around her. 'Ish that all Mr. Shanderson?'

He stretched across her and placed his lips, slightly open, fully on hers, then moved away, leaving her nightdress lying in folds across her legs. He looked gently down at her as he rose to his feet.

'Are you sure there's nothing elsh I can do for you, Mr. Shanderson?' Harriet almost pleaded.

'I'm feeling rather shocked Harriet that you should ask me that question in your condition! Not to mention the state you're in. I think I remember having to compete with a wine bottle once before Harriet. This is certainly not the time. I'm disappointed Harriet, we don't get a lot of opportunity to chat together. Another day maybe?'

He placed a bundle of used notes on the dressing table, then thinking better of it spotted a long white envelope on top of the ship's writing folder. He popped them all inside. 'I'll see you in the morning.'

'Mr. Shanderson,' said Harriet before he had chance to open the door.

He turned around. 'Better this way Harriet. Now, one thing before I go. I think it's about time you called me Joris, well, on the ship anyway,' he replied, a smile starting to break.

'I find that very difficult Mr. Shanderson. Come and give me some leshons in cashe I call you Horashe by mishstake.'

'Harriet I've watched your alcoholic consumption with interest this evening. It might not be such a good idea, especially if you're, well, you know!'

'Hiding the cat,' Harriet half-whispered to herself. 'No, I don't know Mr. Shanderson, I really don't.'

'Besides, your steward thinks I'm your doctor and your friends think we don't know each other! It's all starting to feel very surreal Harriet.'

'You're just shaving yourself for Tricia!' responded Harriet in desperation.

Mr. Sanderson's face changed. 'I beg your pardon Miss Glover, I understood Mrs. Harrington to be married!'

'Oh, yesh, yesh she is. Shorry!' said Harriet twisting at her diamond pendant, looking very worried, completely unable to read him.

He smiled and then started laughing. 'OK,' he said, walking back towards her. 'I'll give you a few lessons. First we'll start with morality, then you can practise my name and then we'll see if you need any other kind of lessons, Miss Glover!'

He kicked the cat's plate to one side before leaping on to the bed to gather her into his arms.

'Why do you leave dirty dishes on the floor Miss Glover, or was it a trap for that charming steward of yours? Hoping he'd land on his back and then be yours for the night?'

'Shuch cheek, cheek, cheek!' exclaimed Harriet, grabbing a pillow and covering their heads.

Mr. Sanderson flung it away, brushed her hair away from her face and kissed her hard, very hard.

'Harriet,' he murmured, 'I wanted us to… A fucking cat! Bloody hell Harriet, I…' Mr. Sanderson was unable to finish his sentence! Suddenly they were leapt on and he found himself tussling with the cat's rear end which seemed intent on depriving him of oxygen! 'Where did this bloody thing come from? Quite unbelievable!' he stuttered.

The cat, back arched, fur on end shot across the bed and down the other side, Harriet knew not where!

Mr. Sanderson jumped off the bed. 'Quite surreal Miss Glover, quite surreal,' he said brushing himself down. He strode towards the door gathering up his bag on the way. He zipped it and snapped the clasp closed. He marched out without looking back.

'Don't you bloody dare come out or thish time I really will throw you over the shide!' Harriet bawled at the cat.

With that she flounced between the covers and fell fast asleep.

Chapter 31

Daylight saw Harriet well and truly hungover and in the foulest of moods.

'That bloody cat!' was all she could say to herself. 'You can stay in the bloody wardrobe all day for that,' she announced to the door. 'You've just ruined everything. Why couldn't you have just stayed under the dressing table or under the bed or wherever you where?' She paused for breath. 'If you don't end up getting me prosecuted before we go home, that's if we get home, I'll be surprised. In any case you're straight in the cats' home. I've had it with you!'

She picked up the breakfast plate Charles had left, opened the wardrobe door just enough to get her hand in and locked it.

There was a knock on the cabin door. Harriet forced herself to open it. It was Molly. 'Are you coming down to breakfast Harriet?'

'I think I'll pass this morning, thank you Molly. A bit of a hangover, unfortunately.'

'What a shame. You must have been feeling quite poorly after your meal. I went off with Percy and Joris to the Omega bar in the end. We did wait for quite a while for you to come back to the restaurant though.'

'Oh sorry Molly, I just crashed out. Did you all have a nice time?'

'Well, do you remember that awful girl in the services who was so rude to poor Percy? Well she's *here*. She's onboard! She was walking past our table with a load of other girls just like her when she spotted Percy. Poor Percy, she deliberately, well I say deliberately because I think it was. She deliberately slopped her beer all over his sleeve as she was walking past.'

'Oh no! Poor Mr. Fishwick,' said Harriet. 'What did he do?'

'Well that incredibly good looking man, Horace, I mean Joris rounded them all up taking them back towards the bar and I could just see him talking to her in a very serious manner. Joris came back to us with an apology from her to Percy which we both persuaded him to accept and then he made his excuses. I expect he would have found himself some gorgeous young lady to keep him company for the evening by then, don't you Harriet?'

Harriet winced. Her legs went weak at the thought of being, oh, so close to him.

'Shall we keep you a seat by us on the coach Harriet?' Molly moved on. 'We're off to Bruges today you know.'

'I'm afraid I won't be able to do that one Molly,' said Harriet. 'Apart from anything else I think I'd better keep an eye on the cat. I don't want anything to go wrong now since we're back in Southampton tomorrow.'

'Harriet, please don't miss Bruges dear. It's the best part of the trip. Look, let me stay with the cat, I've been there before. You go along with Percy and make the most of it. I'll be alright, it's a lot of walking for me anyway. I'll just put my feet up here.'

'No, no thank you, Molly. You're so kind but I wouldn't dream of it. I don't think I'm up to it anyway. You go with Mr. Fishwick and I'll look forward to hearing all about it.'

Molly patted her on the arm and went off to breakfast.

Harriet closed the door behind her and sat on the end of the bed with her head in her hands. She wondered if she would see Mr. Sanderson today. She hoped against hope Molly would tell him at breakfast that she was staying in her cabin all day. He would surely realise that she would have one big hangover!

'Yes, he'll come and see me, I know he will,' she said to herself. 'And you can bloody well stay in there. I mean it!' she said out loud to the wardrobe door.

This time Harriet would be measured, far more measured. This time Harriet would be completely sober. She would sit next to him and just listen to what he had to say. She would apologise for her behaviour last night.

Harriet began to feel better. She picked up his bow tie he'd left on the bedside cabinet and held it close to her mouth. She wondered and wondered what he would have said had he not been so rudely set upon by the cat. She thought back to the times that he'd almost tried to say something to her, the hints, the glances. Oh how he could hold her completely in one of those looks!

Harriet finally admitted to herself that she had fallen, utterly, totally in love.

The sun was shining in the clear blue sky and the wind had dropped to nothing. Harriet opened the balcony doors and sat down on the patio. She decided they would sit together, all day they would sit together and talk. Closing her eyes she stretched back in the chair and let the sun warm her face. Relaxing into its gentle heat the remnants of turmoil from the night before slowly disappeared while she waited.

She looked at her watch. It had been ten minutes and still no sign of him. Harriet had to do something. She needed to see what was going on. She weighed up the rail at the edge of the balcony. It really was very high up. Harriet had looked down from it only once since boarding the ship and had retracted quickly for fear of going over. She steeled herself for another try. 'Just to see if the coaches for Bruges have left,' she said to herself. She placed her feet well back and arms outstretched she rested her hands on the solid wooden rail. She forced herself to look down just in time to see the coaches driving away along the flat dreary road. She looked around her at the tanks and chimneys and stark utilitarian flat-roofed buildings, all differing shades of grey. In between, as far as the eye could see the ground was chequered with odd squares of rough, flat grassland adjoining acres of empty scruffy concrete sporting the odd green tufts of life; pathetic offerings from its derelict neighbours. The sea birds flew low and circular in constant patterns over the scrub and Harriet decided there couldn't be a drearier port anywhere else in the world.

Her eyes pulled back to the side of the ship and she noticed a black taxi drawing up almost vertically below her. It looked odd as it sat alone with its engine ticking over.

Then Harriet saw someone striding away from the ship towards it, black holdall in one hand, briefcase in the other. She gasped. 'It's him!' she said out loud. 'He's leaving the ship!' The tears filled her eyes as she saw him get into the black cab and close the door behind him. She watched it drive along the road and out of the docks until it was out of sight. She flung herself on to the bed and lay still for a long time, feeling the dampness from her tears on the pillow.

She decided she needed the cat. 'You soddin` well don't deserve it,' she snuffled, staring at the wardrobe door. 'It was all your fault so you can just come out and make me feel better.' She turned the key in the lock and opened the door wide. 'Oh don't start playing hard to get now,' she sniffed, 'I meant what I said about the cats' home.' But still the cat didn't come out.

'Oh sod you then,' said Harriet, 'just stop there!'

Then she had a very queasy, uneasy feeling.

'Supposing it's not in there at all?' The thought frightened her.

She undid the catch and swung the other door open. The plate of food was still there sitting on the shredded newspaper. She bent down and rummaged along the back but couldn't feel anything. She panicked. 'OK so you didn't go in there after all. You're under the bed, aren't you just?'

Harriet scrambled on her hands and knees. The covers were getting in the way. They sat on her head and trailed her shoulders as she peered along the dark floor in her struggle with the three sides of the large bed.

She just couldn't see it. 'Come out you stupid thing,' she howled, 'and I promise I won't take you to the cats' home.' But the cat wouldn't come out. 'Stay there then!' she snapped as tears started to stream down her already flushed cheeks. 'I'll never get you out from under there, the bed's far too big!' Harriet gave up and climbed back in.

She sobbed herself to sleep.

Chapter 32

It was 3pm when Harriet finally stirred to the repeated knocking on the cabin door.

'It's only us Harriet.' She could hear Molly's voice becoming more and more anxious. 'We're back! Percy and I were just wondering how you are feeling now, weren't we Percy?'

'We certainly were my dear!' replied Mr. Fishwick with gusto.

'Oh, I'm coming. Just a minute. Sorry,' said Harriet as she opened the cabin door. 'Please do come in. Did you both enjoy your trip to Bruges?'

'Oh it was nice enough but far too much walking,' complained Mr. Fishwick.

Molly didn't answer, she just looked at Harriet in dismay. 'Oh Harriet dear, whatever is the matter? You've been crying.' Molly sat her on the end of the bed and put her arm around her. Harriet refused to allow the next surge of tears to gather. She swallowed the huge lump that was threatening to choke her. 'The cat's gone under the bed and I can't get at it!' she blurted out to them both.

'The cat?' queried Mr. Fishwick. He gave Harriet a puzzled look. 'There is a cat. There isn't a cat. There is a cat! Oh dear, I hope I didn't take two pills by mistake this morning. Do tell me I'm not going funny Molly. I'm very disadvantaged being so hard of hearing.' He reached for his bottle hoping the gin might refresh his memory.

'No, no, Mr. Fishwick, I'm terribly sorry I misled you,' replied Harriet. 'You're not going funny at all.'

Mr. Fishwick beamed a huge smile and breathed an enormous sigh of relief.

'Look Percy, Harriet's cat somehow got itself into her luggage and the poor girl's been worried sick ever since. We must get it out from under there right away. Mum's the word, Mr. Fishwick,' said Molly.

'Mum's the word indeed!' declared Mr. Fishwick. 'I feel deeply for you my dear,' he said looking at Harriet. 'This could put you in a very serious position.'

His words were enough to open the floodgates. Harriet sat on the bed holding one soggy tissue after another to her face. She caught a glimpse of herself in the dressing table mirror. Her nose had become swollen and red, matching her eyes.

'Now look what you've done!' said Molly glowering at Mr. Fishwick. 'You've frightened the life out of her.'

Suddenly he shot over to Harriet and immediately threw his arm around her, pinning her to his chest. 'We were up against much worse than this during the war my dear. Much worse! Now don't you worry! Stand by chaps! I've the very thing, you'll see!'

'Oh, just let go of her will you Mr. Fishwick and get on with it,' said Molly, 'the poor girl can hardly breathe!'

Mr. Fishwick vanished from the cabin leaving Molly to console Harriet as best she could. 'Come on Harriet, let's have a proper look under there, shall we?'

That suited Harriet, at least it would give her chance to hide her face.

They both got down on their hands and knees coaxing and cajoling the cat in a desperate attempt to get it out.

In a tick Mr. Fishwick was back, armed with his golf club and a yard brush that had been inadvertently left outside on his patio. He passed Molly the golf club and he took hold of the long bristled brush. 'You poke from that side Molly and I'll have a go from this side. Sweep it back and forth all the way across. We'll soon get the little bugger out!'

Molly raising her eyebrows glanced at Harriet. She was pleased to see a little grin breaking out on Harriet's face.

'I've got it!' shouted Molly, ample backside perched in the air.

'Are you sure?' queried Mr. Fishwick.

'I just felt it with the end of this golf club. I know when I've just poked a cat!' she said. Then she gave one more shove on the handle.

'Ouch!' yelled Mr. Fishwick rolling backwards to Harriet's feet. 'You've just thrust that lump of iron into my bloody balls!' Mr. Fishwick could hardly bring himself up from the floor.

Immediately Harriet doubled up. She flew out of the cabin without explanation, held the door ajar with her foot and wiped the tears away with her sleeve as she tried to stifle her laughter.

'Well I'm most terribly sorry Mr. Fishwick!' Harriet could hear Molly's indignation. 'I didn't know you were half way under the bed with that damned brush!'

'I was only trying to find the little bugger! Get out you swine!' ordered Mr. Fishwick resuming his position.

'There's no need to be abusive Mr. Fishwick,' replied Molly, most upset. 'I'm doing my best. I'm not as nimble as I used to be.'

'Not you, you stupid woman! The cat! I'm talking to the cat!'

Harriet couldn't contain herself, she let her foot go and the door banged shut. She flew down the corridor hands on aching ribs until she was well out of earshot. She arrived at the bottom of the stairs by the lifts, then turned left and crashed through the three sets of doors to the outside deck. Fortunately for Harriet it was quite deserted. She collapsed into a hard white plastic chair, put her head in her hands and laughed uncontrollably. It was some time before she recovered her equilibrium.

'Poor Mr. Fishwick,' she said to herself. Harriet knew it wasn't really funny at all and in the knowledge that very soon she was going to have to go back she tried very hard to focus on the pain he'd had inflicted on him. 'After all,' she reminded herself, 'it *was* all because of me and that stupid cat!'

She glanced down the deck and saw a group of noisy youths, arms laden, trailing the corner looking for somewhere to sit. She looked away and then did a second take. 'I think that's the one who's got it in for Mr. Fishwick,' she said to herself. 'Time to go!'

At speed, Harriet shot through the three sets of double doors, turned right at the staircase by the lifts and marched back along the lengthy corridor. She arrived at her cabin to see Molly just starting to open the door.

'Ah! There you are Harriet. I do hope you're feeling better now. Percy and I have combed the place from top to bottom and there's no sign of it. It must have got out Harriet,' Molly informed her, looking very worried indeed. 'We're determined to find it Harriet. We've got to start searching the ship, we're only here because we didn't want to lock you out of your cabin.'

'Oh, I'm ever so sorry,' Harriet said suddenly realising how selfish she'd been.

'No, no, not at all!' said Molly. 'It's given Percy and I a chance to sort our differences out, hasn't it Percy?'

'Well my dear,' he said, walking over to Harriet. 'I don't know what came over me.'

'Pain!' declared Harriet. 'It does that to people,' she said wondering where this sudden insight had come from.

Mr. Fishwick smiled, impressed with Harriet's unprecedented degree of understanding. 'Still no excuse! I apologise unreservedly to you both again, for my unforgivable outburst.'

Harriet, suddenly feeling very insecure at the thought of being locked out of her cabin, picked up her key card. Mr. Fishwick straightened his back, then suddenly shot his elbows out to place his hands either side of his waist. The brush and golf club whipped through the air, giving Harriet and Molly precious little time to get out of the way.

'What are you up to now, Mr. Fishwick?' said Molly, impatiently. 'You're a menace with those things.'

'Link up ladies, we're off to find the cat. It's got to be somewhere!' he said.

Chapter 33

For such a huge ship capable of accommodating over three thousand people the corridors were always surprisingly deserted. This was most fortunate for them since, to say the least, they looked somewhat strange striding along together, brush and golf club in tow.

'We'll try the outside deck first,' commanded Mr. Fishwick marching them straight up the never ending corridor and then left to the three sets of double doors. 'There are plenty of nooks and crannies out there alright for it to hide in.'

Harriet and Molly agreed. They came to the stairs and the lifts and then turned left again to reach the doors. Harriet held them open for Molly and Mr. Fishwick until the last set of doors swung closed behind them. As the fresh air hit them they agreed it would be more expedient to go their separate ways.

'Molly, you continue on towards the bow of the ship and make sure you feel under those grills,' he said, passing her the golf club. 'Harriet, you concentrate on this central part. Get a good look under all those tables and chairs, especially those folded canvas ones.'

'Right!' said Harriet.

'I'll move down towards the stern of the ship as it's getting a bit crowded.' He informed them. 'We'll report back here in, say,' he looked at his watch, 'fifteen minutes.'

For the next quarter of an hour Harriet, desperate to find the cat, lifted everything and anything that would move but to no avail. She was just scrambling up from under the last deckchair when she saw Molly coming towards her.

'There's nowhere out there that hasn't had a good poke with this. I don't know what handicap he is Harriet but this thing's not going to help his golf. It's a handicap in itself especially when you're looking for a cat. I keep getting that flat bit at the bottom stuck in things. I nearly pulled one of those grills right up just now.'

Harriet smiled. 'I'm sure he's well handicapped by now Molly. You shouldn't be let loose with one of those things.'

'Did you think it was funny, Harriet?' Molly asked trying to stop her shoulders from shaking.

'I thought I was going to die laughing!' admitted Harriet. 'That's why I disappeared.'

They walked a little towards the doors.

'Come on Percy, we'll not get any joy here,' said Molly whose feet were starting to give way.

'Look, there he is!' exclaimed Harriet. 'Whatever is he doing?'

'He's brushing the deck right by that group of young people on the end,' Molly said, unable to believe her eyes. 'I think it's that lot that were in the bar last night. He'd do well to stay away from them.'

'Oh, he's just stopped anyway. He's coming now,' said Harriet very relieved.

She remembered seeing them earlier on and didn't want this to become yet another public exhibition.

A triumphant Mr. Fishwick arrived.

'I've spotted it!' he exclaimed. 'I've found the damned thing!'

Harriet flooded with indescribable relief.

'Where? Where is it?' asked Molly, unable to contain herself.

'Well we're going to have to take it very steady,' advised Mr. Fishwick. 'It's behind all the gubbins that crowd of yobs have slung behind their chairs. I can just see its tail sticking out.'

'However are we going to get at it?' asked Harriet, now daunted by the logistics of the situation.

'We'll walk down casually, all of us,' said Mr. Fishwick, 'and we'll wait for them to move.'

'But what if they don't move?' asked Molly. 'We could be there `til midnight and my feet are killing me!'

'If they don't move then I'm going to have to pretend I lost something there earlier on and ask them if they'd mind me having a look. Then I'll take off this jacket and scoop the cat up in it. We'll be gone before they can turn round. We'll exit from the stern.'

'Don't you think it might be better if I do it?' suggested Molly, eyeing up the damp soup stains on his jacket. 'If it's the same crowd of yobs, you don't want to irritate that awful girl all over again, Percy.'

'Irritate her! I'll more than irritate her!' Percy declared.

'It's them alright!' Molly suddenly declared. 'That offensive girl's right on the end there. Just look at her waving her arms around and showing off. If I looked like that I'd be inclined to stay quiet. Oh, do let me handle it, Percy.'

'No, no!' insisted Mr. Fishwick. 'I'll do it. Apologies have been accepted, she'll be only too pleased to cooperate.'

Harriet looked at Molly. They really weren't convinced.

'Just let's chatter nonchalantly among ourselves as we walk down,' suggested Mr. Fishwick. 'When we get past them we'll stand by that table near the lifebuoy. It'll give us a perfect view.'

And so it did. Harriet and Molly could see a pile of bags, coats and jackets stuffed behind the chairs and more of the cat's tail out from under than Mr. Fishwick had suggested. It was curled round on the deck. Harriet could hardly believe her eyes!

'No they're not looking like they're going to move, any of them,' observed Mr. Fishwick 'We'd better go in for the kill before it wakes up.'

That made sense to Harriet.

Mr. Fishwick, jacket over arm, carefully placed the brush against the lifebuoy and the three of them sauntered over as casually as they could.

'Er, excuse me,' Mr. Fishwick touched his forehead, 'my good lady and I were walking here this morning,' he said, pointing to Molly, when she had the misfortune to mislay her diamond ring. We've searched and searched but you know the joints in this decking, we've had no luck. She's convinced she lost it in this corner. She took it off, you see, whilst we were sitting here. Would you mind?' The wayward looking girl actually raised a smile.

'No norra tall,' she said and as they were hitching their chairs forward to give him space, Mr. Fishwick plunged his jacket over the tail and grabbed the lot. To his utter horror it all went very flat in his hands.

'Hey! This old geezer's trying to pinch my Davy Crockett hat!' the raucous girl shouted.

'No, I thought I saw the ring. Trying not to damage it. So sorry!'

Mr. Fishwick dropped the lot, grabbed his jacket, snatched the brush and flew. Harriet, Molly and the golf club were already out of sight.

'Come back baldy! Tryin' to get yer own back wer yer? I don't want me prize 'at anywhere near that derty ol` jacket!' she shouted. At that pace, her words were lost on Mr. Fishwick.

It was some time before he caught them up. He arrived panting as he spotted them ducking under the end of a protective canvas hanging off a row of chairs.

Fortunately they were stacked right next to the opposite sets of doors on the other side of the ship.

'Quick!' said Mr. Fishwick, 'back to the cabin in case they come after us.' The three of them flew past the lifts and the stairs, turned left into their corridor and at breakneck speed arrived outside Harriet's door.

'Key, Harriet, Key! Have you got your key card?' Molly gabbled.

Thank goodness Harriet had made a point of remembering it. She pulled it out from her back pocket, pushed it into the slot and without delay swung the door open.

Mr. Fishwick banged it closed behind him.

They fell onto the bed, puffing and panting.

'What went wrong, Percy?' Molly said when she could find enough breath to enable her words.

'It wasn't the cat! It was a bloody Davy Crockett hat! It was that girl's!'

'Whatever would she want a hat like that for?' questioned Molly. 'Shaped just like a saucepan with a fur tail. It's a man's hat, anyway! There's something very strange about her.'

'Certainly is,' agreed Mr. Fishwick.

'I was convinced it was the cat,' said Harrriet, 'its tail was curled on the deck. She sleeps just like that! Anyway, thank you so much for trying Mr. Fishwick, and you, too, Molly. Wherever she went, I think she's gone for good. At least I won't have to worry about customs. You two mustn't do any more searching. It's had its last chance. I'm so grateful to you both but it's taken over the holiday and I feel dreadful about it.'

'Oh we haven't finished yet, have we Percy?' said Molly suddenly finding her second wind. 'We'll have a cup of tea and start again. They'll not be bothered to chase us. It took them all their time to budge their chairs forward!'

'You're probably right,' agreed Mr. Fishwick, obviously up for the challenge. 'Put the kettle on my dear.' Harriet had already done it.

A short tea break saw them back in the corridor.

'Now let's think,' began Molly. 'It's not going to get into any of the cabins. The doors close too quickly of their own accord. No I reckon it's been under the bed Harriet and slipped out behind the cleaning lady. No doubt we'll find it in the store cupboard at the end here.'

'Good thinking Molly,' praised Mr. Fishwick, still very anxious to make amends for his misjudgement, 'but how are we going to get in there?'

The three of them stood staring at the strong metal door now imprisoning the cat.

'Press your ear against it Harriet,' commanded Mr. Fishwick, 'just listen carefully.' Harriet did as she was told.

'No, nothing. I can't hear anything,' she said.

'Oh it's probably asleep,' said Molly. 'Cats are always doing that. They find a nice cosy place, always somewhere they shouldn't be and hijack it for the rest of the day.' She started rattling the handle.

'Ah! Can I help you?' came a voice from behind. All three turned round looking very guilty indeed. 'You want something?' enquired Charles, focussing on Harriet. 'We are off the duty now you know? Ah, I see you been crying. Have you? That condition make you very sensitive you know.'

'Oh no! Er, I mean yes,' answered Harriet, rubbing her eyes.

'Could I possibly have another towel? A dry one please. Mine don't seem to dry very well and Mr. Fishwick wants to return this brush which was left on his patio.' Harriet felt very pleased with herself for suddenly aspiring to a perfectly legitimate request.

'We don't do wet towels,' said Charles starting to smile. 'If I give you a towel it will be a dry one anyway. Those towels should be changed every day. If you don't have your cabin cleaned you have wet towels, you know.'

He rummaged inside his pocket, produced his key card and slid it into the lock. The cupboard was dark, narrow and deep. 'Now this isn't my thing you know, I'm not very sure where to do the look!'

'Not to worry,' said Mr. Fishwick taking command again. 'Do we just slam the door to close it when we've finished?'

'No, no, no, not a slam or a bang! Just close it behind you like you do your cabin door, OK?' replied Charles. 'Be sure to keep it open when you are in there though. This one waiting for the mend, you know. It won't open from the inside.'

'I'll hold it open,' volunteered Molly.

'I'll leave you to it then,' agreed Charles and off he went anxious not to waste any more of his spare time than necessary.

The three of them beamed at each other.

'Well done Mr. Fishwick,' said Harriet and Molly nodded in agreement.

Mr. Fishwick shrugged his shoulders making a token effort to dismiss the compliment without much success. He positively beamed as he found the light switch.

'You hold on to the door then, Molly,' he ordered as he propped the brush up against it.

Mr. Fishwick wanted to keep it open and wasn't taking any chances. He started rummaging amongst the tins, packs and boxes while Harriet helped herself to a clean towel.

'Puss, puss out you come you little bugger!' Harriet and Molly could hear him say as he disappeared into the depths of the store.

'I can hear voices,' said Harriet suddenly panicking. 'It sounds just like them! Oh no! Mr. Fishwick come out quickly. It *is* them, they're coming up the corridor,' Harriet hurriedly warned him.

Mr. Fishwick shot out and the three of them flew up the corridor with just time to hide round the corner before the angry girl followed by a loud-mouthed, gangly, tattooed youth came into view.

'At least there's only two of them,' Molly whispered after a quick squint. 'Oh listen it sounds as though they've gone in the cupboard.'

With that Mr. Fishwick shot off and Harriet and Molly could hear the brush clattering to the floor as he banged the door closed behind them.

'He's shut them in,' Harriet declared. 'He's shut them in!'

'Quick!' said Molly, 'Back!'

Mr. Fishwick beckoned them and the three of them shot up the corridor and scrambled into Harriet's cabin.

'What on earth made you do that Mr. Fishwick?' asked Harriet still unable to believe what had just happened.

'I don't know,' said Mr. Fishwick. 'I think I just wanted them out of the way. I have an intense dislike of that strange girl.'

'Well we all have Percy,' said Molly still astounded, 'but there's no way they can let themselves out. Charles told us the lock needed fixing.'

'That's why I did it,' explained Mr. Fishwick, with a note of impatience in his voice. 'It'll teach them a lesson. Rude, foul-mouthed lot!'

Harriet looked at Molly covering her mouth with her hand. 'How long are you going to leave them in there Mr. Fishwick?' she asked.

'For as long as it takes someone else to get them out!' replied Mr. Fishwick in no uncertain terms.

'Will anyone hear them, though?' said Molly looking very concerned. 'These corridors are so lonely.'

'Well they'll have to wait then until the cleaning ladies do their morning round,' he replied.

'All night?' asked Harriet.

'If necessary! We had to put up with a lot worse than that in the army. Conscription, that's what they need. Conscription. That'd teach them a bit of discipline!'

'But their friends are bound to come looking for them,' said Harriet, starting to feel worried about any possible repercussions.

'So!' snapped Mr. Fishwick. 'They don't know it's got anything to do with us.'

Harriet put the kettle on again and silently cursed the cat. Oh she would be so, so glad to be off this ship.

'What about dinner?' said Molly, who couldn't let go. 'We'll see the rest of the gang then, won't we?'

'Then we won't go down to dinner!' retorted Mr. Fishwick. 'We'll stay put until "lights out" so to speak! Maybe Harriet could persuade Charles to bring some extra cold meats, er, on account of her condition?!'

'No! No! Percy. We told you didn't we?' and then she hesitated. 'Or did we, that Harriet hasn't got a condition. It was all about Charles making the wrong assumption on account of her wanting food for the cat!' Molly tried to explain.

'Pregnant, not pregnant! Cat, no cat! It's all getting too much for me. I think I need to lie down,' Mr. Fishwick said, stroking his forehead in bemusement. 'Do you mind my dear?' He grabbed his jacket, pulled his bottle out from the inside pocket and slugged away for all he was worth. Then he kicked off his shoes, stretched himself out full length on the bed and went to sleep.

Molly despaired.

Harriet looked across. 'Wrong man,' she thought and then the true reality of her folly came home to roost. 'Whatever must he think of me? Lying there, desperate for him, like some cheap tart!'

Molly kicked off her shoes too. 'You don't mind do you Harriet? It was quite some trip round Bruges today.'

'No, of course not,' said Harriet, 'your feet must be absolutely killing you by now.

That damned cat! If I found it now I really would throw it over the side.' She had another quick look under the bed.

Molly laughed. 'It's given us a bit of fun though Harriet. You can't deny that.'

'I don't think it's over yet,' said Harriet. 'What shall we do about dinner?'

'Oh we'd be on pins! Give Charles a ring Harriet and see what he can do for us.'

Harriet lifted the phone and dialled 101.

'Yes!' came Charles` unmistakable voice, 'How may I be of service to you?'

'Charles, it's Harriet speaking,' she said.

'Ah Harriet, don't you worry now. We are coming to get you and your two friends out, see?' Then it suddenly occurred to him. 'How you phone me from that cupboard? I told you to be careful of the door. All afternoon I pretend it was not me that let you in. Now all the ship know you are all in there!'

'But we're not in there Charles, we're in my cabin!'

'Who is that in the cupboard then and how they get in there?'

'I don't know,' said Harriet scratching her head.

'You not tell me the lies Harriet?' he continued.

'No! We must have forgotten to shut the door.'

'That door close without you shutting it?'

'Yes, but Mr. Fishwick propped it open with the brush. It must've fallen over.'

'Ah, I see!' he said, now more satisfied with the explanation.

'Well whoever they are in there they ask for it!' he concluded. 'It was just my favour to you, you see?'

'Yes, yes,' said Harriet, 'and we're so grateful Charles. Could I ask just one more favour, please?'

'Oh yes and what is that?' he enquired, a hint of suspicion in his voice.

'Our dear friend Mr. Fishwick is exhausted. He's done much too much walking round Bruges today with very little to eat. He can't move and we mustn't leave him in this state. He needs food Charles, desperately!'

'Who exactly with you now?' he asked.

'Just Molly and Mr. Fishwick,' replied Harriet.

'I'll arrange for evening meal for three in your cabin Harriet. Don't get upset in that condition you know!'

'Oh Charles, you're the kindest, nicest man on earth! How can I ever repay you for all you've done?' Harriet said trying to repress her guilt.

'Don't you mention it. It is my job to make sure you want to cruise with us again!'

From the expression on Molly's face Harriet knew she'd got the gist of the conversation.

'Gosh!' she said, replacing the receiver and pointing to the ceiling. 'That's a service reserved only for those in the penthouse suites paying penthouse money!'

'How wonderful! You are such a clever girl Harriet,' praised Molly. 'Now let's just hope those two don't find the cat while they're stuck in there.'

Harriet went sick. She knew with the identity microchip Mark had insisted on having inserted into the poor thing, the cat would literally be out of the bag! She couldn't deny ownership.

It was starting to feel very warm in the cabin. Harriet opened the patio doors. The sun had been on their side of the ship for most of the day.

'Good idea Harriet,' said Molly, 'let's drink our tea out there.'

Glad that some of the pressure was off, they sat down together and chatted whilst Mr. Fishwick's tea went cold at the side of the bed.

'And what was Bruges like?' asked Harriet, feeling a little sad that she'd missed it.

'Well, as you know Harriet, I've been before a couple of times but there's so much of historical interest there. There's always something new to discover.'

Molly had another sip of tea and then stretched forward to put her cup down on the patio table. Unconsciously Harriet did the same. They were comfortable in each other's company and at that moment Harriet decided she would like to keep in touch with her.

'The strange thing is Harriet, I've never done a boat ride on the canals before. We could never be bothered waiting in those long queues. Far rather spend the time in the churches. Oh Harriet, there's one in particular, hundreds and hundreds of years old. It's full of statues and paintings and old musty timbers and dank stone walls. But the *atmosphere* Harriet. The original atmosphere's still there, trapped in time. It's like going back centuries into a completely different world. It's quite an experience. Just goes to show though,' she said thoughtfully, 'it's more than just a building Harriet, that place is alive with over a thousand years of prayer and devotion. You breath it in and you come out wondering.'

Harriet was now really sorry she'd missed out. 'And the canal trip?' she asked. 'Did you enjoy that, Molly?'

'Well, Percy, you wouldn't believe it! I told him to throw it away, but as we know, he didn't. Wearing that hat with tomato soup all over it, he had a bit of a stumble into the boat which sent huge waves across the canal and plenty of a panic on board, I can tell you. Anyway, once he'd recovered from that and we all settled down it was good, really good, apart from his damned golf club getting in the way. For the life of me I don't know why he had to take that. Mind you the chap driving it was a bit of a card. In his broken accent he told us we were all his hostages for the next thirty five minutes and then we were bombarded with his non-stop jokes until Percy forgot to duck under one of the very low bridges. He just spotted him in his mirror and yelled something at him in his native tongue! Poor Percy flung himself to the floor whilst his hat floated away towards the canal bank. Best place for it, I thought. Then he suddenly shot up and swiped that blasted golf club past everyone's heads! I don't how he didn't blind anybody! He stretched across, swung it over the water and managed to hook it on. It was absolutely drenched, Harriet! The damned thing was dripping all over us as he swung it back in. We were terrified we were all going to end up in the canal. We were all clinging to the sides of the boat. My word he got a roasting from the chap at the wheel.'

'Poor Percy!' laughed Harriet. 'No wonder he's exhausted.'

'Oh he gave it him alright! There was no need for a translator. It made him turn round, anyway. Do you know Harriet I couldn't wait to see his face. From the back you could see his long wavy blonde hair and when he turned round, well, he reminded me of our new friend. Strong handsome features and lovely twinkling blue eyes.'

Harriet felt a pang going right through her.

'It's a shame he couldn't join the trip Harriet. He told us at breakfast he had some business to attend to abroad and for whatever reason, he didn't actually say, it suited him to cross the channel this way. Strange he was allowed to use this as a ferry though. Must have had a word with the Captain!'

Harriet hardly heard. She stared across the wasteland again. She knew that if she were to paint a picture now this would be the only thing she could aspire to.

'It seems as though he enjoyed his evening though,' Molly continued. Harriet suddenly switched from the view, all her senses heightened as she went to full alert.

'Did he?' she asked eagerly.

'Oh yes! I asked him did he find himself a nice young lady to keep him company and he smiled that lovely smile of his. "That would be telling Molly!" he said.'

Harriet sank back in her chair. 'He smiled, he smiled!' she said to herself. 'He smiled that gorgeous smile of his.' Harriet was beside herself with joy! Then as quickly as it came it evaporated. 'Maybe it was just a smile at Molly. He never really said anything. He smiles at everyone.' Harriet needed to know more.

'So he wouldn't say any more?' began Harriet.

'Oh he did! I wasn't letting him off the hook that easily,' admitted Molly nudging Harriet's arm. 'I said to him, "Well I hope you didn't fall for our hippie friend after charming her into apologising." '

'And what did he say then?' asked Harriet, anxious and impatient.

'He said, "The best I could get out of that one was an apology by proxy, if you don't mind!" Oh Harriet, if I were twenty years younger I'd fall for him myself! For a minute I thought I'd made him quite cross and then his face broke out into that gorgeous smile. My heart leapt Harriet. Just leapt!'

'And then what did he say?' Harriet couldn't wait to get the words out.

'Well I said if it wasn't her, then who was the lucky girl who took his fancy?'

'Yes, yes,' gabbled Harriet, 'and then what?'

'And then he said, "She was too beautiful to describe. Too gorgeous to contemplate. I hope I meet her again one day." ' Molly finished with a sigh.

Harriet became ecstatic. She didn't think this surge of most exquisite joy could ever be hers again.

'We haven't seen anyone on this ship that could remotely aspire to that description, have we Harriet?' Molly said, a little offhand.

'No. No!' replied Harriet. She definitely didn't see herself that way.

'You know Harriet, it's not much fun being available at my age. Anyway Harriet, if you don't mind dear I'll just pop next door to freshen up before our butler arrives. You don't mind me leaving you with Mr. Fishwick for a few minutes, do you?'

'No, not at all,' said Harriet looking over to him. 'He's swigged quite a lot of that gin, though. I do hope he wakes up for his evening meal.'

Chapter 34

Molly disappeared and Harriet, still feeling euphoric completely blanked Mr. Fishwick out. She twirled in front of the mirror and then flung herself on the bed in sheer joy.

Mr. Fishwick leapt into the air as Harriet landed. 'What, what the devil's happening?' he said, still half asleep.

'Oh, Mr. Fishwick, I'm most terribly sorry! I forgot you were there for a moment.'

Mr. Fishwick gave a huge yawn and started rubbing his eyes. Then, unfortunately for Harriet he came to extremely quickly.

'Ah, aha, my dear!' he said. 'You don't have to apologise to me you know. I felt from the moment I saw you there was something between us. Since losing my wife my dear, I've been so lonely. I died with her, you understand? You've given me a new lease of life Harriet, my lovely. How my heart ached when I thought you were expecting a little one and oh how the relief overcame my confusion when Molly explained it all. Harriet! This cruise was meant to be! There's someone up there smiling down on us my dear. Do you believe that, too?'

Harriet was absolutely aghast. He'd been so kind to her, especially as he was still grieving for his wife. How could she hurt him now, especially as he'd attributed it all to divine intervention.

All of a sudden Harriet could hear Molly thumping on the door. 'Hurry up Harriet! They're coming!'

Harriet could hear loud, angry voices and shot off to open it.

Molly threw herself in. The yard brush came flying in after her.

'Ere give that to the ole geezer and tell 'im to stick it where the sun don` shine! We know it was 'im that locked us in, the ole plonker.' Harriet struggled but just managed to slam the door on the hysterical pair.

Molly staggered to the bed, dazed.

Mr. Fishwick couldn't believe how divine providence could allow such a crass interruption.

Harriet thanked her lucky stars for the break.

'A cup of tea! A nice cup of tea will see us right,' she announced. She put the kettle on determined not to make any eye contact whatsoever with Mr. Fishwick.

'Just as well we're dining here tonight,' spluttered Molly as she sat up to take the tea from Harriet.

'Too right, I'm not leaving this cabin until they're off the ship in the morning,' declared Mr. Fishwick.

Harriet's heart sank. 'I can't spend the night in here with him!' she panicked. Her stomach started churning over. She began to think it was her punishment for last night. All the joy she'd had from Molly's words were fast disappearing.

'But you can't sleep here in Harriet's cabin Mr. Fishwick,' began Molly.

'Oh, I don't think Harriet will mind at all, will you my dear?'

Harriet felt sick.

'No, no, Mr. Fishwick,' said Molly, 'I absolutely insist you come back to my cabin. I promised to go through the lifeboat drill with you, remember? We haven't done it yet.'

Harriet couldn't contain her relief.

'Most kind Molly but I wouldn't dream of troubling you. We leave the ship in the morning. Hardly worth it,' he replied.

Harriet felt sick again.

'Rubbish, Percy! The ship could sink tonight,' retorted Molly.

'Then that would be our destiny,' he said turning to Harriet.

Harriet was appalled. 'Mark, Mark my fiancé once had the most awful experience at sea. That was the last night of the cruise, too. He said he would've drowned if it hadn't been for knowing the lifeboat drill!' That was the best she could come up with.

'Oh, so you're engaged to be married my dear?' queried a very crestfallen Mr. Fishwick. 'Then I'd be more than happy to accept my fate.'

Harriet felt dreadful. She wrapped her right hand around her left in anguish and then realised she wasn't even wearing an engagement ring.

'Then we'll do lifeboat drill here, if Harriet doesn't mind,' Molly said, not in the mood for any nonsense 'Anyway I'm not in too much of a hurry to venture out with that pair on the loose.'

Harriet breathed an enormous sigh of relief. 'Oh, good old Molly!' she said to herself. 'At least it will give me some breathing space.'

Mr. Fishwick reached for his gin bottle and for the next thirty seconds started drinking it like water. Harriet and Molly looked across to one another.

'Switch the television on Harriet, if you don't mind dear. Now Percy, put that bottle down,' demanded Molly snatching it from him, 'and we'll watch this lifeboat drill very carefully together.'

She pulled him over to the settee. 'There! Harriet won't mind passing our tea over. Would you mind dear?'

Harriet smiled and nodded.

'I see Harriet that you are not wearing an engagement ring,' said Mr. Fishwick touching her hand as she passed him his cup.

'Whatever has that got to do with anything Mr. Fishwick?' blazed Molly. 'Just concentrate on watching this! First I have to cope with being bawled at by those two idiots and then that flaming yard brush flies past me nearly knocking me for six and now you decide to be obstinate. Mr. Fishwick I really am about to lose patience!'

Harriet couldn't have been more pleased to see Molly putting Mr. Fishwick well and truly in his place, if she'd done it herself. He settled down to the film and gave his undivided attention to Molly as she explained the obvious to him.

The three of them became engrossed. Molly insisted on letting it run three times to make sure Mr. Fishwick knew exactly what to do in the event. Molly was just considering a fourth run when there was a loud knock on the door. They each looked at the other.

'They're not back again are they?' they almost said in unison.

The cabin went very quiet.

The knock came again. They could just hear Charles calling for Harriet.

Harriet rushed to the door and held it open for him as he wheeled in the trolley laden with hot covered dishes on the top and a selection of the most tempting of sweets on the bottom.

'There!' he said, 'I hope this will be suitable for you three. They got them out you know. I happened to be going by and I see they were very angry. They said there's a thief on board. Some old devil try to steal the girl's very expensive retro hat you know. I shrug my shoulders. I know nothing. I pretend it not me that opened the door in the first place.'

Mr. Fishwick, looked up, now doubly chastened.

Harriet and Molly helped him to wheel in the trolley.

'This smells good, Charles,' said Molly, 'it really is most kind of you!'

'I'll second that!' announced Mr. Fishwick.

Charles stood back and smiled, appreciating the gratitude. Impulsively Harriet flung her arms around him and gave him a kiss. 'Oh Charles,' she said, 'whatever would we have done without you, you dear, dear man!'

Molly caught Mr. Fishwick in an envious glance. 'Mr. Fishwick,' she said, 'help me unload this now, before it gets cold!'

Harriet swiftly closed the door behind Charles.

'Oh Harriet! Would you believe it?' exclaimed Molly. 'He's laid a couple of bottles of wine down here. Three in fact.' Molly heaved herself from the bottom of the trolley and placed them on the dressing table.

'Right,' said Harriet, 'let's just forget about everything for a little while and enjoy this.'

'I'll toast to that,' declared Molly.

'Me too,' said Mr. Fishwick, his reply a little half-hearted. He looked longingly at Harriet, then switched to his gin bottle. He caught Molly's eye and thought better of it.

They chattered and laughed, wined and dined for the next three hours or more. Then Harriet made some coffee.

'No thank you my dear, shame to curtail the evening just yet!' said Mr. Fishwick, now into the swing of things.

Harriet lifted the empty bottles. 'All gone I'm afraid. We've drunk them dry!'

'Well I've had plenty,' declared Molly.

'Me too,' agreed Harriet, who'd taken it a lot easier than the night before.

'I think I've probably had a bit more than I should've, though,' confessed Molly. 'How about you Percy?'

'I'm not about to spoil a good evening by even thinking about it,' Mr. Fishwick declared. He eyed the confiscated gin bottle, struggled to his feet, and grabbed it. 'You ladies don't mind if I…' He didn't wait for a reply. The bottle had already hit his mouth.

'No Percy, we don't mind at all do we Harriet?' said Molly winking at her.

'You've had a very tiring day Mr. Fishwick. It'll help you to relax,' encouraged Harriet.

Having been given the green light from them both he slowly emptied the bottle of its contents. In disbelief, he tried again for the last dregs and sheer disappointment brought him to his feet.

'I need to lie down Harriet my dear. Is that all right with you?'

'Of course it is Mr. Fishwick,' replied Harriet, resolving, whatever happened, not to go anywhere near him.

He dropped the bottle into the waste paper bin as he staggered to the far side of the bed. He heaved himself in and promptly lost consciousness.

'Thank goodness for that!' exclaimed Harriet. 'We won't be far behind him. Not in there though!' she said, pointing to the bed.

'Don't you worry dear,' said Molly fishing in her handbag for her key card. 'You slip next door to my cabin. I'll lie down here, there's plenty of room for us both. He's not going to wake up for a long time.'

Harriet paused only to thank Molly then she was out like a shot! She lay on Molly's bed and with hardly a second to bask in oh such sweet, sweet relief, she fell fast asleep.

Chapter 35

Next morning Harriet awoke to Molly thumping on the cabin door. She jumped off the bed. 'I'm coming Molly. Are you all right?' she asked as she opened it to let her in.

'No, no I most certainly am not Harriet!' Molly stormed as she marched past. 'That man! Do you know Harriet in the middle of the night he rolled over and over on that bed until he found me.'

Harriet looked at her, suddenly feeling a bit uncomfortable.

'Then he started stroking my hair and feeling my face, telling me I was his one and only love, Harriet. Good job I had my clothes on, indeed! He said we we're destined to be together. My word he's a fast worker Harriet. Too fast for me! I thought I had a soft spot for him, but I'm not so sure now.'

'Did he actually wake up Molly?' Harriet asked, sure that Molly had been the unwitting recipient of his advances. Harriet was starting to feel very guilty. It should have been her!

'Come to think of it Harriet, I don't think he did but I was half asleep myself and it's hard to remember. I do know he completely ignored my protests, though. Now there's a thought,' Molly continued, 'he could have been dreaming about his wife, poor soul. Oh Harriet, I'm so glad he didn't hear me ranting and raving at him.'

'I wouldn't worry Molly,' said Harriet. 'After downing that bottle of neat gin last night he probably won't remember a thing.'

Molly crossed her fingers and smiled. 'You know Harriet, I'm feeling a bit sad at the thought of leaving this ship. We've had such a good time haven't we?'

'We certainly have Molly,' agreed Harriet, beginning to rise again on Mr. Sanderson's unbelievable words. 'I'm still worried about the cat though. I'm sure those two would have found it if it'd been in the cupboard.'

'I would have thought so,' said Molly, 'they were in there long enough.'

'I'm jolly glad I haven't got to get it through customs, anyway,' continued Harriet, 'but I'd like to know where the damned thing is. It's been microchipped Molly. I just know this one's going to come back to haunt me. Not to mention Mark. He'll go absolutely ballistic if he ever finds out why it went missing.'

There was a knock on the cabin door. 'That'll be Charles with the breakfast tray,' said Molly.

'Oh please keep him talking Molly while I try to budge Mr. Fishwick. I don't want him to think I've been in there all night with *him*.'

Harriet slipped past Charles and slid her card key into the cabin door.

Mr. Fishwick was nowhere to be seen. 'He must have decided to go down for breakfast,' she thought, 'I'm amazed he felt up to it.'

Then, just to make sure, she looked in the en suite and then out on to the patio. Finally she lifted the fallen duvet and looked under the bed just in case he'd rolled off. She breathed a huge sigh of relief and then opened the wardrobe door. She suddenly felt violently sick from the stench she'd just released into the cabin.

'Oh no,' Charles mustn't come in here now.'

She stepped into the corridor leaving one foot in the doorway and waited for him.

'Ah Harriet!' he said, passing the tray to her. 'You enjoy your cruise? You come again? Yes?'

'Oh most certainly will!' exclaimed Harriet, 'I can't thank you enough for your kindness. I shall write to the company when I get home and tell them about your most excellent service.'

Charles beamed and shook her hand as she gave him a little kiss on his cheek.

'You have a good journey home, yes?' he said as he moved across to the cabin opposite.

Harried nodded, smiled and went back into her cabin, closing the door behind her.

She shot over to the patio doors and opened them as wide as she could. Fortunately there was a strong offshore breeze blowing straight from Southampton dock and it didn't take long for the cabin to clear.

She hurriedly rolled up the newspapers and their disgusting contents from the bottom of the wardrobe floor. Then she emptied the bits and pieces she'd bought from the ship's very posh 'Cruising Christiana' carrier bag and pushed the bundle into it. She covered it all with layers of scented tissues and then sprayed it and sprayed it with her best perfume. She tried to squeeze it all into her holdall but it wouldn't go. Harriet got impatient. 'You brought the bloody cat, now you can just take its mess!' In despair she gave up. 'I'm just going to have to carry it like this,' she thought, holding it all at arm's length as she dumped it on the patio.

Harriet just had time to eat her breakfast, throw her things into her bag and quickly tidy the bed before Molly knocked on the door.

'Are you ready dear? I believe we greens are going first. Goodness knows when Percy's deck is allowed off, they don't seem to do it in any particular order. Still, the coach will wait for him. Where is he Harriet?' she asked, looking round the cabin.

'I don't know,' said Harriet. 'He wasn't here when I came in so I presume he got himself down to breakfast. Brush and all!'

'Whatever could he have been thinking of going off with that?' said Molly. 'Sure they're not both in the wardrobe, Harriet?'

Harriet laughed. It reminded her to pick up the carrier bag from the patio.

Chapter 36

Molly suddenly looked at her watch. 'Come on Harriet we're not going to be allowed off the ship at this rate if we miss our slot.'

Harriet wanted to have a quick tidy round the cabin but now thought better of it. She grabbed all her luggage, took one last look and then closed the door behind them both. 'I hope I haven't forgotten anything, *like the cat*!' she said to herself as they marched along the corridor towards the lifts. It was a short ride.

Glad to be out, Harriet rearranged her baggage and Molly quickly followed suit as they made for the reception area.

'Gosh Molly,' said Harriet, 'it doesn't seem like two minutes ago we were on our way in.' She suddenly felt guilty about the way she'd treated Mr. Fishwick. She remembered how she'd been only too pleased to follow him around then.

'I wonder if Mr. Fishwick's all right?' she asked Molly.

'Talk of the devil Harriet! Look there, he's standing in that alcove with the brush, would you believe?'

'Oh no!' exclaimed Harriet, 'what's he up to now?'

'Just a minute, Harriet,' warned Molly, stopping in her tracks. 'Pull into here a moment. I can just see that lot about to turn the corner over there.'

They both stepped back into a small recess squeezing in alongside the life saving equipment.

'Wait for it,' whispered Molly. 'Oh no! There goes Mr. Fishwick. He's just stuck that brush handle out, right in their path. Oh! He's off! He's disappeared Harriet!'

'Oh look!' panicked Harriet, 'they're heading straight for it. They haven't seen it!'

The raucous girl and her long thin boyfriend suddenly tripped on the broom handle. They sprawled across the floor, swiftly followed by the rest of them wobbling and jerking until they all went down with a crash. Harriet and Molly could see a huge mountain of heads, bodies, arms and legs all interspersed with suitcases and bags. The corridor was filled with howls of raging indignation.

'It's that bloody brush again!' screeched the tattooed girl. 'I bet it's that ole geezer. Cum on, let's gerrim!'

'We're tryin` to gerroff this fuckin` ship arn we? Cum on we'll miss our turn!' The lanky lad bellowed as he grabbed his last bag. With that they all struggled to their feet and flew up the passageway to the checkout.

Harriet could hardly contain herself. She was about to collapse into one of her uncontrollable eruptions when she stopped in her tracks. She nearly leapt out of her skin. 'That bag he's just picked up. The cat was in it! I saw its tail wagging as he ran. I did Molly, didn't you?'

She turned to see Molly in near hysterics, head down, absolutely doubled up, shaking with shrieks of violent laughter.

She struggled for ages to try to answer Harriet but by the time she'd managed to just about catch her breath, they'd long since disappeared.

'Molly, we're going to miss our turn,' said Harriet. 'Come on, we might just see them checking out if we're quick. It *was* the cat, I'm sure of it.'

'That's just what Percy thought Harriet,' panted Molly, now beginning to calm down, 'and it turned out to be that damned hat, remember?'

'But they've been in that store cupboard since then Molly. It *was* in there after all. Never mind hurling the brush at us. They'd have done better throwing the cat back into the cabin!'

'Well you could be right, Harriet,' said Molly as they gathered all their bags and started walking briskly along the passage. 'Mind you they couldn't have known it was *your* cat Harriet, could they? I wouldn't suppose for one minute that girl's bright enough to associate that hat with a cat, not even a dead one!'

'Oh no Molly!' said Harriet, most alarmed, 'that's just what those types do to cats, isn't it? They taunt them and the next minute they've finished them off.'

It was an uncomfortable thought for Molly, too. She decided to glance behind her. 'Oh look there's Mr. Fishwick running, trying to catch us up. Hold on a minute Harriet, we'd better wait for him.'

It wasn't long before Mr. Fishwick arrived puffing and panting. 'Ah! Ladies!' he managed to say. 'We might just make it.'

'You're not off the same time as us are you Percy?' asked Molly, deciding it was better to pretend the night before had never happened.

'Well I had a little bit of business to attend to,' he snorted. 'Should've gone the one before, but I reckoned a little delay would be worth it.'

Molly looked across to Harriet and their shoulders started to shake again.

'Oh Percy, we saw what you did. You should've seen them all landing in a heap. We wouldn't have missed it for the world, would we Harriet?'

The three of them started laughing.

'That'll teach the little buggers a lesson!' he exclaimed. 'They didn't see me, did they?'

'Oh no Percy,' reassured Molly, 'you were too quick down that corridor.'

The three of them marched on and into the reception area. They finally joined the tail end of the queue after struggling through the crowds who were still waiting for their turn to disembark.

'Missed your turn Sir?' enquired a ship's officer standing guard at the exit as Mr. Fishwick produced his documents.

'The lift was full and these old legs are not what they used to be especially on stairs,' he complained.

Harriet and Molly, standing behind him, refused to look at each other.

They let him through. He turned to share his relief with them both and then all his pent up adrenaline took over to shoot him forward at breakneck speed.

'I didn't think he could move like that,' said Molly, starting to shake again.

'Hidden depths!' laughed Harriet, trying not to let it take hold again.

They watched him, way ahead, already holding the door open for them.

'It's been a smashing cruise, Harriet,' said Molly, 'I'm sorry it's all over.'

'Me too, though it would have been better if we'd not have had to worry about that idiotic cat of mine.'

'I wouldn't even think about it Harriet. Cats have nine lives don't they? You see if it hasn't swum home. You might find it already there when you get back!'

Harriet smiled at Molly. 'If that cat's at home when I get back Molly, then I'll be a bridesmaid at your wedding!'

'Wedding Harriet? Wedding? Who on earth to?'

'Mr. Fishwick of course!' laughed Harriet.

'Oh no Harriet. You've got to be joking!' chortled Molly.

'I'm just about as serious as you,' insisted Harriet.

In a tick they were off the ship, onto the gangway and into the exit hall where Mr. Fishwick had been patiently holding onto the door. To Harriet's great relief, it was devoid of all customs officers. She looked around but there was no sign of the gang.

'At least they'll have got it out,' she said to herself , 'but if they take it to a vet or a cats' home and tell them how they came by it, I'm sunk. It depends how official people want to be. Perhaps it would be better if they *did* finish it off.' Harriet was immediately overcome with a deep sense of guilt at harbouring such a thought. She continued to torment herself as they walked out of one doorway and in through another. She looked down at the ship's posh carrier bag she was holding. 'Bloody cat,' she said to herself, 'I've got to find somewhere to dump this now.'

'Harriet thinks they've got the cat, Percy. You thought you saw its tail wagging out of that lad's bag didn't you Harriet?'

Harriet nodded. 'You were right all along Mr. Fishwick. It was in that cupboard. Pity we didn't get chance to scour the place especially as we've just breezed through customs.'

'You're seeing things my dear,' said Mr. Fishwick, stopping to lean on his golf club. She could feel him putting his arm around her, standing as close to her as he could get away with.

Harriet took a very deep breath.

'I certainly am, Mr. Fishwick!' she stuttered as she looked up to see Mr. Sanderson coming towards them. Harriet's legs turned to jelly. She was almost grateful to Mr. Fishwick for inadvertently propping her up.

'Look Harriet. It's our friend! I wonder what he's doing here?' said Molly, turning to Harriet, eager to share her excitement.

Harriet didn't have time to answer.

'Good morning!' he greeted, smiling at all three of them.

'Whatever's brought you back, then?' enquired Molly, her curiosity getting the better of her.

He glanced over to the large desk at the far end of the hall. 'A little bit of left luggage,' he said. Then, he forced Harriet away from Mr. Fishwick and drew her to his side. He looked straight into her eyes, his voice serious. 'And a lot of lost property!'

Mr. Fishwick looked utterly crestfallen. Then he rose to his full but limited height and waved his golf club.

'We shared the same bed last night!' he spluttered, most indignant, glowering at Mr. Sanderson.

Harriet went bright red.

'Well, she was desperately trying to get someone into it!' replied Mr. Sanderson as lightly as he could.

'Oh come on Percy, we'll miss that coach,' insisted a very embarrassed Molly, dragging him off by the arm. 'I'll give you a call Harriet.'

Chapter 37

Still in the grip of Mr. Sanderson's strong arm, Harriet nodded and waved goodbye to them both as he ushered her towards the left luggage desk. She couldn't bring herself to speak. Her mind was numbed from the constant highs and lows of her emotional existence. She half-heard, half-saw him collecting a couple of cases and a carrier bag. In her daze she tried to rationalise his actions.

'Of course he wouldn't have been able to take everything with him to wherever he was going, especially if he was off to Switzerland,' she thought. Immediately she pushed it all from her mind. At this moment in time he was hers, all hers. This was going to be the most beautiful journey she'd ever had in her life.

'Where are you taking me?' she finally managed to say.

'Home, Harriet. I'm taking you home and on the way back you've got some explaining to do young lady!'

Harriet hardly heard him.

She looked up at him conscious of his arm still around her as they walked towards the exit. She could feel herself trembling from the whole mix of emotion that always swamped her when she was close to him. She still couldn't bring herself to speak. She could feel her head brushing his shoulder as they walked along towards his car. She looked down at his highly polished shoes. 'Shoes, significant shoes,' she thought recalling the wine shop when all the brochures had fallen at his feet. Harriet could scarcely believe that her break away had taken her to him. She looked up at him again.

He caught her glance with a smile. 'Harriet, you did want a lift home, didn't you?'

'Oh yes, thank you, Mr. Sanderson. I'm just so taken by surprise!'

'Well I was always going to have to come back to pick up the car,' he said as he put the key in the boot lock. 'Shove it all in here Harriet.' He threw his own luggage in. Harriet, now feeling flustered and a little disappointed at his need to return anyway, pushed it all in. She turned round to see Mr. Sanderson holding the front passenger door open for her.

'Car, significant car!' she said to herself. 'How many times has this car reduced me to a quivering wreck?' As he closed the door her shaking hand grabbed at the seatbelt and she struggled to get the end into the clasp. Floundering she looked across at him as he eased himself into the driving seat.

'Just a tick Harriet, you've got that twisted.' He undid the clasp and let the belt ride to its sitting position. Harriet just melted. Then he stretched over and gently slid it over her shoulder and across her chest to her waist where he clipped it into place.

'Is that secure now Harriet?' he asked. He leaned over again. She could just feel the brief touch of his hand against her breast as he ran it down the strap. Harriet flushed. She smiled shyly at him unable to come to terms with her blatant behaviour at their last encounter.

She watched him start the engine and her eyes followed his hand as he pushed the gear lever into first. Then with a swift turn of the wheel they were away.

'Comfortable there Harriet?' he enquired.

'Very much so, thank you,' replied Harriet feeling absolutely lost for words. She wondered if he was going to mention that evening on board. 'It's a nice day,' she continued, looking out of the window at the blue sky.

'It certainly is Harriet,' replied Mr. Sanderson, 'especially now I've finally got you to myself, at last! Or is that cat up your jumper?' He beamed a huge smile across as he changed down gear in readiness to negotiate the approaching roundabout.

'It certainly isn't Mr. Sanderson!' Harriet protested. 'In fact, I think I know where it is.'

'You do Harriet?' he queried, taking a swift look left before proceeding. Harriet watched his hand now back on the gear lever. She noticed how quickly he moved through to top gear and how rapidly he gathered speed as they dominated the outside lane of the motorway.

'Oh please don't go so quickly,' she said to herself, 'this journey will be over before it's begun.'

He looked across at her again. She noticed his eyes narrow slightly and then start to twinkle. 'Where is it then Harriet?' he laughed.

'It's not funny Mr. Sanderson. A gang of horrible youths stole it from the linen cupboard down the corridor from us. Goodness knows what they'll do to it and if they don't someone's sure to find its microchip and the next thing I'll be on trial for trying to smuggle a cat on board.'

'Is that what you tried to do Harriet? Are you so attached to the damned thing that you had to take it away with you?'

'Of course not, Mr. Sanderson! Somehow it found its way into my holdall. I didn't have a clue it was there until I opened it. It spent most of its time in the wardrobe, though. It didn't have any choice!'

'Not the night before last. It certainly wasn't in the wardrobe then Harriet!'

Harriet could feel herself going bright red just as he turned to look at her.

He laughed again. 'Do you remember anything of that night Harriet?' he enquired, his face suddenly becoming more intent.

'Not a lot,' she replied, hoping against hope he'd believe her. She watched intently as he swung into the middle lane to let a wagon get past.

'Bloody idiot!' he swore as he moved back to the outside lane. He looked across at her again. Her gaze was fixed to his hands on the steering wheel. 'The confidence, the precision he's got,' she thought. 'He's just so masculine, so gorgeous! I wonder if he'll tell me what he was going to say that night?' She recalled lying on the bed wanting him with an intensity of passion that almost frightened her. As she looked across to him she knew that this was the only direction her life could now take.

'We're looking for the exit at junction two Harriet,' he said as he eased off the accelerator to change lanes. 'Keep an eye open once we're off here for the A442.'

Harriet focussed her eyes on the signs. They turned off the motorway but there were so many of them she became completely flummoxed.

'Damn! We've missed it! We're heading back towards the motorway. Miss Glover that wasn't too much to ask, or was it?'

Harriet was mortified. She could get this from Mark any day of the week. She took a deep breath and then she felt his hand on hers. 'Sorry Harriet,' he said, 'this isn't easy for me you know.'

Harriet squeezed his hand. 'It's just that I'm probably the world's worst navigator. You weren't to know. Sorry.'

He returned his hand to the steering wheel and smiled gently at her. 'I think we'll do a bit of a detour here, if that's OK with you,' he said as he took a sharp left into a country lane, 'Let's see if we can find somewhere half-decent for coffee shall we?'

'Oh that would be nice,' said Harriet delighted she'd managed to slow the trip down.

She looked out of the window and spotted a field filled with the blues, whites and pinks of spring meadow flowers. She remembered the picture on her calendar. She found it inconceivable that she was with him. She glanced at the blonde curl overlapping his collar, its deep sea green a perfect backcloth to the pale gold of his hair.

She loved the way his collar sat on the neckline of his beautifully knitted Aran jumper. She was more used to seeing him in suits. She watched his arms, strong, as he manoeuvred the car round the twists and turns of the lane and she noticed how his legs, somehow too big for the car took up every last ounce of movement there was left in his black cord trousers.

'Ah just what we're looking for,' he said and Harriet looked up to see a thatched cottage sporting some kind of hotel sign in the distance.

'Lovely!' said Harriet. 'This is such a pretty place. Did you manage to see that field? It was just a haze of spring flowers.'

'Missed that one Harriet. Where was that then?'

'Just across that way, back there.'

'We'll have that coffee and then you can show me,' he smiled.

Chapter 38

The sun felt warmer than usual for the time of the year and Mr. Sanderson let go of Harriet's hand to take his sweater off.

'Can I carry anything for you Harriet?' he asked looking across at her jacket. 'You've got to be roasting in that!'

Harriet slipped her jacket off and was glad of her light open stitch mohair jumper which allowed her to cool down quickly.

'That's very pretty, Harriet,' said Mr. Sanderson looking down at her as he took hold of her hand again. 'You suit white lace.'

'But it's black Mr. Sanderson,' said Harriet viewing the soft woolly cuff against her wrist. Then she remembered she was wearing the holey one. 'Could I have my jacket back again for a moment, please? I just need a tissue.'

'You'll roast Harriet. There's no point. I've already seen it,' he said. 'Well it's the second time, as a matter of fact. The first time it was strewn across your bed!' He stopped.

Harriet could feel the colour flooding to her cheeks. She looked to the ground and then felt his hand gently lifting her face towards him.

'You didn't seem to mind at the time Harriet. In fact…'

Harriet stopped him in his tracks. 'Mr. Sanderson I barely remember the evening and if my behaviour was in any way inappropriate I apologise now.'

He looked down at her and smiled. 'On the contrary it could have been very appropriate Harriet if it hadn't been for one small thing.'

'Oh and what was that?' Harriet was beginning to feel a little nervous.

'In a minute Harriet. In a minute!' he said.

'No, nothing, nothing can spoil this wonderful day,' she thought, trying to reassure herself as she desperately waited for an answer.

'Ah, what's this?' he said as a turnstile suddenly appeared in front of them. 'Maybe we should follow this footpath. Is that about right Harriet? Will this take us to your field of flowers?'

'I hope so,' replied Harriet, taking his hand as she stepped over. He caught her as she jumped down and then he kept her in his arms. He pressed her closely to the full length of his body and then melted a lasting kiss into her lips, then he drew himself away and put his arm around her shoulder. For some time they walked along the grassy footpath without a word spoken.

For Harriet earth had just become heaven and heaven had become earth, they were indistinguishable. She floated on the magical mix of perfection that is so esoteric to lovers. Then she spotted the flowers.

'Over there!' she said. 'I can just see the whites, blues and pinks through the gaps in that hedge.'

They followed the footpath to the field and Mr. Sanderson pushed open the creaky, old five-bar gate.

'Should we be in here?' Harriet asked him, a hint of concern in her voice.

'Should we be anywhere Harriet? I'd say probably not!'

He scooped her up and then laid her gently down in the flowers. He lay beside her for a moment and then took her in his arms and kissed her as he smoothed her hair away from her face.

'Harriet,' he said, 'my sweet, sweet Harriet, I've wanted you for so long.'

She heard his words singing in her ears. She started to feel dazed as his kisses became laced with a strong, passionate intimacy. Harriet lay in his arms, her mind blown away. She felt every part of her body desperately opening for him. She wanted to lie completely exposed in all the flowers. He had to take her, now!

Then she felt him easing himself away. 'I'm finding this one of the most difficult things I've ever encountered in my life Harriet, but it's not going to do, is it?'

Harriet, her eyes hardly able to open, looked at him. 'Because?' she whispered.

'Because of many things my darling, not least of which, this.' He ran his hand across her skirt and then placed it firmly below her waist. 'When's it due Harriet?'

Harriet could hardly believe his words. 'Oh no, it's not,' she whispered desperately. 'Mr. Sanderson....'

'Skip the formality Harriet, Joris will do nicely,' he interrupted. She took a deep breath. This wasn't going to be easy.

'Joris, I'm not pregnant!'

'According to that waiter chap you most certainly are!' he insisted.

'No, he just assumed it because I needed extra food in my cabin to feed the cat. It worked so I let him believe it.'

Mr. Sanderson cleared his throat, raised his eyebrows and briefly stroked his chin.

He replaced his hand and moved it slowly down her body. Then he lay on top of her kissing her desperately before forcing himself to stop. He pressed his hand firmly back on her abdomen.

'That's a relief Harriet,' he said. 'Save that one for me!'

Harriet looked straight into his eyes. 'Well it might not just work straight away Mr. Sanderson, I've been trying for months and months and no luck.'

'Really Harriet?' Mr. Sanderson said with a note of surprise in his voice. Then he gave her the broadest of smiles. 'Oh Harriet, that's why I've fallen for you! I don't mean now. I can't risk getting you pregnant just yet, though conception in the flowers certainly has its appeal. No Harriet. We've both got a bit of sorting out to do before we go there, wouldn't you say?'

Had he just said those words to her? Harriet was deliriously happy. She smiled across at him as she watched him pick a handful of green stalks, trailing their coloured heads across his palm. She lay back in the flower studded grass bathing in its scent whilst the birds, as if celebrating her joy sang her their prettiest of songs.

Mr. Sanderson scattered the flowers across her skirt, then he bent forward and carefully undid the top button of her jumper. He slipped his hand into her white lace bra and then slowly moved it back to open the next button, just giving himself room to kiss her soft pale skin. She felt the warmth of his lips against her breast and she desperately wanted all of him now. Suddenly she felt him pull away. She looked down to see his hand move to his waist. He started to open the buckle on his belt. She could feel him breathing in as he pulled the strap back into his hand. Then he stopped.

'This isn't going to do Harriet. It's not going to do at all.'

Harriet watched his eyes, his face. She'd never seen him like this before.

He lay back again and drew her very close. She could feel his lips in her hair. He looked into her eyes as he slowly undid the next button on her jumper. He slid his fingers under her bra strap, slipping it off her shoulder. She could feel him gently taking the full weight of her breast into his hand.

'This is most definitely not going to do Harriet,' he whispered.

She lay quite still. Her eyes were closed. He looked down at her. He lifted her breast to his lips then gently lowered it back into her white lace bra. He returned the strap to her shoulder and then put the button he'd just undone back into its buttonhole. Harriet opened her eyes. He smiled at her.

He lifted two buttercups from the array of flowers on her lap and threaded them through the buttonholes left open in her jumper. Then he took her by the hands and brought her to her feet. They stood, arm in arm, gazing at the haze of beauty around them. In silence they retraced their steps to the Inn. There was nothing more to say. Harriet knew they were both so very much in love.

As they neared the Inn Mr. Sanderson steered her towards the door. He looked at his watch. 'Do you know Harriet it's almost midday. We might just as well have a bite to eat here before we hit the road.'

'That would be lovely,' replied Harriet ducking under his arm as he held the old wooden door open for her.

They found a table for two in an alcove overlooking the garden. Mr. Sanderson pulled the chair out for Harriet and they both sat down.

He picked up the menu and turned to the wine list. 'Can I get you anything?' he asked, smiling at her.

'Just a mineral water, please.'

'Very restrained Harriet. I'm having a half of lager, at least join me in the other half,' he laughed.

'A better idea!' she said, knowing full well it wasn't one of her favourite drinks.

She watched him walk over to the bar and took a very deep breath. She knew that this had to be a life-changing day for her. 'Oh Harriet, that's why I've fallen for you!' his words floated through her mind. 'This is so, so serious,' she told herself. 'Men never admit that. Well maybe during sex, or straight after maybe, but never in the face of such restraint.'

She thought about Mark, but the thought faded as fast as it had come.

Then she remembered what else Mr. Sanderson had said. 'Save that one for me!' He actually asked me to wait for him.' In her heavenly transportation Harriet was having the greatest difficulty trying to absorb it all.

'Lost in thought Harriet?' Mr. Sanderson enquired as he placed the two lagers on the table. He put his arm around her and lightly kissed her cheek before he sat down. Harriet thanked him and they raised their drinks. 'To us,' he said. 'To us,' returned Harriet. She could scarcely believe how things had moved on since they last raised glasses together.

He handed her the menu.

'Oh, just a bagel for me please.'

'Are you sure Harriet, have another look. I was reading the board at the bar, they've certainly got a decent selection.'

Harriet looked across to the board and through the menu again. 'No, I'm not very hungry really, a bagel will be fine, thank you.'

'Only if you promise to join me one evening for the finest of wining and dining. Promise?'

'Promise!' smiled Harriet as she saw him catch the waiter's attention.

'So you've been doing your utmost to get pregnant, Harriet?' Mr. Sanderson suddenly said.

Harriet knew her cheeks were starting to colour. 'Well, er not really, just take a few chances sometimes,' she said feeling highly uncomfortable with the subject.

'No more chances, Harriet!' he announced. 'We don't need any complications, besides I've got something I want to ask you.'

Harriet could feel her legs going to jelly again.

'Ye-es?' said Harriet very cautiously, her heart leaping at the prospect of a proposal.

'Amanda Woods will be leaving us for a while and I would like you to stand in as my deputy.'

Harriet went flop inside as the sweet tension of anticipation ran to the ground.

'Oh, er, where is she going?' stumbled Harriet.

'She's opted to do one of these work sabbaticals for three months. She's exchanging to Canada. It's not a straight exchange, we'll get a supply in, but I need someone who knows the score to deputise for me especially as I'm in the throws of getting Starboard Marine North West up and running.'

Harriet felt her heart sink. How could he switch to work, just like that? She looked at him trying desperately to hold on to all they'd just had.

'Have a think about it Harriet.'

'Oh no, that will be fine Mr. Sanderson. I'll do my very best. Thank you for the opportunity.'

'I'm sure you'll make a grand job of it Harriet. Just don't go knocking Mr. Brown off any ladders, will you? The place couldn't run without him!' He smiled the broadest of smiles. Harriet was too flustered to rise to the bait.

'Mind you Harriet, you seem to have a penchant for irritating little elderly gentlemen.'

'Whatever do you mean?' Harriet asked.

'Our friend Percival. He was very irritated when I met him this morning.'

'That wasn't me, that was you!' spluttered Harriet.

Mr. Sanderson started laughing. 'So you *did* sleep with him last night did you? He certainly had you up tight and close when I arrived!'

'No I certainly did not!' Harriet protested. 'He was legless by the end of the evening so I slept in Molly's cabin. Molly ended up on the edge of my bed trying to escape from him. Didn't he just roll up to her in the middle of the night whispering sweet nothings into her ear thinking it was me! That's why she dragged him off in such a hurry.'

Mr. Sanderson couldn't stop laughing. 'Oh Harriet, you are adorable!' he said and he took her hand across the table and squeezed it hard before excusing himself.

Harriet, now feeling deliriously happy again, looked at her drink. The glass was almost full. He'd just taken her back to their magical haze of flowers with his compliment, she most certainly wasn't going to offend him now. Quickly she looked behind her to see if there was any potential for offering the tall rubber plant gracing the bay window a quick half.

'Ah a nice big pot a bit short on soil, nice and damp though,' she thought. Swiftly she took the glass off the table and poured the lot away. She turned round to see Mr. Sanderson just closing the gent's door behind him.

'Presume you're OK Harriet?' he enquired as he came back to the table.

'Yes thanks, I'm fine!'

'Oh you girls! You'll probably need the loo when we're miles from anywhere, especially after downing that in one!' he said, looking at the empty glass. Harriet's colour returned. They picked up their things and walked to the door.

'Thank you so much for lunch,' Harriet said as he held it open for her. He smiled across at her and they walked towards the car

'That's funny,' declared Mr. Sanderson turning a backward glance as he opened the car door for her. He pointed at the bay window where they'd just been sitting. 'That plant was as straight as a die when we came in!'

Harriet's heart sank. 'Oh no,' she thought, 'it's as drunk as Mr. Fishwick!' She half- turned expecting to see it completely flopped over. To her relief it was standing as tall and as straight as before. She looked up at Mr. Sanderson to see him laughing.

Then she suddenly realised he was oh so much smarter than her.

They made their way back home, the motorways eating the miles before them. Harriet sat back delighting in the musical interlude Mr. Sanderson had chosen to share with her. She basked in the soft grey leather interior of his expensive car. She couldn't quite believe she was in it, with *him*. It afforded her a privacy, an intimacy, almost a right to be a part of him, a part of his world.

'Who would ever have thought it could have ended like this?' she thought.

She wanted to say so much to him now. She wanted to pin him down. She wanted to be his and she wanted to know exactly what his plans were for them both. After all, he'd all but declared his hand.

She watched him intently as he gathered speed. She became addicted to watching the ease with which he slid in and out of lanes, always his foot down hard as he commanded priority over all else. It seemed to Harriet that he was pushing the Mercedes to its absolute limits but she felt safe, so very safe in his hands.

'You'll like the first track on this one,' he said, pressing yet another button on the dashboard. 'Just listen carefully. It's particularly appropriate.' He leant over and touched the buttercups still in her jumper.

Harriet closed her eyes as the music filled the car. 'Is this Tchaikovsky?' she asked.

'It is! "Waltz of the flowers" from the Nutcracker, Harriet.'

'I recognise this,' she said as the next track cut in. 'It's from Sleeping Beauty,' she smiled.

'Even more appropriate Harriet, you did close your eyes.'

She blushed as looked across at him and caught the full force of his smile as he reached for her hand.

'For ever, this day will be ours Harriet,' he said. 'Our perfect day.'

* * *

As the road signs took on their increasing familiarity Harriet tried desperately to hold them back. She wasn't ready to go home. Apart from school she didn't really know when she'd see him again. He'd mentioned dinner, but not when. This was the first day of her new life, there was no going back now.

'Our perfect day,' she thought. 'He's so right. It has been absolutely perfect.'

Then just for a moment she felt hollow, empty. 'Is that all it's going to be, just one perfect day in a lifetime?' She looked across at him and made a silent plea, 'Please don't break my heart.'

Harriet needn't have worried. As he drove into the coach station she caught his smile. 'Thanks Harriet for bringing me home. You can work that one out for yourself. Oh and can you manage dinner tomorrow evening?'

Harriet smiled and nodded.

'I'll pick you up at seven.'

He parked the car and stretched his legs before letting Harriet out.

'Good trip?' he asked, still smiling at her.

'Good trip,' she agreed, 'I can't thank you enough.'

He caught hold of her hand. 'I'd rather have travelled down with you as well. Why wouldn't you come with me Harriet?'

'I just decided you were out of my life forever.'

'Thought as much, Harriet. You certainly don't make things easy for me,' he said stopping to kiss her on her cheek. Then he opened the boot and carried her luggage as they walked towards her car.

'Everything here?' he asked as Harriet loaded it all on to her back seat.

She did a quick check. 'Yes that looks about right, thank you,' she said closing the car door.

'Thank you so much for everything,' she whispered, looking into his eyes.

'Absolutely all my pleasure. Drive carefully my darling, see you tomorrow evening at seven.'

He kissed her a quick goodbye as she settled herself into her car. She waved at him and watched him walk over to his silver Mercedes. She started the engine, backed out and eased herself forward. Then she drove slowly past him, waving as he got into his car. At that moment Harriet felt she needed driving lessons. Her mind was so completely afloat she felt she'd almost forgotten how to drive.

Necessity forced her to focus as best she could. In exquisite euphoria she followed the wispy white clouds along the magical blue sky as they danced their dance in jubilation all the way home.

Chapter 39

Harriet drove onto the path and sighed in relief. She knew she shouldn't have been driving in such a state. Her concentration had been spasmodic, erratic. That irresistibly gorgeous hunk of a man was swimming in her head and she really was quite helpless to change the frame.

She struggled to open the car door and felt it hit the fence as she finally squeezed herself out. She went round the other side and grabbed all her luggage separating out the ship's carrier bag.

'That one can go straight in the bin. Disgusting thing! Thank goodness it went in his boot,' she said to herself, walking over to the front wall. She lifted the lid and hurled it in, noticing that it hadn't yet been emptied. 'They should be here any minute. It's almost 5 o'clock,' she thought, looking at her watch.

She fished in her pocket to retrieve her keys, gathered the rest of her luggage and opened the front door. Then she suddenly remembered Belinda Oxfordshire and the second viewing. 'Gosh, I wonder how that went?' she asked herself. 'At least she couldn't complain about the cat.'

At that moment Harriet heard a very familiar sound. 'Meow, meow…'

'Starting to hear things now! I'm going like Mr. Fishwick.' She dumped all her stuff down in the hall and then she thought she heard it again. Her stomach suddenly started churning. 'Oh no! I'm becoming unhinged in my euphoria. Wherever that damned cat is, it certainly isn't here,' she told herself sternly.

She popped her head into the front lounge and then the dining room. 'Just as I left it, all nice and tidy. I wonder if she's going to buy it?'

Then she pushed the kitchen door open and fell flat on her face.

'Bloody Nora!' she screeched in a state of utter shock. She looked across to see the tail end of a cat vanish through the cat flap.

She picked herself up. 'Bloody cheeky cat!' she said out loud. 'Bloody get out and stay out. You don't live here!' Then it suddenly crossed her mind that all the cats in the neighbourhood had probably had free lodging since she went away. 'I know just how Mr. Fishwick must have felt now. It's not very nice feeling as confused as this.'

Suddenly she saw the cat flap beginning to open again. Before she could get her foot across, it was in. Back again!

'It's *you*!' she exploded. 'How the bloody hell did you get here?'

For a moment Harriet thought she was dreaming. 'Oh no, this is all too much! Are you real, or am I hallucinating?' Then she quickly reassured herself that she couldn't trip over a figment of her imagination and anyway the cat was now well and truly trying to get on the right side of her. She bent down for fear of going over again as it pushed in and out of her legs, purring to capacity. It jumped on her lap and started licking her face. She took it in her arms and hugged it and hugged it. Her vision blurred as the tears filled her eyes. 'It's a pity you can't talk, you stupid cat!'

She carried it into the hall and noticed several flashes on the answer machine.

'Not now,' she said, 'first a nice cup of tea. Just *how* did you get home?'

The cat, nuzzling her neck, meowed loudly. Harriet began wondering how those two nightmarish youths could possibly have managed to return it in such record time.

'Unless they sent it by special delivery, but who'd take it in? There's no card through the letterbox, no official record of its arrival.' Her mind starting going round and round trying to come up with a plausible explanation. 'One thing's for sure. I'm glad Mark insisted on that microchip.'

She tried to put the cat down as she heard the bin wagon clattering and banging at the front gate.

'That's good. Glad to be rid of your mess,' she told it, finally managing to let go. 'I'll just take that round the back.'

With the cat glued to her legs Harriet wheeled the bin down the side path and placed it under the housing by the kitchen window. She forgot the back door was still locked so she wandered down the garden, the cat meowing at her feet.

Harriet looked across at the lilac bush. She recalled seeing his shiny black shoes stood alongside her. How things had moved on since he'd taken her upstairs and laid her on the bed. She wondered why such most precious moments of her life were destined to take place in an alcoholic haze. 'Not today though. It's been just perfect!' She wanted tomorrow evening to come quickly.

'Come on cat!' she ordered. 'Back to the front. We'd better play the messages in case there's something from Mark.' Then it suddenly occurred to her she'd hardly given him a thought since she'd got in.

They walked round to the front door. The cat shot in front, sniffed the luggage, jumped up and for a second sat on her black bag. Harriet closed the door behind them. She pressed the button for the first message.

'Oh hello Harriet, it's Mummy here. Do hope you and Mark are enjoying your weekend away. Daddy and I are fine, but I must tell you this little piece of news Harriet. Geraldine was on the phone going over the guest list and it seems they've invited a local celebrity to the wedding. I believe he's very rich Harriet. Not only is he a big figure at the golf club but he has friends in very high places. I believe he's on good terms with the Prime Minister, Harriet. Apparently he makes huge donations to charity. What a good man! I don't know how Geraldine found it all out, but she says James has been told by someone he's up for a knighthood. Apparently he's head of one of the local schools Harriet. I just wondered if you've heard of him at all. The wedding should be fun Harriet. It seems he's single and Samantha and Gabriella are both out to get him. Poor chap! Perhaps you should look out for him Harriet and take him under your wing. Yes, do that Harriet. I can't wait to meet him.

Anyway give me a call when you get home. Love to you all.'

The message stopped and Harriet was completely speechless.

'Friend of the Prime Minister? He can't be!' she finally said to herself. 'Surely not. Due for a knighthood? He never said.'

Then it occurred to her just how little she knew about him. 'In spite of his social conscience, I never could quite understand why he should want to teach in that school,' she thought. Harriet was dazed. She was still trying to fathom out how the cat had got home and now this. She thought about him for a moment. Certainly everything about him sported class and wealth. 'Then why, oh why should he be interested in me?' Suddenly all her confidence dwindled. She felt the need to confide in the cat.

'I don't know why he didn't go over with Tricia to Switzerland, do I?'

'I don't know why he left the ship or where he went to either, do I?' The cat started licking her hand.

'I do know why he wouldn't make love to me, though. He didn't want to risk getting me pregnant!' The cat suddenly drew its tongue back and started meowing at her.

'No, I didn't tell you that. Forget I said it!' she said wagging her finger firmly at its little black nose. Harriet found herself taking a very deep breath, then she heard the key in the front door.

'Hi Hat, I'm home! Come on give us a kiss.' It was Mark.

'But I thought you weren't back until Thursday at the earliest?' Harriet said automatically moving to his outstretched arms.

'Haven't you picked up the message yet, Hat?' Mark replied, giving her a big hug and a kiss.

'No, I've not been back long myself really.'

'Made a pig's ear of parking that thing Hat. How did you manage to get out?'

'With great difficulty! Anyway, did you have a good trip?'

'Not bad, not bad,' he said. 'Most of them are still down there trying to validate that ridiculous hypothesis of theirs. They'll never do it Hat, our data doesn't even show a trend. I came back with Kevin and Nigel, as we were obviously becoming surplus to requirements. We've left Paul Meadows down there arguing the toss.'

'And what about Melissa Scott, is she still there?' Harriet couldn't help herself.

'Well no actually. We've all arranged to meet at Kevin's tomorrow evening. They want us to comb the data again to see if it's flawed in some way.'

'So why does *she* have to be there?'

'Oh she's got all the previous data lined up. Records going back donkey's years. Goodness knows how far we've got to take it. It's all a pain Hat.'

'Oh right,' said Harriet seizing the opportunity. 'So you won't mind Mr. Sanderson picking me up tomorrow at 7 o'clock then?'

'What for? It was only last week you were all set to hand in your notice! What's that lard ball up to now?'

'Well, I've actually got some news for you,' Harriet suddenly remembered.

'News? What kind of news Hat and what's it got to do with him?'

'He wants me to stand in as deputy whilst Amanda Woods takes a sabbatical.'

'It's taken you long enough to tell me. You must have known before you broke up. So why does he have to pick you up at seven tomorrow night? It's work Hat. Work! You'll be seeing him on Monday anyway won't you?'

Harriet leapt at the ready-made excuse.

'Well, that's precisely the point Mark! He won't be in on Monday. He said he's got a lot to get sorted before the official opening of Starboard Marine North West next weekend and he wants to go through where we're at with the parenting classes. I've got a feeling he's really appreciated me bailing him out at that first meeting last week and that's why he wants me to deputise.'

'So where's he taking you Hat?' Mark shot her a suspicious look.

'Oh I think we'll just go through it all over a drink.'

'What's wrong with the dining room, Hat? I won't make mincemeat of him just yet!'

'And what's wrong with the dining room for your little get-together?' Harriet said, accusingly. 'I should quit Mark while you're ahead!'

'You daft bat Hat.' Mark's expression changed. 'Why should I be chasing anyone else when I've got you?' He took her into his arms and gave her a long, warm, affectionate kiss.

She looked at him, smiled and hugged him very closely.

'Do you really mean that?'

'Of course I do Hat. Are we in a permanent state of pre-menstrual tension these days, or what? I love you Hat and I missed you.'

Harriet snuggled right up to him. 'I love you too,' she said, happy that the equilibrium was restored. Harriet couldn't deny that she loved him in a warm, comfortable way.

'We'll always be a matching set, Hat and Glovers,' he laughed

'No shoes, though,' she thought as she looked down to her feet. Mr. Sanderson's were the only shoes in the world that could set her heart dancing.

Then she looked at Mark's feet and a pang went through her.

'It's not as if I've got to make any decisions immediately,' she reassured herself.

The phone rang.

'I'll get it!' said Mark, suddenly letting go of her.

'No! It's probably for me!' insisted Harriet, striding right past him.

'Hello,' she answered briskly.

'Oh hello, it's Melissa Scott speaking. Is Mark back yet?'

Harriet could feel herself starting to bristle.

'No I'm afraid he isn't. Can I take a message?'

With that Mark took the phone off Harriet.

'Just this minute through the door, Melissa! Harriet's just passed the phone over.'

Harriet fumed as she watched him listening to whatever it was she wanted.

'No, no of course it's no trouble Melissa. Hope you can get your car sorted out soon. Pick you up about quarter to seven then tomorrow night.'

'Oh not again!' blazed Harriet. 'You must have encouraged her. She could only have been in five minutes herself and there she is, can't wait to phone you.'

'It's work Harriet,' said Mark firmly. 'Just as yours is work.'

Harriet felt a pang of guilt.

'She's having problems getting her car started again so she's taking it in for some diagnostic testing.'

'Surely they'll lend her a courtesy car, won't they?'

'Well I don't know, do I?' said Mark starting to feel very impatient with Harriet. 'Think about it, will you? I have to work with the woman, I can hardly say "no" can I?'

Harriet just started to calm down when the phone rang again. This time Mark got there first.

'Yes, good evening,' Mark said very abruptly. 'I'll just pass you over.'

'Who is it?' Harriet mouthed to him as she went to take the phone from him. Mark threw his eyes up.

'Oh Hello,' Harriet half-whispered. She started to look very crestfallen.

'Oh no, that's fine.' Mark could hear her say. 'Not to worry, I know you've got a lot on at the moment. Thank you for letting me know.' She put the phone down.

Mark looked very pleased with himself. 'All off is it Hat?'

'Something's cropped up, I expect I'll just have to get on with it myself. All part and parcel of my new job.' She tried to sound as cheerful as she could.

'When does it start Hat?'

'I don't know. He didn't really say.'

'You don't know? Well don't you be doing his job for him without getting properly paid. I've met his type before. You want to watch yourself with him Harriet.'

'And just what do you mean by that?' Harriet demanded feeling herself starting to flush.

'I wouldn't trust him as far as I could throw him,' Mark replied.

'You don't need to,' said Harriet, deliberately missing the point. 'You don't work for him, I do! I know he can be awkward sometimes but he has a very difficult job to do. In fact he's got far more strings to his bow than any of us could ever have imagined.'

'Oh yes? Like what?'

'Don't be so cynical Mark. If you don't believe me just listen to this!'

She pressed the button on the answer machine for Mark to hear her mother's message.

'Well, how do you know it's him? There are plenty of schools in the borough. It could be anyone,' said Mark in very sceptical tones.

'Of course it's him!' Harriet said. 'Samantha and Gabriella told me that James had invited the chap from the golf club, the one who'd just opened Starboard Marine North West.'

'In that case have as little to do with him as possible, Harriet. In fact I'd feel a lot happier if you gave in your notice on Monday. We'll manage.'

'I don't want to give my notice in on Monday. I've just been offered a promotion and that's all you can say!'

'Your mother's got no more sense than you, either. Take him under your wing indeed. Knock him for six, more likely!'

Now feeling totally depressed Harriet pressed the button for the second message.

'Only me `arriet!' came Tricia's voice. 'Sorry you're not there. Oh `ave I got so much to tell you! Catch you later.'

'She wants to watch herself, too!' Mark shouted.

'Oh give over,' Harriet said, now in a really bad mood. She pressed the button again for the final message.

'Good day Mr. and Mrs. Glover, Mr. Roberts of Bryce Rae Roberts here. Just to update you with regard to the second viewing of your property, which we conducted on your behalf on Tuesday afternoon at four, at the request of a Ms Oxfordshire and a Mr. Sanderson, we believe. Would you be so kind as to call the office at your earliest convenience?' The message ended.

Harriet was completely dumbfounded.

'What on earth is he talking about? He's getting mixed up, he's got to be. They were the agents for the corner showrooms Mr. Sanderson bought. He wouldn't be coming *here* to view *this* with Belinda Oxfordshire.'

'Don't bank on it Harriet. It sounds to me like he's got a finger in every pie. Don't be taken in Harriet.'

'Of course he hasn't,' protested Harriet. 'They get everything wrong. He's definitely mistaken.'

Mark shrugged his shoulders.

'Anyway, where's your message then?' she said trying to change the subject.

'I definitely left one. I bet I got the end of the tape. It's probably run out thanks to your mother. It's high time we replaced that old thing.'

'Oh don't start on her now. She's only passing the news on.'

'Huh?' grunted Mark. 'Anyway you'd better give the estate agents a ring and find out what's been going on.'

'I'm not,' said Harriet looking at her watch. 'Anyway it's nearly ten to six they'll be well closed by now. I'll do it in the morning.'

'What are we doing about dinner, anyway?' Mark suddenly asked.

'There's nothing in. You'd better get some fish and chips,' Harriet answered.

'Why me?' Mark complained. 'I haven't just come back from a luxury cruise! You could just as easily go.'

'I want to start getting sorted out. You won't empty your suitcase all on your own, will you?'

Mark suddenly grinned at her. 'OK then Hat. I'll pick up a bottle of wine as well, shall I?'

'That's the best thing you've come up with since you came in. Make it two!'

Chapter 40

Harriet put the plates in the oven to warm and took all the luggage upstairs. She wasn't in the mood for sorting anything out so she tipped everything into the linen bin for the wash and then carefully hung her white suit up in the wardrobe before doing the same with Mark's suit and tie.

There was too much going on in her mind to dwell on Melissa Scott for the moment. She was glad Mark was home in spite of his attitude to Mr. Sanderson. In some ways it made her feel more secure. 'He wouldn't give *him* a thought,' she reassured herself, 'if he was really in love with *her*!'

She wondered why Mr. Sanderson had put her off tomorrow night. She was starting to feel the prospect of her new, exciting life beginning to drift away. 'He was always well and truly out of my league, anyway,' she reminded herself. She felt a huge cloud of sadness suddenly swamp her. 'I can't let go of my dreams. I won't let go of them,' she vowed as she remembered all he'd said, all they'd had between them.

She closed the case and put it back in the bottom of the wardrobe before getting to work on both sets of toiletries. 'Oh I can't stand this job!' she snapped to herself, sitting the numerous toilet bags open and upside down on the bathroom window sill. She just popped the two toothbrushes back into the rack when she heard Mark letting himself in.

'These look good tonight, Hat,' he called up the stairs. 'Come on before they get cold.'

Harriet went straight down and quietly returned the old black holdall to the cupboard under the stairs.

'Look Hat,' said Mark, trying to make amends. 'Look how white that fish is tonight. Makes a change from some of that yellowy-grey stuff we've been getting lately.'

'It smells nice too,' said Harriet, half-heartedly; giving him a hand with the second white paper parcel.

'Ah glasses. That's all we need now.' Mark rummaged in the wall cupboard to find the pair of oversized ones the girls had bought them for a laugh, a few years ago.

'You should have bought three bottles if we're going to be using these!' Harriet said, a smile suddenly overtaking her.

'I did!' said Mark. 'I think we're both in need of it.'

Just as they sat down to enjoy their meal the phone rang.

'Leave it!' ordered Mark. 'They'll leave a message if it's that important.'

They lifted their glasses just as the ringing gave way to Mark's voice cutting in, inviting whoever it was to leave a message after the tone.

They both sat with ears pricked, waiting.

'Jolly good!' exclaimed Mark. 'The tape's definitely run out. Cheers Hat!'

'Cheers Mark!' she said.

'How was the cruise then Hat?' Mark enquired as they tucked into the fish and chips. 'I bet you'd have enjoyed it a lot better with me.'

'Not if you'd been in one of your moods,' said Harriet beginning to feel irritated again.

The alcohol didn't seem to be doing much for her. She was desperately wondering if that had been Mr. Sanderson phoning back to say he could make it after all.

'I need to see him, urgently,' she said to herself. 'I can't wait until Monday!'

'Yes, sorry Hat,' apologised Mark. 'I can't stand his type. Just as long as he didn't put those buttercups in your jumper!'

Harriet looked down. She'd forgotten all about them. She picked up her wine glass and drank quickly from it in an attempt to ignore the question. Then she started coughing and spluttering.

'Steady on Hat!' Mark said, as he placed his knife and fork down. Then he shot off his chair to give her a good thump on the back.

'Gone down the wrong way,' Harriet managed to say as she watched the two buttercups shoot from her jumper and land in her wine glass.

'Don't bother answering that one Harriet.'

'Oh, finish your dinner Mark, for goodness sake!'

He looked out of the kitchen window at the buttercups and daisies growing in the lawn. 'I must get that grass cut.'

Mark was as good as his word. He went off to the shed while Harriet loaded the dishes into the sink. She fished her buttercups out of the wine glass and ran them under the tap. Then she pressed them very carefully into a piece of kitchen towel. She went over to the calendar on the wall and gazed at the picture, hardly able to believe her dream had come true. He had actually picked the meadow flowers and strewn them over her skirt. It seemed like a million years ago now. Slowly she opened the folded paper and took the flowers in her hand. A sharp pang went through her. 'Significant beautiful flowers,' she said to herself as she went to get her handbag. She placed them between the last page and the hard cover of her address book. She choked back the lump that was starting to form in her throat. 'He can't do this to me,' she thought.

Her tears dripped into the washing-up water as she watched Mark through the window, mowing the grass. She wedged the last plate into the dish rack and went to get the tea towel. She'd just put the last fork away in the cutlery drawer when the phone rang again. She rushed to answer it.

'Oh, Hi Tricia,' she said, blowing her nose. 'Got your message but haven't had chance to phone you back yet. Sorry.'

'Oh that's alright `arriet. You `aven`t caught a cold `ave you, `arriet? Only I`ve been blowin` my nose all day, not with a cold, though. With `im! `e`s broken my `eart `arriet! Well `e did but I'm getting over it now. Now I just feel mad with `im. I couldn't wait any longer to tell you. You wouldn't believe it!'

'Oh!' Harriet exclaimed, suddenly feeling better. 'Just a minute Tricia, I'll take this in the front room. Mark's mowing the grass and I can't hear a thing.'

Harriet shot to the lounge and picked up the extension.

'That's better Tricia. I was hoping you'd had a nice time.' Harriet knew that was a lie but didn't know what else to say.

'Nice time? You've got to be joking `arriet,' she screeched.

'Oh dear!' said Harriet. 'What happened Tricia?'

'Well there I was with my own suitcase and that bloody big thing of `is, sitting there, eyes glued to the door waiting for `im to come. I can't tell you `ow many times I looked at that airport clock. Everyone was queuing up to check in and I thought if `e doesn't come soon `e's going to miss the flight! Honestly `arriet I was cursin` `im. I tried to get `im on the moby and all I could get was leave a bloody message. I can tell you `arriet I left `im a few messages alright!'

'Oh gosh,' said Harriet. 'Poor you. So what did you do?'

'Well I didn't know what to do, did I until my moby started ringing.'

'Was it him, then?' Harriet interrupted

'It was `im alright only asking me to go over on my own. Well `e did say an urgent matter had cropped up and `e'd do `is very best to meet me over there. But in any case I was to take the suitcase to that big bank. Er, what was it called now? Swiss Rollards, or something like that, anyway I know it reminded me of a cake. Bloody cheek of `im `arriet, my arm was already droppin` off `umpin` it round the airport!'

'Did you know where to find it Tricia?' Harriet enquired starting to feel very uncomfortable.

'No, I didn't `ave a clue! That's what I told `im and `e said I would be met at the airport by Johansson and he would take me straight there. So I said to `im, well I didn't so much as say, I shouted, "So what's inside this bloody thing that's makin` it so `eavy?" I told `im my arm was droppin` off, `arriet and there was me thinking there was a lovely present in it! I dreamed about that all the night before. I dreamed he'd taken me in his arms and then opened the case to give me such a beautiful matching set. All diamonds and emeralds. I should be so lucky `arriet. I didn't even get to see in the bloody thing!'

'Gosh,' said Harriet, 'what did you do then?'

'Well, I `ad to go didn't I? I plonked both cases on that thing, that belt thing; ooh I can't remember what you call it. Anyway they disappeared whilst I was strugglin` to get my passport out at the same time as I was trying to give my ticket in. I was glad to see the back of that `eavy thing I can tell you! My arm's never been the same. Anyway I got on the plane and thought just my luck for this thing to crash, but I'm glad to say it didn't, nor did the one on the way back, I'm glad to say again! You can never be sure about these things can you `arriet?'

'No, no of course not. So was Johansson there to meet you?'

'It's a bloody good job `e was, I can tell you. `e was standin` right by the bit where the cases came off the belt holdin` up a big brown round board with his name chalked on in white. `e had that many little white dots on it I thought it just looked like a haggis `arriet. You know, where those bits of white, is it fat or suet, just sort of stick up a bit under the skin?'

149

'Oh yes, I know. He was probably trying to make it stand out so you wouldn't miss him.'

'Miss `im!' shouted Tricia. 'Miss `im! I'm tellin` you `arriet he was as big as two sideboards stuck together! I was really scared to get in the car with `im. Anyway he took me to the bank and gave me a sealed envelope to hand in with the suitcase. So I said to `im to keep hold of mine while I put some more make-up on so as not to get them mixed up. It wouldn't `ave done for me to `ave no clean knickers in the morning would it?'

'Certainly not!' agreed Harriet. 'How did you get to your hotel then?'

'Well good job `e'd been told to wait for me because I didn't have a clue where I was. Anyway I only `ad to push those big wooden doors open and someone took it all off me before I even got to the counter. You couldn't see me for dust getting` out of there, I can tell you. All of them speakin` foreign! I couldn't understand a word they said.'

'Johansson spoke English, then?' Harriet asked.

'`e was quite good I 'm surprised to say. We `ad a few problems with some of the things `e was trying to say in the bar at night and when I couldn't understand `im he started using his hands. Then he wouldn't put them away `arriet! Wrong man, I said to myself. Really furious with my boss, well our boss `arriet, I was!'

'I bet!' agreed Harriet. 'Did he manage to get over to you then?'

'Didn't he just `arriet? He arrived at the hotel at precisely 11.55am. I know because I looked at my watch. Good I thought. Now we're going to `ave some quality time together, if you know what I mean!'

Harriet didn't answer.

'Anyway,' continued Tricia, 'not a bit of it! `e tried to charm me a bit but really `e just wanted to know in the shortest possible time whether I'd got that soddin` case into the bank! Mind you, `e did take me in `is arms and give me a kiss before he went half an hour later. Did you get that `arriet? Half an hour later! He left at exactly 12.25. I know because I looked at my watch again. Anyway `e did say I was a star. A star `arriet! What the bloody `ell does that mean? I felt like a bloody star stranded in the sky I can tell you, havin` to kill the next six hours before I could get on the flight home. I was furious with `im! `e could manage to fly there and back in a few hours no doubt and there was I bloomin' well stranded with me pre-booked ticket and I wasn't lookin` forward to gettin` back in that car with Johansson I can tell you! `e wanted to wait in the airport lounge with me until the flight `arriet. I told `im to bugger off! Gosh his `ands were big! Am I glad to be back. I haven't dared tell Bob anything about it. I think `e'd go and land `im one!'

'Land who one Tricia?' Harriet asked, now feeling lost for more appropriate words.

'Both of them,' I would say, 'but it was that Joris Sanderson, and I don't care `ow you say it, that exposed me to all that aggravation. Oh `arriet, `e's left me feeling all of a dither. `e said those lovely words to me. A star is something twinkly and very precious, don't you think `arriet? You know `arriet that man's made me feel like a yo-yo. I'm up and down with `im all the time! Sometimes `e gives me that look of `is, you know, when someone looks as if they can't wait to get you to bed and I just know `e's fallen for me. Other times like now, I'm really left wondering. Just between you and me `arriet, please don't tell Bob, but I 'd decided to give `im my all. Bloody fat chance!'

'Oh Tricia,' began Harriet now feeling extremely uncomfortable. 'I am sorry you've been through all that. I'm sure it will all sort itself out when you get back to work.'

'Well that might be difficult as `e's never `ardly there! The only man I ever get to see down there these days is Tarquin Bridgewater. Do you know `arriet `e's a real pest, always askin` if Joris `as left anythin` for `im. I never know what the bloody `ell `e's talking about! Anyway, sorry `arriet, where was I? Oh yes `im! `e's left me with all the organisin` of that flamin` openin` next weekend. Goodness knows who `e won't be `avin`! It wouldn't surprise me if we saw the Prime Minister there! And `aven't I just got to be doing all the refreshments `arriet. Well after the way `e's treated me they'll all be lucky to get a stick with a sausage on the end…up their bums!'

Harriet exploded with a fit of the giggles. 'Good job we can laugh,' she said. 'Anyway why don't you let me give you a hand with the food?'

'Oooh that would be brilliant `arriet. I'll pop round and we'll go through it together shall we?'

'That's fine by me. If you see the car on the drive, just call in.'

'Thanks for listening `arriet!' said Tricia. 'You're a real mate. Must go Bob's just come in.'

'Bye Tricia,' said Harriet. 'Thanks for phoning!'

A bemused Harriet put the phone down. She tried to stop herself from feeling pleased Tricia hadn't been able to advance her claim on Mr. Sanderson, although she felt for her, she was fighting for her own rights to have him all to herself. She needed to unravel just where Mr. Sanderson was at with Tricia. She tried to convince herself that *she* was the one he'd actually *chosen* to be with. 'He could so easily have flown out with her but he was doing his utmost to try to give *me* a lift,' she thought. 'But he did say he was going down that way so maybe for some reason he needed to be on the ship. No, no, that would be much too much of a coincidence. He definitely wanted to be with *me*.'

Harriet struggled trying to piece it all together.

'So he left the ship after breakfast. He must have been taking that taxi to the airport. I suppose it would make it about right him getting there at lunchtime. But he only stayed half an hour, so then where would he have gone? He had to get back down to Southampton today to pick up his car, so where would he have gone from Switzerland?' An uncomfortable thought crossed her mind. She suddenly remembered the message from Bryce Rae Roberts. She looked around her. 'Oh no, not here! Not viewing this with Belinda Oxfordshire, I hope.'

She scratched her head.

'No, he's made a mistake, he doesn't even know her. Definitely not! And giving Tricia the eye indeed, kissing her and calling her a star!'

Then all he'd said to her came to mind. 'Our perfect day, Harriet.' She could afford to give a little to Tricia.

She went back into the kitchen and suddenly noticed she'd left the phone off the hook in the hall when she'd shot into the front room. She quickly replaced it. She couldn't hear Mark mowing any more and she'd hoped he hadn't overheard.

'Oh Hat,' he called, as he opened the back door. 'Did Tricia say Bob was in?'

'Yes,' Harriet replied, her heart sinking. 'Tricia's just gone off the phone. She heard him coming in.'

'Oh good, I'm just going round to pick up the winch. I want to go down to the club tomorrow, and I'll need it.'

'What now?' said Harriet. 'He'll be having his dinner.'

'Oh it won't take a tick. See you in a minute,' he said, kissing her cheek as he picked up his car keys.

'I think I'll give the girls a call while you're out,' Harriet said. 'I need to know just when they're coming up for that grand opening. I hope the lads will stay as well. We can all bung up for a couple of days, can't we?'

'No we bloody can't!' said Mark. 'It's bad enough having to ingratiate ourselves with that lard ball without having to listen to it five-fold! Just keep shtum Harriet.'

Fortunately for Mark both phone calls revealed that all the expenses were on Starboard Marine North West and Tristan and Sebastian had invited the girls to join them at their hotel for the weekend. Harriet felt very disappointed. Her babies would rather be in a hotel than at home. She hoped it had nothing to do with her inebriated state last time they were up. Harriet felt by now they were probably both well and truly ashamed of their mother.

She sat down in the lounge and the cat jumped up onto her lap. 'Pepper, if you could talk would you still keep my secret?' she asked stroking its black velvety nose. She pushed her little head hard into Harriet's hand.

'Of course I still love Mark,' she said, 'but this feeling is something different. Just imagine there was a huge black male panther living next door and it oozed charm, intelligence and good looks. In fact it had everything a little female cat like you could ever dream of and all the other lady cats around fancied it. What would you do?'

The cat turned on her lap to face her.

'This is uncanny,' Harriet thought. 'I swear she can understand every word.'

'Not fettered by convention you'd be off like a shot, wouldn't you?'

The cat started to purr very loudly.

'Well, that's exactly how I feel. That man has utterly and completely taken me over. I would do absolutely anything for him. He is just the most adorable hunk of male anyone could ever dream of! Oh why can't he make it tomorrow night?'

Pepper yawned and reversed herself again as if she was starting to get bored with Harriet.

'It's no good yawning at me,' Harriet said, 'you were the one that interrupted us, remember? If you hadn't leapt on top of us we'd have well and truly been an item. Well I think we would.'

The cat dug its claws into her knees and started a rhythmical exchange, which was both flattering and painful at the same time.

'Well I'm not fettered by convention either you know,' Harriet suddenly declared. 'I'm as free as you are. I'm not married. Mark's had his chance!' She took a deep breath.

'Anyway what about your secret? You've got one big secret haven't you? Just how did you get home? Wait 'til I tell Molly!'

The cat suddenly jumped off her knee.

Chapter 41

The next morning Harriet and Mark woke to the cat nuzzling between them. They could feel her little wet tongue moving from one to the other in long sweeping licks down each of their cheeks.

'What's this all about then Pepper?' said Mark, yawning and stretching as he started to come to.

Harriet rubbed her eyes. 'Soft cat! Just leave him alone so he can get out of bed and make a cup of tea.'

'She's obviously missed us,' said Mark, ignoring Harriet's comment. 'Was she alright when you got back Hat? You did remember to leave her some food didn't you?'

The cat stood up on Mark's stomach and started wagging its tail back and forth.

'No Hat. Look she's wagging her tail to say no.'

'Oh don't be so ridiculous Mark! I'm going to make the tea.'

The cat followed Harriet down stairs and persistently rubbed against her legs until she was forced to feed her.

'OK, OK, I was going to do it while the kettle was boiling,' she said, feeling obliged to offer it an explanation. She reached for the tin and turned away while she opened it. Harriet couldn't stand the smell of cat food. Then she filled the kettle and stood on the cold kitchen floor with her arms wrapped around her waiting for it to boil. She thought she heard the paper come through the letter box. 'That's a bit early. It's the school holidays,' she thought. Then she remembered this new kid had told her he'd rather be up and out so he could enjoy the rest of the day.

The kettle boiled and Harriet made the tea. The cat returned to her ankles whilst she still had the bottle of milk in her hand. 'Oh sorry Pepper,' she said, now distinctly feeling the cat had some kind of power over her. 'Let me get your saucer.' Over full, she wobbled it to the floor.

'I'm off, I'll just get the paper and then I'm back to bed.' The disinterested cat continued licking her milk.

Harriet went to the door but couldn't see anything on the floor. 'That's strange,' she said to herself, looking down again. Then at the very foot of the door on the mat she noticed two buttercups. Her heart leapt! 'There's only one way they'd get there!' She bent down and picked them up. She held them close to her chest and then floated in a dream back to the kitchen to put them in water. She hid them on top of the filing cabinet in the cupboard under the stairs. Harriet was in heaven again.

'Tea, Mark,' she announced as she finally lay the tray on the dressing table.

'No paper, Hat? I thought I heard it.'

'So did I, but it wasn't there when I looked.'

'Maybe he put the wrong one in and then pulled it out quick,' Mark said. 'Are all fourteen year old lads thick, or do we somehow attract them?'

'Well he's not thick enough to want to lie in bed during the holidays,' said Harriet as she put Mark's tea down by the bed and looked at the clock. 'It might be just a bit early even for him, though. Don't worry, it'll come.'

Harriet got back into bed, smiling. She was floating on air again. The reassurance that had just dropped through the letterbox was oh so sweet. 'Fancy him coming here, this early in the morning to do that,' she thought. Harriet couldn't get over it. 'He's so romantic!'

She looked across to Mark, still smiling. 'In a million years you'd never dream of doing that,' she said to herself.

'You look like the cat that's got the cream Harriet. Pleased to see your mood's improved.'

'Oh yes, sorry Mark,' she said. 'It's just that Pepper's been very demanding since we got back. Sometimes I think I come a poor second.'

'What a load of old rubbish!' grinned Mark. 'Didn't you get my presents then?'

'What presents?' asked Harriet, puzzled.

'You must have seen them when you went to get the paper.'

'No there wasn't anything there,' replied Harriet, her mind focussing on at least a small carrier bag housing some coloured tissue paper with something nice inside it.

'I posted you two buttercups through the letterbox last night when I'd finished cutting the grass. My romantic gesture was obviously wasted on you Hat!'

'I'd better go and put them in water then,' she said trying to suppress her fury as she jumped out of bed.

She shot down the stairs, went to the front door and then marched back to the kitchen and ran the tap. She retrieved them from the cupboard and placed them on the window sill.

'Thanks a bunch Mark!' she fumed to herself. 'How could I have been so stupid? As if Mr. Sanderson's got the time to do things like that. I wonder what Mark's playing at?'

Harriet heard the letter box go again. 'That's got to be the bloody paper this time!' she thought.

'Sorry about that, you nearly got the wrong one before.'

She could just hear the lad's voice through the letter box as she pulled it out. She took it up to Mark, resisting the urge to fling it at him.

'Why did you do that then?' she asked.

'I did it because I love you Hat,' replied Mark. 'Don't ever forget it.'

'I know!' she said as she got back into bed, her anger rapidly giving way to despair.

'And what about you Hat?'

Harriet searched her soul for the truth. 'Well of course I do.'

'Are you sure about that Hat?' Mark questioned putting his arm around her.

'I'm sure,' Harriet answered, 'I've loved you for a long time now.'

'You make it sound like a duty, Hat, like you'd love your granny!'

'Well, I must admit, we have known more exciting times.'

'But that's life, isn't it Hat? The thrill of the chase soon evaporates. Everything settles down to a reasonable, workable equilibrium.'

'Well you haven't exactly caught me yet, have you Mark? If I'm still being chased I'm certainly not finding it very thrilling. Maybe you should stake your claim now, before anyone else does!'

'Meaning?' said Mark, pulling her closer to him.

'Meaning we're still not married. Meaning I'm still single because you can't bring yourself to commit. Meaning if someone else came along and I found him completely irresistible and he felt the same way about me, of course, then I am completely free, like the cat, to do my own thing. Unless you want to make an honest woman of me!'

'Make an honest woman of you Hat? Impossible! Anyway don't we beat the tax man living in sin?'

'No we bloody don't!' exclaimed Harriet. 'You can't use that one anymore!'

'Come here Hat,' said Mark pulling her back towards him. 'We stay together precisely because we do love each other. We don't need to be tied by a bit of paper. You see if that makes any difference to Bob and Tricia in the end. We'll still be together long after they've divorced.'

'And what makes you think they're going to get divorced?' Harriet asked, wondering just how much he'd heard of last night's conversation.

'You should remember to put the phone down Hat when you take the call in the lounge. She was squawking and warbling on about that lard ball non-stop. I couldn't help but hear.'

Harriet gave him a sideways look.

'I am allowed to come back in to wash my hands after mowing the lawn, aren't I?'

'Of course you are,' declared Harriet, stretching her arms. It was definitely time to get up.

'Hat are you doing a wash today?' said Mark on the way out of the bathroom. 'I'd like my sweater back for tonight. I can't think why you dumped it in the bin in the first place. It wasn't even dirty!'

'OK, OK, point taken. You can have it back if you like, now!'

'Not after it's been sitting in there with all that lot, thank you,' objected Mark. Harriet, now dressed, stomped past him and came back with the bin in both hands.

'You shall have your sweater for Melissa.'

'Oh, you should talk!' Mark retorted.

'Meaning?'

'Meaning exactly that. There's something different about you Hat.'

'No!' exclaimed Harriet. 'It's just your imagination. Maybe you're trying to make yourself feel better about something?'

'And you're not even trying. Don't forget to give the estate agents a call.'

With breakfast over, Harriet went into the hall and picked up the phone. She decided there and then she wouldn't enquire as to exactly who came to view the house. 'No point,' she reassured herself. 'They've obviously got mixed up.'

Harriet wanted to leave it, just there.

'Good morning,' she said, 'thanks for the message. How did the second viewing go then?'

Harriet switched her weight to the other foot while she waited for the 'Just a minute, I'm only here on a Thursday and Friday' girl to get the file.

'Any luck?' mouthed Mark as he brushed past Harriet on his way to the front door.

'Oh Hello. The asking price? We've been offered the asking price? Right! That certainly is good news. No, I don't think we'll have any problems with that. Thank you very much indeed.'

Mark stopped in his tracks.

'She wants it. We've got a buyer at last!' exclaimed Harriet. 'Even if it is *her*!'

Harriet was unable to contain her delight.

Mark flung his arms around her and almost lifted her off the floor as he swirled her round in the narrow hall.

'Great news Hat! It's just what we both need, a new start.'

'Maybe you're right, Mark,' agreed Harriet, burying her head in his neck, 'maybe things have just got on top of us lately.'

'If we can find the right place then you should be able to give up work Hat. We might just get you pregnant once you're not having to worry about that dump!'

'But I can't be an unmarried mother again Mark. Not at my age!'

'Leave that one with me Hat. Just leave it with me for the moment,' said Mark kissing her lightly on her lips.

Harriet went back to the kitchen and without sorting it loaded all the washing into the machine. 'This is reality,' she told herself as she pushed the door hard in order to close it on the overloaded quick wash cycle. She thought about Mr. Sanderson and how magical it had all been. 'But he can't make it tonight.' Then she thought about Tricia, 'I wonder just how many there are of us out there feeling like this about him? Not only are those disagreeable girls intent on making a beeline for him but my mother, my own mother's even succumbed. She hasn't even seen him! Not to mention Molly. This is a hopeless case. The sooner I get out of that school the better!'

She looked at the calendar. The month had now changed. She realised she needed to turn over the picture of Switzerland, with its beautiful spring flowers. 'That's it.' she thought. 'It was nothing more than a picture on a calendar.'

She knew she was kidding herself. 'No, I can't give up on all we've just had together.' She recalled watching him, so masculine as he flung the car from lane to lane, his strong hand on the gear lever, his head turned, glancing at her, smiling. She felt the same urgent need for him surge through her body. She knew she was helplessly in love but she didn't know where it would take her.

She jumped as her thoughts and feelings were suddenly interrupted by the phone ringing.

'Hello,' she said, hoping against hope it would be *him*.

'No chance,' Harriet groaned to herself as the man's voice turned out to be Mr. Bryce, no less, from the estate agents.

'Oh yes, I returned the message. We're delighted with the news,' said Harriet.

'Pardon? These people turned up out of the blue?' Harriet took a deep breath.

'No, no Mr. Bryce this was a second viewing for Miss Oxfordshire. Pardon? You're saying a Mr. and Mrs. Pendlebury came to see it on Monday and offered the full asking price after just one viewing? I wasn't told that! It was Mr. Roberts that left the message.'

'I don't think the error would be of Mr. Roberts' making Mrs. Glover.' came the swift response.

'What about Miss Oxfordshire then?'

Harriet shoved the cat into the kitchen with her foot and closed the door on it as she listened to Mr. Bryce.

'Oh, so she wanted to discuss it with her partner but she felt sure they would definitely come back with an offer. Did you tell her she was too late?'

Harriet felt a huge sense of satisfaction that Belinda Oxfordshire had been pipped at the post.

'Mrs. Glover, we never turn away potential buyers. These are exceedingly early days. Should Miss Oxfordshire come back to us we'll listen to all she has to say. They are cash buyers Mrs. Glover whereas Mr. and Mrs. Pendlebury are in a very long chain. Leave the decisions to us Mrs. Glover, that's what you're paying us for!' Harriet heard Mr. Bryce put the phone down.

'Well!' she declared out loud.

Mark came back into the hall. 'What's up now Hat?'

'Well that was Mr. Bryce on the phone. I thought that Thursday and Friday girl was talking about Mz Oxfordshire, but it seems that the offer came from a Mr. and Mrs. Pendlebury who viewed it on Monday, but we're supposed to wait while Belinda Oxfordshire and her partner chew it over because they're cash buyers. But, and just listen to this! We're not allowed to have any say in it as Mr. Bryce will decide who's best to go with.'

'Well, he must have given a good reason,' declared Mark, face straight.

'Only that the Pendleburys are in a long chain and Ms Oxfordshire and her partner are cash buyers,' retorted Harriet.

'Sounds like a good reason to me Hat. Just leave it for a while and we'll see how it goes.'

'Well, as far as we're concerned we accepted the offer this morning. I'd rather not sell to Belinda Oxfordshire if we don't have to. I wouldn't trust that Mr. Bryce or any of them in that office as far as I could throw them.'

'Leave it be Hat. We're going to have to go along with it. After all that's what we pay them for.'

'Huh,' said Harriet, 'you sound just like him!' She stomped off to the kitchen with Mark close behind.

'Washing's finished!' Mark grinned as he opened the back door.

Harriet ignored him. The orange light looked at her. She pressed the button and out it went. Then she opened the door and let the whole lot fall into her lap. On her knees she struggled to the tumble dryer and threw it all in.

'I've never heard so much fuss about a bloody jumper!' she moaned to herself.

Harriet returned to the hall and stood staring at the phone, willing it to ring.

'He can't just do this to me,' she said to herself, 'he can't leave me in pieces like this.'

'What's up Hat?' declared Mark as he swung open the kitchen door. 'Practising being a statue? We'll have to paint your face grey as well as those old clothes you're wearing and you can stand outside Starboard Marine North West on Saturday with a collection tin and make us a fortune!'

'What are you talking about now, Mark?' declared a very irritated Harriet.

'Oh, you know what I mean. Actually we saw a couple of those in Stratford. Differing versions of Shakespeare. What a laugh! You should have seen the kids jump when they finally flickered an eyelid.'

'And when did you go to Stratford, Mark?' Harriet queried.

'Oh, it was just on the way back. We decided to do a bit of a detour before picking up the motorway.'

'Oh, I see!' said Harriet, her hackles beginning to rise.

'What do you see exactly Hat?' demanded Mark starting to sound annoyed.

'You didn't tell me you'd been jollying all over the place.'

'And what haven't *you* told me about *your* trip, Harriet? I wouldn't mind knowing all of the rest.'

Harriet looked down. It was definitely time to keep quiet.

'I'm off to the sailing club. I'll get a bite of lunch there. See you later Hat.'

Harriet didn't have time to reply. She heard him close the front door behind him.

She went back into the kitchen and watched the tumble drier struggling to turn its heavy wet load round and round. She couldn't believe how quickly the ecstasy of yesterday had now turned. The desire to be with him now saturated her in longing, frustration, anger and irritation.

She looked down at her clothes. 'What did Mark mean by "those old clothes"? I wonder how smart Melissa the green looked all the time they were away.' She rolled her sleeves up, opened the back door and sauntered around the garden. She looked across to the lilac bush. 'Not my favourite day,' she thought. 'It's pay back time.'

Harriet was completely demotivated. She turned the television on and sat down with a pen and paper in an attempt to make some kind of plan for the buffet on Saturday. 'Why should I be doing this for him? I 'll do it to help Tricia out but that's all. It's certainly not for him,' she tried to convince herself. 'In fact, as soon as I've given Tricia a hand with it all, I'm off. He can have every female there swooning over him, but I won't be one of them!' she vowed.

Harriet went back into the kitchen and watched the drum throwing its lightening load round and round. She turned the knob back to 120 minutes. 'Must make sure this precious jumper is nice and dry for Melissa,' she said to herself. She looked across at the two buttercups in the small glass of water on the window sill and then went into the understairs cupboard in the hall to her handbag hanging on the hook. She undid the zip and took out her address book, opening it at the last page. Her fingers touched the buttercups and she swallowed hard as a huge lump came into her throat. In the dark cupboard she brushed the first gathering of tears away. 'My life is such a mess!' she cried to herself. In the comfort of her home, in the comfort of her life, Harriet knew she had everything. Knew she had nothing. 'That man. That man! What can I do? What should I do? He's turned my world upside down and inside out!'

She sniffed the tears back and returned to the kitchen. 'I'm a wet rag in the tumble drier of life. Only he's turned the heat off. I'll never be anything else.'

Her profound thoughts were suddenly interrupted by the cat shooting in through the cat flap.

'And you're no bloody help! Who knows where we'd be now if you hadn't gate-crashed the party.'

The cat did a smart about turn and shot out again.

Harriet opened the back door, she hadn't finished with it yet.

'Just stay out there all day and all night will you? For the rest of your life would be even better. That's if you've got a rest of your life. I haven't decided what I'm going to do to you yet you interfering old busybody!' Harriet, unaware her voice had become louder stopped abruptly as she felt a tap on her shoulder. She turned to see Mr. Sanderson beaming at her.

'Oh golly!' she exclaimed quickly brushing away the residue of tears from her eyes. 'Where did *you* come from?'

'I tried the bell but you obviously didn't hear it because you were out here shouting at some unfortunate soul!' Mr. Sanderson laughed.

'It's the cat. I was shouting at the cat.'

'Obviously did the trick Harriet. It's nowhere to be seen!'

'Let's hope it's finally got the message then,' she said trying to pluck up the courage to look him straight in the eyes.

'Are you trying to lose someone else's cat for them now, Harriet?' He gave her a mischievous grin.

'I'd rather not talk about cats, if you don't mind Mr. Sanderson.'

'I do hope you're not going to shout at me like that Harriet,' he said, watching her face go very red indeed. 'Shall we step inside a moment?'

Mr. Sanderson pushed open the door and Harriet, dumbfounded, followed him into the kitchen.

'Your better-half not back yet, Harriet?' he enquired.

'Er no. Er, I mean yes. He came back yesterday. He answered your call I think.'

'Ah yes, of course he did. Sorry about that Harriet. These things crop up you know.'

'I'm sure they do Mr. Sanderson,' replied Harriet, rolling up her sleeves and hoping there was no trace of tears left on her face. 'Mark's gone down to the club for the rest of the day.'

He nodded and smiled and then looked towards the window sill at the two buttercups sitting in the water filled glass.

'Sweet memories Harriet!' he declared.

'Just memories?' replied Harriet, all her resolve rapidly disintegrating. For the moment she was most grateful that Mark had picked them. She couldn't bear the thought of Mr. Sanderson knowing his had ended up in her glass of red wine.

'Trust me Harriet. There will be a time for us.' He moved forward, taking her gently into his arms. Harriet felt the warmth of his soft woollen sweater against her cheek. She looked up at him and then felt the fullness of his open lips softly resting on hers for the briefest of moments. Then her legs weakened as he pressed his kisses deeper and deeper, forcing her lips apart, sending her head spinning.

'Harriet, my darling, please trust me. I know it's unfair asking you to wait, but there are so many complications in my life. I've got to get them sorted before I can make the change of direction I want.'

He relaxed his grip, took her by the shoulders and looked straight into her eyes. She watched his eyes twinkle and sparkle before she drowned helplessly in their unparalleled shade of deep, clear blue.

'I do trust you. For as long as it takes I'll always trust you,' Harriet whispered.

Mr. Sanderson stood back, shot her a uniquely serious glance and then smiled.

'I hope my bow tie isn't in there,' he said pointing to the tumble drier, a huge grin breaking across his face.

'In there!' exclaimed Harriet. 'Why should it be in there?'

'Precisely Harriet,' he said. 'So do you know where it is Miss Glover? I'll need it tonight!' He started to laugh at the perplexed look on her face.

'Oh of course, you left it in my cabin! I remember packing it away now. I'll just go and have a look.'

Harriet shot upstairs. She riffled through the drawers but couldn't find it anywhere. Then she suddenly remembered emptying her whole case into the linen bin. 'What am I going to do now?' she thought, embarrassed at having to fish it out of the tumble dryer after all. She suddenly had an idea and shot downstairs.

'Er, I think I know where it is but I'll just need a minute or two to get it. It's just about lunch time so how about I make us both a sandwich and I'll find it while the kettle's boiling.'

'Sounds good to me,' Mr. Sanderson declared as Harriet ushered him into the lounge.

'There, the television's still on. You can watch that while you're waiting if you like. I won't be a minute,' said Harriet.

Harriet closed the door behind her, shot into the kitchen and pulled the tumble drier door open. She tugged at all the washing until it landed on the kitchen floor in one large over-dried ball. She scrambled into the middle and started untwisting sleeves and legs from knickers and bras. Then she spotted the end of a black thin stringy thing refusing to budge from its nesting place. Harriet gave a huge pull and fell backwards as it shot out, clinging for dear life to her newest skimpy bra. Just as she was about to unravel it, the kitchen door opened. She scrambled to her feet.

'Ah you've found it Harriet! What on earth have you done to it? What's that it's obviously become so attached to?'

Harriet blushed.

'Harriet, it looks like a piece of stringy black liquorice. What on earth have you done to it?' Mr. Sanderson declared, taking it from her and dangling the inseparable items over her head.

'I'm terribly sorry, Mr. Sanderson.' Harriet still scarlet, looked down at the floor. 'I'll get you another one. I promise!'

'Not in time for this evening Miss Glover. Are you trying to sabotage my night out?'

In a flash he was smiling and Harriet breathed a huge sigh of relief.

'No, I mean it, I really will get you another one. I am really sorry.'

'In that case I feel duty bound to get you another one of these,' he declared. 'Unfortunately the colour's run. I hope the rest of your washing hasn't turned black, Harriet.'

Harriet had been too flustered to notice. She watched him push the entangled bra and bow tie into his pocket.

'We'll just have to down-market a bit Harriet. I'll pick you up at seven.'

'What about lunch Mr. Sanderson?' asked Harriet as he began to open the back door.

'Another time, thanks, Harriet. We'll do dinner this evening.'

With that, he was gone.

Harriet could hardly believe he'd been and gone. Her head was in a complete spin. 'Now I really do feel like I've been in there!' she said to herself picking up all the washing from the floor. She wasn't feeling like a wet rag anymore, though. She was totally elated.

'Trust him? I'd trust him to the ends of the earth.'

She recalled being taken in his arms. 'Oh that kiss. Boy, does he know how to kiss!' Harriet swooned to herself as the cat's nose cautioned its way through the cat flap.

'OK, it's OK to come in. I absolutely forgive you,' she said to it as it finally came through. 'There's just nothing you can do to ruin our relationship now. Understand?'

For a couple of moments the cat meowed round her legs and then shot into the lounge.

Harriet popped the kettle on and made a quick sandwich. 'This will be the best lunch I've ever had,' she said to the cat as it reappeared. 'Well, apart from yesterday's that is, with him. Oh go on then, you can have something too.' She proceeded to sprinkle some dry cat food onto a saucer and pushed it under its nose. 'Oh and some milk. Now please leave me alone and let me dream in peace.' The cat did just that.

Harriet settled down to the news with her lunch beside her feeling so very happy. She wondered why he was able to keep the dinner date after all. Then she decided it didn't matter. All that mattered was that she was going to be with *him*. She sat gazing at the television, unable and unwilling to concentrate as the usual batch of political mud slinging came to an end.

'And finally,' she heard the newsreader say, 'is this the most generous tip ever recorded for a cruise liner?'

Harriet pricked up her ears. 'The Christiana docked in Southampton yesterday with a special surprise onboard for Charles Ormerod, one of the ship's stewards. Apparently one very generous passenger left him a tip of three thousand pounds in gratitude for performing a very special service to her. Intrigued? So are we! We hope to bring you more on this story as it unfolds. Watch this space!'

Harriet went white and absolutely sick.

'Oh no!' she said out loud. 'I completely forgot about the money. I forgot to leave him a tip, that was the envelope for it!'

She sat dazed, staring at the screen as the weather forecast started.

'Oh no, what am I going to do now?'

She thanked her lucky stars they hadn't both been there together, watching it.

'At least *he* won't have seen it. I just hope he doesn't pick it up on the evening news.' Harriet's stomach started churning over and over.

'How could I have been so stupid?' she asked herself again and again. 'Just when I thought the problem was solved. Wherever am I going to get three thousand pounds from, now?'

The thought of confessing all to Mr. Sanderson was a complete no no. She could see their newly cemented relationship disintegrating before her eyes.

'And Mark. What if he gets to hear about it? Oh, I've never been in such a mess!' She panicked. She only hoped Charles would keep quiet. He still thought she was pregnant.

The cat, licking its lips, sauntered in, sat beside her and waggled its bottom. It usually did when it was about to leap onto somebody's lap.

'Oh no you don't!' declared Harriet, pulling her half-eaten plate of sandwiches towards her. 'If it hadn't been for you driving me to distraction I would most certainly have remembered to pick it up.'

In her heart Harriet knew that this was untrue. She began to feel completely irresponsible.

'That man, he's succeeded in draining every ounce of common sense I ever had out of me!' she balled at the cat. 'You certainly didn't help though. The next thing I know there'll be another runner at the end of the news wanting to know who was responsible for the stowaway cat!'

Harriet decided it was probably better not to watch the television for a few days. Her head started to hurt as she stormed through the possible consequences of her folly.

Done thinking, Harriet decided to give Tricia a call. 'Can you come round?'

'Great minds think alike `arriet! I was on my way. Oh `arriet, guess who's just been to see me?'

'Who?' asked Harriet nervously.

'Ooh that gorgeous hunk of a man! I was just watching the television with my Cornish pasty and the doorbell went just when the news finished. Well I say finished but it was almost finished because `e came in and wouldn't talk to me `til `e'd finished staring at this thing that was on about a three thousand pound tip being left to some steward or other on a ship that had docked in Southampton yesterday. Ooh it wasn't you by any chance, was it `arriet? Didn't you come back there yesterday?'

Harriet nearly choked.

'Only joking `arriet! It must have been somebody really rich like Tarquin Bridgwater I would say! Anyway he stood there just staring at it with all this stuff to give me about Saturday in his `ands.'

Harriet was speechless.

'I said `ave you come to see me or `as your own telly broken down or something. So he said "Sorry Tricia!" and shoved the lot at me. Then, and this is definitely the best bit, he put his arm right round my waist and kissed me on the cheek. Then he said "What a scatterbrain!" I said I `ope you're not talking about me. "No, no!" he said "I can't believe anyone would be so stupid as to do that!"

Do you know `arriet he looked absolutely furious. Anyone would think it was `is money that had been given away. Then he smiled that smile and said he'd pop in and see me at work tomorrow. Ooh `arriet! I can `ardly wait! Anyway it's a bit silly me talking like this as it's costing money and I'll be round in a tick. We don't really want you to be too scared to look at your bill do we? Ooh, isn't that funny `arriet? Good job your Mark's not called Bill isn't it, `arriet? See you soon!'

Harriet didn't have time to say goodbye. Tricia just went. She couldn't believe that Mr. Sanderson had just seen it all, especially standing next to *her*.

'And what was he doing putting his arm round her and kissing her on the cheek when he'd just told me to trust him?' Harriet fumed to herself. 'A scatterbrain and stupid! So that's what he really thinks of me. Bloody cheek!

Well, he needn't think I'm dining with him this evening!' she vowed to herself.

Harriet just had time to tidy up and try to recover herself when the doorbell went.

'Hi Tricia,' she said.

'Hi 'arriet!' replied Tricia. 'It's really good to see you again. Thank you so much for listening to me yesterday. I came off the phone thinking poor 'arriet having to listen to me moaning. But there you are! I'm just like a yo-yo! I'm up again now! The difference between two phone calls, eh 'arriet!'

Harriet just about managed a smile. 'You're up and I'm down. *Well* down,' she thought as she stepped aside to let Tricia in.

'Just look at this lot 'e's given me 'arriet. I thought I'd bring it with me so we can go through it in case it says anything about when 'e wants the refreshments to be served. I expect 'e wants a champagne reception maybe with those canary things 'arriet.'

'You mean canapés Tricia,' said Harriet, feeling utterly and totally drained.

'Oh yes that's it. You are clever 'arriet! I can't think why 'e's fallen for me, I'm just not of 'is calliper at all.'

This time Harriet couldn't be bothered. Besides she knew it was not very polite to correct other people's malapropisms. She tried to sit on her sense of irritation as she allowed the worry of her complete folly to take over. Then she suddenly felt sorry for her. 'Poor Tricia,' she thought as she watched her tottering into the lounge. 'She could never have fancied Mark that much if she's so smitten with Joris Sanderson.' A sense of relief overcame her followed by a huge pang of jealousy. 'She's stealing my dreams instead now!'

They sat down together and Tricia proceeded to open the file sending a flutter of loose sheets to the floor.

Harriet bent down to pick them up. 'Ah this looks like it might be the order of the day,' she said as she popped it on top and passed them all over to her.

'Thanks ever so much 'arriet,' smiled Tricia. She sat back on the sofa assuming a more comfortable reading position.

'Just a minute 'arriet! What's 'e saying 'ere? I don't believe it! "The Mayor and dignitaries of the Borough will welcome the Prime Minister who will be escorted by Joris Sanderson and Belinda Oxfordshire." What's he doin' with another woman on 'is arm? I'm supposed to be the one 'e fancies!'

Harriet was shocked. 'Let's have a read Tricia,' she demanded impatiently. Harriet's jaw dropped as she read it. 'Bloody Belinda Oxfordshire! What's she doing there?'

'Eh steady on 'arriet. You don't know 'er do you?'

'No, I don't actually know her but she's been to see this a couple of times. What the heck has *she* got to do with *him*?'

'Been to see what 'arriet? Oh do tell me!' pleaded Tricia.

'The house, you know, a viewing! We think she and her partner want to buy it. Well, that's if they ever get round to making their minds up.'

'Who's her bloody partner then?' declared Tricia suddenly feeling very outraged. 'It better not bloody well be `im I can tell you!'

Harriet went white and then she suddenly recalled the name Ted with great relief.

'No Tricia, I seem to recall her referring to a Ted. Yes she definitely said Ted.'

'Oh thank goodness for that. I just don't think I could cope with `im 'aving anyone else in his life!'

Harriet nodded in agreement whilst frantically trying to work out the connection.

'Just a minute Tricia, I think I remember her saying something about them expanding their business and floating it on the stock exchange. She said it was a very appropriate metaphor.'

'Metaphor? What's that then?' enquired Tricia looking very blank.

'Oh it's when you describe something using something else.'

'You what `arriet? I don't get what you mean.' said Tricia, screwing her face up.

'Floating, floating on the stock exchange as in boats float! She's obviously something to do with the business,' said Harriet.

'Oh, I see and she wants to buy your house? Not bloody likely `arriet! You're not going to sell it to `er are you?'

'Not bloody likely!' agreed Harriet. 'We've already had an offer from another couple and I'm going to make sure we go with them. Oh no, I've just remembered!'

'Remembered? Remembered what `arriet? Go on tell me. I `ope you're not remembering something else to take my Joris away from me,' panicked Tricia.

'Well,' began Harriet, 'there was a message from the estate agents when I got back saying "With regard to Miss Oxfordshire and Mr. Sanderson's second viewing." Oh don't tell me he hadn't made a mistake after all.'

'What exactly do you mean `arriet? Made a mistake?'

'Well, Mr. Sanderson bought the premises for Starboard Marine North West through the same agent and I thought they were getting their wires crossed,' Harriet explained.

'So they both came to see it together while you were away. What a bloody cheek `arriet! Didn't `e even tell you? And what about that bear fellow she mentioned? Oh what was his name now? Ted. That's it, Teddy bear! Trust me to remember the wrong bit. Where was `e then if `e's supposed to be `er soddin` partner? Oh `arriet I've waited all my life, well ever since I first got interested in boys, I suppose I was about twelve. Anyway I've waited since then for the love of my dreams and I've found `im `arriet. I really `ave found `im! `e's taken my heart and everything else away. Oh `arriet, do you know just how I feel?'

'I know just how you feel,' sympathised Harriet, 'and worse,' she thought.

'Well I'm not letting that, come `ere, what's `er name again?' Tricia reached for the sheet. 'Belinda Oxfordshire. Huh, Belinda Oxfordshire indeed! I'm not letting that one come between us. Our love is just like a little bud `arriet. It's just about to burst into full bloom. She needn't think she's going to blow all the petals away. There `arriet, I think there's a few pretty good metathingys in there, don`t you? Oh what was that bloody word again, `arriet?'

'Metaphor, Tricia. Metaphors,' Harriet reminded her.

'You are such a good friend `arriet!' declared Tricia. 'I can tell that you can really feel my pain. It's all over your face.'

Harriet suddenly felt a surge of affection, guilt and intense jealousy.

'Come on Tricia, we'd better not lose the plot here,' she declared, suddenly pulling herself together in a flash of common sense.

'I `aven't a clue what the plot is `arriet,' Tricia exploded, 'never mind lose it! I went to Switzerland with that bloody big case for `im. `e's no right to be carrying another woman on `is arm, especially as I'm `is little star!' Tricia stood up and stomped her way across the room to the window. 'Just looking to see if I can see `im. `e said something about coming to see you.'

Harriet's heart jumped. 'See me? What now?!' she exclaimed.

'Just a tick `arriet!. Am I getting confused? `e's got me in such a state I can `ardly remember what `e said.'

Harriet took a very deep breath.

'Oh no! Oh yes `arriet! That was it. When I told `im I was going round to yours, `e said on second thoughts would I pass the message on to you that `e would now be spending this evening calculating `is losses.'

'Right,' declared Harriet. 'Thanks for that Tricia.'

'Can't think what `e was goin` on about. If it makes any sense to you `arriet, I'd be surprised,' said Tricia.

Harriet desperately trying to stay calm, shrugged her shoulders and chewed the end of her pen. 'Come on Tricia, back to these refreshments. We'd better make an effort if the Prime Minister's going to be there.'

'Prime Minister, me arse!' angered Tricia. 'I've a good mind to give `em all haggis on a pitchfork and poke `ers right up `er bum!'

Chapter 42

With Mark having popped back only briefly for his sweater, and out all evening, Harriet sat down alongside the cat hoping for some answers to her ongoing dilemma. She didn't know where to start unravelling the threads of fear, anger, passion and jealousy that were entangling her mind. She felt like she had some insidious love virus thrusting its unrelenting pangs of pain through her body which now ached and ached for the only cure she'd just thrown away. 'How could I have been so stupid?' she asked herself over and over. But every attempt at rationalisation simply ended on the bed that night in the ship's cabin.

She pushed the cat off her knee. She curled her arm around her head and buried her face in the cushion. Then the doorbell went.

'Oh no it's him!' she panicked to herself. 'I look a mess!'

The doorbell went again.

'Better get it over with,' she choked, as she smoothed her hair and straightened her clothes.

'Good evening luv,' came a deep, distinctly northern voice through the gap she'd just made opening the front door. 'We're from Internews TV.' With that he pushed his foot into the doorway and thrust a ball of matt, grey fur on the end of a long wire, into Harriet's face. 'Don't try to close the door luv. We're going live in just ten seconds.' Harriet could hear the countdown in the background, ..3, 2, 1!

'What on earth do you want?' she spluttered.

'We wanna congratulate you live for leaving the biggest tip ever on a cruise ship. Oh and of course, we wanna know why?'

Harriet desperately tried to close the door. She could see a gang of people with cameras and wires trailing back to the front slope all leading into a big grey van with 'INTERNEWS TV' plastered on the side.

'Get your bloody big foot out of my front door you swine!' she raged. Then she stamped hard on his toe just as she felt the cat leaping from nowhere onto her right shoulder before launching at the angry face glued to the door's edge. Harriet seized the opportunity and slammed it closed. She put the bolt on and flew to the back door to do the same thing. She ran round the whole house closing all the curtains and just stayed long enough in the bedroom to peep through a crack the two edges of curtain had made before widening out down the radiator. She could just see him nursing his head as he hopped towards the gate. In a flash the drive was cleared and Harriet spotted another man banging something down onto the small blackboard he was holding. Then to her horror she saw the reporter pointing up to the window. He started talking rapidly into his microphone with his left hand first pointing to his head and then his foot. Harriet didn't wait to see any more. Shaking, she flew down the stairs and turned the television on. 'It's our house! Oh my goodness, it's our house!' she said out loud.

'Well once again we apologise for the disruption to our transmission. As you can see we risk life and limb to bring you the hottest of stories! We just wanted to praise her generosity. There's got to be a good reason why this lady won't talk. Watch this space folk. We'll be back! This is Simon Barnes for Internews TV from, 4 The Willows, Crosport.'

Harriet, trembling, turned the television off. Oh how she wished Mark was home and then she was relieved he wasn't. She jumped as she heard the phone ringing. 'I'm not answering that!' she said to herself and promptly switched on the answer phone. She ran upstairs and peered through the same crack in the curtains to see them driving away.

Then the phone rang again. She flew downstairs and heard Tricia's voice through stifled giggles attempting to leave a message. Harriet picked up the receiver.

'Oh `arriet you are there after all, aren't you? `arriet whatever were they doing on your doorstep? They got the wrong person, didn't they?'

Harriet could hear her taking a deep breath. 'Oh just a minute `arriet, I must blow my nose. Oooooh my sides are aching. That was the funniest thing I ever saw in my life. You certainly gave `is toe what for `arriet and the cat….! It was as if you already `ad it there in waiting. Well done `arriet! That got rid of `im alright! Maybe we should take it to Starboard Marine North West on Saturday, we'll hide it in my office behind my one way mirror. It might just go for that Belinda Bear!'

Harriet could hear screeches of laughter down the phone again.

'Oh, but the funniest thing `arriet was just seeing you peeping from the bottom of the curtains in your bedroom window. Do you know that reporter was raging. We're going to `ave to protect you `arriet! Ooh, must go I can `ear Bob coming. Shame `e missed it! Still it might be on the 10 o'clock news. See you Saturday, `arriet!'

Harriet, still shaking, replaced the receiver, hardly aware that she hadn't actually said anything to Tricia. The phone went again. This time she let it run.

'It's Molly, Harriet. That wasn't you on Internews TV was it? I said to Percy surely Harriet didn't leave Charles all that money and was that your cat Harriet? How on earth did it get back? Anyway I'll look forward to hearing from you Harriet. Oh, by the way, you went off with our gorgeous friend, too. Lucky you Harriet! Bye bye for now dear, oh and Percy sends his regards.'

The phone rang again. 'Harriet it's Mummy. Daddy and I are very worried about you. What on earth was that all about? It was your house wasn't it Harriet, only they all look the same in your road. It certainly looked like you, especially when you stamped on that poor man's foot. You had that very same expression on your face when you used to do it to poor James when you were little. I'm not sure he's quite forgiven you. Anyway Harriet phone us just as soon as you can. Daddy and I are very worried.'

Harriet felt her mother's displeasure mingling with both anger and concern. 'Well I didn't ask to be put in this position,' she heard herself arguing back in silent spurts. 'All I need now is for *him* to phone!' Before the sentence was barely finished she jumped as her prediction was fulfilled.

'Not answering Miss Glover?!'

'OH YES I BLOODY AM!' balled Harriet, snatching the receiver from the wall, 'and you can think what you bloody well like. I've actually had it. Do you know that Mr. Sanderson? I've had it with you and the cat and anyone you'd care to name. I actually don't care any more!'

'Not a wise statement, Miss Glover. Have you forgotten just to whom you are speaking?'

'I probably have,' raged Harriet. 'I should've done it long since!'

'Miss Glover, there could be very serious implications arising from this bout of cheap publicity.'

'Cheap publicity?' stormed Harriet. 'As if I asked for any of it!'

'Not the point Miss Glover. It's absolutely imperative that you do not disclose who gave you the money. It goes without saying that you do not say why it was given to you either, of course.'

'Well, I'm not that stupid Mr. Sanderson, I've no intention of speaking to any of them.'

'Good! Now,' Mr. Sanderson snapped, 'I trust you will find some way of squaring this loss with that Bastard woman. I do not need any, I mean any, adverse publicity right now. Do you understand, Miss Glover? And get that damned cat put down before it flies at anyone else!'

Harriet fumed. She heard him bang the phone down. Now she was definitely glad Mark was out. She was strangely relieved. She'd just taken that man out of her life, for good!

She shot upstairs and peered through the crack in the curtains again. 'It's safe now and I don't bloody care if it's not!' she said out loud as she swung open the bedroom curtains. As fast as she'd closed them she flew round the house opening the rest of them. She didn't like being plunged into unaccustomed darkness.

Harriet went off to find the cat. 'Brilliant cat,' she thought. 'She needs rewarding for being able to suss out despicable, horrible men!'

She went to the cupboard and spotted a tin of salmon. 'This shall be yours! Pepper, where are you?'

In a tick the cat like lightning crashed through the cat flap and started nuzzling her legs before trying to clamber up the cupboard door to the worktop.

'Just a minute,' Harriet said. 'Hang on. There. It's all yours now and well deserved too!' Barely able to fend the cat off she just managed to place the saucer on the floor before she heard Mark opening the front door. She jumped. She wasn't expecting him back so soon.

'Hi Hat!' he breezed and then he turned on his heel to peer down at the green flashes lighting up the answer machine in the hall. 'Had a good day then? What on earth have you given the cat now?'

Without waiting for an answer he went to the play button.

'No!' screeched Harriet, 'I've already played them!' With that she double clicked the delete button shoving Mark out of the way as she did so.

'OK Hat. Keep your hair on! All from the lard ball were they?'

'No. Of course they weren't!' declared Harriet. 'I'm just sick of the phone. Every call is a load of hassle at the moment.'

'Load of hassle, Hat? What's been going on?'

'I don't want to talk about it,' she snapped. 'Anyway you're early.'

'Not pleased to see me then Hat?'

'Oh of course I am. You'll never know how pleased I am to see you!' She flung her arms around him and pressed herself very hard into his chest.

'Come on Hat. The cat's making me hungry. Let's go to the Indian takeaway and then pick up a couple of bottles of wine.'

'Brilliant!' said Harriet.

Mark backed the car out and Harriet tried desperately hard to forget the drama on the drive that happened less than half-an-hour ago. She hoped against hope he wouldn't hear of it and was only thankful he was driving home at the time.

'Mark?' she enquired as they set off down the road. 'Mark, why did you come home so early?'

'It wasn't going anywhere Hat.'

'And what about Melissa Scott? Did she go home early too?'

Mark scratched his head. 'We all decided to call it a day Hat. Mel was the only one that wanted to stick with it, as it happened.'

'Mel,' thought Harriet, feeling herself starting to seethe inside. 'I bet she wanted to stick with it! Anyway since when has he been calling her Mel?'

Somehow Harriet managed to refrain from asking the question. She looked across at him. His driving was predictable, safe. It didn't have the flair of Mr. Sanderson's. Harriet was pleased. She felt immediately reassured. Mark's driving could never turn Green Melissa on.

Mark took his left hand off the steering wheel and reached for Harriet's hand. 'Daft bat Hat! We were wasting our time but I came home early because I wanted to be with you. I've missed you Hat!'

'Missed you too,' said Harriet as Mark retrieved his hand to change gear.

'Oh look Mark! There's a parking space right outside the shop. Quick! Go for it!' said Harriet.

'Don't *do* that to me!' Mark replied in a very loud voice. 'I've got a dirty great van up my backside!'

'Oh, too late now, somebody else has pinched it. Now we'll have to walk miles.'

'Oh,' said Mark, 'somebody's just pulled out behind him.' He swung the car into the service road fronting the shops and parked in the newly created space right outside the takeaway. He looked at Harriet and grinned.

Harriet thumped his arm as they got out of the car. 'You get the meals and

I'll pop along to get the wine.'

'Your usual?' called Mark as Harriet marched off. She nodded as she hurried to the end shop on the row.

'He'll be ages in there,' Harriet thought, 'I'll take my time choosing.'

The shop was busy and Harriet pushed the door open to a gathering of excited chatter around the counter. She browsed the reds and then the whites and then decided she would need a basket for the four bottles she intended to buy. She went to the neat stack alongside the counter.

'Excuse me, could I just reach for a basket, please?' Harriet asked as she stretched her arm between the people.

'I'll pass you one love,' said the tall, jolly round faced chap from behind the till. He lifted it over the heads of the growing, excited gathering.

'Did you see it love?' he said. Just on the Internews TV programme not much more than half-an-hour ago. Wow! Did that girl and her cat give him a mauling! There's going to be more. They won't leave her alone now. This could be the latest soap! Come to think of it she looked a bit like you. It wasn't you was it love?' The chatter stopped instantly and everyone stopped to look at Harriet.

'Sorry, don't know what you're talking about. I'm just on my way home from work.'

'Oh!' said the jolly assistant looking a bit put out. 'That's hard luck love, it should be on again later. Bloody funny though! That's just what we need round here to cheer this miserable place up.'

Harriet thanked him for the basket. She resisted the urge to drop it and run. Instead she stared long and hard at the labels on all the wine bottles in the shop, totally unable to concentrate.

'Do you need any help there love?' came the same jolly voice from right behind. 'Let me recommend this.' He thrust a merlot under her nose.

'I'll take two of those, please,' she said, 'oh and these as well.' She passed the basket over to him and kept her head down as he checked them out.

'I'll take those, thanks,' came Mark's voice from over her shoulder. 'I think she's been treading the grapes in here.'

'Cheek!' said Harriet, as she held open the shop door for him. 'You've only just arrived yourself.'

'Have they been telling you all about that woman leathering that TV reporter then? I didn't quite get the gist of it, they were all talking at once,' Mark asked. 'Apparently the takeaway was in uproar. They were all watching it live in there. We might catch it on the news later, Hat.'

'Not a chance!' Harriet said to herself. Whatever it took, Harriet would ensure that the television would not go on all evening.

Chapter 43

'Very nice too!' said Mark as he awoke to the cup of tea Harriet had just placed on the bedside table.

'It's only a cup of tea Mark,' said Harriet not desiring any special attention after last night.

Mark looked at her. 'Very nice too! I was rather hoping we might… He cleared his throat. I didn't think we were in the frame for such an evening of unbridled passion, Hat. I've never seen you lying completely naked on the hearth rug before. Well, let's be honest Hat we're usually watching the 10 o'clock news. Come here you little sex goddess, let's have some more!'

'Oh for goodness sake Mark, grow up. I'm not in the mood. That was last night. I missed you that's all. It doesn't do any harm to spice things up occasionally.'

'Oh, I've grown up alright Hat, I'm just about as grown up as they come! Come here.' He heaved himself up from the pillow with his elbow, swung his arm out and promptly swiped his tea off the side.

'Now, just look what you've done! Tea all over the place! Well, you clear it up and throw the sheets in the wash too. Men! No control over anything!'

Harriet got back into bed and sipped her tea, much relieved and most thankful for Mark's clumsiness. 'Yes, I drank far too much last night. I'd never had behaved in such a way normally. Still we are married,' she thought. 'Oh no we're not! How could that one have slipped my mind?'

Harriet began to regret her performance. She thought about the night on the ship. She regretted that, too.

'Right!' she determined. 'No more sex before marriage!'

She thought of Mr. Sanderson. 'Now that would be different. Oh what on earth have I done talking like that to him?'

She turned over on the pillow. She closed her eyes. She lay naked on the rug again and Mr. Sanderson took her completely away, time after time, after time.

'Gone back to sleep Hat?' Mark chirped up. 'I've had to go and make another cup of tea. I noticed you didn't offer.'

'You knocked it off!' retorted Harriet.

'You've changed a bit since last night,' said Mark, sharply.

'Due to your complete insensitivity,' retorted Harriet.

'My insensitivity?' queried Mark

'Yes, your insensitivity!' Harriet threw back.

'What are you going on about now?' said Mark, feeling exasperated. 'I seem to remember it was you who was up for it last night.'

'I'm talking about now, this morning. Totally insensitive! Typical man! We girls didn't do ourselves any favours surrendering our virginity before marriage. I've decided to leave it all out until somebody chooses to marry me!'

'A bit late for that Hat, you can't return to that state,' replied Mark

'No, thanks to you I can't. I should've known better. I'll always blame you and those bloody light bulbs. What's wrong with marriage anyway?'

'Oh, so this is where it's going, is it? Come on, let's get up.'

The room filled with a deep, sullen silence as the bed accommodated itself to the final vibrations of emptiness.

Harriet stormed down the stairs. She decided to feed the cat before getting washed. No way did she want to share the bathroom with him!

The phone rang and Harriet's heart leapt. 'I'm sorry, so, so sorry,' she desperately rehearsed as she went to answer it.

'Harriet! Ah, you're there? Look Harriet, Daddy and I are worried sick about you. What's going on? Just tell me it wasn't you Harriet on the television last night. Only Geraldine's been on the phone and I felt so foolish, I couldn't tell her. Goodness knows what she thinks if I can't recognise my own daughter.'

Harriet sank into a chasm of deep disappointment.

'Are you there Harriet? Don't tell me there's something wrong with this line now. I couldn't get you last night, either. Harriet. Are you there?'

'Just about,' replied Harriet.

'What on earth do you mean Harriet? Just about!'

'Just about this!' snapped Harriet surfacing rapidly from her bitter disappointment. 'Just about this! Tell Geraldine to keep her snooty nose out of it!'

'How very rude Harriet, that's not like you. I hope you've recovered yourself before you see them all on Saturday. Geraldine was saying just how much they're all looking forward to the grand opening of that marina place. Oh and it *is* that headmaster of yours that will be opening it on Saturday. I hope you weren't trying to keep that from me. Surely you must have known it was your boss James was talking about. For heaven's sake Harriet don't go being rude to him as well. You might lose your job! Don't forget you've still got that mortgage to pay off. It's not as if Mark's got a job like James'. You've *got* to work Harriet. It would be far better if he married you Harriet seeing as he's totally dependent on you working.'

'Couldn't agree more, Mummy!' exclaimed Harriet, delighted her mother had completely sidetracked herself. 'Sorry, Mummy, Mark's just come over to the phone.'

'Oh I'd better go,' panicked Harriet's mother. 'Give him my love!'

'Who were you trying to get rid of Hat?' grinned Mark as he descended the stairs. 'Gosh you do shout when you're annoyed.'

Harriet lowered her eyebrows and glowered at him. 'It was Mummy actually. Geraldine thinks we should get married.'

'And you told her to keep her snooty nose out of it. Well done Hat! Quite right too!'

Mark suddenly swung his arm around Harriet and kissed her flushed cheek. 'Stay in today Hat and don't answer the phone either. Think of the planet. Hurricane Harriet's arrived! See you later.'

Harriet managed a reluctant wave from the narrow gap as she closed the door behind him. Now she felt annoyed with absolutely everyone. She stomped up the hall in her nightdress to the sound of the phone again. 'Not *him*, no it's not *him*?' the reality flashed across her mind. She couldn't bear the utter disappointment again.

'Simon Barnes! Oh no, what if it's Simon Barnes from Internews TV?' She quivered over the receiver. 'I'll give him what for!' she suddenly decided in a rush of determination.

'Yes!' Harriet exclaimed.

'Is it wise to commit yourself to anything until you've heard the question, Ms Glover?' Harriet went slightly dizzy and very wobbly at the knees. Elation gripped her and she could feel her hands beginning to tremble. In the brief silence that followed Harriet's mind was made up. It was still yes, yes, yes, and no problems explaining to mummy! She would be delighted that at last her only daughter was to be married.

'Hm, er, are you still there Ms Glover?' came the concerned voice at the other end of the phone.

'Oh, of course I am!' spluttered Harriet, 'And I'm so, so sorry.'

'Of course you are Ms er Mrs. I believe, Glover!' came the delighted response.

'Mr. Bryce, er, oh I'm ever so sorry, I haven't yet introduced myself, er I'm Mr. Roberts managing director of the firm, er where was I, oh yes! Er Mr. Bryce and myself were discussing your dilemma, although we can hardly call it that, of having two prospective purchasers for your property and I have the greatest of pleasure in informing you that Ms Oxfordshire and her partner have now offered the full asking price. As a cash buyer it would be nothing short of foolish to reject it. However, you've obviously seen the folly of your ways and we'll get on to Ms Oxfordshire right away to tell her the good news. Good morning to you Mrs. Glover.'

The call was terminated before Harriet could get over the shock. For all the world he'd sounded just like Mr. Sanderson. She was outraged.

'What a cheek!' she said out loud. 'What a bloody cheek!' She quickly did a 1471 and pressed 3 to redial but it bleeped its smug rhythm of dashes at her. 'Engaged. It's bloody well engaged! He's probably told her by now. How dare he presume we've accepted the offer. Mark doesn't even know about it yet.' Harriet's thoughts crashed round her head as she tried to find their house brochure with the telephone number on.

'Good morning,' she snapped to the unsuspecting assistant. 'I've just been called by your Mr. Roberts whose presumed an acceptance of an offer on our property when I haven't even talked to my hus... husband yet.'

'Just hold one second, please,' came the detached voice on the other end. 'I'll see if he's available.' Harriet took a deep breath while she waited.

'How dare Mark do this to me when in the middle of a crisis. Having to lie about my status! Typical of Bryce Rae Roberts, too, getting it wrong in the first place. They wouldn't be told!' The thought fuelled her boiling anger.

'So sorry, he's on the other line. Would you like to hold or can I ask him to call you back?'

'No,' snapped Harriet. 'No thank you, I'll call again later.'

Harriet rushed to the kitchen drawer and scrambled through its miscellaneous contents to find Mark's mobile number. 'Well, don't get in the way then!' she hissed back at the cat as an assortment of paper clips, screws and elastic bands shot into its fur. 'That's your trouble, getting in the way! I wouldn't be in this mess if it weren't for you, getting in the way!'

She had to phone Mark.

'Hat I'm breaking the law. Do you realise? Hang on just let me turn into here. What's up now Hat? Someone bitten back already?'

'That Belinda Oxfordshire's offered the full asking price and bloody cheek, they've told her we've accepted.'

'Sounds good to me Hat. What's your problem? We want to get moved, don't we? So you can give up work and spend every evening naked on the hearth rug. Wow Hat, I'm still dazed. You're gorgeous when you're angry!'

There was a threatening silence. Mark knew it was totally the wrong thing to say. 'Only so we can have our third Hat. Remember? That's what you wanted. Give up work and have another baby.'

'Not before marriage,' Harriet stormed.

'Come on Hat, you're not letting that Geraldine wind you up, are you? We'll get moved and sorted out. Must go Hat. Just leave things where they are, OK. You don't mess about with cash buyers. Must go or I'll be into flexi-time. See you later.'

'No point in telling him!' Harriet complained to herself, unable to rationalise Mark's common sense approach. She knew he was right, of course, but she couldn't bear the thought of selling the family home to someone even remotely connected to Mr. Sanderson.

'Oh, how could I have been so dim as to mistake that obnoxious man Mr. Roberts for Mr. Sanderson?' she thought. 'Well he did start off calling me Miss Glover, I'm sure he did. He sounded just like *him*! You hear what you want to hear, I suppose, especially in this state.'

At least he'd reconstructed her response to his own ends. She was momentarily grateful for that. It made her feel marginally less foolish but then she was riled at the thought of Miss Oxfordshire having viewed it with *him*.

'Just what was that all about?' She couldn't come up with the answer.

Rattled and perplexed Harriet, with a scowl on her face, went upstairs to shower and dress before phoning her babies for comfort.

'No never heard of her,' replied Rachael, 'certainly Tristan's very involved in the business and I can't say I can recall him speaking of her.'

Harriet's heart sank. 'Are you sure Rachael? I know she's going to be there on Saturday at the grand opening.'

'I wouldn't worry about it Mummy,' said Rachael reassuringly. 'I'm sure her money's as good as anyone else's. Why don't you phone Clare? She might know of her. Sebastian seems to be more on sales than Tristan, probably knows more people. Guess what Mummy? Ben phoned out of the blue! Wants to get together for old times sake. No way. I told him we're off to meet the Prime Minister. See you Saturday, there. Won't have time to call home first.'

Harriet replaced the receiver frustrated Clare was out. She'd already left a message for her prior to phoning Rachael. She grudgingly resigned herself to the fact that she wasn't about to find out any more about Ms Oxfordshire, today at least.

She sat down, still riled at the thought of Belinda Oxfordshire being so obviously connected to Mr. Sanderson. She tried to rationalise her feelings without success. She certainly didn't want to become involved with her in a formal sales transaction. She felt nervously irritated. She didn't want to see that Simon Barnes again, either. She jumped at the sound of cars passing by and daren't look out to see which car door had slammed yet again for fear of a further visitation from Internews TV. She switched the answer phone on to defend herself from the rest of the world. She went to the cupboard in the dining room and after clattering the miscellaneous collection of glass dishes managed to retrieve a piece of paper and a pen. She decided it was time to draft her letter of resignation.

Harriet knew she couldn't ever work for him again. She baulked at the thought of serving notice. 'Acting deputy indeed. For him. No thanks!' she thought. 'Let him have his beloved Belinda and the trail of other demented women too weak to know better. I'm out!' Suddenly she was very pleased she had a buyer for the house. Suddenly she'd had enough. 'What does if matter if she *is* the one who buys it? *He's* not part of my life anymore. It's time to grow up.'

Harriet kept the letter short and to the point. 'And, if at all possible, I wish to forfeit salary in lieu of notice,' she concluded, very unsure of just how that would work.

Feeling extremely pleased with herself Harriet went on to the computer, typed it up and printed it off. 'Right! He'll get that on Saturday, whether he likes it or not,' she decided. 'Oh Saturday. Better phone Tricia. We haven't finalised the buffet yet.'

'Buffet? What bloody buffet `arriet? `e can jolly well get that Belinda woman to do it. Who does `e think we are `arriet? `e's a two-timer alright! He's broken my `eart `arriet and I've got something to give `im on Saturday. Just sealed the envelope now. I'm not working for `im any more. `e can get some other poor sucker to carry `is back breakin` stash of loot over to Switzerland. I'd like to know where `e gets it all from. It isn't from Starboard Marine North West I can tell you `arriet! I `ardly ever serve anyone. When I'm not behind my one way mirror, all I do is dust, dust, dust! Well I'm sick of dustin` bloody ropes `arriet! Oh. `Scuse me. I think I've got that wrong. I'm so confused now I don't know what you bloody well call them. `e keeps saying they'll all turn into sheets, with that look on his face. Ooh Harriet, like `e just wants to get me in between some!'

Harriet could hear Tricia swallowing hard.

'That's why I keep dustin` them `arriet so `e'll come over and look at me like that. No, no `arriet! I'm not going to weaken. Never did get that, `arriet. What's ropes got to do with sheets? Obsessed with sex, I'd say! Can't get bed out of `is mind, `arriet. Well, `e's not `aving me `arriet. Thank goodness I've resisted `im all along. To think `arriet, I was on the brink of leaving my Bob and the kids for `im!'

Harriet, certainly not in the mood for explaining sailing terminology to Tricia, suddenly panicked at the thought of him receiving two letters of resignation. 'He'll think we've planned it together,' she thought. 'Oh no, I can't go there!'

'Harriet. Are you there? You've gone a bit quiet `arriet.'

'Sorry, Tricia,' replied Harriet, 'just don't think we can opt out of all that at this late stage.'

'Course we can `arriet! I've already phoned that "All about Buffets" place. I said, "What do you do?" and she said, "How many for?" and I said, "There'll be at least a thousand because the Prime Minister's going to be there." "Are you sure you want to cater for everybody?" she said and I said, "Yes. There's got to be plenty to go round." Then she said, "Who's paying for all this?" and I said, "My boss. Don't you worry now `e's got plenty of money!" Well `e `as, `asn`t `e `arriet?'

'Oh Tricia. It's going to cost an absolute fortune! We can't dump him in it like that.' Harriet panicked.

'Well, no. I did think better of it. I went for `er cheapest option, only £6.00 per `ead `arriet and told `er to do five hundred. I told `er we could always cut the sandwiches in `alf if we're short. That'll serve `im right `arriet. I've tried to work it out but I can't be bovvered. Let `im do the sums eh `arriet.'

'Good thinking,' praised Harriet, 'are they laying it out as well?'

'Too right `arriet for that price, whatever price it is. So we won't need to hang around there too long `arriet. I'm very pleased to say!'

'Thanks so much Tricia,' said Harriet, greatly relieved to be off the hook. 'See you there at ten, then.'

'Ooh! Don't be late `arriet!' Tricia warned, now regaining some composure. 'I'd rather you were there when `e `as to pay the bill.'

Harriet decided she would rather not be there when he has to pay the bill. She did a quick calculation in her head. £3000! The irony was not lost on her. She still had to get her head round paying Mrs. Bustard yet.

Chapter 44

'What do you keep fiddling with that bag for Hat? You keep opening and closing it like you've got a nervous tic,' Mark demanded as he rummaged in the drawer for a suitable tie.

'I'm not!' said Harriet, irritated Mark had noticed. She'd decided not to tell him about her letter of resignation until she'd actually done it. She didn't want to inflame his desires. She certainly didn't intend to repeat last night's performance in a hurry. No, she most certainly wasn't intending to make a habit of it!

'Does this dress look OK?' she suddenly asked Mark. 'That's the trouble with dark blue velvet, it shows all the bits.'

'Come here Hat, let me brush you down,' Mark grinned.

'Get your hands off me!' demanded Harriet in her best teacher tone. 'Anyway if we don't hurry up we're going to be late.'

'Only trying to help, Hat. Just come back here,' ordered Mark, unravelling the clothes brush from a bundle of ties. 'You look like you've been having an affair with the duster.'

'That just about sums it up,' Harriet thought as she relied on the brush to perform a detached, dispassionate job.

'No! Just keep your other hand to yourself Mark,' she warned. 'I'm not in the mood!'

'Not because we're about to see that lard ball, I hope, Hat. Anyway, who's all going to be there, apart from the PM? Huh. I'll believe that when I see it. Let's go.'

Harriet looked out of the window whilst Mark drove along the old familiar route that would normally have led her to school.

'Which corner is it on, Hat?'

'Right by the traffic lights,' came Harriet's response, as they just changed to green.

'What are you turning down here for?' she suddenly announced. 'You've gone right past it!'

'You told me to turn right, Harriet!' returned Mark in equal tone.

'No Mark, couldn't you see the place on the corner? I said it's right by the traffic lights.'

'Precisely. That's just what I did!'

'I didn't say turn right by the traffic lights, did I? I said its right by the traffic lights!'

'Very funny Harriet. Where now?'

'Quick, turn left here. Go straight ahead then left again and then left again on to the main road. We should be able to park on the road if we're lucky.'

Harriet hardly heard Mark's ongoing selection of choice words as she recalled her own folly at repeating the self same cycle again and again just to get a glimpse of *that* man.

She opened her bag and nervously ran her hand across the top of the letter.

She hadn't spoken to him since that last call. How would he be with her? She suddenly felt quite weak at the thought of seeing him. A sharp pang caught her breath as it spread deep into her chest. She felt the anguish of folly surge through her. She lay in the field of flowers again and surrendered to the full weight of his body on hers. Oh how she wanted him again. He'd taken her mind away, and left her drained from the physical need to feel him deep inside her. She wanted him to penetrate her whole being, to fuse together, to unite as one; mind, body and soul. "Save that one for me!" His words came back to her. 'That's the only way babies should be made,' she thought, 'by two people, desperately in love.' Oh how she wished she hadn't been so stupid.

Steeped in thought she didn't notice Mark struggling back and forth trying to get the car parked into a very narrow space. 'Sod this for a game of soldiers!' she heard him say, before he finally managed it. 'That was a bit of a bugger!' he exclaimed, glancing behind him as he locked the car door.

They walked along the pavement following a long line of parked cars.

'Just look at that lot in there! Thanks for telling me about the car park Harriet. You know I hate leaving that thing on the main road. You do realise that was a struggle, don't you? We'll have to wait until everyone's gone. I'm not going to be able to get that thing out in a hurry.' They moved along.

'Mr. Sanderson wouldn't have had any difficulty,' she thought.

'All about Buffet's, eh?' continued Mark spotting the delivery van. 'All about that lard ball more like.'

Harriet looked down. She felt herself blush. It was as if he'd been able to read her thoughts.

'She's just taken enough in there to feed an army and that other girl's coming back for more!' His mood lightened. Harriet thought it must have been due to the prospect of being fed.

'Hang on Hat, we're all going to be on the telly tonight. Internews TV. Good job I brushed you down!'

Harriet froze. She didn't want to come up against Simon Barnes again. She didn't want Mark to hear of her encounter with him the night before last. 'Oh look!' she said, 'isn't that Rachael's car?'

'Sure is,' said Mark, 'and that glamorous one, just going in, isn't she the one that's going to buy our house?'

'Look,' said Harriet, choosing to ignore the comment. 'You go and find the girls. You might spot James and Geraldine too. We're late. We must be. I was supposed to meet Tricia before all this lot arrived.'

With that Harriet hurried off to the side entrance. She kept her head down for fear of bumping into Simon Barnes and his television crew. She pushed the door open and was greatly relieved to see Tricia tottering her way in and around the buffet tables, making superficial adjustments as the two white aproned girls filled them with remarkable speed.

'Cor, 'arriet! Am I pleased to see you. I thought you weren't coming. 'e's paid them 'arriet. I sent that one with the dark hair over to 'im as soon as she came in. "'e's the one you want to see," I said, "that tall chap with the blonde hair. The one that's talking to the Prime Minister." "Oh! He's gorgeous!" she said. "Not so gorgeous to those that know him!" I said, and we do, don't we 'arriet. Don't we just know 'im indeed? Ever since I got 'ere 'e's been swanking around anything in a skirt. I've definitely made the right decision and even if 'e tries to win me back my mind's made up!'

Harriet looked down.

'That blonde piece of string that's just arrived 'arriet, ooh come over here and peep through there at 'er. She's tied 'erself in knots all round 'im. That was another good metathingy, wasn't it 'arriet? Anyway she spotted 'im alright. In that crowd. I ask you? Straight over she went and kissed 'im full on the lips in front of everyone!'

Harriet felt herself starting to rage with jealousy. 'That's Belinda Oxfordshire! She's the one that's buying our house.'

'You're joking me 'arriet. You 'aven't caved in I 'ope! You're never selling to 'er and 'er teddy bear boyfriend. I wouldn't. I most certainly wouldn't! Anyway what was she doing viewing your house with my boss? Ex-boss, I mean. From this afternoon, that is. I 'aven't quite decided how to give 'im my letter yet.'

'That I intend to find out! If I get the chance I'll speak to her,' returned Harriet, taking another look through the half opened hatch, only to observe that Mark had got there first.

'Shove over 'arriet!' Tricia suddenly chirped. 'Let's have a look. Wow I've never seen so many people. Look 'arriet there's Tarquin Bridgewater. It was so funny when 'e 'eld your girdle up for all to see at Burns' night. Good job most of us were a bit squiffy, eh 'arriet. Let's 'ope 'e behaves 'imself today. You 'aven't got anything else in your bag you don't want the world to know about, have you 'arriet?'

'I hope she hasn't Mrs. Harrington!' came a familiar, charming voice. 'Miss Glover, I suspect, is now watching her step very carefully. Very carefully indeed!'

Harriet and Tricia turned round with a start. He shook his head at the tables.

'What is it with you two? Trying to bleed me dry at £3000 a throw!' He turned to Harriet. 'For heaven's sake Miss Glover don't go anywhere near Internews TV. In spite of your outburst you have legal contractual obligations to fulfil and I don't wish you to cause me any further embarrassment.'

He turned to Tricia. 'Mrs. Harrington under no circumstances were you given permission to sanction caterers intent on feeding half the nation!'

Tricia shot to the corner of the room, rummaged in her bag and then handed him the letter.

He swiftly thumbed it open, glanced across the paper, smiled and put his arm around her. 'Not necessary Mrs. Harrington. How would I manage this little lot without you?' He stood, legs astride, face serious tearing it to shreds. He gave it her back. 'Let's be sensible shall we?'

He walked off.

Tricia looked at Harriet. She saw the onset of tears. Harriet immediately put her arm around her. 'Don't upset yourself Tricia. He'll get over it.' she comforted.

'No `arriet.' declared Tricia. 'These are tears of joy!'

'Are you sure you really want to share him with all that glamour out there?' Harriet queried. She'd been completely wrong-footed.

'Oh `arriet. I'll settle for any little crumb he offers!' replied Tricia, her face glowing.

'I know just what you mean,' Harriet thought as she moved away towards the laden tables. She could feel the tears filling her eyes and swallowed hard to stop them. 'Why oh why had he been so easy on Tricia and so hard on her?' Harriet didn't want to work the answer out.

'You alright `arriet?' Tricia suddenly piped up from the other side of the room. 'Only you've gone very quiet. I know you think I'm very silly for going back on giving my notice in, I could tell by your face, but `e needs me `arriet. You `eard `im say! Look, don't worry about it. `e's not. I'm not. So why should you?'

'No, Tricia. You're right.' replied Harriet trying hard to smile.

'I've got far too many other things to worry about,' she said to herself, hoping that Tricia in her euphoria, had failed to pick up on Mr. Sanderson's sharp words to her. All she wanted now was to find Mark and go home.

'I think we're all done in `ere `arriet,' Tricia suddenly declared. 'Let's go and get a look at the Prime Minister, shall we? Ooh `arriet, this is so exciting!'

'I think not,' Harriet thought as she followed her out of the room. 'The last person I want to see is the Prime Minister.' Then she corrected herself. 'No, the next to last person I want to see is the Prime Minister!' She tried hard to terminate her thoughts. She was going to have a job spotting Mark in such a huge crowd, she'd never seen so many people. She was glad of that. It gave her some cover. 'Tricia was right. We've probably under-catered.' Harriet kept her head down as she followed Tricia through the crowds.

Suddenly Harriet felt a tap on her shoulder. She turned and called Tricia to stop.

'Good show, wouldn't you say?' came the cultured voice of Belinda Oxfordshire. 'I've just been speaking to your husband, such a charming man!' She glanced at Harriet's left hand. 'Oh I do beg your forgiveness. You two still not married?'

Harriet could feel herself going incandescent with rage.

'And you are..?' she said, peering down at Tricia lowering the brim of her designer hat.

'Oh I'm Tricia, Mr. Sanderson's PA. Very pleased to meet you!' replied an over- enthusiastic Tricia thrusting her hand out.

'Oh what a beautiful diamond ring!' Tricia burst out, as the long white hand stretched forward. 'So you're engaged then and who's the lucky man?'

'That would be telling,' retorted Belinda. A small mysterious smile crossed her lips as she tossed her head towards Mr. Sanderson now standing on the platform next to Tarquin Bridgewater and the Prime Minister.

'Oooh so you've got a secret then 'ave you?' enquired Tricia suddenly feeling too disturbed to remember not to drop her h's in such company.

'That's a lovely pink hat you're wearing,' Harriet suddenly declared in an immediate attempt to distract Tricia. Then she suddenly remembered just who might have bought it for her. The thought of the cruise immediately made her knees shake. She recalled the carrier bag left in the boot of Mr. Sanderson's car while he passed her hers, full of the cat's rubbish. The other one would definitely have been for Belinda!

'Oh this. Oh no, this is last year's model. I've been so busy what with expanding the business and house hunting I just haven't had time to shop. Actually, I asked Joris to bring me one back from his last trip to Switzerland.' Harriet just knew it. 'He's such a sweetie, says it's gorgeous and wanted to give it me there and then but I insisted on him giving it me in the church. I just wanted to save the surprise for somewhere special.'

'In the church?' shouted Tricia beginning to feel very annoyed. Harriet glanced across trying to catch her eye. She wasn't sure where this was going.

'Yes. We're going to a wedding up here actually in a couple of months time. Poor Joris. I'm surprised he remembered the hat after that episode with the cat!'

Harriet froze. 'The cat. What cat?' she finally snapped.

'Thought you would have noticed it in your garden, actually. He hasn't got the foggiest how it got there, but when he came back from Switzerland he opened one of his cases, his black holdall I think, and the beastly thing jumped out! Put me in mind of that cat of yours to look at. At least the end of its tail did! Just as moth eaten I'm afraid. He dumped it in your garden when we came to view the house. Said something about Miss Glover being good with cats and would be bound to take it in. Sorry you didn't. Still it won't bother Joris. He's like me. We can't stand the things! Anyway, speaking of your house, we are delighted that you've accepted our offer. Not that you were likely to turn down the full asking price, especially as it needs such an enormous amount of work.'

'What do you mean enormous amount of work? 'arriet and Mark 'ave spent a long time doin' that 'ouse up, 'aven't you 'arriet?'

'Still, it's not in our best interests to buy no-brainers,' continued Belinda.

Harriet, puzzled, threw her a sharp glance.

'Oh! It's not just yours, we're making offers all the time.'

'We're making offers all the time,' the words buzzed round Harriet's head. Tricia nudged her.

'Oh, so you make all these offers together then do you?'

'Correct,' came her certain reply.

'And who would that be with then?' enquired Tricia, well overstepping the mark.

'Now, that also would be telling!' she beamed and then threw the smile towards Mr. Sanderson.

Tricia and Harriet could hardly contain their fury. Tricia, having just recovered, albeit, a less than perfect equilibrium was not up for having it shattered. She shot a knowing glance at Harriet, who by now was seething.

Belinda Oxfordshire turned to Harriet. 'Yes, Mark was saying how delighted you both are and it means you will be able to give up work Ms Glover. Bit of a relief for Joris, I would say. Anyway, I don't blame you for that. One of the most beastly jobs on the planet, I should think! Even the PM can't understand how Joris got involved in education. Joris was boning him last night over dinner about funding for parenting classes or something equally boring. He reminded Joris of the state of the economy and told him not to make waves!'

'Make waves? `e wouldn't know `ow,' Tricia burst forth. 'I've never seen `im in a boat. Anyone who calls ropes sheets doesn't exactly know much about sailing, I'd say.'

'Not literally,' said Belinda Oxfordshire, curtly. 'Metaphorically speaking.'

'Oooh not those bloody metathingies again! I can't be doin` with them myself.'

Tricia had beaten Harriet to it. She'd just pre-empted Harriet's furious response.

She could see her winding herself up in an irrational tangle as Belinda Oxfordshire's porcelain features began to express extreme impatience.

'Actually Joris is very well known as a highly accomplished yachtsman in the circles that matter,' Belinda declared, looking down her thin straight nostrils at Tricia. 'I'm surprised you didn't know that, working for him in the capacity you do.'

'Oh Joris just tells me the things I need to know, but that's between `im and me and the sheets. Don't ask me what though. That would be telling!'

Harriet looked back at Tricia to avoid witnessing Belinda Oxfordshire's rapidly deepening colour. 'We'd best find Bob and Mark, Tricia before the speeches start,' bristled Harriet, her rage giving way to disbelief at Tricia's outburst.

Too late. All three felt themselves being ushered from behind by at least four insistent, burly men and led from the front by Tarquin Bridgewater.

'And where are we supposed to be going now?' demanded Tricia as they were shunted towards a makeshift platform. 'Fuck off Fatty. If your tryin` to kidnap us I'll scream for my Bob! Get your porky big bum out of my way will you?'

'Ah, Simon Barnes "Internews TV" here. I think we caught that one.' All of a sudden Tricia was face to face with a black cylindrical microphone head perched on the end of a long stick.

'Ere, `arriet hold this a minute,' she said, passing her handbag over. 'And you. Get that broomstick out of my face. Give it back to `er where it belongs!'

Belinda Oxfordshire's face turned puce.

Harriet went white, slipped her own bag off her shoulder and without thinking promptly dumped them both on the edge of the platform where she could see Mr. Sanderson and the Prime Minister striding towards them.

'I said bring her to me,' she heard Mr. Sanderson shout across to the freshly insulted bodyguard as he pointed his finger towards Belinda Oxfordshire.

'Sorry guv,' came the reply, 'thought you said, "Bring me the three!" Too much noise in here. Deafening!'

'No, no!' came the insistent voice of the Prime Minister. 'Any friends of Belinda's are friends of mine.' In an attempt to reinforce the sincerity of his announcement, head in the air, grinning, he gathered speed, unwittingly scooped up the strap of Harriet's bag with the toe of his right foot and went hurtling over the other one straight off the platform into them all.

With the contents of her bag thrown into the air, Harriet's world went into slow motion. The cameras rolled.

'What a scoop!' She heard Simon Barnes congratulating himself from his hands and knees as he collected up all her belongings. 'These yours, Miss?' he asked tugging at her left elbow in an attempt to raise her from the floor. 'Just a minute,' he triumphed as he came face to face with Harriet. 'You're the one that stamped on my toe! The one with the mad cat that flew at me!' he balled. 'Oh no, you're certainly not having that one back!' he suddenly announced as he grabbed the letter marked 'Mr. Sanderson'. 'Well, not until you tell me the story behind that £3000 tip!'

'That's rubbish, rubbish, rubbish!' retorted Harriet.

'Ere! You just give that to me!' demanded Tricia, snatching it out of his hand. '`ow dare you steal that from my friend, even if it is rubbish.'

Desperate to retain some degree of elegance Belinda Oxfordshire leant against Tricia's side as she stumbled her stilettos into whoever else was left on the floor. She finally managed to stretch to full height. 'Ah for Mr. Sanderson, I see. Well, if it's rubbish and I'm sure it is, let me relieve you of it,' she said, whipping it out of Tricia's hand. In a flash she tore it to shreds. 'Joris certainly doesn't have time for reading rubbish!' she declared, glancing back at Harriet as the pieces fell to the ground like disillusioned confetti. She marched off towards Mr. Sanderson who was still brushing the Prime Minister down as they remounted the platform.

'Bloody cheek `arriet,' stormed Tricia. 'That was your letter. How dare she do that. The snooty old cow!'

'Out, Tricia. Just let's get out of here. We'll walk home if we have to!'

Before the rippling hiatus could reach the peripherals of the room Harriet and Tricia, clutching their bags, had shut the side door behind them, crossed over at the traffic lights and half-ran, half-walked in panting bursts along the main road.

'Aven't we got enough money between us to get a taxi, `arriet?' puffed Tricia as they headed towards Whellread's the newsagents.

'Let's check it out here,' suggested Harriet looking over her shoulder, pushing Tricia through the door of the wine shop.

'Just a pound I keep for the shopping trolley. I thought as much,' Tricia groaned. 'I don't suppose taxi drivers do plastic?'

'Well done Tricia,' panted Harriet. 'Put yours away. There's a cash machine next door. I'll draw some out while you phone the cabbie. Look there's a number up there.'

'It's an emergency!' Harriet could hear Tricia saying as she came back into the shop. 'Come to the wine shop now!' She turned to Harriet. 'He wants to know where it is,' she whispered.

'Tell him it's next to Whellread's on Brompton Road.'

Tricia spat it out, turned her mobile off and sighed at Harriet. 'He'll be at least three minutes.'

'Just time to get some of this,' puffed Harriet, thrusting two bottles of red wine into Tricia's arms. Sweeping another two off the shelf she went to the counter and declared she'd have another four of the same before handing her card over.

They heard the blast of the horn just as the little square box reluctantly agreed to accept Harriet's pin number. 'Tell him I'm coming,' she ordered Tricia. 'Quick, now!'

Tricia disappeared while Harriet waited endlessly for the receipt to slowly shunt its way through the till. Finally the demand to remove her card appeared. She stumbled out of the shop, laden with clinking bottles. 'Just a moment,' she said, 'need to go back for the others.'

'Off to a party, then?' enquired the huge, shiny headed man as he loaded the rest of the bottles on to the front seat.

'You might say that,' replied Harriet, relieved to be sitting down. '4 The Willows please.' She turned to Tricia, 'Is that OK?'

'Ooh yes thank you `arriet, I've no desire whatsoever to go `ome by myself. Goodness knows what time Bob will be back.'

They watched the taxi drive off as Harriet delved in her bag for the front door keys. 'Ooh, you `aven't lost them `ave you, `arriet? That's all we need! We could `ave gone to ours if you've lost them, `arriet. Come `ere. Let me `ave a look.'

'Well *I* can't find them. Let's hope that revolting man hasn't picked them up.' Harriet said as she handed her bag over.

'Which one `arriet? The place was *filled* with revolting men as far as I could see.' Tricia rummaged away. 'Cor, those big burly bouncers. Reminded me of that `orrible man who was supposed to be looking after me in Switzerland. What would Tarquin Bridgewater want with them, `arriet? That slime-ball boss, er ex-boss, of ours, or should I say mine, since I've decided `e can keep `is snooty piece of string, seemed to know them very well, too, I'd say. Looked like the Mafia to me. What would `e be doin` with the Mafia eh `arriet? Most probably where `e gets all that money from, I'd say! Wouldn't you `arriet? No I can't find them in `ere. We'll `ave to go and sit in your shed `arriet. My feet are killing me.

I'd never be able to walk back to ours.'

With a nod of the head Harriet led Tricia round the back. They were just beaten to the side gate by the cat with its tail in the air. Harriet threw it a disgusted look as it shot through the cat flap. How it ever managed to survive the flight to Zurich and back in Mr. Sanderson's black bag she would never know. She was now doubly furious with him for making her think he knew nothing of its return. She pulled open the shed door, stumbled over the bikes as she dragged the garden chairs from the back, opened them and echoed Tricia's sigh of relief as they both flopped down. She pulled out the nearest bottle of red wine from the carrier bag at her feet and unscrewed the top as she passed it to Tricia. 'All yours,' she said.

'Ooh, thanks `arriet,' declared Tricia immediately wrapping her lips around the bottleneck. 'That's better!'

'Too right it is,' agreed Harriet, kicking her shoes off. 'They'll never find us here.'

'Oooh,' said Tricia, 'you don't think those Mafia men will be looking for us, do you `arriet?'

'Of couse not,' smiled Harriet. 'Just a joke, Tricia.'

'Oh, of course you're joking `arriet. They're far too busy putting all that stolen money into the washing machine. That glamorous piece of knotted string irons it and then gives it to `im, whose name will never touch my lips again.' She held her bottle to the shed window. 'Hmm not `alf way through this one yet and another three to go,' she delighted.

'Sure is, sure are,' declared Harriet, struggling to get it right and suddenly trying to suppress a giggle.

'What you laughin` at `arriet? This `as traumatised, see `arriet a big word doesn't `ave to be a metathingy at all does it? Where was I? Oh yes, traumatised me, it `as. Apart from seeing Miss Stringything, that is, struggling and wobbling all over the place trying to get up off the floor. Ooh was that just so funny, `arriet? It was worth all the trauma just to see `er land on her bum!'

Their mirth increased in direct proportion to the emptying bottles of wine. Somehow Harriet had a vague feeling she'd been here before but she was having the greatest difficulty trying to remember just when. She moved her mind to the more pressing question. 'You were shaying Tricia about Mzzzzzz Oxfordshire ironing the dosh. Then what does she do?'

'Oh `arriet! I told you she gives it to your boss. There, I'm not too drunk to remember that I'm never going to use `is name again!'

'Well neither am I,' positioned Harriet, nonplussed by her evaporating passion. 'Then what?'

'Well, where would she put it once it's been ironed `arriet?'

'I could tell her where to put it without her bothering to iron it first,' retorted Harriet.

'Oooh that's really rude `arriet! I didn't know you could be rude like that,'

Tricia giggled. 'Anyway I reckon she gives it back to `im all freshly laundered and `e gives it to me to stash away in that Swiss bank account of `is!'

'Sho what happens next?' slurred Harriet.

'He spends it all on bloody big `ats and diamond rings for `er. That's what `appens next, `arriet!'

'Of courshe he does,' laughed Harriet, 'you're shuch a clever girl.'

In a complete fog, Harriet turned to Tricia only to find the compliment lost on her. She was slumped in the garden chair fast asleep.

'Now,' Harriet mused to herself in an attempt to get to the bottom of it all. 'There's shomething not quite right about laundering money in a washing machine. What can it be?' She tried and tried but couldn't round up her thoughts in any cohesive fashion to try to find the answer. She drifted off to the rhythm of the rotating drum as it flung the notes round and round and round.

Chapter 45

'No, haven't a clue where they are Clare,' Mark declared as he picked up the phone. 'Bob's here now. No sign that they've been here or to Bob's. Oh don't worry Clare, two of them together, nothing like that is likely to have happened. You see if they don't turn up soon. No, no. We'll leave it twenty-four hours before we tell the police. No, look, there's absolutely nothing you or Rachael can do. You must all go back as planned and as soon as we get any news at all we'll phone.'

Mark placed the receiver down and shrugged his shoulders at Bob. 'I suppose we should have made more of an effort to find them,' he said, 'but it was jam-packed in there.' He glanced at his watch. 'We might just catch the news before we go looking again.'

Bob shadowed Mark into the lounge.

'And following the break,' Mark and Bob listened intently, 'how the Prime Minister made a comeback after taking to the floor.'

They waited to hear it out.

Mark turned the television off in stunned silence.

They'd just watched and heard, along with the whole nation, Harriet and Tricia making complete and utter fools of themselves.

'I don't believe it,' stormed Mark.

'Nor me,' reciprocated Bob. 'What the hell were they doing making complete arses of themselves like that? No wonder they've gone missing!'

Between them Mark and Bob experienced a tangible sense of relief. At least there was an explanation for their disappearance.

'Just wait until she gets home,' boiled Mark. 'What was that bloody letter all about? Watch this space indeed! What's all that got to do with some fool leaving a £3000 tip?'

'Let's go,' declared Bob, equally furious. 'We've lost all credibility with the sailing club and anyone else you can care to mention. Not that I'm bothered about that arsehole she works for.'

'Too right!' agreed Mark. 'I've been playing second fiddle to him for long enough.'

'Really?' came Bob's immediate response. 'Exactly my feelings!'

They continued their utterances of disbelief as they drove in and out of all the side roads for a good hour.

With no luck Bob decided his best course of action was to go home and wait. 'Any news and I'll call you straight away,' he told Mark as he pulled away from the kerb.

Mark went inside, his concern mounting. It was coming up to twenty-four hours since he last saw Harriet.

The phone went. Mark grabbed it.

'Now it's no good pretending it wasn't you this time Harriet,' came her mother's voice. 'We've just seen you on the news again, Daddy and I. Wasn't it enough stamping on that poor man's foot without having to trip him up as well? You sent the Prime Minister flying too, Harriet. The Prime Minister of all people! Such a good man. Daddy and I wouldn't be as well off as we are if it weren't for him. You do realise that, don't you Harriet? Anyway, I've been on to James, fortunately he didn't know a thing about it, said the place was bursting at the seams and they were all at the back. He did recall them all looking a bit shaky though when the speeches started. He sends his apologies for not seeing you. Apologies indeed Harriet. Better that he didn't. He'll know why when he watches the late news tonight. Goodness knows what that charming boss of yours makes of it all. I only hope you haven't spoiled James and Geraldine's relationship with him. He's coming to the wedding you know. Harriet it's high time you told that Bohemian boyfriend of yours to grow up and marry you. The sooner you're out of that school the better. You'll end up ruining that poor man's career!'

'I'll pass the message on,' Mark replied, with great restraint, 'she's *out*!' He took great pleasure in whamming the phone down on the bluster that followed. He paced up and down the hall venting his anger on the worn carpet as he thumped along its thinning tread. He went to the lounge window and craned his neck, but it was no use, there was no sign of them. He went to the kitchen and stared out of the window at the garden shed. Then he suddenly noticed the windows were all steamed up.

Without hesitation he strode over the grass and flung the door open.

Harriet and Tricia woke with a jolt.

'Ooooh me `ed,' groaned Tricia, 'and I'm stiff all over.'

'Me too,' mumbled Harriet. 'Have a bit of consideration Mark,' she complained, 'you wouldn't be feeling that brilliant if you'd been sleeping on one of these all night either!'

'Your choice,' Mark snapped, eyeing the bottles before he slammed the shed door, leaving it to swing open.

Harriet and Tricia looked at each other as they heard the car engine start.

'Oooh `e looked cross didn`t `e `arriet? I hope `e doesn't get to Bob before I do. Ooh me `ead. It feels like the inside of this shed but it's all clangin` around.'

'He was cross,' declared Harriet, 'very cross!' Harriet lifted her head from her hands and made several attempts to heave herself out of the garden chair.

'Mind them bottles `arriet. `ow many did we `ave? Let's see now, one, two, three, four… Oh no. Not four between us? I `ope we `aven't got alcoholic poisoning `arriet.' She stretched forward in an attempt to clear a path for their feet. 'Ooh I can`t move `arriet. I feel very ill indeed.'

Harriet tried again. She felt less intimidated now Tricia had managed to clear the way and she heaved herself up only to flop down again.

'Oooooh `arriet, I think I'm goin` to be sick,' Tricia suddenly declared.

'Hang on!' panicked Harriet and with sheer grit and determination she managed to lift herself up. She put her arm around Tricia and pulled and pushed until she came out of the chair. They both staggered to the open door.

'Behind that bush!' She heaved the words out to Tricia just in time as they tried to hurry across the lawn to the lilac by the dining room window.

'He'd have to clean his shoes this time!' Harriet suddenly thought as she peered through the branches to the ground in front of her. 'Déjà vu. Of course,' she said to herself suddenly remembering where her thoughts had been trying to take her yesterday evening.

It was some time before Harriet and Tricia felt confident enough to leave the protection the shrubbery afforded.

'I think I'll be alright now,' said Tricia as she backed out into the open space. 'Ooh my `ead's still goin` though. `ow about you `arriet?'

'Just leave me to die,' groaned Harriet. 'I'll never touch it again.'

'Oooh no, not again!' They both fled back to the shrubbery.

* * *

'Where are they now?' came Mark's impatient voice as he and Bob peered into the shed.

'They haven't buggered off again, have they?' snapped Bob.

'Better bloody not have! Probably inside by now,' declared Mark, opening the back door.

'Oooh they're back,' Tricia whispered to Harriet. 'What shall we do?'

'Go right in and apologise for nothing,' Harriet suddenly decided.

'Too right `arriet,' said Tricia, 'only I `ope they don`t shout. My `ead couldn't stand it.'

'Just a tick,' Harriet said, 'wasn't that the car doors slamming? I think they've gone. Quick into the house.'

Harriet grabbed two bottles of water from the larder cupboard by the back door. 'It should help,' she mumbled as she passed one over. They went to the front room window and just saw Bob's car disappearing out of sight.

'Yes, let them pick up their own pieces,' Mark said to Bob as they drove along. 'They're around there somewhere. Too done for to be able to have gone far. Tomorrow morning will be soon enough.'

'Couldn't agree more,' said Bob. 'It'll give the pair of them a taste of their own medicine.'

Harriet and Tricia flopped onto the sofa with great relief.

The phone rang and the cat pestered for food without success. It was only the sound of Tricia snoring loudly into her ear that finally woke Harriet up at exactly 6pm.

She took the empty bottles into the kitchen and suddenly realised Mark wasn't there.

'I must `ave woke myself up snoring` Harriet. I do `ope I didn't wake you up as well,' Harriet heard Tricia saying from right behind her.

'No, no Tricia. I was coming round anyway. How are you feeling?'

'Ooh heaps better I should say,' replied Tricia, 'what about you?'

'Oh, me too, thanks,' declared Harriet, reaching for the cat food.

'Is that yours Harriet?' Tricia declared, suddenly making a supreme effort with her pronunciation to convince herself she was well on the way to recovery from the night before. 'Or might it be that stray, glamour face was telling us about yesterday?'

'This is definitely our very own flea bag,' Harriet replied, desperately wanting to open her heart to Tricia and tell all, but something was holding her back. She felt bad that Tricia had so openly confided in her and had a momentary tussle with the sympathy and affection she felt for her and, even now, the need to hold *him* to herself.

'Hungry Tricia?' Harriet enquired as she opened the tin of cat food.

'Too right Harriet. That'll do if you've got nothing else.'

Harriet laughed. She shooed the cat from her feet. She banged the dish down on the floor. 'There,' she said depriving it of its usual stroke. 'Eat that!'

'Soup OK?'

'Oh lovely, thanks Harriet. Can I do anything to help?'

'There's some ham in the fridge and the rolls are in there,' said Harriet, pointing to the bread bin. 'You can get that chocolate cake out while you're there, if you like. Thanks Tricia.'

They sat over the table desperately trying to piece their shreds of memory together in an attempt to finish the bizarre jigsaw of yesterday. Neither could see how they had done anything wrong.

'In actual fact, 'arriet, it was that Belinda woman who 'ad no right to snatch your letter and tear it up like she did. She was fantasising 'arriet. Thinks everyone's after 'er Joris. Who was it for, 'arriet? She obviously can't read, you've got more sense than writin' 'im a letter 'arriet, 'aven't you?'

Harriet had to come clean. 'Actually it was my letter of resignation too, Tricia,' she confessed.

'Well what a coincidence 'arriet, 'ave you 'ad enough of 'im as well?'

'Sure have Tricia!'

'Well you couldn't write it in a story could you 'arriet? 'im tearing mine up and 'er tearin' up yours. Maybe we're not destined to resign just yet 'arriet.'

Harriet reluctantly agreed as those 'legal obligations' passed through her mind.

'That was lovely, thank you,' said Tricia, 'still no sign of them 'arriet,' she continued, as she helped clear the kitchen table.

'Not to worry, they'll be back soon enough. Let's go and put our feet up,' said Harriet glancing at the answer phone as she came out of the kitchen.

'Ooh, you've got messages there 'arriet.'

'Not interested,' declared Harriet as she pressed her finger long and hard on the delete button. 'It's about time we had a bit of peace.'

'You know Tricia,' began Harriet as they settled back into the sofa, 'I wonder if he's really, seriously up to something?'

'Up to something?' queried Tricia feeling a tinge of excitement. 'What exactly do you mean by that `arriet?'

'Well,' said Harriet, 'where does he get all this spare cash? He's got to be depositing *money* in that Swiss bank.'

'Well I don't know `arriet but I can tell you I'm not goin` there again for `im. That ugly chap with the big `ands, what was `is name? Johansson, yes, I remember now, Johansson, just looked like one of them bouncers we `ad the pleasure of meeting yesterday. Oh no, I'll threaten to resign good and proper if `e tries to send me there again. That'll do it alright, especially now `e`s already said `e can't do without me.'

Harriet nodded in agreement.

'Anyway `arriet, what was Tarquin Bridgewater doing shoving` and pushin` `is way past us leadin` all those big thugs? We were just like meat in a sandwich, we were. I reckon `e`s up to somethin`, too. Come to think of it why does `e keep pesterin` me askin` if that Joris Sanderson's left anything` for `im?'

'Well we'd be hard pushed to try to work that one out,' said Harriet, 'but there's certainly something very odd about the whole set up. We weren't there long enough to pick up any clues to it all.'

'Glad we weren't,' said Tricia. 'Do you reckon she's washing it or ironing it at the moment?'

'That's it,' Harriet declared, 'that's what I've been trying to remember. Well done Tricia!'

Tricia looked puzzled.

'Money laundering, Tricia. How does he do it if it's not in the washing machine?'

'He might buy `ouses with it `arriet. He might be buying your `ouse with a load of stolen money from those stolen goods. Ooh be careful `arriet I think it's breakin` the law to receive stolen goods. Even if you don't know they were stolen.'

'Just a minute Tricia, I'm sure there's something in the brochure where Bryce Rae Roberts mention money laundering. They ask for identification of people making offers because of that. It can't be. Neither of them would have any trouble in that direction.'

'No, definitely not seeing as they've got plenty of posh people to speak up for them, they `ave. But just a minute `arriet. Stolen goods are sold on the black market, aren't they?'

'Yes,' said Harriet cautiously, 'but then plenty get sold on the open market too.'

'Ah, yes! You think about it `arriet,' continued Tricia, now filled with mounting nervous excitement, 'this is where the Mafia come in I think. Isn't all their crime organised so big wedges of dosh, er that's all the cash from the sale of all the stolen goods, gets laundered? Oh I don't know `arriet, we're back to the washing machine again.'

'Unless, just unless,' said Harriet, 'it's paid into an offshore account where nobody asks any questions.'

'That's got to be it `arriet. Ooh you're not a teacher for nothing. Clever old you. That's exactly what `appens. Oooh `arriet `ave I been the gang runner for a load of criminals? Oooh `arriet I `ope I don't get caught. Even if I told the truth and said I didn't know, it's the same as stolen goods isn't it? I've still been breaking the law.

Oh `arriet I can't cope with all this on top of yesterday.'

'Calm down Tricia,' said Harriet reassuringly. 'He could have been depositing anything into that bank. We don't actually know what, if anything at all is going on.'

'Yes you're right. Absolutely right `arriet. Oooh am I so glad I didn't give `im my all, though. I nearly weakened didn't I `arriet?'

Harriet smiled across at her, not convinced by her own words. 'We can now see him for what he is,' she declared, 'and I've no intention of selling the house to either of them.'

'I think I can hear your phone ringing `arriet,' Tricia said as she felt her panic subside. 'It might be Bob. Shall I answer it for you?'

'Oh go on then,' said Harriet, 'before I phone the estate agents. There's no way we're selling to them.'

'It's that disgusting Simon Barnes, would you believe it?' said Tricia, craning her neck round the lounge door, 'says he's got something for you and can he have a word.'

Harriet jumped up and for a moment was startled into silence. Then she suddenly remembered the missing house keys. 'I'll take it, thanks Tricia,' she answered.

'Yes, thank you very much. I'd be obliged if you could post them through the letterbox immediately together with whatever you found my phone number on. Don't bother bringing that crew of yours along either.'

'You're not getting them as easily as that. You tell me why you gave that steward three grand and then I'll post them through your letterbox.'

'How dare you,' snapped Harriet. 'You've now stolen my keys and I shall inform the police immediately.'

'Your keys! What are you talking about? I haven't got your keys. Heard of cut and paste have you?' came the irritated response.

'What do you mean?' demanded Harriet.

'Well I'm looking at your phone number now on the bit I'm holding up. Finish the story and you'll get every last one of these bits of paper back. Don't and I'll stick them all together again. Our viewers can't wait for the next instalment after last night's programme.'

'That's not your property either,' she snapped.

'Your choice luv!' came the reply.

Harriet slammed the phone down.

'Ooh eh `arriet. What was that all about?' rushed Tricia.

'We were on last night's news,' Harriet exploded. 'That man actually grovelled on his hands and knees to collect every last piece of my letter.'

'Never!' said Tricia. 'Why is he so interested in you `arriet? It was only your letter of resignation after all. It doesn't make any sense to me at all.'

Harriet was greatly relieved Tricia was in a complete fog. She desperately wanted to confide the whole story to her but knew it would probably be the end of their newly cemented friendship.

'You know what these reporters are like, Tricia. They make stories out of nothing.'

'Yes,' agreed Tricia, 'the less they know about what they think they know the better. There `arriet. That's my very own that is. Far more impressive than one of those metathingies wouldn't you say?'

'I would most certainly say so Tricia.'

The phone rang again.

'Yes!' snapped Harriet.

'Oh you're back,' came the girl's voice down the phone.

'Who's speaking please?' Harriet queried impatiently.

'It's Melissa Scott. Mark phoned, he was terribly worried about you. He didn't know which way to turn. I suggested he rang Marcus Cooper. He's always good in a crisis. I don't know whether he did or not. You are so lucky Harriet. Geoffrey just wouldn't have compromised the planet burning off all that fuel for me. I didn't realise just how environmentally conscious he was until we got married. Anyway are you OK?'

'Oh yes I'm fine thank you Melissa,' said Harriet, suddenly warming to her in the light of such good news.

'Mark didn't tell me you were getting married.'

'No he wouldn't. We just went off and did it quietly and we're still waiting to see if anyone in the office notices. They're all totally preoccupied with global warming I'm afraid. At least we've saved the planet a few of its precious resources. People can spend anything up to twenty grand and more on such occasions these days. Not that it's the money it's the environmental cost of producing what it buys that's the issue.'

'Quite,' said Harriet suddenly reminded of Clarissa's rapidly approaching wedding. 'Quite, I couldn't agree more. Anyway congratulations Melissa.'

'Thank you,' Melissa replied. 'If everybody simply delivered a verbal message of goodwill in just that way think of the benefit that would be to the planet.'

'Too right,' Harriet enthusiastically agreed. 'Far less of the Earth's resources, far less recycling. Not that that's much use Mark says.'

'Really, why?'

'He reckons it all ends up in Chinese landfill.'

'Must have a word with Geoffrey tonight about that. I didn't realise we had a sceptic in the camp.'

'That's his nature, I'm afraid,' said Harriet. 'Anyway, must go. Thanks for calling. I'll tell Mark when he gets in.'

Harriet replaced the receiver, now pretty certain Mark's affair had been merely a figment of her imagination. 'I wonder where he is?' she thought. She was starting to get worried.

'Ooh, `ere they are `arriet,' came Tricia's voice as she drew back from the window. 'I wonder if they've spent the night in our shed `arriet?'

'Don't even go there,' ordered Harriet as she went to open the door. Harriet was relieved to be able to hang some guilt on him.

'You didn't tell me Melisa and Geoffrey got married,' she said as soon as she opened the door.

'Melissa and Geoffrey! What on earth are you talking about Harriet?'

'Well not exactly being up for it yourself I suppose you wouldn't have noticed,' Harriet triumphed, delighted she'd managed to take the wind completely out of his sails.

Bob squeezed past them. 'Home Tricia,' he ordered, rounding her up to the front door.

'You just let go of me will you. I've `ad enough of bossy men! Give you a ring `arriet when I get the chance,' Tricia said as she struggled past, glaring at Bob. 'Thanks for everything `arriet.' Her voice faded as he directed her towards the car.

'Well that wasn't very nice, was it?' observed Harriet, trying to retain the moral high ground.

'What can she bloody expect?' retorted Mark. 'The pair of you made complete arses of yourselves!'

'It wasn't our fault actually. All I did was put our handbags on the platform.'

'You and that bloody bag Harriet. You'll end up killing somebody one of these days. Thank your lucky stars it wasn't the mayor that went over. He'd never have survived it at his age. If he'd gone you'd be done for manslaughter!'

'Oh,' said Harriet, going a bit pale. She hadn't thought of it like that.

'I suppose you were too hungover to see the action replay on the news last night?' He didn't wait for an answer. 'I don't know what you've been up to on that bloody cruise but that guy seems to think he's got something on you. What's been going on? A three grand tip. We don't have that kind of dosh Harriet.'

'Don't ask me. You know what these reporters are like,' she said turning away as she felt herself going bright red.

'There's no smoke without fire Harriet. That thing Belinda was tearing up. Was that one of your love letters to *him*? You're making yourself look very stupid Harriet. It's plain for all to see they're engaged.'

'That's not the sort of thing you see, Mark,' Harriet retorted.

'In any case, the sooner you extricate yourself from that lard ball the better. Have you bothered to give the girls a ring? No, I thought as much,' said Mark without waiting for an answer, 'just as well I did.'

'Oh, so they know I'm alright, then?'

Mark ignored the question. 'There's something more going on Harriet otherwise you two wouldn't have scarpered like that. Just get that letter of resignation in tomorrow will you, the sooner you are out of his clutches the better.'

'In actual fact that *was* my letter of resignation,' triumphed Harriet, 'and she had no right whatsoever to tear it up.'

'Why didn't you tell me?'

'I was going to tell you on the hearth rug, actually,' Harriet lied, now desperate to pull out all the stops.

Mark scratched his head. Then he grinned. 'We've got some house hunting to do.'

'It's just as well I didn't get round to phoning the estate agents,' she thought.

Chapter 46

It was Monday morning. Harriet backed off the drive. The unmarked exercise books perched on the rear seat of the car had now collided into their usual heap. She was apprehensive about the day ahead.

'I'll just have to try to keep completely out of his way,' she decided, yet again. She wished she'd got round to writing another letter of resignation. She thought about last night. Her sullen silence last night. Mark was unable to soften sufficiently to want her back on the hearth rug. She was grateful for that.

She glanced across to Whellreads and the wine shop, hardly believing their escapade of two days ago. She pulled up at the traffic lights and looked over to Starboard Marine North West sitting quietly on the corner, as if nothing had happened. She mused at the thought of time, the most powerful force on the planet, nonchalantly tossing and turning human emotion in the wake of change while seemingly leaving everything untouched.

'Oh, if only I could turn the clock back,' she thought, her mind wandering to the field of flowers. ' "Save that one for me!" How could he say that when all along he was bound to Belinda Oxfordshire? So what happened to Ted? She's succeeded where I've failed,' Harriet concluded, miserably.

She continued to the school gates and noticed his car wasn't there. 'Well it was either me or Tricia this morning,' she thought. 'I wonder how she'll get on?'

She slung her bag over her shoulder and struggled to grasp the books from the back seat of the car before closing the door. She automatically glanced behind her. She jumped. She saw Mr. Sanderson driving through the school gateway. Her heart leapt. She hurried to the entrance door and desperately tried to heave it open without her customary half turn. Relieved, she made it. She all but ran along the corridor to her classroom. Already chattering mothers, anxious to be rid of their offspring were collecting outside her room. She kept her head down. She didn't know how she was going to deal with Mrs. Bustard today.

Barely at her desk, the door swung open. He closed it with a bang. He marched straight over. Harriet hardly dared to look up. He handed her a plain white envelope. 'Make sure that Bastard woman gets this will you and get her to sign the chitt inside.' He strode to the door, reached for the handle and glanced back. 'That's nine grand between the two of you Miss Glover in only as many weeks. Oh, I suggest you clear that with Broadbent's first. We don't want any rebounds. And don't, I repeat don't put it in that blasted bag of yours. It's sheer good fortune no one was hurt.' With that he slammed the door behind him and then opened it again. 'Try to keep it off the national news, as well, will you?' He marched off. Harriet had never seen him so furious. She knew it was all over between them.

'Sara Atkins, Daniel Bustard, Sabaru Cam...' Harriet reeled off the names on the register but her heart wasn't in it. She was trying to force herself to think. She could feel herself sinking into a deep depression. She tried to draw on every reserve she had to stop herself from going there. She must check with the secretary and see if there had been anything from Broadbent's in relation to Mrs. Bustard relinquishing her claim.

'Big question,' she thought. 'How am I going to get to Alice's office without risk of seeing *him*?' Not wishing to get involved with Mrs. Bustard either, she decided to leave it until home time.

The day dragged and dragged. The children received as superficial an education as Harriet could manage. As soon as the bell went she flung her bag over her shoulder and marched down the corridor to Alice Atkin's office.

'Er, I'll just check that with Mr. Sanderson,' she said.

Harriet swallowed hard.

'Oh sorry,' she continued, 'Mr. Sanderson's not there. He's been out most of the day. I should have remembered. Hang on I'll just go through the in tray. Ah, just a minute. Yes, that's what we're looking for.'

She lifted the A4 sheet and briefly read its contents. 'Do you want me to copy it?' she asked Harriet.

'No, that's OK, thanks, I might still catch Mrs. Bustard if I'm quick. Thanks Alice.'

Harriet went back to the classroom to find Mrs. Bustard standing by her desk with Danny by her side. Her stomach started to churn as she suddenly thought about the news. Without any doubt Mrs. Bustard would have seen her on Internews TV, both times.

'Ah, Mrs. Bustard,' greeted Harriet, acting for all she was worth. 'Just the person I wanted to see. I've got something for you from Mr. Sanderson, actually.'

She rummaged in her bag and took out the small grey key belonging to the drawer in her desk. 'Just a minute.'

She unlocked the drawer and opened the large sealed white envelope Mr. Sanderson had given her. She placed her hand in and ran it over the neatly bound packs of used notes to retrieve the receipt. 'This is your settlement, Mrs. Bustard. Can you just check the contents and sign this for me please?'

'Well I never! I thought this was goin` to be just between you and me.'

'It was but it would seem Mr. Sanderson had the same idea.'

'Money's the same. It doesn't matter where it comes from.'

'Quite!' agreed Harriet.

'Danny,' shouted Mrs. Bustard, pen in hand, 'Danny we can `ave that there holiday now, babe. Butlins `ere we come. Wait till I tell our Bert!'

Harriet observed her efficiency as she leafed through the notes. 'Three grand there alright! You're a good'n Miss Glover,' she said, patting Harriet on the back. 'It was you, wasn't it? `e'd never have done this on `is own. You talked `im round to keep it all official. Well I'd rather be takin` it from `im. `e's got plenty judgin` by that swanky car `e drives.'

'Top of the range,' said Harriet as she took the signed receipt from her.

Mrs. Bustard immediately started fumbling in her bag. 'And I've got something for you Miss. Nearly forgot about it, I did.' She was beaming all over her face. '`ere, this is yours. Remember when our Dannybabes went runnin` back to you with this?' She thrust a much crinkled lottery ticket into Harriet's hand. 'He got them all mixed up, didn't he? I think you'll find you've won somethin` on that. Don't bother givin` me mine back, that fuckin` line never wins a thing. C'mon Danny get out of that sand before I box your ears. Wait till your Dad `ears this.'

She'd dragged Danny across the school playground and away before Harriet had barely chance to thank her. Harriet sat down, ticket in hand. She looked across at the numbers. Yes, that was her winning line alright. She could feel the tears starting to fill her eyes. Mrs. Bustard could so easily have claimed the money for herself. She remembered the parents' meeting and Mrs. Bustard cheering her on.

'Perhaps that's what did it,' Harriet decided, reaching for the box of tissues on her desk.

'Shall I come back?' the cleaning lady said as she clanked her bucket inside the doorway.

'Oh no, that's OK, you can come in. I'm going home now.'

'That was so kind of her and not even a mention of the news,' she thought, blowing her nose as she drove out of the school gateway. Her spirits were considerably lifted. She felt a huge surge of gratitude to Mrs. Bustard and decided there and then she didn't want to resign. She suddenly felt desperate for the deputy post. She wanted to steer those parents' meetings herself. She wanted to make a real difference to their lives. She hoped against hope Mr. Sanderson hadn't changed his mind.

She took her customary glance at Starboard Marine North West as she stopped at the lights. She wondered if he was still there. She knew Tricia would be well home by now. 'I'll phone her just as soon as I get in,' she thought. She could hardly wait.

'Ooh I've got some good news for you `arriet!' Tricia said just as soon as she'd picked up the phone.

'Bob didn't tell you off then?'

'Oh yes `e did and I told `im where to go. I said I'd divorce `im if `e didn't shut up.'

'So, it's Mr. Sanderson then. He's charmed you back into his arms,' said Harriet, 'you will have seen him today?'

'No `arriet, just that nosy Tarquin Bridgewater again. Am I sick of `im?' said Tricia impatiently, 'and even if I `ad seen *`im*, `e'd never charm me back into `is arms. I don't get you `arriet? That wouldn't be good news anyway. `e `asn`t been near all day. No, they took away that platform, didn't they `arriet and guess what? I brushed up more than `alf the pieces of your letter that must `ave slid underneath when she tore it up. I put them in my bag for you `arriet.'

'Oh thanks Tricia, you're an absolute angel.'

'Well `e can `ardly blackmail you with `alf a letter can `e? Anyway when I tried to piece my bits together, I mean yours `arriet, they didn't make any sense, so `is aren't going to either, are they `arriet?'

'Oh Tricia, I don't know how to thank you,' declared Harriet.

'Don't even mention it. Any more signs of `is little tricks `arriet? I'm sure `e`s up to something with that Tarquin Bridgewater.'

Harriet thought for a moment. All that cash he'd given her, *again*.

'Certainly is Tricia!'

'Oh `e `asn`t been down to that launderette again `as `e?'

'Well, he's definitely been somewhere,' Harriet said. 'You could be right. I wonder if he's offloading it to Tarquin Bridgewater for some reason?'

'Ooh `arriet, that's probably it! I wonder just what they're both up to? Anyway `arriet, `ow come that Joris Sanderson's such good buddies with the Prime Minister? And you said `e`s up for a knighthood. Why would `e be `honoured like that?'

'Well I believe he does a lot of charity work. I presume it's in recognition of that.'

'Like spreading `is favours round for free you mean `arriet? That's the only kind of charity work `e does. Can't get bed and sheets out of `is brain!'

Harriet laughed. Tricia was so good at putting her over-strung emotions into perspective.

'Well he might do proper charity work as well,' Harriet suggested, suddenly feeling the need to defend him. 'He does have a very genuine concern for the disadvantaged around us.'

'I wouldn't say Tarquin Bridgewater's disadvantaged with a boat like that, `arriet. `e`s got plenty of money `e `as. But `e would `ave wouldn't `e if our friend's shoving bunches of dirty fivers at `im. No wonder `e`s always asking me if our Joris `as left `im anything. Yes `arriet, that's it! `e`s givin` all that stolen money to `im, but then what does *`e* do with it `arriet?'

'That's the part that doesn't make much sense,' replied Harriet. 'Tarquin Bridgewater certainly doesn't need the money for himself. He's got to be a part of a distribution chain.'

'Ooh `arriet what a story we could tell if we `ad all the answers. I bet Internews TV would find that little lot very interesting. I don't think they'd be too bovvered about the missing `alf of your letter, then.'

'I'm sure they wouldn't,' agreed Harriet, half tempted to tease Simon Barnes into further enquiry just to get him off her back.

'Oooh, aren't we clever `arriet? We know their little game. Must go `arriet, I can `ear my Bob coming in, `e mustn't `ear us. Just keep watching `im at work, like me `arriet. That's when `e decides to turn up, that is.'

Harriet replaced the receiver wondering how near the mark Tricia was. Something in her didn't want to know. 'If she's right it's no wonder he doesn't want me anywhere near Internews TV!'

Suddenly Harriet was filled with remorse at causing him so much grief. Why, oh why did she hit back at him like that? After all it wasn't his fault that Danny had ended up with the playhouse on top of him. It wasn't his fault she'd left the first lot of money in the cabin. It wasn't his fault she'd managed to provide Internews TV with their best shots of the year.

She didn't suppose the PM would be best pleased either, that undignified struggle to his feet now exposed to the whole nation. Fortunately he'd got out from under before Belinda Oxfordshire had chance to stab him with those stiletto heels as she'd surfaced to snatch her letter with those long, white fingers. Harriet could still see the huge diamond flashing as she tore it to pieces. Then it suddenly struck her. It was on her right hand. 'She's not engaged to anyone,' Harriet triumphed. 'I must phone Tricia again.'

In the second it took Harriet to get to the phone she'd thought better of it. 'Tricia's right off him, she wouldn't be interested.'

She picked up her bag and rummaged for the lottery ticket Mrs. Bustard had given her before sitting back down on the sofa. 'I'll return it. I'll give him every last penny back.'

* * *

Harriet arrived at school the next morning feeling a whole lot better. She could hardly wait to get to the Post Office to claim the money. She was very grateful to Mrs. Bustard. At least she'd have something good to tell him and the chance to apologise.

She saw his car parked in its usual spot by the door. She was pleased he was there. Today she would teach to the best of her ability just in case he should pop into her room. Oh how she wanted to see him again, like she'd never wanted to see him before.

'Miss Glover,' she heard him say as the entrance door closed behind her. 'A quick word, if you don't mind.'

'Yes of course Mr. Sanderson.' She followed him into his room. Suddenly her confidence vanished. She felt very apprehensive, too apprehensive to say sorry, though with all her heart that's what she wanted to do.

'Miss Glover,' he repeated striding to the window. His strong masculine figure outlined by the early morning sun sent that predictable wave of weakness through her.

'Yes Mr. Sanderson.' She responded as if she'd just taken up a new appointment.

He looked sternly across at her, then turned to face the window. 'Belinda Oxfordshire who was acting on behalf of the company, Starboard Marine… Er, you did realise that, didn't you?'

'No, Mr. Sanderson,' declared Harriet.

'Damned estate agents!' he cursed. 'That's why I'm telling you myself. They seem incapable of relaying accurate information. Where was I? Ah yes! The company now has a considerable property portfolio, it's part of our investment strategy. Belinda, as a company employee, deals with all that side of it. For reasons best known to herself she now feels it's not such a good investment after all. As it happens I disagree with her and consider it highly unethical to withdraw the offer at this stage. However, she's having none of it and as that's what we pay her to do, being the company surveyor, I feel we've got to go along with her decision. Besides the directors don't see it as a problem and I haven't got the time to make waves, I'm afraid.'

'Oh,' said Harriet a bit shocked. 'When she first came to view she gave me the impression she was buying for herself and Ted, her fiancé.'

'As I've just said, she was purchasing on behalf of the company Miss Glover. But yes, they were going to be based up here for a little while until we got this new branch established. Ted was our business consultant and accountant until they split. Unfortunately I've been forced to take over the reins. You didn't think I wanted to invade your privacy by viewing your house from choice, did you?'

Harriet's heart went out to him. 'No, I don't, I mean I didn't Mr. Sanderson,' was all she could manage to say.

'I'm very sorry this has happened especially as I seem to remember the agent mentioning there was another offer on the table which you turned down in favour of ours. Unfortunately you backed the wrong horse Miss Glover.' He turned to face her and looked straight into her eyes. 'Try not to do it again!'

Harriet could feel herself blushing.

'Now, did you manage to get that Bustard woman to sign that chitt?'

'Yes,' said Harriet as she struggled with the zip on the inner pocket of her bag. She handed it over, wanting so much to take his hand.

'Thanks for that, Miss Glover. One less irritation out of the way. Speaking of which, Amanda's leaving at the end of the week. Have a word with her will you. She'll give you the low down on the job. I'll inform the office you'll be starting on Monday.'

'Yes, thank you,' Harriet said, politely.

She rushed to her classroom, placing her head in her hands as she sat down to the desk. She needed more time than this to absorb all that had just gone on.

The bell rang. Suddenly Danny came bursting through the door, banana in the air, with the rest of the class clamouring behind.

'He's pokin' us all with that banana Miss!' came the indignant voice of Simon Clarke. 'Look he's got Melanie in the eye and she's cryin` now.'

Hyper, Danny rushed around the circular tables bumping into the others as they tried to grab their chairs. 'He's just `it me on the nose with it now!' balled Sabaru Camaboolla.

'Stop it Danny Bustard! Come here this minute!' ordered Harriet. 'Are you OK Melanie?' she said noticing her eye was very watery. She reached for a tissue and put her arm around her. Her eye had gone quite pink.

'That was very naughty Danny! Whatever is the matter with you this morning?' I think your nose will be alright Sabaru. I suggest you leave it alone.'

Harriet's stomach was starting to turn as she watched the intermittent bubbles of green snot explode from her nostrils every time she touched it. 'Get that banana out of my face, Danny!' Too late, she turned round sharply and caught it straight in the eye. It started to water profusely.

'Ah, look what he's done to Miss,' came a delighted voice from under the table.

'On your seats immediately!' boomed Mr. Sanderson raising the file he was carrying as he slammed the classroom door closed.

'I'll take that!' he said, snatching the banana from Danny's hand. He glanced at Harriet and then at Melanie still cradled in her arm. 'I suggest you go and sort yourselves out Miss Glover while I hold the fort.'

Harriet, holding Melanie's hand left the stunned and silenced class to empathise with her young pupil.

She cautiously opened the classroom door as she returned with Melanie who was still rubbing her eye. At great speed Mr. Sanderson left the room. All heads were down as her class got on with their work. It remained like that for the rest of the day. Harriet was grateful for that. It had given her some unexpected space to mull over all he'd said.

The bell rang for home time. 'I wan' me banana back Miss. That Mr. Sandcastles put it in 'is pocket. I'm tellin' me Mum of 'im!' Danny winged at Harriet as she watched them file out of the room.

'What's up with yer now?' enquired Mrs. Bustard. 'You can't stay happy for more than two minutes can yer, *you*? We're goin' to Butlins don't forget. If you be'ave yourself!'

'It's me banana. 'e stole it from me!'

'Who stole it from you?'

''im!' he said pointing his finger at Mr. Sanderson now walking down the corridor towards them.

'Me poor little Dannybabes. One minute we're bein' told 'ow to give yer 'ealthy food and the next 'e's snatchin' it off yer. Just wait there a minute will youse. I'll sort 'im out if he's bin pickin' on yer!'

Harriet quickly ushered the last child out of the room and closed the door on Danny as Mrs. Bustard bristled up the corridor. She steeled herself for the inevitable.

'Are you sure you can handle all this, on top of that lot?' Mr. Sanderson said passing her the deputy's job file. 'They're certainly a lively bunch, not to mention their parents.'

So painfully aware that the promise of the morning was never destined to get off the ground she rubbed her eye. She could feel herself blush. She looked up. 'I'm terribly sorry Mr. Sanderson and I do appreciate you helping me out like that. I can only assume Danny was excited about now being able to go to

Butlins. That's the way he came in I'm afraid.'

'Well, it's not the way he's gone out. I'm just not having this sort of nonsense! For once his mother appears to have come on side. She says he's not going anywhere near the place until he says sorry. Expect an apology in the morning Miss Glover!'

That was it. He was gone. Harriet gathered the file with her books and bag and walked quickly down the corridor.

She fished in her bag for her spare keys, the only ones she had left, and hurried to the car before she could meet him again.

Head in a whirl, she drove home. What a day it had been. She turned into the drive and was grateful to turn the key on the engine and engage with the silence of the late afternoon. She sat for a few moments to reflect on Mr. Sanderson's words. She looked across at the house and back to the 'For Sale' board struggling to retain its vertical stance against the red brick wall. 'If only I'd known,' she thought. 'If only I'd known. The last thing he needed was that outburst!' She thought about the cat and how easily it could have created mayhem for him had it been discovered. It had been her fault. He'd not rebuked her. She desperately wanted to make amends. She thought about the lottery money and then thought better of it. After seeing him today she didn't think she'd have the courage to give it to him. She tussled with herself and decided the only way she could do it was to give that deputy post everything she had.

Harriet got out of the car. She suddenly felt the brush of fur and the nuzzle of a little wet nose against her calves as she stopped to put the key into the front door. The cat bounded ahead and then back again in and out of her legs as she put her things down. 'You've got a lot to answer for,' she said out loud catching its little black triangular head with a stroke as it jumped up in an attempt to cling to her swinging bag. 'And don't think I don't know how you got home either. You were lucky not to have suffocated in his black bag. Stupid cat!'

Her conversation was interrupted by the phone. It made her jump. She wanted it so much to be him.

'It's Mummy, Harriet. No wonder you didn't phone back! What on earth is going on Harriet? We've just watched the local news bulletin and they've shown the whole thing again, only this time that awful man Simon Barnes has invited us all to help him piece together the mystery letter. He reckons it holds the clue to why you left that steward all that money. He says if he hasn't got the answer by Friday we're "to watch this space!" '

Harriet do you realise how you've embroiled not only your boss who is about to be knighted but the Prime Minister too. Poor unfortunate man in the wrong place at the wrong time. Can't you just put an end to all of this Harriet and tell us why you left the darned man such a lot of money. I didn't know you had any to throw around. Goodness knows what Mark and those grandaughters of mine think. Mind you, he's as much to blame! If he'd married you like James and Paul married theirs you might not have gone on such a bender at your age. Speaking of which I expect the menopause has got a lot to do with it. Harriet are you still there? I do hope you're alright Harriet.'

'Don't worry,' Harriet said trying to reassure her almost hysterical mother. 'That pratt's got the wrong end of the stick completely. Just watch him make a complete fool of himself on Friday and that will be the last you'll hear of it.'

'Well, I'd rather like to know what was in the letter Harriet. Who was it to?'

'Mr. Sanderson, actually. It was my letter of resignation.'

'Oh, thank goodness for that Harriet! Is that all? So Mark's going to marry you then? Well, all's well that ends well. I knew I could rely on you both to be sensible in the end. Daddy sends his love. Must go!'

'Bye Mummy,' said Harriet, grateful for the lack of opportunity to get a word in.

She looked down at the flashing green light. 'Messages. I don't need them,' she told the cat who was now meowing loudly at the kitchen door. 'OK you'll be fed in a tick. Just let me catch these.'

'Good afternoon,' came the same voice that sounded far too like Mr. Sanderson's for Harriet's liking. 'Bryce Rae Roberts here. Please would you call the office immediately, we have an important message for you.'

'That can wait,' Harriet told the cat. 'We know exactly what that's all about.'

She listened for the next message. 'Harriet dear, it's Molly. Do phone back when you get a moment. Mr. Fishwick and I have got some splendid news! By the way Harriet you've managed to get yourself on television again. We're dying to find out what happened at that grand opening. How did everyone manage to end up on the floor? It was such a special occasion, too, with the Prime Minister there. You know Harriet I had a very strong feeling there was far more to our handsome friend than meets the eye. I knew when he left the ship like that he more than likely had friends in high places. What a pity it all went so wrong. Good job our Prime Minister's a decent sort of chap. I'm sure he'll have taken it all in his stride. We saw you having a go at that snivelling reporter Simon Barnes, though Harriet. I can't stand him! Well done Harriet! Oh Harriet, I can't wait to tell you the news. Percy and I are to be married. Well, you did promise to be our bridesmaid Harriet if the cat got back. Clever little thing going for that hideous man like that. Percy and I are bursting to know what happened. How on earth did it find its way back? We haven't fixed the date yet dear but we're looking at a late autumn wedding. As soon as we've booked everything I'll let you know. After seeing him on telly Percy's determined to track down our gorgeous friend. No doubt he'll be wanting to invite the PM too! What a coincidence dear that you should meet up with our gorgeous friend again. Well maybe not if he just happened to open that marina place in your area and of course he did give you that lift home. Lucky you Harriet! You've got such a lot to tell us. Anyway, must go, I think that's Percy ringing the doorbell. Do phone dear!'

Harriet paused for breath as the message ended. She found it hard to believe just how much truth there had been in her joke. 'Wow!' she thought, 'Mr. Fishwick and Molly getting married!' Harriet smiled to herself as she recalled Molly's horror at his nocturnal advances when she'd kindly swapped cabins and beds for her. 'Of course I'll be a bridesmaid, I couldn't be more thrilled for them both. And you can just get down,' she said to the cat. 'Just one more message to play.'

Harriet pressed the button. 'Ooh `arriet it's me. I `aven't seen `im for more than two seconds all week, I'm very pleased to say. Of course `e gave me one of those looks and I was quite impervious to `im. Well, for the first second I was and then I felt myself going funny all over! I `ad to be very strict with myself `arriet until I remembered that `aughty piece of string tying `erself in knots all round `im and I soon came to my senses.

Anyway `arriet I'm really phoning to tell you that cheeky Simon Barnes actually came in `ere trying to find out all about you. I saw `im through my one-way mirror before `e could see me so I was ready for `im. I was just brushing the floor, so I stopped and leaned on my brush. I told `im to go and get lost and `e threatened to piece your letter together live on Internews TV if `e `asn`t found out any more by Friday. I told `im `e should do just that and there was no use `im going round to yours because you'd gone away abroad for a few weeks.'

'Nice one, Tricia,' Harriet said.

'Anyway `arriet call me if you get any clues as to where all that money's coming from. It ain`t from this till that's for sure. I might just see if I can't get a peek at `is accounts. Keep you posted `arriet.'

Harriet, no longer able to fend the cat off, went into the kitchen and put the kettle on to boil while, at arms length, she opened a tin of cat food. She heaved. It wasn't doing anything to improve the state of her stomach, after being in such turmoil all day. She took the milk from the fridge and wobbled the over-full saucer to the floor. 'There, that's you sorted,' she said and proceeded to make herself a cup of tea before returning all the calls.

'Mr. Bryce speaking,' came the pompous voice down the phone. 'Bad news I'm afraid.'

'Too right it is!' retorted Harriet, 'especially as you completely disregarded my wish to go with Mr. and Mrs. Pendlebury in the first place.'

'Ah, you already know Mrs. Glover. It's not our usual practice to leave such information on the answer phone. I do wish vendors and purchasers would refrain from communicating in this way. We'd have far fewer offers falling through if everybody let the agents get on with the job they're supposed to do.'

'Exactly!' declared Harriet.

'I'm not sure I like your tone,' came the response.

'Just agreeing with you,' said Harriet suddenly remembering her manners. 'Any chance you could contact Mr. and Mrs. Pendlebury to let them know.'

'Just a minute. Let me get the hot box out. Ah, yes, here we are. No, terribly sorry Mrs. Glover they've gone on to purchase another one of our properties actually, not too far from you. Not to worry! We'll re-advertise yours and do another round of mailshots.'

'Thank you very much,' replied Harriet. 'I'll let you return to the job you're *supposed* to do.'

She felt better for getting that off her chest. 'Silly man,' she thought. She never wanted to sell to Belinda Oxfordshire in the first place. She decided to ring Molly next and save Tricia to the end.

It was gone five by the time Harriet had finished making the calls. She returned to the kitchen with the empty cup. She was pleased she'd decided to come clean with Tricia about Mr. Sanderson's working relationship with Belinda Oxfordshire. Besides she wanted to tell her how deflated Mr. Bryce was when she'd told him she already knew the sale was off. She knew Tricia would find it hilarious.

'Serves 'im right! Well fancy 'er calling it off just because of our little scrum. It's all come right for you in the end, 'arriet. You didn't want 'er to buy your 'ouse, anyway. What a cheek, though! Fancy them buying your 'ouse as an investment for 'is company. It's starting to make sense 'arriet. I really do wonder if that's 'ow 'e gets all that money laundered, buying 'ouses. Maybe 'e pays Tarquin Bridgewater to suss them out, but 'e never came to yours, did 'e? No, 'e must 'ave another job to do like you said 'arriet, passing the money on. But who to 'arriet? Anyway, 'e's a spiv 'arriet. That Joris Sanderson is most definitely a spiv! I don't believe it's only work with them two either. Not the way she was pouring 'erself all over 'im. Am I glad I've gone off 'im and I'm going to make sure I stay off 'im.' Tricia had said.

Harriet wasn't too sure if Tricia's resolve to remain out of love with Mr. Sanderson would last. Anyway she knew how hard that could be. She hoped Tricia's rapidly evolving insight into the Starboard Marine North West set-up would turn out to be her over-active imagination, but she had her doubts. Tricia was right, things were starting to fall into place.

'If she's right, it's certainly good reason to go off him,' she said to herself, but she knew in her heart nothing could extinguish the surging pain she continuously felt. She thought about Simon Barnes and cursed him for ever considering Charles Ormerod's story to be newsworthy. She would be so glad when Friday's 4 o'clock news was over. It would all be out of the way once he'd made himself look such a fool. With some trepidation she found herself looking forward to it. She'd invited Tricia round though. She didn't want to see it by herself.

Fortunately Molly had been too excited about her wedding to want to linger on Harriet's run-in with Simon Barnes but her stomach churned over again as she recalled Molly asking her to pop into that new marina place to get Mr. Sanderson's phone number.

'…just in case Percy can't manage to get hold of him. Oh we do so want him to come to our wedding Harriet,' she had said.

The thought of Mr. Sanderson turning up at Molly's wedding with Belinda

Oxfordshire was almost too much to bear. Any shreds of hope Harriet had managed to glean from the day dwindled as she recalled Tricia's words. She too, had now convinced herself that out of *that* business relationship full blown love was rapidly blossoming. 'Why else would Belinda Oxfordshire have thrown so many hints out? Why would he have bought her a hat?' she asked herself. She wished with all her heart she hadn't squandered her chances in a fit of fury.

Chapter 47

'So she pulled out then,' grumbled Mark as he gulped his morning tea in bed. 'I bet it's down to that lard ball, Hat. I couldn't quite see those two making a pad for themselves here.'

'I've already told you it was a business decision, Mark. It wasn't anything to do with Mr. Sanderson. In fact he took a dim view of it all, especially as we let Mr. and Mrs. Pendlebury go. Or should I say *you* did. I never wanted to sell to that Mz Oxfordshire in the first place.'

'Cash buyer Harriet. Her money's as good as anyone's.'

'I wouldn't be too sure of that either!' returned Harriet.

'You can't be too sure of anything in this world,' declared Mark, especially if there's an accelerated compound effect on global warming. Oh, by the way Hat, I forgot to tell you. It's ages off yet but they're asking, in the first instance, for volunteers to join the Antarctic expedition in September. They've got to replace the team that are down there now. I quite fancy it myself. Watch a few icebergs melting. Would you mind Hat? We'll be away for three months. Back home for Christmas. Think of the honeymoon we could have on that hearth rug when I come back.'

'You've got to be married before you can have a honeymoon, Mark!' Harriet said, stomping out of bed. 'And I suppose Melissa will be going?' Harriet paused, 'But with Geoffrey this time.'

'They got married and didn't have a honeymoon which makes your statement totally illogical Harriet.'

'You always manage to sidestep the issue Mark. Well you go and do your own thing for three months and I'll do mine. You never know I might just be married when you get back!'

'Well it certainly won't be to that name dropping lump of lard. He's well and truly spoken for!'

Harriet slammed the bathroom door closed and felt the hot spray of water from the shower mingle with her rapidly emerging tears. Maybe her mother was right. Maybe she *was* on the verge of the menopause. She knew she couldn't get a handle on letting Mr. Sanderson go. She knew she was being totally irrational. Totally illogical. She desperately wanted to blame her hormones. 'If only Mark would marry me. Mummy is absolutely right. I know I'd settle down. I wouldn't even be looking at anyone else. It's all Mark's fault.'

Then she thought of Tricia. 'Just how much difference would being married make in the face of meeting someone like Mr. Sanderson?'

Harriet heard Mark shout a perfunctory goodbye before closing the front door behind him. 'He's gone to work without getting washed,' she thought, 'green at least.'

She went down to the kitchen and met the trail of his discarded clothes on the floor. She spotted he'd used the dishcloth for a flannel. 'How disgusting,' she said to the cat, before getting ready for school. 'At least I won't have to cope with all this when he goes.' She left it all there. She didn't want to be late for school.

Harriet went, determined to spend as much time as she could with Amanda. This was the one positive thing she had in her life and was she going to make a go of it.

It seemed that she would be left pretty much in charge of the whole school as according to Amanda, Joris would be focussing as much as possible on his other business.

Harriet was very grateful to Alice Atkins who'd popped along to reassure her that she would take on all the admin work Mr. Sanderson liked to do, but he'd specifically requested that Miss Glover be totally responsible for directing and planning the parenting classes. Harriet was to have a completely free rein. She could hardly wait for Monday.

For the rest of the week Harriet's mind was set on how she'd turn the whole school round. She hadn't seen Mr. Sanderson and didn't want to until she could prove her worth. Highly motivated, she was enlivened by the task in hand. She decided she'd probably be a lot better off with Mark out of the way too, in September. She hoped she'd get the chance to see this thing right through.

This work was going to be totally demanding. This was Harriet's baby. She'd been given it and she would nuture it until every parent of every child in the school felt their own success. Then she'd watch the pride in each child as the demands of home and school synchronised to make sense of this world of learning they'd been thrown into. There would be positive results, starting with a completely new school uniform. Then a school magazine. The children would become involved with school discipline and friendship, curriculum planning, outings, fund raising, school meals, playtime activities... The list was endless. Harriet could see a way in which all the children could contribute to all the aspects of school life.

This was what she needed. A complete break from all the emotional turmoil that had governed her life for so long. A serious task that would not only energise herself but all the teaching staff. They would need to drive this together if she was to pull if off.

With the humdrum of the teacher's day out of her system, Harriet completely forgot it was Friday afternoon.

The doorbell rang. Harriet gathered up the post on her way to answering it.

'Hi 'arriet!' Tricia greeted. 'You didn't forget I was coming round, did you? Quick 'arriet turn the telly on. We're in for a laugh.'

They rushed into the lounge and Harriet turned the television on just in time to catch the local news.

'Ooh 'arriet, I can't wait to see 'im making a fool of 'imself. 'is 'alf of your letter definitely doesn't make any sense.'

'Maybe he's already discovered that Tricia,' said Harriet, nervously. 'I hope he hasn't got anything else up his sleeve.'

The doorbell rang.

'What a time to be visited,' Harriet complained.

'Keep watching `arriet. I'll get rid of them just as quick as I can.'

As fast as Tricia disappeared Harriet watched the screen. She could feel herself turning to jelly. She saw Tricia opening her own front door to a huge fluffy microphone being pushed at her face. She could hear Tricia's irate voice in stereo.

'Bloody `ell! What are you doin` `ere? Of all the bloody cheek! Didn't I tell you `arriet `as gone off abroad. I'm only `ere to feed the cat.'

'Abroad eh? Now that's beginning to make sense. We've gleaned more than she thinks. Goes on a cruise, leaves a wad of hush money to the steward,' came the sneering voice of Simon Barnes. 'She wouldn't happen to be terminating that pregnancy out of sight of her husband by any chance? You can't blame us for following this one through, luv. She mixes in high places!'

Harriet went ice cold and felt very sick as she watched the triumphant expression on Simon Barnes' face.

'So how come you were up front with the rich and famous at that grand opening? Oh sorry luv, of course you're the cleaner down there. It would have been discrimination to leave you out.'

'Discrimination? You insulting bugger!' raged Tricia opening the door to get just close enough to kick him hard at the zip in his trousers. 'Now you get your bleedin' foot out of this door if you don't want another one.'

He did. Harriet didn't know whether to laugh or cry as she saw him crouched over, holding himself. He hobbled down the path shouting at the crew to 'stop the bloody cameras rolling!'

Tricia, red in the face and trembling with fury flew back to the television to see the last of the crew scramble into the back of the van as the words 'INTERNEWS TV' simultaneous with the outside, shot swiftly past the hedge.

'Ooh `arriet, I feel much better now. Wasn't I a good shot? I didn't think I was capable of such things. What a bloody cheek `e's got! Thinks I'm the soddin` cleaner down there just `cos I `ad a brush in me `and when `e came in. I'll `it `im with it next time!'

Harriet put her arm around Tricia and they started to shake hysterically. They rolled around between the sofa and the floor in pain as the tears streamed down their cheeks. It was only the sound of the phone ringing that brought Harriet to her feet.

'Oh, so you're not abroad then? Congratulations Harriet!' came her mother's frosty tone. 'It would have been nicer if you'd told Daddy and I first. Of course that's why he's finally got round to marrying you. You could hardly give birth out of wedlock at your age, though goodness knows they do anything they like these days. Like that common friend of yours kicking that poor man where it hurts. Not that I've got much time for him with his preposterous innuendo but I didn't care for *that*. I do hope you aren't going to spend these menopausal years with that awful girl constantly brawling on Internews TV Harriet, I've got the

Womens' Institute to think of! Don't forget I've got a lot of friends there that watched you grow up Harriet.'

In absolute pleats Harriet shrieked and sobbed down the phone.

'Now don't get upset Harriet, of course we still love you, Daddy and I. We'll get over it. Just you look after yourself. It is Mark's isn't it?'

Harriet heard the receiver go down without waiting for an answer. 'Just Mummy,' she said to Tricia, creased double, 'having a go!' She was so hysterical it never even crossed her mind to deny any of it.

They turned to the television and read the runner at the bottom of the screen. Breaking news: Simon Barnes assaulted by local cleaner.

'Ooh `arriet, you don't think I'll get into trouble do you?'

'Of course not Tricia. We've got too much on him. Pregnant indeed!'

'I thought you'd been `iding that one from me, for a moment `arriet.'

'No, not at all,' declared Harriet. 'How dare he make false accusations. He's invading our privacy. Any trouble from him and we'd just threaten to sue.'

Tricia immediately felt very much better. 'Ooh I do `ope that's the last we'll `ear from `im `arriet. Bloody cheek calling me a cleaner when I'm a PA. I went to college for six weeks to train to be a secretary. How dare `e insult my professional status.'

'Ooh ay Tricia,' replied Harriet, 'guess who's just driven up?'

'They've not come back, `ave they? Well what a bloody cheek. I'll give `im another one, only `arder this time.'

'No Tricia it's Mr. Sanderson. Quick! Into the cupboard under the stairs,' ordered Harriet.

'He'll see my car `arriet. You'll `ave to answer it.'

'No we bloody well won't,' said Harriet grabbing Tricia by the arm. They squashed into the small cloaks cupboard under the stairs and waited for the doorbell to ring.

Two short rings were swiftly followed by one long one.

'Is `e ever going to take `is finger off?' Tricia whispered. Harriet was just about to answer when they heard a push on the front door.

'Tricia, you couldn't have closed it properly,' panicked Harriet.

'Not wise to leave the front door open Miss Glover, it could have been anybody!'

They both scrambled out of the cupboard to Mr. Sanderson standing in the doorway. He shot them a knowing glance.

'We were just looking for my keys, weren't we Tricia? I lost them last weekend and I haven't been able to get into my filing cabinet since. There's stuff in there I want to use in school next week,' finished Harriet, desperately trying to gain some credibility.

'Oh yes, we most certainly were Mr. Sanderson,' said Tricia suddenly trying hard with her pronunciation. I came round especially to help you didn't I Harriet? You can see for yourself Harriet's filing cabinet is right at the back of that cupboard. You 'ave to mind you don't bang your 'ead on the inside of the stairs though to get at it. I've been bumping my 'ead all afternoon 'aven't I Harriet trying to find those flippin' keys. We've been in there all the time, we 'aven't even 'ad time to watch the news. Have we 'arriet?'

'Really?' said Mr. Sanderson, taking a bunch of keys from his pocket and handing them over to Harriet. 'I think you'll find these are yours, thanks to Belinda. She noticed they'd been kicked to somewhere or other. You might see your way to thanking her Miss Glover.'

Before Harriet could say anything he turned, closed the door behind him and got back into his car.

'Phew! That was a close shave,' said a most relieved Harriet as she checked the keys on the ring. 'Thanks Tricia for that brilliant back-up.'

'Think nothing of it 'arriet! It was my pleasure. I was convinced 'e'd come round to give us a going over after that news bulletin. Of course 'e wouldn't 'ave known I was 'ere, would 'e, but 'e might 'ave been going to 'ave a go at you 'arriet.'

'Exactly!' said Harriet.

Before they'd had time to fully appreciate the sense of relief the doorbell went again. Harriet answered it.

'See me in my office at 7.30 prompt on Monday morning Miss Glover.' He marched off, got into his car and drove away.

Harriet hurried back to Tricia. 'It was him, back again.'

'Yes, I said to myself that's funny, I thought you'd just gone. I thought I was seeing double just now when 'e drove off. Mind you 'arriet if there was two of 'im we could 'ave one each, couldn't we? Isn't 'e gorgeous? Oh I'm 'avin' a terrible time trying to get 'im out of my system 'arriet. I mustn't weaken. Don't let me weaken 'arriet. Oh sorry 'arriet. What did 'e want?'

'He wants to see me on Monday morning at half past seven. I thought he was away.'

'So did I,' said Tricia. 'Oooh, but that's early. It doesn't sound very good does it 'arriet?'

'It certainly doesn't,' agreed Harriet.

'He definitely told me 'e was going away, though. He must 'ave got unpaid leave or something?'

Harriet nodded in agreement. 'Story was he wanted to get Starboard Marine North West up and running, but how he squared that one with the authorities I'll never know.'

'How he squares goin' away with getting our place up and running, I'll never know either,' said Tricia, "e's a law unto 'imself, 'e is.'

'I'm just hoping against hope he didn't see the news.'

'Me too,' agreed Tricia, 'otherwise we're both in the soup!'

Chapter 48

Out early on Monday morning, Harriet was at least grateful that Mark had appeared blissfully unaware of the doorstep traumas of Friday afternoon. She wished she could say the same of Mr. Sanderson. She stopped at the lights and looked across to Starboard Marine North West. She wondered what was going on in his life. She recalled him telling her how complicated things were for him. Oh how she wished she could help.

The lights turned to green and as she drove off she rehearsed morning assembly in her mind. First day of acting as deputy head. This was not the start she'd envisaged. He wasn't supposed to be there. Her thoughts turned to Tricia. She remembered he'd said the same to her. 'Not at Starboard Marine North West either, then, so it's nothing to do with getting that up and running.' Her thoughts ran away as she tried to work out where he was going and who with. By the time Harriet drove through the school gateway she was convinced that Mr. Joris and Mrs. Belinda Sanderson would be returning from their world cruise honeymoon just in time for Clarissa's wedding.

She parked the car alongside his and looked at her watch. Twenty five minutes past seven. Just time to dump her things in the classroom.

Harriet smoothed her hair, twisted her skirt round to recentre the front seam and pulled her jumper down before knocking on Mr. Sanderson's office door.

'In!' she heard his sharp command.

She struggled for a few seconds with the old silver ball handle and died a thousand deaths wondering what he must have been making of the rattling knob on the other side. It had never done this to her before.

'You've finally managed it Miss Glover! Close it behind you will you.'

Harriet gave it a sharp turn and to her utter horror the knob came off in her hand. The door was firmly shut.

'Good start Miss Glover,' he snapped as he lifted the phone. 'Brown should be around somewhere.' He hammered the caretaker's extension key without success. 'That damned man can never be found,' he stormed as he banged the receiver down. He looked at Harriet clinging on to the doorknob. 'Just put it on the desk will you!'

Harriet obeyed and looked across to see Mr. Brown coming across the playground.

'There he is Mr. Sanderson,' Harriet said pointing towards the window.

Mr. Sanderson pushed hard to open the old wooden frame and called over.

'Mr. Brown! Come and get us out of this damned place immediately will you?' He reached for the handle. 'It came off in Miss Glover's hand. No surprises there!'

Mr. Brown touched his cap. 'Just let me get my tools Sir. I'll be right with you.'

Harriet watched him retrace his steps as Mr. Sanderson turned to face her.

'I'm terribly sorry Mr. Sanderson.' The colour flooded to her cheeks.

'It's not that you should be apologising for Miss Glover. So you were pregnant all the time?'

He scanned her from head to toe and then his eyes rested below her waist at the now twisted seam of her skirt.

Harriet was stunned into utter silence.

'I told you the last thing I needed was that damned reporter snooping around. Do whatever it takes to get him out of my life!'

She could hear Mr. Brown turning his screwdriver on the other side of the door. Oh how she wanted to get out of that room.

'Nearly there sir,' came the confident but breathless voice.

They both jumped as Mr. Brown suddenly shot the door open.

'That will be all Miss Glover. By the way, slight change of plan. I'll be popping back from time to time.'

'A quick word, Mr. Brown,' he said moving towards him as Harriet left the room.

She shot to her classroom. 'I've got to go back. I've got to tell him,' she thought. She could feel herself trembling. Surely he couldn't think that of her? She'd explained it all to him. How could he go on a throw away line from the likes of Simon Barnes? How did he even get to see the news almost at the same time as arriving at her house? Harriet's mind was whirling. 'He must have wanted to say more than that to ask me to see him so early.' How she cursed that door handle.

She summoned up as much courage as her shaking body would allow and walked the never ending corridor back to his room. The door was open. Mr. Brown was brushing up the bits of wood and sawdust from the floor.

'He's just gone, if it was him you wanted.'

'Oh no, thank you,' Harriet said, 'it's quite alright.'

Harriet knew it wasn't quite alright at all. She had to take assembly and face the hundred and one new tasks the day would bring. Her stomach sank and she began to feel quite ill. How ever could she put the record straight? She didn't know when she would see him again.

She couldn't bring herself to stay in his office any longer than it took to gather the paperwork for the day which she took to the staff room while the supply teacher took over her class for the morning. She was grateful not to be losing her class altogether. She needed that familiarity and anyway it provided the base for launching her new ideas. By the time Harriet got home she felt it had been the longest day of her life.

She jumped when she heard Mark's key turning in the door.

'Bob's livid!' announced Mark as soon as he pushed the lounge door open. 'Yes, just bumped into him at the petrol station. Apparently the girl behind the till recognised Tricia. Told him she'd just caught a glimpse of that reporter from Internews TV on Friday afternoon on their doorstep wanting to know which rich and famous person had made her pregnant, said she didn't realise Tricia was a cleaner. When the girl said "Fancy it happening to the likes of her," he said he hit the roof!'

Harriet went cold.

'I don't blame him either,' stormed Mark. 'I hope you had nothing to do with this Harriet. Just as well it wasn't our doorstep. He'll keep going until he's got some dirt to dish up. Believe you me he'll use every trick in the book!'

Harriet walked over to the window. It was better to look anywhere than at Mark's sceptical face. 'That girl's probably got it all wrong. Tricia's *not* pregnant,' she declared.

'She'd better not be!' said Mark. 'Bob would divorce her before she could turn round. I wouldn't put it past that lard ball either!'

Harriet didn't answer. The thought was just too painful.

Chapter 49

For the next eight weeks Harriet stepped up the parenting classes and delighted in the enthusiasm and cooperation she got from all the parents and staff. She was amazed at how easily her ideas had proliferated into positive change and how much they, and the children had to give as they all pulled together to make the difference the school needed. She hadn't seen sight nor sound of Mr. Sanderson during that time inspite of his intention to keep popping in. She knew he would be avoiding her. All her energy became absorbed in her mission to turn the school round and she fed on the success that was evident everywhere, from the palms in the foyer to the artwork on the walls, she was loving every minute. The school magazine acted as a magnet, a focus in print where both children and parents could proudly read of their success. Since she'd got the parents into using the school computers, and after talking nicely to Mr. Brown, she'd completely zoned one of his little rooms to store all those boxes and bags of stuff no longer destined for the car booty, now on their way to an internet auction. The school funds were growing rapidly. She'd begged and pleaded with local businesses for sponsorship to widen the children's horizons, and got it. There was now money for a variety of extra-curricular activities including sailing. Harriet had had to swallow hard to approach Tarquin Bridgewater, but she'd managed to secure his full cooperation in gaining the use of the sailing club. How pleased she was that Mark and Bob had agreed to help out the qualified instructor with the children.

'You're a good'n Miss Glover!' she could hear Mrs. Bustard say in the back of her mind. 'She's a good'n that Miss Glover!' she could hear Mrs. Bustard say to the crowd in the corridor. Harriet was so grateful to her for she knew in her heart of hearts Mrs. Bustard was the one with the influence. The one the parents would listen to. The key player in all of it.

She hoped Mr. Sanderson would be pleased. Tricia hadn't seen him either. He'd definitely gone somewhere. Harriet wanted so much for him to be pleased with her. To her surprise she'd actually been so busy she'd hardly missed him. It was just when she stopped to think, like now, that the emptiness and longing set in.

The phone rang. It was Tricia. 'Ooh `arriet! Just guess who turned up today?'

'Not him?' returned a shocked Harriet.

'Well not `im on `is own that is, but `im with that long grinning lamp post.'

Harriet had heart sink. 'Oh,' she said.

'Yes `arriet, wouldn't be surprised if she wasn't behind me getting into all that trouble with my Bob when `e thought I was pregnant. I `aven't quite worked it all out yet `arriet especially as my Bob refused to tell me where `e got the story from only that it was to do with my work and that TV reporter, but I wouldn't mind betting she `ad something to do with it. I nearly lost my `usband `arriet over all that.'

'That wouldn't do, Tricia,' said Harriet, observing how Bob had not missed the opportunity to rein her in.

'`ad it been your Mark with you I could've understood it after that nasty experience on your doorstep. Well you know why we `aven't `eard any more from `im, that Barnes slime ball, don't you `arriet?'

'No,' replied Harriet who hadn't wanted to tempt fate contemplating it.

'My Bob went straight down there with my test thingy written **NOT PREGNANT** all over its window and `e said `e`d land `im one if `e ever so much as came near the place again. It seems to `ave worked `arriet. Thank goodness!'

'Thank goodness,' agreed Harriet, thinking Simon Barnes had obviously presumed Bob to be Mark. 'Good on your Bob, Tricia!' Harriet knew she would be eternally grateful to him.

'I'll say,' said Tricia, 'anyway `arriet, take a deep breath. This is what I really wanted to tell you, apart from all `is accounts looking alright to me, sorry to say.'

'Go on,' demanded Harriet unable to bear the suspense.

'They're engaged! Against my better judgement I `ad to congratulate them `arriet. Whatever does `e see in that long streak of liquorice? I bet she's got some kind of `old over `im. Yes, that's it! She blackmailed `im into it! Am I glad my Bob didn't divorce me `arriet. `e was the only man I'd `ave ever left `im for. He's broken my `art `arriet. I can't get it out of my mind. I was " `is little star" `arriet. Remember?'

Harriet could feel the tears welling in her eyes and a large lump got stuck in her throat.

'Are you alright `arriet?' asked Tricia, 'I think the line's gone a bit funny. I can `ardly `ear you.'

Harriet swallowed hard. 'I'm OK thanks Tricia,' she said, 'I just can't believe it either.'

'He asked me to save that one for him.' Harriet cried to herself as she put the phone down. 'That's all he wanted of me, just to wait for him. That's why he's done it. He couldn't possibly have fallen in love with *her*. She's enticed him. I bet she's even made things up about me.'

Then she had a thought. 'She must have been the one who saw the news and then couldn't wait to phone *him* about it, no doubt embroidering it along the way.

Mr. Sanderson wouldn't possibly have had time to see it, he was too soon round here. Yes that's it. That's definitely it! Tricia was right and wrong. It was *me* Belinda Oxfordshire had it in for. It was that garage girl though, not listening properly, thinking Simon Barnes was having a go at Tricia that got her into trouble with Bob.' Harriet suddenly felt very sorry for her. She knew that garage girl had inadvertently most definitely done her a huge favour. She began to feel bad about it. For the world she hadn't wanted Bob and Tricia to carry the flak. 'How worse can things get?' she asked herself.

Harriet sank into the sofa and sobbed her heart out. Her thoughts ran wild.

'Maybe she didn't entice him at all. Maybe he just wants a wife of the right social standing, someone who fits into his social circle. I'm not sophisticated enough for him.'

All the work she'd done in the school now counted for nothing. She just wanted to see him again to explain. She was desperate to see him. She didn't know how long it would be before he married Belinda Oxfordshire.

The phone rang. She picked it up.

'Be late tonight Hat,' came Mark's voice, 'don't bother waiting up for me.'

Harriet couldn't remember what she'd said to him in reply. She didn't care. She went back on to the sofa and broke her heart crying.

The cat jumped onto her lap. Then it clambered up her jumper and started licking her face. The tears bagan to glisten as they dropped on to the end of its whiskers. 'Oh Pepper,' she sobbed. 'What have I done?'

Chapter 50

In the face of losing Mr. Sanderson to Belinda Oxfordshire Harriet lost all enthusiasm for the task in hand. She was glad she'd given it the huge push it needed to get it off the ground and was very grateful the momentum was such that it really didn't need her input any more. She continued to do her deputy job as best she could, but her mind was elsewhere. There wasn't a day gone by in which she wasn't constantly looking for him.

'Any sign of Mr. Sanderson?' she had asked Amanda on various occasions. 'It's strange,' she would say, 'you two are like ships in the night. One of these days he'll actually get to see you!'

Harriet didn't need such confirmation. She knew he was avoiding her as if his life depended on it. Then one day, just one day they met in the doorway. He was going out and she was on her way in. For a split second they froze. Harriet was so taken aback she opened her mouth to speak and all the wrong words came tumbling out.

'You're engaged Mr. Sanderson!' she said

'And you're pregnant Miss Glover!' he replied.

Harriet had lost her one opportunity to put things right. He'd marched past her and driven off before she'd even stepped off the old metal rim that held the sunken doormat in place. No wonder she was down.

Mark was convinced she was in the doldrums because they were having to start all over again with the house sale. 'Never mind Hat,' he would say, 'something will turn up. It won't be long before you can leave that dump. It'll always be a dump Hat, no matter what you think you've done to it!'

Of course Harriet rose to the bait every time. They'd had more rows over her new job than enough. Mark was beginning to feel sidelined. He was looking forward to escaping to the Antarctic.

There was a wedding to go before that, Harriet kept reminding him. Oh how she didn't want to go to Clarissa's wedding. She didn't know how she would cope seeing *them* together, *engaged*. She didn't want to see James and Geraldine either. No doubt Belinda Oxfordshire would befriend Geraldine. They had a lot in common. 'Not all of it nice,' Harriet said to herself. She couldn't bear the thought of seeing Paul and Susan. Pregnant Susan, ripe with impending motherhood. 'If only I were really pregnant,' she thought in despair.

She'd managed to squash that very rumour running through the school via Mrs. Bustard who, of course, had informed her of the gossip in the first place.

'Don't worry though Miss Glover. I'll soon put `em straight. You're one of us you are. You, your friend and the cat. Just what we would've all done between us. Gone for `im good and proper!'

Harriet was convinced Simon Barnes had provided exactly the catalyst she'd needed to enable her to bond with the parents. She still had to tell her mother though. Just for the moment she couldn't bring herself to do it.

Anyway she'd had a busy week at school. The last one before the summer holidays was usually fraught but with Harriet's extra responsibilities she'd worked long hours to ensure an easy return for Amanda in September. She'd hoped against hope to see him before they broke up, but nothing. She had to face the next six weeks dreading the wedding at the end of it. She flipped the calendar over to August and stood transfixed to the ring she'd pencilled around the thirty-first. Her heart was breaking to see him, but not with her. She turned to September. Mark would be away the very next day. 'I can still call it off Hat, if you want, but you are going to be a bridesmaid at that wedding. You wouldn't want *me* there anyway.'

'Too right,' Harriet had replied, 'always the bridesmaid, never the bride!'

'Well you never know Hat, you did say you might be married by the time I get back,' Mark had joked.

'Not any more,' Harriet thought, 'he's someone else's now.'

She decided to let Mark find out for himself. She couldn't bear the 'I told you so!' bit from him. Of course he'd been right all along. Looking back Harriet could see it too. She was absolutely all over him at the grand opening. Mr. Sanderson had only spoken of his business relationship with her. Harriet had never wanted to read between the lines. She was glad that Mark had planned to be out sailing for most of the weekend. She just wanted to be miserable on her own.

She returned to the calendar and flicked back to Switzerland and the fields of flowers. The tears filled her eyes. She'd managed to lose the dream of being with him for ever.

Chapter 51

'Are you certain those girls have got all their accessories to go with those dresses tomorrow?' her mother queried anxiously down the phone.

'That was all sorted last weekend,' said Harriet. 'Just at the moment I'm knee deep in Mark's stuff. He's off on Sunday.'

'Oh of course he is Harriet. I've had nothing but Geraldine fussing about for weeks. If she's not on the phone she's ringing the doorbell. Daddy and I are starting to get a bit tired of it. I'm quite sure everything will work out and we'll all have a wonderful day tomorrow.'

'Not me,' thought Harriet. She just wanted it all over. She was going to have to be cheerful to everyone, including her babies. How she wished they lived nearer. How she needed them now.

She took her outfit out of the wardrobe. She'd been able to buy a size smaller and put it down to all the chasing around she'd been doing at school. She held the pale blue dress and jacket to her shoulders before trying on her new straw hat. 'I need to get my hair washed,' she thought as she flicked the blonde strands back under the blue brim. She took her shoes out of the box. She'd been so pleased at how everything had been such a close colour match. She'd been determined to outdo Belinda Oxfordshire at this wedding. She had set her mind on being irresistibly stunning for Mr. Sanderson. Now she couldn't even bear to see him.

'Ready Harriet!' called Mark as he came up the stairs for his wallet. 'Gosh Hat you look absolutely beautiful. It makes me proud you're mine.' Harriet let the remark go as he took her in his arms. 'Wish I wasn't off tomorrow Hat. Still it'll soon pass. Wear it for me when I get back will you?' Harriet didn't answer. He kissed her on the cheek as she pulled away.

'Right then Hat. Better go or we'll be late.'

The sun was shining as they drove up to the church.

'Looks like they've all come up in Tristan's car,' Mark said as he pointed to the black Audi parked by the gate. 'It'll be good to see them all again Hat. Promise not to go missing on them this time.'

'Very funny,' said Harriet, definitely not in the mood. She wanted to see her girls as much as Mark did Explanations were never much good over the phone.

They managed to park at the end of a long line of cars skirting the church. Harriet straightened herself as she got out. They walked up the winding path flanked either side by gravestones and flowers. She looked across to the back of the church where she could just see the tops of three or four cars in the private car park. As they wound their way towards the church entrance the hedge dipped. She suddenly went wobbly. His silver Mercedes was unmistakeable as she stretched her toes to read the personalised number plate.

'What are you doing now Hat?' Mark said as he pulled her towards him. 'Come on we are *late*.'

'Just made it before the bride,' declared the smiling vicar. He pushed a carrier bag into Harriet's hand. 'Be an angel will you my dear and make sure this gets to which ever guest put it down. You wouldn't believe the lost property we get at weddings.'

Harriet relieved him of it and hurried in behind Mark as he strode up the aisle to the front of the church. They pushed past their girls and the boys to sit in the empty space alongside the wall. Then their pew suddenly housed a flurry of waves and smiles and hushed whispers which quickly halted to the commanding chord of the organ as the unfolding score of Widor's Toccata resounded throughout the lofty building.

Harriet got a lump in her throat. She always did at weddings.

'Alright Harriet?' her mother whispered from the pew in front.

'Lovely lilac hat Mummy,' said Harriet, to Mark digging her in her ribs with his elbow. She pulled away from him. He'd just spoilt the moment. 'Shush,' she could hear him muttering. She felt irritated.

She looked across to the bridegroom. Harriet had only met him a couple of times and she wasn't at all fussy on him. He was tall and very thin, a bit of a Hooray Henry. 'Poor unfortunate chap to have been christened so. Well he could always change his name or his voice, or both,' she mused to herself, 'but not his ears.' She observed the back of his head wasn't unlike the shape of the doorknob she'd managed to pull off in her hand, 'and a good gust of wind behind those ears would most certainly see him up in the belfry.' Harriet had to stifle a giggle as Clarissa struggled up the aisle on James' arm.

A princess she wasn't. Harriet couldn't believe the miles and miles of white organza wrapped around her. It was wider than the width of the aisle and Harriet could see it getting trapped between poor James' legs as he finally managed to park her alongside Henry.

The two hefty bridesmaids panted to a stop behind them and Harriet noticed one of the bustles beginning to lean to the left. She hoped it would stay there, at least until they got out of the church.

The music stopped and the vicar took command.

The church silenced to respect the traditional exchange of wedding vows.

* * *

'Wasn't it a beautiful service?' 'Such a lovely wedding!' 'Clarissa and Henry were made for each other!' Harriet could hear the whole host of complimentary observations filling the church porch as she tried to keep her head down in an attempt to avoid Belinda Oxfordshire and Mr. Sanderson. Carrier bag in one hand and pushing Mark forward with the other, she managed to steer him away before getting involved in any family photographs.

'What's the hurry Hat?' asked Mark. 'You didn't have to shove me quite so hard through that lot, did you?'

'Oh most of the photographs will be taken at the reception,' declared Harriet as she spotted Bob and Tricia in the crowd at the church gate. Harriet continued to drag Mark on, managing Tricia a wave just before she threw a handful of confetti over them both. 'Your turn next `arriet?' she could hear her say as they hurried past.

Covered in confetti they got into the car. Mark was furious. 'She'd have saved that for the bride if we hadn't got there first.'

They struggled to remove the tiny paper bells and horseshoes from their hair.

'Now look at the car. I only cleaned it this morning,' Mark snapped.

They drove off to Birchdale Hall. 'We'll have to do a detour,' Harriet declared. 'We can't arrive before the bride and groom.'

'Then what were you pushing and shoving me out of the church for Harriet? What a waste of petrol. You'll never save the planet.'

Harriet looked at him in disbelief. 'You're beginning to sound like Melissa Scott.'

After another twenty minutes of polluting the atmosphere with unnecessary carbon (according to Mark) they finally drove through the grand entrance of Birchdale Hall and just managed to squeeze into the last space in the car park.

'Good grief!' said Mark, 'Just how many people have they asked? Now we'll have to fight our way to our table, wherever that is. Don't forget that carrier bag either. Next thing you'll have the vicar after you.'

Harriet got out and threw her new dainty blue leather handbag onto her shoulder before picking up the carrier bag. She saw the fancy writing on the side and immediately recognised it. "Cruising Christiana" it read.

'Oh no, I haven't got to give it to *her*, I mean *him*, have I?' she suddenly said out loud.

'Who?' answered Mark. 'Are you psychic, or something?'

'I just think I know who it belongs to, that's all,' diverted Harriet.

'If you know who it belongs to it'll save asking everyone then, won't it Hat?' he replied in his usual logical fashion.

'Well I certainly am not going looking for either of them.' Harriet said to herself. 'She can jolly well do without it.' Harriet was suddenly very pleased that Belinda Oxfordshire had been denied the pleasure of being crowned with her new hat in church.

They went in through the grand entrance hall to be met by Rachael and Clare. 'Over here,' they chorused. 'We're all sitting with Samantha and Gabriella and that gorgeous chap Joris from Starboard Marine North West. You know Mummy, the one Uncle James met at the golf club, the one who was at the meeting at home when you were in the shed Mummy,' gabbled Rachael. 'Oh and his fiancee! Worse luck! I thought he was supposed to be single. It didn't take her long to get her claws into him.'

'Your mother knows exactly who he is Rachael. She's not that off the planet that she doesn't know who's supposed to be in charge of her school.'

Harriet glowered at him.

'Oh, of course,' said Rachael, 'wish he was *my* boss.'

Harriet almost went to pieces at the thought of them all sitting together and it took all her courage to enter the dining room. It was lavish to the extreme and no expense had been spared on the flowers and trimmings for Clarissa's big day.

'We're right up there, next to the top table,' declared Clare as they wound their way round the scores of beautifully laid tables. For a moment they reminded Harriet of the cruise. She clutched the carrier bag close to her side and hoped nobody would notice it as they made their way to the far end of the room.

Tristan and Sebastian rose to greet them and then pointed to their name cards on the table. 'I don't know where the others are,' declared Tristan. 'Anyway, you're next to Belinda I think Harriet, Mark is next to you.'

Sebastian shot round and pulled the chairs out for them both to sit down. Harriet caught the wave from her mother sat next to Henry's parents on the top table. Then she saw Belinda Oxfordshire talking to Geraldine. She clutched the carrier bag between her legs and started chattering intently to Mark. She wasn't going to look sideways if she could at all help it.

'I think you know Mummy and Daddy already,' announced Clare as Belinda Oxfordshire finally resumed her seat. 'Yes, of course,' she declared thrusting her hand out, looking straight at Mark. 'Lovely to meet you again. Joris!' she called over. 'Come and say hello to Mark and Harriet.'

Mr. Sanderson walked across. He looked superb. Harriet was filled with a raging jealousy that seemed to cripple her from head to toe. She'd never experienced anything like it before. This gorgeous man was *hers*. Their eyes met, he shook hands with them both and sat down.

'There's a bit of a niff in here,' Belinda suddenly declared. 'I do hope the first course isn't fish!'

They all wined and dined while Harriet constantly chatted to Mark to excess. 'Harriet, I'm trying to eat,' he said.

She looked down at her plate. For the fifth time her plate had been collected at the end of each course, hardly touched.

As the speeches ended, out of the corner of her eye Harriet could see Belinda Oxfordshire starting to drape herself all over Mr. Sanderson. She heard him clear his throat a couple of times as if he were just a bit uncomfortable.

'So where did you put that hat then my darling?' she heard her whisper.

'And I would like to make one final toast!' James' loud, sudden announcement made Harriet jump. 'It seems appropriate on such an occasion as this to congratulate our friends, Belinda and Joris on their engagement. Toast Belinda and Joris! Every happiness!'

'Belinda and Joris!' came the united chorus.

Harriet was seething. How could her brother do this to her?

Then her mother decided to stand up, a little too flushed Harriet thought.

'It's not quite over yet! I'd like you all to raise your glasses again but this time to Harriet and Mark. To their forthcoming marriage,' and then she coughed slightly, 'and their new baby!'

'Well well,' said Mr. Sanderson shooting a stern glance at Harriet.

'I told you darling, remember? You wouldn't believe me.' Harriet just caught Belinda Oxfordshire's loud whispers.

'You what?' snapped Mark as everyone stood up to toast them.

'She's drunk!' said a stunned Harriet.

'Oh where's my hat darling? Stop playing about!' Harriet heard the stage whispers again.

'*It's bloody well here!*' stormed Harriet as she grabbed the carrier bag from under the table, turned it upside-down and plonked it straight on top of her head. She whammed the base flat against her crown and then pulled at the empty bag only to find herself shaking all the damp smelly old shredded newspaper bits, full of cat's mess, over her. It draped her head and sat like rags on her shoulders. Harriet was shocked. 'And just in case anyone's in any doubt, I'm *not* pregnant and I don't recall this commitophobe ever *asking* me to marry him!'

'My bustle's come off!' she heard Samantha whine.

'That's because your arse was too big for the pin!' she shouted and stormed out of the dining room leaving it in stunned silence.

Her mother suddenly stood up to address the whole room. 'Don't mind Harriet. It's the menopause. Carry on everyone!'

Chapter 52

'Just as well I got a lift home Harriet,' Mark declared the next morning. 'I can't believe you made such a spectacle of yourself. So I'm a commitophobe, am I? Well this time you've got it in one Harriet. Just at the moment you are actually the last person I'd marry, or anyone else would marry after that performance, I'm quite sure.'

'Mummy was drunk,' Harriet replied. 'It's her fault!'

'Not her fault poor Belinda got covered in that lot!'

'What happened then?' Harriet asked, suddenly trying to suppress a fit of the giggles.

'It's not funny Harriet. She ended up blaming it on that lard ball of yours. She reckoned you'd cooked it up between the pair of you to get rid of her.'

'Paranoid as well!' declared Harriet.

'Oh, he made it quite clear it was nothing to do with him. She soon fell back into his arms once he'd managed to calm her down but they left pretty soon after that.'

'Oh,' said Harriet.

'Well she could hardly stay covered in that lot. I can't think why that lard ball would be taking a bag of cat crap to a wedding. A posh bag at that. "Cruising Christiana" eh? What else have you been up to Harriet?'

'I'm single Mark. I can please myself!'

'Well this one certainly isn't mine.'

'What one?' questioned Harriet, starting to feel all of yesterday's anger returning.

'This baby, the one your mother announced to the whole world.' he stopped and thought for a moment. 'It never was anything to do with Tricia, was it? That garage girl mixed her up with you, didn't she?'

'Think what you like,' Harriet stormed. 'I'm **NOT** pregnant!'

'Where did your mother get it from then?'

'Rumours. How does anyone know where they start?'

They heard the beep of the car horn outside.

'I'm off and the South Pole isn't far enough as far as I'm concerned.'

The front door banged shut and from the window Harriet watched him load his cases into the boot of Paul Meadows' car. A huge pang went through her. What had she done?

Chapter 53

It was the start of the autumn term. It was with some trepidation that Harriet drove to school the next morning. At least she would be relieved of her deputy duties, she'd be very pleased to see Amanda again. She was terrified of meeting Mr. Sanderson. He was bound to be there on the first day back.

'Well it was *him* that told me to put all my stuff into his boot. *He* took all my luggage out. Not my fault he gave me the wrong carrier bag back. I didn't know I'd put the bloody hat in the bin.' She tried to justify it all to herself. Then she couldn't help herself. The magical journey home from the cruise took her mind away just as she pulled up at the traffic lights outside Starboard Marine North West. She looked across and felt the all too familiar lump rising in her throat. "Wait for me Harriet." he had said, "Save that one for me!" Where was he now Mark had gone? She cursed Simon Barnes for ruining her life. He'd obviously pestered Charles Ormerod to give him an answer. She was upset. He'd been the perfect steward. She owed him so much. He didn't deserve any backlash after being so kind to her. Things had gone too far. She couldn't write that letter of appreciation now. 'Oh, the bloody cat.' Harriet continued to herself. 'None of this would have happened if it hadn't been for that damned cat!'

But it was all she'd had for company last night. It had nuzzled into her neck as she'd cried herself to sleep.

Harriet drove through the school gateway. His silver Mercedes was parked in its usual place by the entrance door. Harriet could feel it in her bones. This was going to be the worst day of her life. She just hoped the new vibrancy of the school would distract him from Saturday's events.

She needn't have worried. He didn't even take morning assembly. Amanda did it. She'd seen him drive out of the gates as they'd all filed into the hall.

Amanda had popped in to see her. 'Looks like you've made an impression on him Harriet,' she'd said. 'He wants *you* to continue with the parenting side of it all. I just don't know how you've managed to turn this place around. It's absolutely amazing!'

Well at least that was something. If he stayed out of her way and just let her throw herself back into it all it would help her get through the next three months, Harriet had thought.

And that's exactly what he did.

Oh, she'd seen his car on occasions so he must have been popping in, but it was pretty much the same as before, only this time Harriet made extra sure there wasn't going to be the remotest chance of meeting him in the doorway, or anywhere else.

She dreaded hearing of his forthcoming marriage from anywhere. She was just grateful that no one had, as yet, mentioned it at school.

Harriet busied herself mending bridges with all her family. Of course the arrival of the new baby proved a major distraction. Harriet was grateful to Susan and Paul for producing their tiny daughter at such an apposite time.

'Mummy was right!' she'd been glad to be able to tell her girls, 'The menopause certainly plays havoc with the hormones.'

'Why don't you try HRT?' a very concerned Clare had suggested.

'It might come to that,' Harriet had said, but her monthly cycle was as regular as clockwork. She *knew* she wasn't in any way ready for any of that. She knew for her condition, Mr. Sanderson was the only cure.

Most disappointed of all was Harriet's mother. No marriage and no baby. 'Well what a way to let Daddy and I know, Harriet,' she'd said, 'mind you it was my fault in the first place. I'd had goodness knows how many glasses of champagne and that was before all that wine with the meal. I can tell you Daddy was very cross with me. Mind you, he never would have blamed you Harriet. You'll always be his special little girl. Anyway I hope you'll take a lesson from it all and start acting your age. It might help if you stop going round with that common girl!'

But that was the last thing Harriet wanted to do. Their friendship was well and truly cemented in the face of Mr. Sanderson's forthcoming marriage and Tricia now worshipped Harriet for what she'd done. She only wished she'd been there, 'to see `er get what she deserved!'

Harriet had half expected Mark to phone, but nothing. 'It's the end of the road,' she'd said to herself, 'there'll be a lot to sort out.' Yet there was something in her that was just a little relieved the house was still unsold. They'd been together a long time.

Harriet tried desperately hard not to let it get to her. She had sewing to do. She'd promised Molly she'd make her own bridesmaid's dress. She wouldn't hear of Molly spending a fortune buying one. It was not long to go now, it was nearly the end of October and Molly, coincidentally had timed their wedding to fall in half term. Harriet was very grateful for that. It would give her time to organise herself. Although she'd given Molly his phone number, she thought it unlikely she'd see Mr. Sanderson and Belinda Oxfordshire there. Molly hadn't mentioned him again. Even if Mr. Fishwick had contacted him Harriet just knew he wouldn't wish to expose his darling fiancee to *her*.

Harriet had chosen pale blue again. It suited her blonde hair and Molly agreed it would look just fine with her ivory suit.

She stitched and stitched, grateful for the noise of the clattering old sewing machine in the empty house. She was glad of the cat now. She must stop spoiling it. It was starting to put on weight.

Sewing away, she smiled to herself as she recalled those plummy girls. She'd sat for hours making those dresses. She was glad she'd chosen a nice simple elegant long dress for herself. No bustles to fall off. It was coming together nicely. It would go well with the shoes and bag she'd bought for Clarissa's wedding.

Chapter 54

Harriet sat on the train looking out of the window at the hazy blue sky of the late autumn day. She liked this time of the year with its shortening days offering the street lamps a chance to shine a little earlier each evening. She loved the intensity of colour the lowering sun gave to the fields and hedgerows. She loved the early morning mist and the wet grass sparkling with the dew drops refracting the sunlight; shining like millions of tiny diamonds in all the colours of the rainbow. There was a mix of nostalgia and anticipation about the season, a self-generated excitement that was there for the taking.

Harriet thought about Mr. Sanderson and the brief respite that had just been granted her from that constant ache suddenly vanished. She looked out of the window again. The magic had disappeared. Once again she was only going through the motions. She thought about Mr. Fishwick and felt a deep sense of compassion as she remembered his words. Just like him, she knew that something had died within her, too, when Tricia had phoned with news of *that* engagement.

The train pulled into the station and Harriet gathered her bags together to join the queue of waiting passengers ready to descend to the platform. She spotted Mr. Fishwick in the crowd by the steps and met him half way as he came over to meet her.

'It's good to see you again my dear,' he greeted. 'It doesn't seem five minutes ago we were all on that cruise. Things have moved on indeed.'

'Oh yes,' said Harriet, 'I'm absolutely delighted you and Molly are getting married. It couldn't have happened to a nicer couple.'

Mr. Fishwick touched his hat and ushered her to his car. 'Molly's place isn't too far from here,' he said as they drove off. 'If you don't mind I'll just drop you at the gate. Not lucky to see one's bride before the wedding!'

With a wave of his hand he drove off. Harriet put her bags down to open the white painted wrought iron gate. She liked Molly's house. It was big and old and stood in its own grounds.

'Harriet dear, what a joy it is to see you again. Have you had a good journey? Sometimes those trains are not all they should be, you know. Such a pity Mark's away. It's so good of you to come on your own.'

'It's all my pleasure Molly,' replied Harriet. 'You're blooming. You look lovely!'

'Oh thank you Harriet. Wait until you see my outfit. In my ivory and your blue we're both going to look a picture standing together.'

'You've lost a lot of weight Harriet dear. Are you alright?'

'Needed to,' replied Harriet, 'especially for your wedding. Wouldn't have wanted to saddle you with a plump bridesmaid.'

Molly laughed. 'Do come on in dear and make yourself at home.'

The house was buzzing with people. Big people and little people. Two or three generations worth. Harriet couldn't remember their names.

'Now then, I want you all to look after Harriet. Make her feel at home. If it wasn't for Harriet I doubt very much if Percy and I would be getting married this day!'

'Good old Harriet!' somebody shouted and everyone joined in.

'Now you've got a wedding car all of your own Harriet,' Molly said as she led her up the stairs to show her where to get changed. 'You'll be following my car to the church and then all you'll need to do is stand by me and look pretty. The same car will take you to the reception which is only two minutes from here. We thought we'd hang the expense Harriet! We've gone for The Manor House on the top of the hill by the river. The colours of those trees up there are exquisite at the moment and the gardens are still beautiful.'

'Sounds lovely,' said Harriet, 'I've been so looking forward to this day, to seeing you and Percy again.'

'And of course we've been looking forward to seeing you, too, but I'm just dying to hear about that cat of yours. You've certainly got lots to tell us. Any more TV appearances to come Harriet? It's better than any soap I've ever watched!' Molly said, laughing.

'I hope not Molly. Wow, have I got a tale to tell? Definitely for another time, though.'

'Yes,' agreed Molly, 'we'll make a better job of keeping in touch once this is all over.'

Harried hurried to get changed. Time was going very quickly now and she was just able to put the final touches to her hair before she heard a knock on the bedroom door.

'Coming,' she said as she went to open it.

It was Molly standing in the doorway with a bridesmaid's bouquet of beautiful creamy white rosebuds and pale pink carnations. Harriet could just see the softest hints of lilac and blue flowers nestling in the delicate green fern that ran its way in and out and then around the whole bouquet. Harriet was amazed. She'd never seen quite such a beautiful creation before.

'Thank you Molly. It's absolutely beautiful.'

Molly smiled, 'Thought you'd like it Harriet. It *is* beautiful. It just put me in mind of you as soon as I saw it. Quite lovely.'

Harriet smiled and blushed a little.

'You look absolutely stunning Harriet,' she said, passing the flowers over to her.

'And so do you,' declared Harriet holding the flowers in both her arms, cradling them like a baby. She looked down at them and then back at Molly.

'They used to say I was a good looker, just like you Harriet. I know people of my generation are always saying it, but I really do wish I was your age and know what I know now.'

'You still are a good looker, Molly, without a doubt. I hope I look as good as you when I get to your age. I'll never be as nice as you though.' Harriet smiled at her and continued. 'Thank you so very much Molly. Thank you for everything.

It's a long time since I've felt as good as this.'

Molly's expression changed to concern. Harriet hadn't meant to do that to her.

'Your outfit is so superbly tailored, so tasteful Molly,' she said, wanting to rewind the conversation.

'Thanks Harriet.' Molly suddenly smiled again. 'Actually I had this specially made. I must say I am pleased with it.'

'So you should be!' Harriet bent her head to smell the flowers. 'They're so beautiful Molly, you've put a lot of thought into this wedding.'

Molly kissed her on the cheek. 'Oh, just before we go,' she said, passing Harriet a small gift box. 'Just a little something for doing the honours Harriet.'

'But you shouldn't have Molly, that's so very kind of you.'

'Go on, open it!' said Molly.

Harriet undid the wrapping paper and smiled as she read the gift card. She lifted the lid on the box to see three tiny charms ringed together on a silver chain. She nudged the tiny silver bundle with her finger to see a cross, an anchor, and a heart. A tear slid down her cheek as she took Molly into her arms. 'Thank you,' she said, 'it's just so delicate, so very special.'

'I got it from a little shop next door to that church I was telling you about in Bruges. Let's put it on. Would you mind wearing it just for me, Harriet?'

Harriet smiled and nodded. She undid the clasp on the diamond pendant around her neck and laid it down on the dressing table. She took the silver chain from the box and put it on. 'It's lovely, it really is, thank you so much Molly.'

Molly smiled, a wide smile of approval. 'Let's go, shall we Harriet? The cars are waiting.'

Harriet stood behind Molly in the church listening to the rector reading the vows of marriage that would join her to Mr. Fishwick. She thought the words were dignified and beautiful.

'Now they're married,' Harriet said to herself as she walked behind them to witness the signing of the register. She swallowed hard.

'Why had this never been her destiny?'

The organ resumed playing in the cathedral like building and Harriet followed Molly and Percy down the aisle of the over packed church.

'Molly must be very well known around here,' she thought, slowing down as they came to the point in the aisle that branched right towards the door. She glanced across to the other side and suddenly felt her heart miss a beat. She saw Mr. Sanderson sitting on the end of the last pew. Her legs went to jelly as she felt the colour drain from her cheeks. She immediately looked at the floor. She couldn't tell if he was on his own. Whoever was next to him had her head down. Harriet could only see the large sweeping brim of a pale green hat.

She felt sick. She was actually having such a lovely time until now. She hoped against hope Molly hadn't seated them together.

The couple of minutes drive to The Manor House seemed like eternity to

Harriet. She got out of the car not quite knowing where to go next. Suddenly she felt a strong arm around her waist. She immediately turned to see Mr. Sanderson. Her feet left the ground.

'I feel sure Molly will have placed us together, he smiled. 'You're looking exceptionally beautiful today Miss Glover!' He kept his arm around her as he walked her from the wedding car to the hand carved solid oak door of the manor. He stepped forward, pushed it open and leant against it to allow her through.

He steered her around the tables heading towards the top of the room. He glanced at the name cards either side of Molly and Mr. Fishwick and then along to the end of the table.

'Ah yes! Here we are Miss Glover.'

She didn't dare look back for fear of seeing Belinda Oxfordshire behind them.

Mr. Sanderson pulled the chair out for her to sit down and then he sat alongside her. Theirs were the only two settings at the end of the table. No sign of a name card for Belinda Oxfordshire.

'Oh!' she thought. 'This gorgeous man in his dark suit and bow tie!' She noticed the curl of blond hair just resting on his pristine white collar. It immediately sent shivers down her spine. Oh! She watched his strong hands casually rearrange the empty glasses and looked down to see the edge of his jacket touching her dress as he moved his chair closer. She recalled watching him drive. His strong legs still leaving little room for manoeuvre in his smart black trousers as he stretched back and forth before placing both hands just short of his knees. Harriet was in complete meltdown. 'This beautiful, beautiful man,' she said to herself as she caught his gorgeous smile.

'That's a grand job you've done at school Miss Glover. Keep the good work up!'

She could feel herself blushing. 'Thank you,' she managed to say. Those were the only words willing to come. Her mind was racing to try to find something she could say without compromising herself. Every attempt at conversation just ended in a quick smile and a glance away.

'You're exceedingly quiet Miss Glover,' he finally said to the sound of chairs being moved as people started leaving their seats.

'Splendid meal wouldn't you say?'

'It was lovely,' agreed Harriet. 'Molly and Mr. Fishwick have put a lot into making this a very special day.'

'Yes, all over bar the shouting!' He was smiling at her. 'Oh, of course, that was the last wedding we were at. You're not about to make another spectacle of youself, I hope!'

For the second time Harriet felt sick. She knew it had to come. She looked up at him and saw him starting to laugh.

'Don't bother answering that Miss Glover! A walk in the grounds perhaps, before I take you home?'

He put his arm around her and they wandered down to the river bank. Molly was right. The trees sported their rich autumnal colours to perfection. In silence they followed the gurgling water as it splashed the stones all the way to the little bridge canopied by the deep crimson leaves overhead. He stopped and gently scooped her into his arms. He pressed her close against his chest and then lifted her head. He outlined her lips with his finger before bending his head to kiss her. Then he relaxed his grip and looked into her eyes before drawing her back from paradise.

No words were spoken. He put his arm round her again as they walked over to the car park.

'Lift home Miss Glover?' he asked, smiling.

'Yes, thank you, Mr. Sanderson. I maybe need to collect my things though. Can I go home like this?' she said, tugging at the skirt of her long blue bridesmaid's dress.

He took his jacket off and draped it round her shoulders.

'Leave it on for me Miss Glover. I've never seen anybody look as beautiful as you do today, in the whole of my life.'

He squeezed her hand. 'Don't worry, I'll arrange for your things to be collected.'

They got into the Mercedes and Harriet watched his gold cufflinks glitter in the deep cuffs of his shirt sleeves as the late afternoon sun stole its way through the car windows. He put the car into gear and stretched his right leg full forward to the accelerator as he let go of the clutch. They were away.

Harriet wanted to hold this precious moment in time, still, forever. She didn't know whether Belinda Oxfordshire was still in his life. She didn't want to know. The past and the future were places she didn't want to be. For now he was hers. She choked away each lump as it persistently appeared in her throat. This gorgeous man was all she wanted to live for.

She watched the sun, in and out, sweeping its broad strokes of gold across the rich, green pastures. It was starting to go down now. The shadows were lengthening. Some of them were just clipping the car bonnet as they sped along the lanes. At the horizon the blue sky was deepening, becoming exotic, as it gave way to the clouds, now widening bands of lilac and pink, sparingly outlined in gold. They had almost surrendered their pure white composition to the fast sinking sun. The early evening air was gathering a bank of mist. It was starting to float over the fields. One or two street lamps began to flicker.

'Warm enough, Harriet?' Mr. Sanderson enquired. He felt her hand and touched the button to override the temperature control.

'Yes thank you, Mr. Sanderson,' she smiled, looking across. His window framed the view and closed it down to his profile. Harriet couldn't imagine there to be a better looking man anywhere. 'He's absolutely got it all,' she thought. The need for him became deeply intensified. She felt it taking its familiar course again. 'This gorgeous, handsome man. Does he know exactly what he does to me?' There was no answer. The question was silent in her mind.

The miles ran away. He stopped the car outside her house and turned off the engine. He undid his seat belt and stretched across to undo hers. Gently he kissed her cheek, then he looked down to the silver pendant she was wearing. 'That's nice Harriet.'

'Thank you,' she smiled, 'a bridesmaid's gift from Molly.'

He separated the charms and rested them on his finger. 'Faith, hope and love, words to remember Harriet.'

He took her right hand and opened it. He encircled the tips of her fingers with his, slowly moving them down to feel every curve, every contour before clasping it very tightly. He slipped his hand into his pocket, 'speaking of which,' he said, 'just a small, personal gift in recognition of all you've done for the school, all you've done for me.' He slid a gold ring onto her finger. 'This hand for the moment, just for the moment, Harriet.'

He took a very deep breath and held her in his gaze. She could sense the mix of emotion in him. The twinkle in his eyes not winning out to the stern, hard expression on his face. She struggled to find the right words to thank him.

'I'll see you to the door Miss Glover.'

He got out and opened the car door for her. He put her arm around her as they walked up the path.

'Thank you so much Mr. Sanderson, I really don't deserve such kindness.'

'Nonsense, Miss Glover. I'm indebted to you for all you've done in that school.' Harriet smiled at him. 'It really was my pleasure,' she said, 'and you did bring the cat home for me.'

'I told her to keep that one quiet,' he said, a look of concern suddenly crossing his face. 'Anyway, talking about losing things. I think you've forgotten something.'

Harriet watched him go back to the car. He returned with her bridesmaid's bouquet and handed it to her.

'Just missing a couple of buttercups,' he said. She looked for his smile. It wasn't there. He looked solemn and thoughtful. He waited until she'd put her keys in the door before he walked off. She turned back to wave and tried to secure his image in her mind for fear it should suddenly be taken away.

She went into the empty house and picked up the cat as it nuzzled against her legs. 'Oh Pepper, I've had the most wonderful time,' she cried into its soft fur. I really have Pepper. She sat on the bottom stair and just gazed at the ring on her finger. She wanted to take it off to look at it and then she didn't. 'He's just placed it there, I can't take it off now, can I Pepper?' Then she wondered about Belinda Oxfordshire and quickly pushed the thought to the back of her mind. 'Oh Pepper, it's been the best day of my life and I've got a whole week off to dream about it.'

Chapter 55

The end of half term brought Harriet to the beginning of November and still no word from Mark. He was due home at the end of the month. Harriet knew he was alright because he'd managed to phone the girls a couple of times. 'No mention of you Mummy!' they'd said each time and to her surprise Harriet had always felt uneasy. Not that she'd expected any mention of her. After all this time it was pretty evident their relationship was over.

Still wearing her ring, Harriet drove to school wondering if Mr. Sanderson would be there. She was still in a state of euphoria. For all the world she'd never imagined such a scenario.

'My office, Miss Glover,' he said as he met her in the main doorway. She followed him in, grateful for the new handle, as she closed the door behind her.

'As I mentioned, you've done an exceptional job here Harriet, in a very short space of time. The governors are absolutely delighted! Until we can organise permanent promotion I've recommended you go on to the next pay scale.'

'Thank you Mr. Sanderson,' Harriet said. 'Actually I've really enjoyed it, being able to hand Mrs. Bustard all that money certainly helped to bring her on side. It just followed on from there really.'

'You're far too unassuming Harriet.' He smiled as he moved closer to her. 'Mind you, your brother wouldn't agree. I don't think he knows you quite as well as I do!'

He put his arm around her waist and drew her close.

'Mr. Sanderson, you're engaged! What about Belinda Oxfordshire?' Harriet suddenly spluttered.

'What about Belinda Oxfordshire?' retorted Mr. Sanderson as he moved away to unlock the bottom drawer of his desk. He pulled it open and took out his black bow tie still knotted to Harriet's bra. He placed them on his in tray. 'She found these in my pocket!'

'Oh, so it wasn't anything to do with the hat, then?'

'Well you might say that was the last straw, Harriet!'

Harriet watched his face break into that most gorgeous smile.

'Oh, just one more thing. I've arranged for us both to attend a very special ceremony, sometime following the spring. I want you to wear the blue one Harriet.'

Harriet's heart leapt. He picked up the bra and bow tie. 'Appropriately entwined Harriet.' Then he showed her out of his office.

'Whatever did he mean? It could only be marriage. This ring to that finger.' Harriet couldn't get the words out of her head all day. The 3.30 bell rang and she let the children rush to the door. Mrs. Bustard came bustling in with Danny.

''e said 'e's left 'is banana on the radiator Miss Glover. Go on Danny, ask Miss Glover nicely. Remember those manners we've taught you?'

Harriet smiled and suddenly remembered something. She fished in her bag and handed Mrs. Bustard the creased lottery ticket. 'Take it,' she said, 'without you we'd never have turned this school around.'

Mrs. Bustard's weather-beaten face crinkled into a huge smile and her eyes filled with tears. She put her arms around Harriet as she thanked her. She gathered Danny up and opened the door. 'You're a good'n you,' she said.

Harriet watched them, hand in hand, walk across the playground. A huge lump came into her throat.

Chapter 56

The phone rang at 4 The Willows and the answer machine clicked in.

'Ooh 'arriet. 'ave you 'eard the news? They've just mentioned a Mr. Bridgewater, 'arriet. Something to do with donations and cash for 'onours. 'e denied all knowledge but 'e's up for questioning along with a few more of 'em from that parliament place. It's got to be 'im, 'asn't it 'arriet? I 'ope they don't come askin' me any questions, I 'aven't got a clue what's goin' on. Well we 'aven't 'ave we 'arriet? Them 'onours are not for the likes of us, are they 'arriet? Just for the likes of our friend Joris Sanderson, I would say; those with influence, those in 'igh places. They're from another world those that get them. Oooh 'arriet, it's got to be 'im though. It's got to be that Tarquin Bridgewater. Well fancy that 'arriet, would you believe it? Ooh, what do you think 'arriet?'

* * *

'Hi Harriet, it's Mark. Be back on Friday, they've cut the trip a bit short. By the way Hat I've got something to ask you when I get home and I definitely want you to wear the blue one. Missed you Hat, hope you haven't backed the wrong horse!'

The messages resonated in the empty hall.

Chapter 57

Still touched by Mrs. Bustard, the tears that rolled freely from her eyes painted their picture of joy and sorrow in equal measure against Harriet's flushed cheeks as she drove home.

She wiped them away with her sleeve as she opened the front door to go into the hall. She looked across and noticed the couple of messages flashing on the answer machine. She picked up the post and curious, went straight to the formal brown envelope. She could feel the cat brushing against her legs as she took the letter out.

'You have been recommended for the following award,' she read out loud, then she covered her mouth with her hand and touched her face, nervously.

'Dame Commander of the Order of the British Empire for outstanding services to education? What! Me? No, *he* hasn't. *Surely he hasn't?*' She clenched her thumb and her forefinger between her teeth. She couldn't believe her eyes.

She pictured them both at the Palace, then in the church, then at the Palace.

"I declare you Sir and Dame!"

'No. Those aren't the right words. They won't do!'

It wasn't exactly the very special ceremony she'd hoped for.

She took off the ring and placed it onto the wedding finger of her left hand. She twisted it round and round as she tried to shake off the hollow feeling that had suddenly overtaken her. She could feel it threatening to drain away her joy, her hopes. She caught hold of the tiny silver charms resting at her neck. His words returned. "Faith, hope and love, words to remember Harriet." She removed the ring and took a closer look at it. A shaft of sunlight suddenly shone through the hall window just lighting up an inscription in the gold of its inner face as she went to return it to her other hand. She picked up the magnifying glass still left on the window sill and held the ring up to the light. She could just make out the words as they ran their full circle.

'our perfect day' ne obliviscaris JS

She took a deep breath, smiled, and sighed a very deep sigh before picking up the cat to go and play the messages.

'ne obliviscaris - do not forget'

www.ingramcontent.com/pod-product-compliance
Lightning Source LLC
Chambersburg PA
CBHW061441030726
47503CB00005B/1519